Dear Reading Friends,

I had no idea when I wrote the three HAWK'S WAY novels in this collection, *The Rancher and the Runaway Bride, The Cowboy and the Princess* and *The Wrangler and the Rich Girl,* that they were the beginning of a series that would eventually span twelve books and three generations of Whitelaws. The family tree just before the first book tells you in which order the books were written.

If you're like me, you enjoy continuing stories about the same family because they provide an opportunity to see how people who grow up in the same family experience life so differently from one another, how family can help—or inhibit—a romance and how individuals seek—and find—love for different reasons, even though they were raised with essentially the same family values.

I often write about other members of the same family because I want to know "the rest of the story." What happened to that cold-eyed elder brother or that wounded younger sister? I'm frequently surprised at what the characters do and say, by whom they choose to love and by how love finds them. I'm always glad when they manage to live happily ever after. I hope you'll enjoy these family stories of love and laughter.

Happy trails,

Joan Johnston

Praise for *New York Times* bestselling author

JOAN JOHNSTON

"Multi-talented...poignant and sensitive...
Joan Johnston continually gives us everything
that we want...a story that you wish
would never end, and lots of tension
and sensuality."
—*Romantic Times Magazine*

"Absolutely captivating...a delightful
storyteller...Joan Johnston [creates] unforgettable
subplots and characters who make every fine thread
weave into a touching tapestry."
—*Affaire de Coeur*

"Joan Johnston does contemporary Westerns
to perfection."
—*Publishers Weekly*

"...Ms. Johnston writes of intense emotions
and tender passions that seem so real that readers
will feel each one of them...[she] writes the
very essence of the West..."
—*Rave Reviews*

JOAN JOHNSTON

HAWK'S WAY
BACHELORS

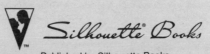

Published by Silhouette Books

America's Publisher of Contemporary Romance

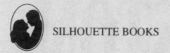 SILHOUETTE BOOKS

HAWK'S WAY BACHELORS

Copyright © 2000 by Harlequin Books S.A.

ISBN 0-373-48415-1

The publisher acknowledges the copyright holder of the individual works as follows:

THE RANCHER AND THE RUNAWAY BRIDE
Copyright © 1993 by Joan Mertens Johnston

THE COWBOY AND THE PRINCESS
Copyright © 1993 by Joan Mertens Johnston

THE WRANGLER AND THE RICH GIRL
Copyright © 1993 by Joan Mertens Johnston

This edition published by arrangement with Harlequin Books S.A.

® and TM are trademarks of Harlequin Books S.A., used under license. Trademarks indicated with ® are registered in the United States Patent and Trademark Office, the Canadian Trade Marks Office and in other countries.

Visit Silhouette at www.eHarlequin.com

Printed in U.S.A.

CONTENTS

Hawk's Way Family Tree

Key:

Hawk's Way

1. Honey and the Hired Hand
2. The Rancher and the Runaway Bride
3. The Disobedient Bride
4. The Cowboy and the Princess
5. The Wrangler and the Rich Girl

6. The Unforgiving Bride
7. The Headstrong Bride
8. The Temporary Groom
9. The Virgin Groom
10. The Rich Girl
11. A Hawk's Way Christmas
12. The Substitute Groom

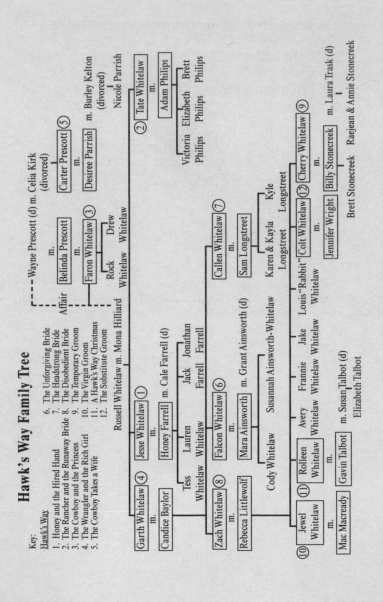

THE RANCHER AND THE RUNAWAY BRIDE

For my editor, Melissa Senate.
Sometimes you find a heap of thread
on a mighty small spool.

One

"May I kiss you good night, Tate?"

"Of course you can, Hank."

"Your brothers—"

"Forget about them! I'm a grown woman. I certainly don't need permission from Faron or Garth to give you a simple little goodnight kiss." Tate Whitelaw stepped closer to the tall cowboy and slipped her arms around his neck. The bright light over the front door didn't quite reach to the corner of the railed porch where she was standing with Hank.

Hank took advantage of Tate's invitation, drawing her into his arms behind one of the massive fluted columns that graced the front of the house and aligning their bodies from breast to hip. She was uncomfortably aware of his arousal, since only two layers of denim—her jeans and his—separated their warm flesh. His mouth sought hers, and his tongue thrust inside. It was more than a simple good-night kiss, and Tate suddenly found herself wishing she hadn't been quite so encouraging.

"Hank—" she gasped, pulling her head back and trying to escape his ardor. "I don't think—"

Hank's arms tightened around her, and Tate found herself in a wrestling match. She struggled to get the heels of her hands to his shoulders to push him away. He gripped her short black hair with one hand and angled her face for his kiss.

"Hank! S-stop it!" she hissed.

Caught up in his lust, Hank was oblivious to Tate's urgently whispered entreaties. Tate had already decided it was time to take desperate action when the issue was taken out of her hands. Literally.

Tate knew someone had arrived on the scene when Hank gave a grunt of surprise as he was jerked away from her. Her brother Faron had a handful of Hank's Western shirt in his grasp and was holding the young man at arm's length.

"What the hell do you think you're doing with my sister?" Faron demanded.

Hank blinked owlishly. "Kissing her?"

"Who the hell gave you permission to kiss her?"

"I did!" Tate said through gritted teeth. Fisted hands on hips, chin up, she faced her brother defiantly. "Who gave *you* permission to interfere!"

"When I see my kid sister getting mauled—"

"I can take care of myself!"

Faron arched a brow, and Tate knew it was because she hadn't denied the fact she was being mauled. Hank had just been a little exuberant, that was all. She could have escaped her predicament without her brother's interference.

To Tate's horror, Garth shoved open the front screen door and asked, "What in blue blazes is going on out here?"

"I found this coyote forcing his attentions on Tate," Faron said.

Garth stepped onto the porch, and if the sheer size of him didn't intimidate, the fierce scowl on his face surely would have. "That true?" Garth demanded of Hank.

Hank gulped. Perspiration dripped at his temple. The color left his face. "Well, sir…" He looked to Tate for rescue.

Tate watched Garth's lips flatten into a grim line as he exchanged a decisive look with Faron. Hank had been tried and convicted. All that was left was sentencing.

"Get your butt out of here," Garth said to Hank. "And don't come back."

Faron gave Hank a pretty good shove in the right direction, and Garth's boot finished the job. Hank stumbled down the porch steps to his pickup, dragged open the door, gunned the engine and departed in a swirl of gravel and choking dust.

There was a moment of awful silence while the dust settled. Tate fought the tears that threatened. She would *never* let her brothers know how humiliated she felt! But there was nothing wrong with giving them the lash of her tongue. She turned and stared first into Garth's stern, deep brown eyes, and then into Faron's more concerned gray-green ones.

"I hope you're both happy!" she snapped. "That's the fourth man in a month you've run off the ranch."

"Now, Tate," Faron began. "Any man who won't stand up to the two of us isn't worth having for a beau."

"Don't patronize me!" she raged. "I won't be placated like a baby with a rattle. I'm not three. I'm not even thirteen. I'm twenty-three. I'm a woman, and I have a woman's needs."

"You don't need to be manhandled," Garth said. "And I won't stand by and let it happen."

"Me neither," Faron said.

Tate hung her head. When she raised it again, her eyes were glistening with tears that blurred her vision. "I could have handled Hank myself," she said in a quiet voice. "You have to trust me to make my own decisions, my own mistakes."

"We don't want to see you hurt," Faron said, laying a hand on Tate's shoulder.

Tate stiffened. "And you think I wasn't hurt by what happened here tonight?"

Garth and Faron exchanged another look. Then Faron said, "Maybe your pride was pricked a little, but—"

"A *little!*" Tate jerked herself from Faron's grasp. "You're impossible! Both of you! You don't know the first thing about what I want or need. You can't imagine what it's like to have every step you take watched to make sure you don't fall down. Maybe it made sense when I was a baby, but I'm grown up now. I don't need you standing guard over me."

"Like you didn't need our help tonight?" Garth asked in a cold voice.

"I didn't!" Tate insisted.

Garth grabbed her chin and forced her face up to his. "You have no idea what a man's passions can lead him to do, little sister. I have no intention of letting you find out. Until the right man comes along—"

"There's no man who'll come within a hundred miles of this place now,'' Tate retorted bitterly. "My loving brothers have seen to that! You're going to keep me a virgin until I dry up and—''

Garth's fingers tightened painfully on her jaw, forcing her to silence. She saw the flash of fury in his dark eyes. A muscle flexed in his jaw. At last he said, "You'd better go to your room and think about what happened here tonight. We'll talk more about this tomorrow.''

"You're not my father!'' Tate spat. "I won't be sent to my room like a naughty child!''

"You'll go, or I'll take you there,'' Garth threatened.

"She can't go anywhere until you let go of her chin,'' Faron pointed out.

Garth shot a rueful look at his brother, then released Tate. "Good night, Tate,'' he said.

Tate had learned there were only two sides to Garth's arguments: his and the wrong one. Her stomach was churning. Her chest felt so tight it was hard to breathe, and her throat had a lump in it that made swallowing painful. Her eyes burned with tears that she would be *damned* if she'd shed!

She looked from Garth to Faron and back again. Garth's face was a granite mask of disapproval, while Faron's bore a look of sympathetic understanding. Tate knew they loved her. It was hard to fight their good intentions. Yet their love was smothering her. They would not let her *live!*

Her mother had died when she was born, and she had been raised by her father and her three brothers, Garth, Faron and Jesse. Their father had died when Tate was eight. Jesse had left home then, and Garth and Faron had been responsible for her ever since. It was a responsibility they had taken very seriously. She had been kept cloistered at Hawk's Way, more closely guarded than a novice in a convent. If she went anywhere off the ranch, one of her brothers came along.

When Tate was younger she'd had girlfriends to share her troubles with. As she got older, she discovered that the females she met were more interested in getting an introduction to her brothers than in being her friend. Eventually, she had simply stopped inviting them.

Tate hadn't even been allowed to go away to college. Instead she had taken correspondence courses to get her degree in business. She had missed the social interaction with her peers, the experience of being out on her own, that would have prepared her to deal with the Hanks of the world.

However, Garth and Faron had taught her every job that had to be done on a ranch, from branding and castrating to vaccinating and breeding. She wasn't naive. No one could be raised on a ranch and remain totally innocent. She had seen the quarter horse stallions they raised at Hawk's Way mount mares. But she could not translate that violent act into what happened between a man and a woman in bed.

So far, she had found the fumbling kisses of her swains more annoying than anything else. Yet Tate had read enough to know there was more to the male-female relationship than she had experienced so far. If her brothers had their way, she would never unravel the mysteries of love.

She had come to the dire conclusion over the past few months that no man would ever pass muster with her brothers. If she continued living with them, she would die an old maid. They had given her no choice. In order to escape her brothers' overprotectiveness, she would have to leave Hawk's Way.

This latest incident was the final straw. But then, kicking a man when he's down is sometimes the only way to make him get up. Tate took one long, last look at each of her brothers. She would be gone from Hawk's Way before morning.

When the front door closed behind Tate, Faron settled a hip on the porch rail, and Garth leaned his shoulder against the doorjamb.

"She's too damn beautiful for her own good," Garth muttered.

"Hard to believe a woman can look so sexy in a man's T-shirt and a pair of jeans," Faron agreed with a shake of his head.

Garth's eyes were bleak. "What're we going to do about her?"

"Don't know that there's anything we can do except what we're already doing."

"I don't want to see her get hurt," Garth said.

Faron felt a tightness in his chest. "Yeah, I know. But she's all grown up, Garth. We're going to have to let go sometime."

Garth frowned. "Not yet."

"When?"

"I don't know. Just not yet."

The next morning, Garth and Faron met in the kitchen, as they always did, just before dawn. Charlie One Horse, the part-Indian codger who had been chief cook and bottle washer at Hawk's Way since their mother had died, had coffee perking and breakfast on the table. Only this morning there was something—someone—missing.

"Where's Tate?" Garth asked as he sat down at the head of the table.

"Ain't seen her," Charlie said.

Garth grimaced. "I suppose she's sulking in her room."

"You drink your coffee, and I'll go upstairs and check on her," Faron offered.

A moment later Faron came bounding into the kitchen. "She's not there! She's gone!"

Garth sprang up from his chair so fast it fell over backward. "What? Gone where?"

Faron grabbed Garth by the shoulders and said in a fierce voice, "She's not in her room. Her bed hasn't been slept in!"

Garth freed himself and took the stairs two at a time to see for himself. Sure enough, the antique brass double bed was made up with its nubby-weave spread. That alone was an ominous sign. Tate wasn't known for her neatness, and if she had made up the bed, she had done it to make a statement.

Garth headed for the closet, his heart in his throat. He heaved a sigh of relief when he saw Tate's few dresses still hanging there. Surely she wouldn't have left Hawk's Way for good without them.

Garth turned and found Faron standing in the doorway to Tate's room. "She probably spent the night sleeping out somewhere on the ranch. She'll turn up when she gets hungry."

"I'm going looking for her," Faron said.

Garth shoved a hand through his hair, making it stand on end. "Hell and the devil! I guess there'll be no peace around here until we find her. When I get hold of her, I'll—"

"When we find her, I'll do the talking," Faron said. "You've caused enough trouble."

"Me? This isn't my fault!"

"Like hell! You're the one who told her to go to her room and stay there."

"Looks like she didn't pay a whole helluva lot of attention to me, did she?" Garth retorted.

At that moment Charlie arrived, puffing from exertion, and said, "You two gonna go look for that girl, or stand here arguin'?"

Faron and Garth glared at each other for another moment before Faron turned and pressed his way past Charlie and down the stairs.

Charlie put a hand out to stop Garth. "Don't think you're gonna find her, boy. Knew this was bound to happen sooner or later."

"What do you mean, old man?"

"Knew you had too tight a rein on that little filly. Figured she had too much spirit to stay in them fences you set up to hold her in."

"It was for her own good!"

Charlie shook his head. "Did it as much for yourself as for her. Knowin' your ma like you did, it's no wonder you'd want to keep your sister close. Prob'ly fearful she'd take after your ma, steppin' out on your pa like she did and—"

"Leave Mother out of this. What she did has nothing to do with the way I've treated Tate."

Charlie tightened the beaded rawhide thong that held one of his long braids, but said nothing.

Garth scowled. "I can see there's no sense arguing with a stone wall. I'm going after Tate, and I'm going to bring her back. This time she'll stay put!"

Garth and Faron searched canyons and mesas, ridges and gullies on their northwest Texas ranch, but not a sign did they find of their sister on Hawk's Way.

It was Charlie One Horse who discovered that the old '51 Chevy pickup, the one with the rusty radiator and the skipping carburetor, was missing from the barn where it was stored.

Another check of Tate's room revealed that her underwear drawer was empty, that her brush and comb and toothpaste were gone, and that several of her favorite T-shirts and jeans had also been packed.

By sunset, the truth could not be denied. At the age of twenty-three, Tate Whitelaw had run away from home.

Two

Adam Philips normally didn't stop to pick up hitchhikers. But there was no way he could drive past the woman sitting on the front fender of a '51 Chevy pickup, its hood raised and its radiator steaming, her thumb outstretched to bum a ride. He pulled his late-model truck up behind her and put on his Stetson as he stepped out into the heat of a south Texas midsummer afternoon.

She was wearing form-fitting jeans and an off-the-shoulder peasant blouse that exposed a lush female figure. But the heart-shaped face, with its huge hazel eyes and wide mouth framed by breeze-ruffled, short-cropped black hair, was innocence itself. He was stunned by her beauty and appalled at her youth. What was this female doing all alone on an isolated stretch of southwest Texas highway in an old rattletrap truck?

She beamed a trusting smile at him, and he felt his heart do a flipflop. She slipped off the rusty fender and lazily sauntered toward him. He felt his groin tighten with desire and scowled. She stopped in her tracks. About time she thought to be wary! Adam was all too conscious of the dangers a stranger presented to a young woman alone. Grim-lipped, he strode the short distance between the two vehicles.

Tate had been so relieved to see *someone* show up on the deserted rural route that the danger of the situation didn't immediately occur to her. She got only a glimpse of wavy blond hair and striking blue eyes before her rescuer had slipped on a Stetson that put his face in shadow.

He was broad-shouldered and lean-hipped, with a stride that ate up the distance between the two trucks. It was a fair assumption, from his dusty boots, worn jeans and sweat-stained Western shirt, that he was a working cowboy. Tate saw no reason to suspect he meant her any harm.

But instead of a pleasant "May I help you?" the first words out of his mouth were, "What the hell do you think you're doing?"

Tate was alarmed by the animosity in the stranger's voice and frightened by the intensity of his stare. But his attitude was so similar to what she had recently gone through with her brothers that she lifted her chin and retorted, "Hitching a ride back to the nearest gas station. In case you hadn't noticed, my truck's broken down."

The scowl deepened but he said, "Get in my pickup."

Tate had only taken two steps when the tall cowboy grabbed her arm and pulled her up short.

"Aren't you going to ask anything about me? Don't you want to know who I am?"

By now Tate was more irritated than frightened. "A Good Samaritan with a bad temper!" she retorted. "Do I need to know more?"

Adam opened his mouth to make a retort, took one look at the mutinous expression on the young woman's face, and shut it again. Instead he dragged her unceremoniously to the passenger's side of his long-bed pickup, opened the door, shoved her inside, and slammed it closed after her.

"My bag! It's in the back end of the Chevy," Tate yelped.

Adam stalked back to the rattletrap Chevy, snagged the duffel bag from the rusted-out truck bed and slung it into the back of his pickup.

Woman was too damned trusting for her own good! he thought. Her acid tongue wouldn't have been much help to her if he had been the kind of villain who preyed on stranded women. Which he wasn't. Lucky for her!

Tate didn't consider herself at all lucky. She recognized the flat-lipped expression on her Good Samaritan's face. He might have rescued her, all right, but he wasn't happy about it. The deep crevices formed around his mouth by his frown and the webbed lines at the edges of his eyes had her guessing his age at thirty-five or thirty-six—the same as her eldest brother Garth. The last thing she needed was another keeper!

She sat back with her arms crossed and stared out the window as they drove past rolling prairie. She thought back to the night two weeks ago when she had decided to leave Hawk's Way.

Her escape from her brothers, while apparently sudden, hadn't been completely without direction. She had taken several ranch journals containing advertisements from outfits all over Texas looking for expert help and headed south. However, Tate soon discovered that not one rancher was interested in hiring a woman, especially one without references, as either foreman or ranch manager.

To confound her problems, the ancient pickup she had taken from the barn was in worse shape than she had thought. It had left her stranded miles from the Lazy S—the last ranch on her list and her last hope for a job in ranch management.

"Do you know where the Lazy S is?" she asked.

Adam started at the sound of her voice. "I expect I could find it. Why?"

"I understand they're looking for a ranch manager. I intend to apply for the job."

"You're just a kid!"

The cowboy could have said nothing more likely to raise Tate's neck hairs. "For your information, I'm twenty-three and a fully grown woman!"

Adam couldn't argue with that. He had a pretty good view of the creamy rise of her breasts at the frilly gathered edge of her blouse. "What do you know about ranching?" he asked.

"I was raised on a ranch, Hawk's Way, and—" She stopped abruptly, realizing that she had revealed more than she had intended to this stranger. Tate hadn't used her own last name to apply for any jobs, knowing that if she did her brothers would be able to hunt her down and drag her back home. "I hope you'll keep that to yourself," she said.

Adam raised an inquiring brow that met such a gamine smile that his heart did that disturbing flipflop again.

"You see," Tate said, "the truth is, I've run away from home."

Adam snorted. "Aren't you a little old for that?"

Tate's lips curled ruefully. "I suppose so. But my brothers just wouldn't let me *live!* I mean, they watched every breath in and out of my body.''

Adam found the thought rather intriguing himself.

"My brothers are a little overprotective, you see. I had to run away if I was ever going to meet the right man and fall in love and have children.''

"Sounds like you could do that better at home than traipsing around the countryside,'' Adam observed.

"You don't know my older brothers! They want to wrap me in cotton batting and keep me safe. Safe, ha! What they mean is, they want to keep me a virgin forever.''

Adam choked at this unbelievable revelation and coughed to clear his throat.

"It's true! They've chased away every single beau I've ever had. Which is only a waste of time and energy because, you know, a man who's born to drown can manage to drown in a desert.''

Adam eyed her askance.

"I mean, if something is destined to happen, it'll happen no matter what.''

Tate waited for Adam to say something, but when he remained silent, she continued, "My older brother, Jesse, left home, too, when I was just eight. It was right after my father died. We haven't seen him for years and years. I don't plan to stay away for years, of course, but then, who knows how long it will take to find my Prince Charming. Not that I have to marry a prince of a man.''

Tate grinned and shrugged. "But it would be nice, you know, to just once kiss a man goodnight, without having my brothers send him packing because he's not good enough for me.''

Tate realized she was talking to fill the silence and forced herself to shut up.

Behind the young woman's bravado Adam saw the desperation that had sent her fleeing from the safe haven her brothers had provided for her. He felt sick inside. Was this the way his younger sister had felt? Had Melanie seen him as an oppressive tyrant, the same way this young woman perceived her brothers?

Tate held her breath as the stranger looked into her eyes. There was an awful sadness there she felt constrained to dispel. So she began talking again.

"I've been looking everywhere for a job,'' she said. "I must have been to fifteen different spreads in the past two weeks. But I haven't had so much as a nibble of interest.

"What I find so frustrating is the fact that most owners don't treat me seriously. I mean, I know I'm young, but there isn't anything I don't know about running a ranch."

"Do you know how to figure the amount of feed you need for each head of stock?" Adam asked.

"Depends on whether you plan to keep the stock penned or let it graze," Tate said. "Now if it's penned—"

Adam interrupted with, "Give me some symptoms of colic."

"A horse might have colic if he won't eat, or if he starts pawing, or gets up and down a lot. Generally an animal that can't get comfortable has a problem."

"Can you keep books on a computer?"

Tate snorted inelegantly. "Boy can I ever! I got stuck with all the bookkeeping at Hawk's Way. So, if you were hiring at the Lazy S, would I get the job?"

"What will you do if you *don't* get the job?" Adam asked instead.

Tate shrugged, not realizing how revealing the gesture was of the fact she wasn't the least bit nonchalant about that distressing possibility. "I don't know. I only know I *won't* go back home."

"And if your brothers find you?"

Her chin took on a mulish tilt. "I'll just run away again."

Adam wondered if his sister was so forthright and disarmingly honest with the man who had picked her up the night she ran away from home. Had that stranger known all about the young woman he had raped and murdered and left lying in a ditch on the side of the road?

Adam's teeth clenched in determination. If he had anything to say about it, the innocent young woman in his pickup would not become another such statistic. And he, of all people, was in a perfect position to help her. Because he owned the Lazy S Ranch.

However, in the months since Adam had put his advertisement in the ranch journal, he had changed his mind about needing a foreman. He had decided to place his country medical practice on hold and put the Lazy S Ranch back in the black himself.

But if he told this young woman he had no job for her, where would she go? What would she do? And how would he feel if he sent her away and she ended up dead somewhere on the side of the road?

"Say, there's the Lazy S Ranch!" Tate pointed at a wrought-iron sign that bridged a dirt road off the main thoroughfare. To her surprise, the cowboy turned and drove across a cattle guard onto the Lazy S.

"I thought you were going to take me into town!" she said.

"I thought you wanted to interview for a job!" he retorted.

Tate eyed the cowboy. She was perplexed. Many western men were the strong, silent type, but the stranger who had picked her up was something more. Aloof. The more distant he was, the more intrigued she became. It was a surprise to find out he had been kind enough to take her directly to the Lazy S.

She could have kicked herself for telling him so much personal information without finding out anything about him—not even his name. When he dropped her off, she might never see him again. Tate suddenly realized she wanted to see him again. Very much.

As the cowboy stopped his pickup in front of an impressive adobe ranch house, she said, "I can't tell you how much I appreciate your giving me a ride here. I'd like to thank you, but I don't even know your name!"

Adam turned to look at her and felt a tightening in his gut as she smiled up at him. Well, it was now or never. "My name is Adam Philips," he said. "I own the Lazy S. Come on inside, and you can interview for that job."

Three

———

Tate was stunned when the mysterious cowboy revealed his identity, but buoyant with hope, as well. She scrambled out of the pickup after Adam, certain that he wouldn't have bothered bringing her here if he didn't intend to at least consider her for the job of ranch fore-man.

"Follow me," he said, heading into the house.

Tate stopped only long enough to grab her duffel bag and sling it over her shoulder before scampering up the three steps after him.

Adam's living room was masculine through and through, filled with massive Spanish furniture of natural leather studded with brass. There was not another frill or a furbelow to soften the room. *No woman has lived here in a long time—if ever,* Tate decided.

She discovered that the adobe hacienda formed a U shape. The two wings enclosed a garden shaded by immense moss-laden live oaks and bright with blooming bougainvillea. A central tile fountain splashed with cascading water.

They finally arrived at Adam's office, which was located at the tip of one wing of the house. The thick adobe walls and the barrel-tile roof kept the inside of the house dark and cool, reminiscent of days gone by when everyone took an afternoon siesta.

Tate saw from the immaculate condition of the office that Adam must be an organized person. Everything had a place and everything was in its place. Tate felt her heart sink. She wasn't averse to order, she just refused to be bound by it. That had been one small rebellion she was capable of in the space in which her brothers confined her.

Instead of sitting on the leather chair in front of the desk, she seated herself on a corner of the antique oak desk itself. Adam refused to sit at all, instead pacing the room like a caged tiger.

"Before we go any further, I want to know your real name," he said.

Tate frowned. "I need a promise from you first that you won't contact my brothers."

Adam stopped pacing and stared at her.

Tate stared right back.

"All right," he said. "You've got it."

Tate took a deep breath and said, "My last name is Whitelaw."

Adam swore under his breath and began pacing again. The Whitelaws were known all over Texas for the excellent quarter horses they bred and trained. He had once met Garth Whitelaw at a quarter horse sale. And he was intimately acquainted with Jesse Whitelaw. Tate's brother Jesse, the one she hadn't seen in years, had recently married Honey Farrell—the woman Adam loved.

Honey's ranch, the Flying Diamond, bordered the Lazy S. Fortunately, with the strained relations between Adam and Jesse Whitelaw, Tate's brother wasn't likely to be visiting the Lazy S anytime soon.

Adam turned his attention to the young woman he had rescued from the side of the road. Her short black hair was windblown around her face, and her cheeks were flushed with excitement. She was gnawing worriedly on her lower lip—something he thought he might like to do himself.

Adam felt that telltale tightening in his groin. He tucked his thumbs into his jeans to keep from reaching out to touch her.

Tate crossed her legs and clutched her knee with laced fingers. She could feel the tension in Adam. A muscle worked in his jaw, and his expression was forbidding. A shiver ran down her spine. But it wasn't fear she felt, it was anticipation.

She was so nervous her voice cracked when she tried to speak. She cleared her throat and asked, "So, do I get the job?"

"I haven't made up my mind yet."

Tate was on her feet and at Adam's side in an instant. "I'd be good at it," she argued. "You wouldn't be sorry you hired me."

Adam had his doubts about that. His blood thrummed as he caught the faint scent of lilacs from her hair. He was already sorry he had stopped to pick her up. He couldn't be anywhere near her without feeling as randy as a teenager. That was a fine state of affairs when he had appointed himself her guardian in her brothers' stead. But he believed Tate when she had said she would just run away again if her brothers tried taking her home. Surely she would be better off here where he could keep a close eye on her.

He carefully stepped away from her and went around to sit behind his desk. Perhaps it would provide a more comfortable barrier between himself and the uncontrollable urges that struck him when he got within touching distance of this engaging runaway.

He steepled his fingers and said, "The job I have available isn't the same one that was advertised."

She braced her palms on the desk and leaned toward him. "Oh? Why not?"

Adam took one look at what her careless posture in the peasant blouse revealed and forced his gaze upward to her wide hazel eyes. "It's complicated."

"How?"

Why didn't she move? He had the irresistible urge to reach out and— He jumped up from behind his desk and started pacing again. "You'd have to know a little bit about what's happened on the Lazy S over the past couple of months."

Tate draped herself sideways across the chair in front of the desk, one leg swinging to release the tension, and said, "I'm listening."

"My previous ranch manager was a crook. He's in prison now, but besides stealing other people's cattle, he embezzled from me. He left my affairs in a mess. Originally, I'd intended to hire someone else to try to straighten things out. Lately I've decided to put my medical practice on hold—"

"Wait a minute!"

Tate sat up and her feet dropped to the floor, depriving Adam of the delicious view he'd had of her derriere.

"Do you mean to tell me you're a doctor?" she asked incredulously.

He shrugged sheepishly. "Afraid so. Over the past few months I've been transferring my practice to another physician who's moved into the area, Dr. Susan Kowalski. Now I have time to supervise the work on the Lazy S myself. What I really need is someone I can trust to organize the paperwork and do the bookkeeping.''

Adam pointed to the computer on a stand near his desk. "That thing and I don't get along. I can't pay much," Adam admitted, "but the job includes room and board." That would keep her from sleeping in her truck, which was about all Adam suspected she could afford right now.

Tate wrinkled her nose. She had cut her teeth on the computer at Hawk's Way, and what she didn't know about bookkeeping hadn't been discovered. But it was the kind of work she liked least of everything she'd done at Hawk's Way. Still, a job was a job. And this was the best offer she had gotten.

"All right. I accept."

Tate stood and held a hand out to Adam to shake on the deal.

When Adam touched her flesh he was appalled by the electricity that streaked between them. He had suspected his attraction for Tate, all the while warning himself not to get involved. His powerful, instantaneous reaction to her still caught him by surprise. He blamed it on the fact that it had been too damn long since he'd had a woman. There were plenty who would willingly satisfy his needs, women who knew the score.

He absolutely, positively, was not going to get involved with a twenty-three-year-old virgin. Especially not some virgin who wanted a husband and a family. For Adam Philips wouldn't give her one— and couldn't give her the other.

Tate was astonished by the jolt she received simply from the clasp of Adam's hand. She looked up into his blue eyes and saw a flash of desire quickly banked. She jerked her hand away, said, "I'm sure we're both going to enjoy this relationship," then flushed at the more intimate interpretation that could be put on her words.

Adam's lips curled in a cynical smile. She was a lamb, all right, and a wily old wolf like himself would be smart to keep his distance. He didn't intend to tell her brothers where she was. But he was betting that sooner or later word of her presence on the Lazy S would leak out, and they would find her. When they did, all hell was going to break loose.

Adam shook his head when he thought of what he was getting himself into. Tate Whitelaw was Trouble with a capital *T*.

"Where do I bunk in?" Tate asked.

Adam dragged his Stetson off and ruffled his blond hair where the sweat had matted it down. He hadn't thought about where he would put her. His previous foreman had occupied a separate room at one end of the bunkhouse. That obviously wouldn't do for Tate.

"I suppose you'll have to stay here in the house," he said. "There's a guest bedroom in the other wing. Come along and I'll show you where it is."

He walked her back through the house, describing the layout of things as they went along. "My bedroom is next to the office. The living room, family room and kitchen are in the center of the house. The last bedroom down the hall on this other wing was set up for medical emergencies, and I haven't had time to refurnish it. The first bedroom on this wing will be your room."

Adam opened the door to a room that had a distinctively southwestern flavor. The furniture was antique Americana, with woven rugs on the floor, a rocker, a dry sink, a wardrobe and a large maple four-poster covered with a brightly patterned quilt. The room felt light and airy. That image was helped by the large sliding glass door that opened onto the courtyard.

Tate sat down on the bed and bounced a couple of times. "Feels plenty comfortable." She turned and smiled her thanks up at Adam.

The smile froze on her face.

His look was avid, his nostrils flared. She was suddenly aware of the softness of the bed. The fact that they were alone. And that she didn't know Adam Philips...from Adam.

However, the part of Tate that was alive to the danger of the situation was squelched by the part of her that was exhilarated to discover she could have such a profound effect on this man. Adam was quite unlike the men her brothers had so peremptorily ejected from Hawk's Way. In some way she could not explain, he was different. She knew instinctively that his kiss, his touch, would be unlike anything she had ever experienced.

Nor did she feel the same person when she was near him. With this man, she was different. She was no longer her brothers' little sister. She was a woman, with a woman's need to be loved by one special man.

Instead of scooting quickly off the bed, she stayed right where she was. She tried her feminine wings just a bit by languidly turning on her side and propping her head up with her hand. She pulled one leg up slightly, mimicking the sexy poses she had seen in some of her brothers' magazines—the ones they thought she knew nothing about.

Adam's reaction was everything she could have wished for. His whole body tautened. A vein in his temple throbbed. The muscles in his throat worked spasmodically. And something else happened. Something which, considering the level she was lying at, she couldn't help observing.

It was fascinating. She had never actually watched it happen to a man before. Mostly, the men she had dated were already in that condition before she had an opportunity to notice. The changing shape of Adam's Levi's left no doubt that he was becoming undeniably, indisputably, absolutely, completely *aroused.*

She gasped, and her eyes sought out his face to see what he intended to do about it.

Nothing! Adam thought. *He was going to do absolutely nothing about the fact this hoyden in blue jeans had him harder than a rock in ten seconds flat!*

"If you're done testing your feminine wiles, I'd like to finish showing you the house," Adam said.

Humiliated by the sarcasm in his voice, Tate quickly scooted off the bed. She had no trouble recognizing his feelings now. Irritation. Frustration. She felt the same things herself. She had never imagined how powerful desire could be. It was a lesson she wouldn't forget.

She stood before him, chin high, unwilling to admit blame or shame or regret for what she had done. "I'm ready."

Then strip down and get into that bed.

Adam clenched his teeth to keep from saying what he was thinking. He didn't know when he had felt such unbridled lust for a woman. It wasn't decent. But he damn sure wasn't going to do anything about it!

"Come on," he growled. "Follow me."

Tate followed Adam back through the house to the kitchen, where they found a short, rotund Mexican woman with snapping black eyes and round, rosy cheeks. She was chopping onions at the counter. Tate was treated to a smile that revealed two rows of brilliant white teeth.

"Who have you brought to meet me, Señor Adam?" the woman asked.

"Maria, this is Tate Whitelaw. She's going to be my new book-keeper. Tate will be staying in the guest bedroom. Tate, I'd like you to meet my housekeeper, Maria Fuentes."

"*Buenos días, Maria,*" Tate said.

"*¿Habla usted español?*" Maria asked.

"You've already heard all I know," Tate said with a self-deprecating grin.

Maria turned to Adam and said in Spanish, "She is very pretty, this one. And very young. Perhaps you would wish me to be her *dueña.*"

Adam flushed and answered in Spanish, "I'm well aware of her age, Maria. She doesn't need a chaperon around me."

The Mexican woman arched a disbelieving brow. Again in Spanish she said, "You are a man, Señor Adam. And her eyes, they smile at you. It would be hard for any man to refuse such an invitation. No?"

"No!" Adam retorted. Then added in Spanish, "I mean, no I wouldn't take advantage of her. She has no idea what she's saying with her eyes."

Maria's disbelieving brow arched higher. "If you say so, Señor Adam."

Tate had been trying to follow the Spanish conversation, but the only words she recognized were "Maria," "chaperon," "Señor Adam" and "No." The look on Maria's face made it clear she disapproved of the fact Tate would be living in the house alone with Adam. Well, she didn't need a chaperon any more than she needed a keeper. She could take care of herself.

Fortunately, it wasn't necessary for her to interrupt the conversation. A knock at the kitchen door did it for her. The door opened before anyone could answer it, and a young cowhand stuck his head inside. He had brown eyes and auburn hair and a face so tanned it looked like rawhide.

"Adam? You're needed in the barn to take a look at that mare, Break of Day. She's having some trouble foaling."

"Sure. I'll be there in a minute, Buck."

Instead of leaving, the cowhand stood where he was, his eyes glued on the vision in a peasant blouse and skin-tight jeans standing in Adam's kitchen. He stepped inside the door, slipped his hat off his head, and said, "Name's Buck, ma'am."

Tate smiled and held out her hand. "Tate Wh—atly."

The cowboy shook her hand and then stood there foolishly grinning at her.

Adam groaned inwardly. This was a complication he should have foreseen, but hadn't. Tate was bound to charm every cowhand on the place. He quickly crossed past her and put a hand on Buck's shoulder to urge him out the door. "Let's go."

"Can I come with you?" Tate asked.

Before Adam could say no, Buck spoke up.

"Why sure, ma'am," the cowboy said. "Be glad to have you along."

There wasn't much Adam could say except, "You can come. But stay out of the way."

"What kind of trouble is the mare having?" Adam asked as they crossed the short distance to the barn, Tate following on their heels.

"She's down and her breathing's labored," Buck said.

Tate saw as soon as they entered the stall that the mare was indeed in trouble. Her features were grim as she settled onto the straw beside the mare's head. "There now, pretty lady. I know it's hard. Just relax, you pretty lady, and everything will be all right."

Adam and Buck exchanged a look of surprise and approval at the calm, matter-of-fact way Tate had insinuated herself with the mare. The mare lifted her head and whickered in response to the sound of Tate's voice. Then she lay back down and a long, low groan escaped her.

Tate held the mare's head while Adam examined her. "It's twins."

"Why that's wonderful!" Tate exclaimed.

"One of them's turned wrong, blocking the birth canal." In fact, there was one hoof from each of the twins showing.

"Surely your vet can deliver them!"

Adam's features were somber as he answered, "He's out of town at his daughter's wedding." Adam couldn't imagine a way to save either foal, entangled as they were.

Tate's excitement vanished to be replaced with foreboding. She had encountered this problem once before, and the result had come close to being disastrous. Garth had managed to save the mare and both foals, but it had been a very near thing.

"I'll have to take one foal to save the other," Adam said in a flat voice.

"You mean, destroy it?" Tate asked. She couldn't bring herself to say "dismember it" though that was what Adam was suggesting.

"There's nothing else I can do." Adam turned to the cowboy and said, "Buck, see if you can find me some rope."

Tate stroked the mare's neck, trying to keep the animal calm. She looked up and saw the dread in Adam's eyes. It was never easy to make such decisions, yet they were a constant part of ranch life.

She was hesitant to interfere, but there was the tiniest chance the second foal could be saved. "My brother Garth went through this not too long ago. He was able to save both foals by—"

Buck arrived and interrupted with, "Here's the rope, Adam. Do you need my help?"

"I'm not sure. I'd appreciate it if you'd stay."

Buck propped a foot on the edge of the stall and leaned his arms across the top rail to watch as Adam knelt beside the mare and began to fashion a noose with the rope.

Adam paused and glanced over at Tate. She was gnawing on her lower lip again while she smoothed her hand over the mare's sleek neck.

Adam found himself saying, "If you know something that can be done to save both foals, I'm willing to give it a try."

He watched Tate's whole face light up.

"Yes! Yes, I do." She quickly explained how Garth had repositioned the foals.

"I'm not sure I—"

"You can do it!" Tate encouraged. "I know you can!"

Her glowing look made him think he might be able to move mountains. As for saving two spindly foals… It was at least worth a try.

A half hour later, sweat had made damp patches under the arms and down the back of Adam's chambray shirt. He had paused in what he was doing long enough to tie a navy blue bandanna around his forehead to keep the salty wetness out of his eyes. He worked quietly, efficiently, aware of the life-and-death nature of his task.

Adam knew a moment of hope when he finished. But now that the foals had been rearranged, the mare seemed too exhausted to push. He looked across the mare to Tate, feeling his failure in every inch of his body. "I'm sorry."

Tate didn't hear his apology. She took the mare's head onto her lap and began chanting and cooing to the exhausted animal—witchcraft for sure, Adam thought—until the mare amazingly, miraculously birthed the first of the foals.

Adam knew his grin had to be as silly as the one on Tate's face, but he didn't care. Buck took care of cleaning up the first foal while Tate continued her incantations until the mare had delivered the second. Buck again took over drying off the foal while Tate remained at the mare's head, and Adam made sure the afterbirths were taken care of.

When Adam was finished, he crossed to a sink at one end of the barn and scrubbed himself clean. He dried his hands with a towel before rolling his sleeves down from above the elbow to the middle of his forearms.

Adam watched in admiration as Tate coaxed the mare onto her feet and introduced her to her offspring. The mare took a tentative lick of one, and then the other. In a matter of minutes both foals were nudging under her belly to find mother's milk.

Tate's eyes met Adam's across the stall. He opened his arms and she walked right into them. Her arms circled his waist, and she held him tightly as she gave vent to the tears she hadn't shed during the awful ordeal.

"Everything's fine, sweetheart. Thanks to you, everything's just fine," Adam said, stroking her short, silky hair. "Don't cry, sweetheart. You did just fine."

Adam wasn't sure how long they stood there. When he looked up to tell Buck he could go, he discovered the cowboy was already gone. Tate's sobs had subsided and he became aware for the first time of the lithe figure that was pressed so intimately against him.

Tate Whitelaw might be young, but she had the body of a woman. He could feel the soft roundness of her breasts against his chest, and her feminine hips were fitted tight against his masculinity. His growing masculinity.

He tried shifting himself away, but her nose buried itself more deeply at his shoulder and she snuggled closer.

"Tate." He didn't recognize the voice as his own. He cleared his throat and tried again. "Tate."

"Hmm?"

If she didn't recognize the potential danger of the situation was he honor bound to point it out to her? She felt so good in his arms!

Before he could stop himself, his hands had tangled in her hair. He tugged and her head fell back. Her eyes were limpid pools of gold and green. Her face was flushed from crying. She had been gnawing on that lip again and it was swollen. He could see it needed soothing.

He lowered his head and caught her lower lip between his teeth, letting his tongue ride the length of it, testing the fullness of it.

Tate moaned and he was lost.

His tongue slipped into her mouth, tasting her, seeking solace for a desolation of spirit he had never admitted even to himself. Her whole body melted against him, and he was aware of an excruciatingly pleasurable heat in his groin where their bodies were fitted together. He spread his legs slightly and pulled her hard against him, then rubbed them together, creating a friction that turned molten coals to fire.

Tate was only aware of sensations. The softness of his lips. The slickness of his tongue. The heat and hardness of his body pressed tightly against hers. The surge of pleasure as his maleness sought out her femaleness. The urgency of his mouth as it found the smooth column of her neck and teased its way up to her ear, where his breath, hot and moist, made her shiver.

"Please, Adam," she gasped. "Please, don't stop."

Adam's head jerked up, and he stared at the woman in his arms. Good Lord in Heaven! What was he doing?

Adam had to reach behind him to free Tate's arms. He held her at arm's length, his hands gripping hers so tightly he saw her wince. He loosened his hold slightly, but didn't let go. If he did, he was liable to pull her back into his arms and finish what he had started.

Her eyes were lambent, her face rosy with the heat of passion. Her body was languid, boneless with desire, and it wouldn't take much to have her flat on her back beneath him.

Are you out of your mind? What's gotten into you? You're supposed to be protecting her from lechers, not seducing her yourself!

Tate could see Adam was distraught, but she hadn't the least notion why. "What's wrong?" she asked.

Her voice was still breathless and sounded sexy as hell! His body throbbed with need.

"I'll tell you what's wrong, *little girl!*" he retorted. "You may be hotter than a firecracker on the Fourth of July, but I'm not interested in initiating any virgins! Do you hear me? *Flat not interested!*"

"Could have fooled me!" Tate shot back.

Adam realized he was still holding her hands—was in fact rubbing his thumbs along her palms—and dropped them like hot potatoes. "You stay away from me, *little girl.* You're here for one reason, and one reason only—keeping books. You got that?"

"I got it, *big boy!*"

Adam started to reach for her but caught himself. He stalked over and let himself out of the stall. A moment later he was gone from the barn.

Tate curled her arms protectively around herself. What had happened to change things so quickly? One minute Adam had been making sweet, sweet love to her. The next he had become a raving lunatic. Oh, how it had stung when he called her *little girl!* She might be small in stature, but she was all grown up in every way that mattered.

Except for being a virgin.

Tate had to admit she was a babe in the woods when it came to sexual experience. But she recognized that what had just happened between her and Adam was something special. He had wanted her as much as she had wanted him. She couldn't be mistaken about that. But their attraction had been more than sexual. It was as though when she walked into his arms she had found a missing part of herself. And though Adam might discount what had happened because she was so young, she wasn't going to let him get away with denying what had happened between them—to her or to himself.

She wasn't some *little girl* he could dismiss with a wave of his hand. Powerful forces were at work between them. Tate had to find a way to make Adam see her as a woman worthy of his love. But how best to accomplish that goal?

Because the physical attraction between them was so powerful, Tate decided she would start with that. She would put temptation in Adam's path and just see what happened.

Four

Adam watched Tate smiling up at the cowboys who surrounded her at the corral while she regaled them with another of her outrageous stories about life at Hawk's Way, as she had often done over the past three weeks. As usual, she was dressed in jeans, boots and a T-shirt with some equally outrageous slogan written on it.

Only this T-shirt had the neckline cut out so it slipped down to reveal one shoulder—and the obvious fact that she wasn't wearing a bra. Anyone with eyes in his head could see she was naked under the T-shirt. The three cowboys were sure as hell looking. The wind was blowing and the cotton clung to her, outlining her generous breasts.

Adam told himself he wasn't going to make a fool out of himself by going over there and dragging her away from three sets of ogling male eyes. However, once his footsteps headed in that direction, he didn't seem to be able to stop them.

He arrived in time to hear her say, "My brothers taught me how to get even when some rabbit-shy horse bucks me off."

"How's that, Tate?" one of the cowboys asked.

"Why, I just make that horse walk back to the barn all by himself!" Tate said with a grin.

The cowboys guffawed, and Tate joined in. Adam caught his lip curling with laughter and straightened it back out.

"Don't you have some work to do?" he demanded of the three cowboys.

"Sure, Boss."

"Yeah, Boss."

"Just leaving, Boss."

They tipped their hats to Tate, but continued staring at her as they backed away.

Adam swore acidly, and they quickly turned tail and scattered in three different directions.

He directed a cool stare at Tate and said, "I thought I told you to stay away from my cowhands."

"I believe your exact words were, 'Finish your work before you go traipsing around the ranch,'" Tate replied in a drawl guaranteed to irritate her already irritated boss.

"Is your work done?"

"Had you been home for lunch, I'd have offered to show you the bookkeeping system I've set up. Everything's been logged in and all the current invoices have been paid. I have some suggestions for ways—"

He interrupted with, "What the hell are you doing out here half-dressed, carousing with the hired help?"

"*Carousing?* I was just *talking* to them!" Tate flashed back.

"I want you to leave those boys alone."

"Boys? They looked like grown men to me. Certainly old enough to make up their minds whether or not they want to spend time with me."

Adam grabbed the hat off his head and slapped it against his thigh. "Dammit, Tate. You're a babe in the woods! You're playing with fire, and you're going to get burned! You can't run around here half naked and not expect—"

"*Half naked?*" she scoffed. "You've got to be kidding!"

"That T-shirt doesn't leave much to the imagination! I can see your nipples plain as day."

Tate looked down and realized for the first time that twin peaks were clearly visible beneath the T-shirt. She decided to brazen it out. "So what if you can? I assume you're familiar with the female anatomy. Besides, you're not my father or my brother. You have absolutely no right to tell me what to wear!"

Since the erotic feelings Adam was experiencing at the moment weren't the least fatherly or brotherly, he didn't argue with her. However, he had appointed himself her guardian in their stead. As such, he felt it his duty to point out to her the dangers of such provocative attire.

He explained in a reasonable voice, "When a man sees a woman looking like that, he just naturally gets ideas."

Tate looked sharply at Adam. "What kind of ideas?"

"The *wrong* kind," Adam said emphatically.

Tate smiled impishly and batted her lashes at him. "I thought you were 'flat not interested' in li'l ole me."

"Cut it out, Tate."

"Cut what out?"

"Stop batting those lashes at me, for one thing."

Tate pouted her lips like a child whose candy had been taken away. "You mean it isn't working?"

It was working all right. Too damn well. She was just precocious enough to be charming. He was entranced despite his wish not to be. He felt his body begin to harden as she slid her gaze from his eyes, to his mouth, to his chest, and straight on down his body to his crotch. Which was putting on a pretty damn good show for her.

"You're asking for it," he said through clenched teeth.

She batted her eyelashes and said, "Am I going to get it?"

"That's it!"

The next thing Tate knew she had been hefted over Adam's shoulder like a sack of wheat, and he was striding toward the house.

"Let me down!" she cried. "Adam, this is uncomfortable."

"Serves you right! You haven't been the least worried about my comfort for the past three weeks."

"Where are you taking me? What are you planning to do with me?"

"Something I'm going to enjoy very much!"

Was Adam really going to make love to her? Would he be rough, or gentle? How was she supposed to act? Was there some sort of proper etiquette for the ravishing of virgins? Not that she had ever worried too much about what was proper. But she felt nervous, anxious about the encounter to come. Finally, Adam would have to acknowledge that greater forces were at work between them than either of them could—or should—resist.

The air inside the adobe house hit her like a cooling zephyr. The dimness left her blind for an instant. Just as she was regaining her sight, they emerged once more into sunlight and she was blinded again. Several more strides and she felt herself being lowered from Adam's shoulder.

Tate barely had time to register the fact that they were in the courtyard when Adam shifted her crosswise in his arms. Grinning down into her face, he said "Maybe this will cool you off!" and unceremoniously dumped her into the pool of water that surrounded the fountain.

Tate came up spluttering. "Why you!" She blinked her eyes furiously, trying to clear the water from them.

"Why, Miss Tate, are you batting your eyelashes at me again? Guess I'll have to try another dunking."

He took one step toward her, and Tate retreated to the other side of the fountain. "I'll get you for this, you rogue! You roué!"

Adam laughed. It had been so long since he had done so, that the sound brought Maria to the kitchen window to see what Señor Adam found so funny. She shook her head and clucked when she saw the new bookkeeper standing dripping in the fountain. She grabbed a bath towel from the stack of laundry she was folding on the kitchen table and hurried outside with it.

She handed it to Adam and said in Spanish, "This is no way to treat a young woman."

Adam's eyes crinkled at the corners with laughter. "It is when she's bent on seducing an older man."

Maria hissed in a breath and turned to eye the bedraggled creature in the pool. So that was the way the wind was blowing. Well, she was not one to stand in the way of any woman who could make Señor Adam laugh once more.

"Be sure you get the *señorita* dried off quickly. Otherwise she might catch a cold."

Maria left Adam standing with the towel in his hand and a smug grin on his face.

Once the housekeeper was gone, Adam turned back to Tate. And quickly lost his smirk. Because if the T-shirt had been revealing before, it was perfectly indecent now. He could easily see Tate's flesh through the soaked cotton. The cold water had caused her nipples to peak into tight buds.

His mouth felt dry. His voice was ragged as he said, "Here. Wrap yourself in this."

Only he didn't extend the towel to her. He held it so she would have to step out of the pool and into his arms. When he encircled her with the terry cloth she shivered and snuggled closer.

"I'm freezing!" she said.

He, on the other hand, was burning up. How did she do it to him? This time, however, he had only himself to blame. He felt her cold nose burrow into his shoulder as his chin nuzzled her damp hair. The water had released the lilac scent of her shampoo. He took a deep breath and realized he didn't want to let her go.

Adam vigorously rubbed the towel up and down Tate's back, hoping to dispel the intimacy of the moment.

"Mmm. That feels good," she murmured.

His body betrayed him again, responding with amazing rapidity to the throaty sound of her voice. He edged himself away from her, unwilling to admit his need to her. In fact, he felt the distinct necessity to deny it.

"I'm not going to make love to you, Tate."

She froze in his arms. Her head lifted from his shoulder, and he found himself looking into eyes that warmed him like brandy.

"Why not, Adam? Is it because I'm not attractive to you?"

"Lord, no! Of course you're a beautiful woman, but—" Adam groaned as he realized what he had just admitted.

"I am?"

What had those brothers of hers been telling her, Adam wondered, *to make her doubt herself like this?*

"Is it because I don't dress like a lady?"

His only objection to the clothes she wore was his reaction to her in them. "Contrary to what you might have heard, clothes *don't* make the man—or the woman."

"Then it must be the fact that I'm a virgin," she said.

Adam felt himself flushing. "Tate, you just don't go around talking about things like that."

"Not even with you?"

"*Especially* not with me!"

"Why not?"

They were back to that again. He turned her so he had an arm around her shoulder, and began ushering her across the courtyard to her bedroom. "I think it's time you got out of those wet clothes."

Tate's impish smile reappeared. "Would you like to help me?"

"Not on your life!" He opened the sliding glass door and gave her a nudge inside. "I'll meet you in the office in fifteen minutes and you can show me whatever bookkeeping wonders you've accomplished today." He turned and marched across the courtyard, fighting the urge to look back.

Once she was alone in her room, Tate let the towel drop. She stared at herself in the standing oval mirror in the corner and groaned. She looked like something the cat had dragged in! No wonder Adam hadn't been interested!

Tate sat down on a wooden chair to pull off her wet boots, then yanked her T-shirt off and struggled with the wet zipper of her jeans. She peeled her silk panties down and quickly began replacing her clothing with an identical wardrobe. All except the wet boots, for which she substituted a pair of beaded Indian moccasins Charlie One Horse had given her for Christmas.

While Tate dressed, she reviewed the events of the past three weeks since she had arrived at the Lazy S. Teasing Adam had begun as a way of making him admit the sexual attraction—and something more—that existed between them. But she had discovered that kidding some folks was like teasing a loaded polecat. The satisfaction was short-lived.

Tate hadn't been enjoying the game much these days, mainly because she had begun to suffer from the sexually charged situations as much as Adam. The problem was, on her side at least, her heart followed where her hormones lead.

She would give anything if Adam was as interested in her as Buck seemed to be. The lean-hipped cowboy had been asking her every day for a week if she would go out with him on Saturday night. Well, maybe she should. Maybe if Adam saw that somebody else found her worth pursuing, he would get the same idea.

Tate had a cheerful smile on her face by the time she joined Adam in his office. He already had the computer on and was perusing the statistics she had input there.

"So what do you think?" she asked, perching herself on the arm of the large swivel chair in which he was sitting.

"It looks good." Of course his office wasn't as neat as it had once been. There were half-filled coffee cups amidst the clutter on the desk, and a collection of magazines and a dirty T-shirt decorated the floor. A bridle and several other pieces of tack Tate was fixing were strewn around the room.

But he couldn't argue with what she had accomplished. Tate had set up a program to handle data on each head of stock, providing a record that would be invaluable in making buying and selling decisions. "You didn't tell me you knew so much about computers."

Tate grinned and said, "You didn't ask." She leaned across him and began earnestly discussing other ideas she had regarding possible uses of the computer in his business.

He started automatically cleaning the debris from his desk.

"Don't worry about those," Tate said, taking a handful of pebbles from him. "Aren't they pretty? I found them down by the creek." She scattered them back onto the desk. "I play with them while I'm thinking, sort of like worry beads, you know?"

"Uh-huh."

Adam forced himself to concentrate on what she was saying, rather than the way her breast was pressed up against his arm. By the time she was done talking about the projects she had in mind, she had shifted position four times. He knew because she had managed to brush some part of his anatomy with some part of hers each time she moved.

Tate was totally oblivious to Adam's difficulty, because she was having her own problems concentrating on the matters at hand. She was busy planning how she could make Adam sit up and take notice of her by accepting Buck's invitation to go out tomorrow evening. She just had to make sure that Adam saw her leaving on the date with the auburn-haired cowboy.

Her thoughts must have conjured Buck, because he suddenly appeared at the door to Adam's office.

"Need you to take a look at that irrigation system to see whether you want it repaired or replaced," Buck said.

"I'll be right there," Adam replied.

Buck had already turned to leave when Tate realized she had the perfect opportunity to let Adam know she was going out with another man. "Oh, Buck."

Buck turned and the hat came off his head in the same motion. "Yes, ma'am?"

"I've decided to take you up on your offer to go dancing tomorrow night."

Buck's face split with an engaging grin. "Yes, ma'am! I'll pick you up at seven o'clock if that's all right, and we can have some dinner first."

The thunderous look on Adam's face was everything Tate could have wished for. "I'll see you at seven," she promised.

Buck slipped his hat back on his head and said, "You coming, Boss?"

"In a minute. I'll catch up to you."

Adam's fists landed on his hips as he turned to confront Tate. "What was that all about?"

"Buck asked me to go dancing at Knippa on Saturday night, and I thought it might be fun."

Adam couldn't very well forbid her going. As Tate had so pointedly noted, he wasn't related to her in the least. But he couldn't help having misgivings, either. There was no telling what Buck Magnesson's reaction would be if Tate subjected him to the same teasing sensuality that Adam had endured for the past three weeks. If Tate said "Please" Buck was damned likely to say "Thank you" and take what she offered.

Adam suddenly heard himself forbidding his sister Melanie from going out on a date with a boy he had thought a little wild. Heard himself telling Melanie that he knew better than she what was best for her. And remembered the awful consequences of his high-handedness. Adam didn't have to like the fact that Tate had decided to go out with Buck Magnesson. But if he didn't want to repeat the mistakes he had made with his younger sister, he had to put up with it.

"Have a good time with Buck tomorrow night," he said. Then he turned and walked out the door.

Tate frowned at Adam's back. That wasn't exactly the reaction she had been hoping for. Where was the jealousy? Where was the demand that she spend her time with him instead? Suddenly Tate wished she had thought things through a little more carefully. Agreeing to date Buck simply to make Adam realize what he was missing wasn't turning out at all as she had hoped.

She felt a little guilty that she had even considered using Buck to make Adam jealous. But since her plan had failed—quite miserably—she could at least enjoy the evening with Buck with a clear conscience.

Tate had gotten the broken water hose fixed on her '51 Chevy, and she used the pickup to drive the ninety miles east to San Antonio that afternoon to go shopping. She could have worn jeans to go dancing, but had decided that she owed it to Buck to show up for their date looking her best.

She found a pretty halter sundress that tied around the neck and had an almost nonexistent back. The bodice fit her like a glove and showed just a hint of décolletage. The bright yellow and white floral print contrasted with her dark hair and picked up the gold in her eyes. The mid-calf length skirt was gathered at the waist and flared at the hem. She whirled once in front of the mirror and saw that the dress was going to reveal a great deal of her legs if Buck was the kind of dancer who liked to twirl his partner a lot.

Buck's smile when she opened the door on Saturday night was well worth the effort spent shopping. She couldn't help feeling a stab of disappointment that Adam wasn't around to see her off. Apparently he had made plans of his own for the evening.

Tate found Buck surprisingly entertaining company. The cowboy had older brothers of his own, and Tate was quick to agree, "Nothing is harder to put up with than a good example!" He and Tate shared older brother horror stories that kept them both laughing through dinner.

The country and western band was in full swing when they crossed the threshold of the Grange Hall in Knippa. The room was fogged with cigarette smoke that battled with the overwhelming odor of sweat and cologne. The sawdusted dance floor was crowded, elbow to elbow, with men in cowboy hats partnered by ladies wearing flounced Western skirts and boots.

Just as they made their way to the dance floor, a two-step ended and the band began playing a waltz.

"Shall we?" Buck asked, making a dance frame with his arms.

"Absolutely!" Tate said, stepping into his embrace.

Tate got another welcome surprise when she and Buck began to waltz around the room. The lean cowboy was graceful on his feet. He led her into several intricate variations of the dance that left her breathless and feeling like a prima ballerina by the time the song ended.

"That was wonderful!" she exclaimed.

"Would you like something to drink?" Buck asked.

"Just a soda, please."

Buck found a seat for Tate at one of the small tables that surrounded the dance floor and forced his way through the crowd toward the bar.

Tate was tapping her foot to another two-step tune and enjoying watching the couples maneuver around the dance floor when she thought she saw someone she recognized. She followed the couple until they turned at the corner of the room.

Tate gasped aloud. It was Adam! He was dancing the two-step with a buxom redheaded woman.

As he passed by her table, Adam smiled and called out, "Hi, there! Having fun?"

Before she could answer, they had danced on past her, and she was left with the trill of the woman's laughter in her ears.

Tate felt sick. *Who was she?* The Redheaded Woman in Adam's arms was absolutely beautiful. No wonder Adam hadn't been interested in pursuing her when he was acquainted with such a gorgeous female.

"What's caught your eye?" Buck asked as he set a soda in front of Tate.

"Adam's here." She pointed him out. "See there. With that redhead."

To Tate's amazement, Buck scowled and swore under his breath.

"What's wrong?" she asked.

"Nothing I can do anything about."

"That's the sort of statement that's guaranteed to get a nosy female's attention," Tate said. "Out with it."

Buck grinned sheepishly and admitted, "All right. Here goes." He took a deep breath and said, "That woman dancing with Adam is my ex-wife."

"You're kidding!"

"'Fraid not."

Tate watched Buck watching the Redheaded Woman. His feelings were painfully transparent. "You're still in love with her."

Buck grimaced. "Much good it'll do me."

"I assume Adam knows how you feel."

"He asked my permission before he took Velma out the first time."

"And you gave it to him?" Tate asked incredulously.

"She isn't my wife anymore. She can see whoever she pleases."

Tate snorted in disgust. "While you suffer in noble silence. Men!"

Tate had been so involved with talking to Buck that she hadn't realized the song was ending. She was less than pleased when Adam and Velma arrived at their table.

"Mind if we join you?" Adam asked.

Tate bit her lip to keep from saying something censorable. She slipped her arm through Buck's, put a gigantic smile on her face, and said, "Why sure! We'd love to have the company, wouldn't we, Buck?"

It was hard to say who was the more surprised by her performance, Buck or Adam. What she hadn't expected was the militant light that rose in Velma's green eyes when Tate claimed Buck's arm. Well, well, well. Maybe there was more here than met the eye.

Adam made introductions, then seated Velma and caught one of the few waitresses long enough to ask for two drinks.

"I didn't expect to see you here," Tate said to Adam.

"I enjoy dancing, and Velma's a great partner."

Tate could imagine what else Velma was great at. She had observed for herself that the redhead had a wonderful sense of rhythm.

Tate was aware of Buck sitting stiffly beside her, quieter than he had been at any time during the evening. How could Adam not be sensitive to the vibrations that arced across the table between the cowboy and his ex-wife?

In fact, Adam was imminently aware of how much Buck Magnesson still loved his ex-wife. It was why he had brought Velma here this evening. Adam knew that with Velma in the room, Buck wasn't liable to spend much time thinking about Tate.

There was more than one way to skin a cat, Adam thought with satisfaction. He had known Tate would rebel against an ultimatum, so he hadn't protested her date with Buck. He had simply sought out a more subtle way to get what he wanted.

Bringing Velma to the dance seemed like the answer to his problem. He was pretty sure Velma was as much in love with Buck as the cowboy was with his ex-wife. He didn't mind playing Cupid, especially if it meant separating Tate from the virile young cowboy.

"How about trading partners?" Adam said, rising from his chair and reaching for Tate's hand.

Before Tate could protest, Buck said, "That sounds fine to me," took Velma by the hand and headed for the dance floor.

Tate wasn't sure what to make of Adam's ploy. She waited until they were half a dance floor away from the other couple before she said, "That was a pretty sneaky thing to do."

"I wanted to dance with you."

"Are you sure you aren't matchmaking?"

Adam smiled. "You could feel it, too?"

"I think he might still love her."

"I'm sure he does."

"Then why did you bring Velma here tonight?"

"I would think that's obvious."

"Not to me."

"I enjoy her company."

"Oh."

He grinned. "And I knew Buck would be here with you."

He sent her into a series of spins that prevented her from making any kind of retort. By the time she was in his arms again the song was over and he was ushering her back toward their table, where Buck and Velma were sitting across from each other arguing vociferously.

"Buck?" Tate didn't want to interrupt, but she wasn't sure whether she should leave him alone with Velma, either.

"Let's get out of here," Buck said, jumping up and turning his back on Velma. "Good night, Adam. I'll see you tomorrow."

As Buck hurried Tate away, she heard Velma say, "I'd like to go home now, Adam. If that's all right with you?"

Tate wasn't sure where Buck was taking her when he burned rubber on the asphalt parking lot. It was a safe guess from the dark look on his face that he had no romantic intentions toward her.

"Want to talk about it?" she asked at last.

Buck glanced quickly at her, then turned his eyes back to the road. "I don't want to bother you with my problems."

"I'm a good listener."

He sighed and said, "Velma and I were high school sweethearts. We married as soon as we graduated. Pretty soon Velma began to think she had missed something. She had an affair."

Tate bit her lip to keep from saying something judgmental. She was glad she had when Buck continued.

"I found out about it and confronted her. She asked for a divorce, and I gave it to her."

"Why?"

"Pride. Foolish damn pride!"

"And you regret it now?"

"My life's been running kind of muddy without her."

"So why don't you do something about it?" Tate asked.

"It's no use. She says that I deserve better. She doesn't believe I can ever forgive or forget what she did."

"Can you?"

The cowboy's eyes were bleak in the light from the dash. "I think so."

"But you're not sure?"

A muscle worked in his jaw. "If I were, I'd have her back home and under me faster than chain lightning with a link snapped!"

Tate had thought they were driving without direction, yet she realized suddenly that they had arrived back at the front door of Adam's house. She saw Adam's truck parked there. So, he was home. And there was a light on in the living room.

She let herself out of the truck, but Buck met her on the front porch. He put an arm around her waist and walked her away from the light.

"May I kiss you good night, Tate?"

Tate drew a breath and held it. This was so exactly like the scene she had played out the night she had left home that it was eerie. Only there were no brothers here to protect her from the big, bad wolf.

"Of course you can kiss me good night," she said at last.

Buck took his time, and Tate was aware of the sweetness of his kiss. And the reluctance in it. When he lifted his head their eyes met, and they smiled at each other.

"No go, huh?" he said.

Tate shook her head. "I like you an awful lot, Buck. I hope we can be friends."

"I'd like that," the cowboy said.

He leaned down and kissed her again. Both of them knew how much—and how little—it meant.

However, it was not so clear to the man watching them through a slit in the living room curtains.

Five

It had taken every ounce of willpower Adam possessed to keep from stalking out onto the front porch and putting his fist in Buck Magnesson's nose. It wasn't just the thought of his sister Melanie that kept him from doing it. There were things he couldn't offer Tate that Buck could.

But he wasn't a saint or a eunuch. If Tate persisted in tempting him, he wasn't noble enough to refuse her. He was determined to keep his hunger leashed at least until he was certain Tate knew what she *wouldn't* be getting if she got involved with him. She was too young to give up her dreams. And there was no way he could fulfill them.

Before Adam had time to examine his feelings further, the front door opened. Tate stepped inside to find him sitting in one of the large Mediterranean chairs before the blackened fireplace, nursing a half-empty glass of whiskey.

"Hello," she said. "I didn't expect to see you again tonight."

"I was waiting up for you."

Tate immediately bristled. "Look, I don't need a caretaker." She wanted a lover. But not just that. A man who loved her, as she was beginning to fear she loved him.

"Old habits die hard."

"What's that supposed to mean?"

"I used to wait up for my sister Melanie."

"You have a sister? Why haven't I met her?"

"She died ten years ago."

"I'm so sorry."

Adam had drunk just enough whiskey to want to tell her the rest of it. "Melanie ran away from home when she was seventeen. She was picked up by a stranger while hitchhiking. He raped her, and then he stabbed her to death."

"That must have been awful for you!" Tate wanted to put her arms around Adam to comfort him, but his body language posted obvious No Trespassing signs.

She used sitting on the couch as an excuse to cross closer to him, slipped off her boots and pulled her feet up under her. She folded her arms under her breasts to give herself the comfort he wouldn't accept.

Then another, more troubling thought occurred to her. "Is that why you picked me up on the road? Because of your sister?"

Adam nodded.

Tate felt as though she'd been physically struck. She hesitated and asked, "Is that why you offered me a job?"

"It seemed like a good idea at the time."

Tate swallowed over the lump that had grown in her throat. "So I'm just a charity case to you?"

Adam heard the pain in Tate's voice and realized he had handled this all wrong. If he didn't do some fast talking, he knew she would be gone by morning. "You can hardly blame me for offering help under the circumstances, can you? I couldn't take the chance that I might be responsible for another young woman's death!"

Tate wasn't so wrapped up in her own feelings that she failed to recognize the significance of what Adam had just said. "How can you blame yourself for your sister's death? What happened couldn't possibly be your fault!"

"Oh, no?" Adam's nostrils were pinched, his blue eyes like shards of ice. "Didn't you tell me that you left home because your brothers made your life miserable?"

"They only did what they did because they love me!" Tate protested.

"So that makes it all right for them to interfere in your life? To aggravate you enough to send you running in that old rattletrap truck?"

It was clear Adam was searching for answers that would release him from the guilt he suffered over what had happened to his sister. Tate found herself equally confounded by the issues he had raised. Was love a good enough excuse for the high-handed way Garth and Faron had acted? What if she had met the same fate as Adam's sister? Would they have blamed themselves for her death?

She knew they would have, just as Adam had blamed himself for Melanie's death all these years. She didn't know what to say to ease his pain. She only knew she had to do something.

Tate stood and crossed to Adam. She knelt on the cool tile floor at his feet and laid a hand on his thigh. She felt him tense beneath her touch. "Adam, I—"

He rose abruptly and stalked away from her. "I'm not in the mood for any teasing tonight."

"I was trying to offer comfort!" Tate retorted.

"Just stay away from me!"

Tate struck back like the scorned woman she felt herself to be. "There are plenty of others who'll welcome my attentions!"

"Like Buck?"

"Like Buck!" That was a lie, but told in a good cause. Saving her pride seemed of utmost importance right now.

"He'll never marry you. He's still in love with Velma."

Since Tate knew he was right, she retorted, "I don't have to marry a man to go to bed with him!"

"Is that so, *little girl?*"

Tate was gasping, she was so furious at the taunting words. But it was clear she could cut her own throat with a sharp tongue. She had certainly dug a hole for herself it was going to be hard to get out of. She took two deep breaths, trying to regain her temper.

Adam didn't give her a chance to speak before he said, "If you're smart, you'll go back home where you belong. Now, before you get hurt."

"Are you firing me?"

Tate held her breath until he said, "No."

"Then I'm staying. If you'll excuse me, I'm tired. I want to go to bed."

Tate had started for the door when Adam quipped, "What, no invitation to join you?"

Tate slowly turned back to face him. She took her time getting from where she was to where he was. She hooked a finger into the opening at the neck of his shirt and looked up into eyes that were both wary and amused.

"I learned at my brothers' knees never to approach a bull from the front, a horse from the rear...or a damn fool from any direction. Good night, Adam."

"We'll talk about this again tomorrow," he said to her retreating back.

"Like hell we will!" she replied.

Tate spent a restless night, tossing and turning as her mind grappled with all of Adam's revelations. What she found most disturbing was the possibility that Adam had merely been tolerating her because he felt responsible for her welfare.

Surely she couldn't have been mistaken about his physical reaction to her! More likely, he was attracted to her, but his feelings of responsibility toward her were keeping him from pursuing a relationship. If so, she would soon cure him of that!

Tate felt somewhat cheered by her decision, and she made up her mind to confront Adam at breakfast. Only, when she arrived in the kitchen the next morning, she discovered that he had already eaten and left the house.

"Did he say where he was going, Maria?"

"No, *señorita.*"

Tate worked hard all day in the office so she wouldn't have time to worry about where Adam had gone. He was bound to turn up sooner or later. He wasn't going anywhere. And neither was she.

However, by seven o'clock that evening there was still no sign of Adam. He hadn't even called Maria to say he wouldn't be home for dinner. Maria was washing up the dinner dishes, and to keep herself busy, Tate was drying them and putting them away. Maria had tried to start a conversation, but Tate was too distracted to keep track of what she was saying. Finally Maria gave up trying and left Tate to her thoughts.

Tate was worried. Where could Adam have gone? She had already checked once at the bunkhouse, but no one had seen him all day.

When she heard a knock at the kitchen door, Tate leaped to answer it. It wasn't until she opened the door that she realized Adam wouldn't have knocked.

"Buck! You look terrible. What's wrong?"

Buck pulled his hat off his head and wiped the sweat from his brow with his sleeve. "Um, I, um."

She put a hand on his arm and urged him inside the room. "Come in. Sit down."

He resisted her efforts to move him from his spot just inside the kitchen door. "No, I—"

"You what?" Tate asked in exasperation.

"I need your help."

"Of course, anything."

"Maybe you better not say yes until you hear what I have to say." He eyed Maria, but was too polite to ask her to leave.

Aware of the tension in the cowboy, Maria said, "I give you some time alone, so you can talk," and left the room. But she made up her mind she wouldn't be gone for long. The nice *señorita,* she was good for Señor Adam. It would not do to let cowboys like Buck Magnesson take what should not be theirs.

Tate turned a kitchen chair and sat in it like a saddle. "I'm all ears."

Buck fidgeted with the brim of his hat another moment before he said, "I've thought a lot about our conversation last night. You know, about whether or not I could forgive and forget what Velma did? And, well...I believe I can."

A smile spread on Tate's face. "I'm so glad, Buck."

"Yeah, well, that's why I need your help. I've decided to go see Velma and tell her how I feel, and I thought maybe if you were along to sort of referee—"

Tate was up and across the room in an instant. She gave the startled cowboy a big hug. "It'll be my pleasure. When would you like to go see her?"

Buck grinned. "Is right now too soon?"

Tate thought about leaving a note for Adam, then rejected the idea. It would do him good to know how it felt to worry about someone who didn't leave a message where he was going!

Maria heard the kitchen door slam closed and came back in to see what Señor Buck had wanted. She frowned and clucked her tongue in dismay when she realized that Señorita Tate had left the house with the handsome cowboy. "Señor Adam will not like this. He will not like this at all."

Maria made up her mind to stay until Señor Adam got back from wherever he had gone and tell him what had happened. Then he could go find the *señorita* and bring her home where she belonged.

Meanwhile, Buck drove Tate to a tiny house with gingerbread trim in a quiet neighborhood off Main Street in Uvalde. She waited anxiously with him to see if Velma was going to answer the doorbell.

Tate saw the light in Velma's green eyes when she saw Buck, and watched it die when she realized Tate was with him.

"I want to talk to you, Velma," Buck said.

"I don't think we have anything to say to each other." She nearly had the door closed when Buck stuck his boot in it.

"I'm not leaving until I say my piece," Buck insisted in a harsh voice.

"I'll call the police if you don't go away," Velma threatened.

"I just want to talk!"

When Velma let go of the door to run for the phone, Buck and Tate took advantage of the opportunity to come inside. Buck caught Velma in the kitchen and pried the phone receiver out of her hand.

"Please, baby, just listen to me," he pleaded.

"Please give him a chance, Velma. I know you're going to want to hear what Buck has to say."

Velma froze when she heard Tate's voice. "Why did you come here?" she demanded.

"Buck thought it might make it easier for the two of you to talk if there was someone else here to sort of mediate."

Velma looked at Buck's somber face. She took a deep breath and said, "All right. I'll listen to what you have to say. For five minutes."

Buck set her down, letting her body slide along his as he did. Tate could have lit a fire from the sparks that flew between them. They belonged together, all right. She only hoped Buck would find the right words to convince Velma he meant what he said.

Five minutes later, Velma was still listening, but Tate could see she was torn between the fervent wish to believe Buck, and the awful fear that he would soon regret what he was saying.

"I don't think I'll ever forget what happened, Velma," Buck said. "But I think I can live with it."

That wasn't exactly the same thing as *forgiving* it, Tate realized. Apparently Velma also noticed the distinction.

"That's not good enough, Buck," she said in a quiet voice.

"I love you, Velma," he said.

She choked on a sob. "I know, Buck. I love you, too."

"Then why can't we get back together?"

"It just wouldn't work."

By now Velma was crying in earnest, and Buck would have been heartless indeed if he could have resisted pulling her into his arms to comfort her. In fact, that was just what he did.

Tate suddenly realized another reason why she had been brought along. Her presence provided the only restraint on the sexual explosion that occurred whenever the two of them touched. Even that wasn't sufficient at first.

Buck already had his fingers twined in Velma's red curls, and Velma had her hand on the front of Buck's jeans when Tate cleared her throat loudly to remind them that she was still there. They broke apart like two teenagers caught necking, their faces flushed as much by embarrassment as by passion.

"Uh, sorry," Buck said.

Velma tried rearranging her hair, a hopeless task considering how badly Buck had messed it up.

"You look fine, honey," Buck said, taking a hand at smoothing her tresses himself. But the gesture turned into a caress, which turned into a fervent look of desire, which ended when Buck's lips lowered to Velma's in the gentlest of kisses.

There was no telling where things might have gone from there, except Tate said, "All right, enough is enough! We'll never get anywhere this way. Buck, you go sit over there in that chair. Velma and I will sit on the couch."

Sheepishly, Buck crossed the room and slouched down in the chair Tate had indicated. Tate joined Velma on the couch. She dragged her T-shirt out of her jeans and used it to dab at Velma's tears.

"Now it seems to me," Tate began, "that you both want to give this relationship another try. So I have a suggestion."

Tate outlined for them a plan whereby they would start from scratch. Buck would pick Velma up at her door, they would go out together and he would return her at the end of the evening. Absolutely no sex.

"You have to learn to trust each other again," she said. "That takes time."

Buck's face had taken on a mulish cast. "I'm not sure I can play by those rules. Especially that 'no sex' part."

It wasn't hard to see why. The sexual electricity between them would have killed a normal person.

"No sex," Tate insisted. "If you spend all your time in bed, you won't do as much talking. And you both have a lot you need to talk about."

Tate chewed anxiously on her lower lip while she waited to see whether they would accept her suggestion.

"I think Tate's right," Velma said.

The negotiations didn't end there. In fact it wasn't until the wee hours of the morning that all parties were satisfied. Tate felt as emotionally exhausted as she knew Buck and Velma were. The hug Velma gave her as she was leaving, and the whispered "Thank you" from the other woman, made everything worthwhile.

Tate rubbed the tense muscles in her neck as Buck drove her back to the ranch. She knew Buck was still troubled, but at least now there was some hope that he and his ex-wife might one day end up together again.

When they arrived at the front door to Adam's house, Buck took Tate's hand in his and said, "I don't know how to thank you."

"Just be good to Velma. That'll be thanks enough for me."

He ruffled her hair as an older brother might, then leaned over and kissed her on the cheek. "You're a good friend, Tate. If I can ever do anything for you, just let me know."

"I'll remember that," Tate said. "You don't need to get out. I can let myself in."

Buck waited until she was inside the front door before he drove his truck around to the bunkhouse.

Tate had only taken two steps when the living room lights clicked on. Adam stood at the switch, his face a granite mask of displeasure.

"Where were you?" Tate accused. "I waited for you for hours, but you never came home!"

Adam was taken aback, since he had intended to ask the same question. "Dr. Kowalski had a medical emergency with one of my former patients. Susan asked me to come because Mrs. Daniels was frightened, and she thought the old lady would respond better if I was there."

"I knew it had to be something important," Tate said with a sigh of relief. "Were you able to help?"

"Yes, Mrs. Daniels is out of danger now."

Adam suddenly realized that Tate had completely distracted him from the confrontation he had planned. His eyes narrowed as he tried to decide whether she had done it on purpose.

"Where have you been all night?" he asked in a cool voice. "Do you realize it's four a.m.?"

"Is it really that late? I mean, that early," Tate said with a laugh. "I was out with Buck. Oh, Adam—"

He cut her off with a snarl of disgust as she confirmed his worst suspicions. "I don't suppose I have to ask what you were doing, *little girl*. If you were that anxious to lose your virginity you should have told me. You didn't have to drag Buck into the picture."

Tate was aghast. "You think Buck and I—"

"What am I supposed to think when you come rolling in at this ungodly hour of the morning with your T-shirt hanging out and your hair mussed up and your lower lip swollen like it's been bitten a dozen times."

"There's a perfectly logical—"

"I don't want to hear any excuses! Do you deny that you spent the night with Buck?"

"No, but something wonderful happened—"

"I don't want to hear the gory details!"

He was shouting by now, and Tate knew that if she had been any closer Adam might not have been able to control the visible anger that shook his body.

"Get out of my sight!" he said in hard, quiet voice. "Before I do something I'll regret."

Tate put her chin up. If this *fool* would give her a chance, she could explain everything! But her pride goaded her to remain silent. Adam was neither father nor brother. Yet he seemed determined to fill the role of protector. She felt the tears that threatened. Why couldn't he see that she only had eyes for one man—and that man was him!

"Some folks can't see any farther than the steam from their own pot of stew." With that pronouncement, she turned and stalked from the room.

Once Tate was gone, Adam swore a blue streak. When he was

done, he felt worse instead of better. He had hoped he was wrong about what Tate and Buck had been doing out so late. He had been stunned when Tate hadn't denied losing her virginity to the cowboy. He felt absolute, uncontrollable rage at the thought of some other man touching her in ways he knew she had never been touched. And the thought that she had found it *wonderful* caused an unbearable tightness in his chest.

He tried to tell himself that what had happened was for the best. He was not a whole man. She deserved more. But nothing he said to himself took away the bitter taste in his mouth. She was his. She belonged to him.

And by God, now that her virginity was no longer an impediment, he would have her.

Six

Suddenly it was Adam who became the pursuer and Tate who proved elusive. She gave him the cold shoulder whenever she met him and made a point of smiling and recklessly flirting with Buck. Because of the way Buck's courtship was prospering with Velma, he had the look of a happy, well-satisfied man. Which left Adam seething with jealousy.

Tate suspected she could lift the thundercloud that followed Adam around if she simply told him the truth about what she had been doing the night she had spent with Buck. But she was determined that Adam would be the one to make the first move toward conciliation. All he had done for the past week was glare daggers at her.

However, there was more than anger reflected in his gaze, more than antagonism in his attitude toward her. Tate was beginning to feel frazzled by the unspoken sexual tension that sizzled between them. Something had changed since the night they had argued, and Tate felt the hairs lift on her arms whenever Adam was around. His look was hungry. His body radiated leashed power. His features were harsh with unsatisfied need. She had the uneasy feeling he was stalking her.

Tate escaped into the office by day, and played mediator for Buck and Velma at night. She refused to admit that she was hiding from Adam, but that was the case. His eyes followed her whenever they were in the same room together, and she knew he must be aware of her reaction to his disconcerting gaze.

Exactly one week from the day Tate had accompanied Buck on his pivotal visit to Velma, the cowboy took Tate aside and asked whether she minded staying home that evening instead of joining them as chaperon.

"There are some things I'd like to discuss with Velma alone," Buck said.

"Why sure," Tate replied with a forced smile. "I don't mind at all."

Once Buck was gone, Tate's smile flattened into a somber line. She was more than a little worried about what Adam might do if he found out she was home for the evening. She decided the best plan was to avoid him by staying in her room. It was the coward's way out, but her brothers had taught her that sometimes it was best to play your cards close to your belly.

Tate quickly found herself bored within the confines of her bedroom. She remembered that there was some work she could do in the office—if only she could get there without being detected by Adam. The light was on in his bedroom across the courtyard. Adam often retired early and did his reading—both ranch and medical journals—in bed.

She was already dressed for sleep in a long pink T-shirt, but it covered her practically to the knees. She decided it was modest enough even for Adam should he find her working late in the office. She tiptoed barefoot across the tiled courtyard, which was lit by both moon and stars, slipped into Adam's wing of the house via a door at the far end, and sneaked down the hall to the office.

It could have been an hour later, or two, when Tate suddenly felt the hairs prickle on her arms. She had long since finished working at the computer. Because the chair in front of the desk was more comfortable than the one behind it—which was as straight-backed and rigid as the man who usually sat there—she had plopped down in it to look over the printout of what she had done. She had one ankle balanced on the front of the desk and the other hooked on the opposite knee.

She glanced up and found herself ensnared by the look of desire in Adam's heavy-lidded blue eyes.

"Working late?" he asked in a silky voice.

"I thought I'd finish a few things."

Tate was frozen, unable to move, uncomfortably aware that her long T-shirt had rucked up around her thighs, and that her legs were bare all the way up to yonder. As Adam stared intently at her, she felt her nipples harden into dark buds easily visible beneath the pink cotton.

Adam's chest was bare, revealing dark curls that arrowed down into his Levi's. His jeans seemed to be hanging on his hipbones. His belly was ribbed with muscle, and a faint sheen of perspiration made his skin glow in the light from the single standing lamp.

Adam was no less disconcerted by Tate's appearance. He had come to his office looking for a ranch journal and found a sultry sex kitten instead. His view of Tate's French-cut panties was wreaking havoc with his self-control. Her crow-black hair was tousled, and her whiskey-colored eyes were dark with feminine allure.

"You ought to know better than to come here half dressed," Adam said.

"I wasn't expecting to see you."

One black brow arched disbelievingly. "Weren't you?"

Adam abruptly swept the desk clear of debris with one hand while he reached for Tate with the other. Papers flew in the air, cups shattered, Tate's handful of pebbles pinged as they shot across the tile floor. The last paper hadn't landed, nor the pinging sound faded, when he set her down hard on the edge of the desk facing him.

Tate's frightened protest died on her lips. Adam's fierce blue eyes never left hers as he spread her legs and stepped between them. He yanked her toward him, fitting the thin silk of her panties snugly against the heat and hardness of his arousal.

"Is this what you had in mind?" he demanded.

"Adam, I—"

She gasped as rough hands smoothed the cotton over her breasts, revealing nipples that ached for his touch.

"Adam—"

"You've been teasing me for weeks, *little girl*. Even I have my limits. You're finally going to get what you've been asking for."

"Adam—"

"Shut up, Tate."

He seized both her hands in one of his and thrust his fingers into the hair at her nape to hold her captive for his kiss.

Tate didn't dare breathe as Adam lowered his head to hers. Her body was alive with anticipation. Though she had wanted this ever since she had first laid eyes on Adam, she was still a little afraid of what was to come. She wanted this man, and she was certain now that he wanted her. Tonight she would know what it meant to be a woman, to be Adam's woman. The waiting was over at last.

Adam's anger at finding what he considered a sensual trap in his office made him more forceful with Tate than he had intended. But after all, she was no longer the tender, inexperienced virgin of a week ago.

However, somewhere between the moment he laced his hand into her hair and the instant his lips reached hers, his feelings underwent a violent transformation. Powerful emotions were at work, soothing the savage beast. When they finally kissed, there was nothing in his touch beyond the fierce need for her that thrummed through his body.

Tate was unprepared for the velvety softness of Adam's lips as he slid his mouth across hers. His teeth found her lower lip, and she shivered as he nipped it and then soothed the hurt. His tongue teased her, slipping inside, then retreating until she sought it out and discovered the taste of him. Dark and distinctive and uniquely male.

Tate was lost in sensation as each kiss was answered by a streak of desire that found its way to her belly. Her breasts felt full and achy, yet she was too inexperienced to ask for the touch that would have satisfied her body's yearning.

Sometime while she was being kissed, Adam had released her hands. Tate wasn't quite sure what to do with them. She sought out his shoulders, then slid her hands down his back, feeling the corded muscle and sinew that made him so different from her.

Her head fell back as Adam's mouth caressed the hollow in her throat. The male hands at her waist slowly slid up under her T-shirt until Adam was cupping her breasts. Tate gasped as his thumbs brushed across the aching crests. Her body seemed alive to the barest touch of his callused fingertips.

"I want to feel you against me," Adam said as he slipped the pink T-shirt off over her head.

Before Tate could feel embarrassed, his arms slid around her.

He sighed with satisfaction as he hugged her to him. "You feel so good," he murmured against her throat.

Tate's breasts were excruciatingly sensitive to the wiry texture of

Adam's chest hair. She was intimately aware of his strength, of her own softness.

Adam grasped her thighs and pulled her more snugly against him. She clutched his shoulders and held on as his maleness pressed against her femininity, evoking feelings that were foreign, yet which coaxed an instinctive response.

A guttural groan escaped Adam as Tate arched her body into his. His hands dug into her buttocks, trying to hold her still.

"You're killing me, sweetheart," he said. "Don't move!"

"But it feels good," Tate protested.

Adam half groaned, half laughed. "Too good," he agreed. "Be still. I want to be sure you enjoy this as much as I do."

"Oh, I will," Tate assured him.

Adam chuckled as he slid his mouth down her throat. He captured a nipple in his mouth, sucked on it, teased it with his tongue, then sucked again, until Tate was writhing with pleasure in his arms.

He took one of her hands and slid it along the hard ridge in his jeans, too wrapped up in the pleasure of the moment to notice her virginal reluctance to touch him. "Feel what you do to me," he said. "I only have to look at you, think about you, and I want you!" His chin rested at her temple, and he was aware of the faint scent of lilacs. He would always think of her from now on when he smelled that particular fragrance.

It didn't take Tate long to realize how sensitive Adam was to her barest touch, and she reveled in her newfound feminine power.

When he could stand the pleasure no longer, Adam brought each of Tate's hands to his mouth, kissed her wrists and her palms, then placed her hands flat on his chest. "Lift your hips, sweetheart," Adam murmured as he tucked his thumbs into her bikini panties.

She did as he asked, and an instant later Tate was naked. She hid her face in his shoulder, suddenly shy with him.

Adam's arms slipped around her. "There's no need to be embarrassed, sweetheart," he teased.

"That's easy to say when you've got clothes on," she retorted.

Adam laughed. "That can be easily remedied."

He reached between them and unsnapped his jeans. The harsh rasp of the zipper filled a silence broken only by the sound of her labored breathing, and his.

Tate grabbed Adam's wrist to keep him from pulling his zipper down any more. "Not yet," she said breathlessly.

She couldn't help the nerves that assailed her. Adam seemed to think she knew what to do, and perhaps she had led him to believe it was so, but she was all too aware of her ignorance—and innocence.

He dragged the zipper back up but left the snap undone. "There's no hurry, sweetheart. We have all night."

Tate shivered—as much from a virgin's qualms as from anticipation—at the thought.

Adam settled her hands at his waist and lifted his own to gently cup her face. He angled her chin so that she was looking up at him. "You're so damn beautiful!" he said.

"Your eyes." He kissed them closed.

"Your nose." He cherished the tip of it.

"Your cheeks." He gave each one an accolade.

"Your chin." He nipped it with his teeth.

"Your mouth."

Tate's eyes had slipped closed as Adam began his reverent seduction. She waited with bated breath for the kiss that didn't come. Suddenly she felt herself being lifted into his arms. Her eyes flashed open in alarm.

"Adam! What are you doing? Where are we going?"

He was already halfway down the hall to his room when he said, "I want the pleasure of making love to you for the first time in my own bed."

Tate had peeked into Adam's bedroom, but she had never been invited inside. It was decorated in warm earth tones, sandy browns and cinnamon. She had remembered being awed by the sheer size of his bed. The antique headboard was an intricately carved masterpiece, and the spindles at head and foot nearly reached to the ten-foot ceiling.

The quilt that covered the bed was an intricate box design Tate had never seen before, but the craftsmanship was exquisite. Tate grabbed Adam around the neck to keep from falling when he reached down to yank the quilt aside, revealing pristine white sheets.

"Now we can relax and enjoy ourselves," he said.

Adam laid her on the bed and in the same motion used his body to mantle hers. He nudged her legs apart with his knees and settled himself against her so that she was left in no doubt as to the reason he had brought her here.

"Where did you get this bed?" Tate asked, postponing the moment of ultimate truth.

"It's a family heirloom. Several generations of my ancestors have been conceived and born here."

But not my own, Adam thought. *Never my own.*

Tate felt the sudden tension in his body. "Adam?"

Adam's features hardened as he recalled what had happened over the past week to cause him to be here now with Tate. She had made her choice. And he had made his. He wanted her, and she was willing. That was all that mattered now.

Adam's kiss was fierce, and Tate was caught up in the roughness of his lovemaking. There was nothing brutal about his caresses, but they were not gentle, either. His kisses were fervent, his passion unbridled, as he drove her ruthlessly toward a goal she could only imagine.

Tate was hardly aware when Adam freed himself of his clothes. She was so lost in new sensations that the feel of his hard naked body against hers was but one of many delights. The feel of his hands...*there.* The feel of his lips and tongue...*there.*

Tate was in ecstasy bordering on pain. She reached with trembling hands for whatever part of Adam she could find with her hands and her mouth.

"Adam, please!" She didn't know what she wanted, only that she desperately needed...*something.* Her body arched toward his, wild with need.

Just as Adam lifted her hips for his thrust, she cried, "Wait!" But it was already too late.

Adam's face paled as he realized what he had done.

Tate's fingernails bit into his shoulder, and she clamped her teeth on her lower lip to keep from crying out. Tears of pain pooled in the corners of her eyes.

Adam felt her muscles clench involuntarily around him and struggled not to move, fearing he would hurt her more. "You didn't sleep with Buck," he said in a flat voice.

"No," she whispered.

"You were still a virgin."

"Yes," she whispered.

"Why did you make me think— Dammit to hell, Tate! I would have done things differently if I'd known. I wouldn't have—"

He started to pull out of her, but she clutched at his shoulders. "Please, Adam. It's done now. Make love to me."

Tate lifted her hips, causing Adam to grunt with pleasure.

Now that he knew how inexperienced she was, Adam tried to be gentle. But Tate took matters out of his hands, touching him in places that sent his pulse through the roof, taunting him with her mouth and hands, until his thrust was almost savage. He brought them both to a climax so powerful that it left them gasping.

Adam slid to Tate's side and folded her in his embrace. He reached down to pull the covers over them and saw the blood on the sheet that testified to her innocence.

It made him angry all over again.

"I hope you're pleased with yourself!"

"Yes, I am."

"Don't expect an offer of marriage, because you're not going to get it," he said bluntly.

Tate fumbled for a sheet to cover herself. She sat up and stared at Adam with wary eyes. "I don't think I expected any such thing."

"No? What about all those dreams of yours—meeting the right man, having a nice home and a gaggle of children playing at your feet?"

"Geese come in a gaggle," she corrected. "And for your information, I don't think my dream is the least bit unreasonable."

"It is if you have me pictured in the role of Prince Charming."

Tate flushed. She toyed with the sheet, arranging it to cover her naked flank.

Adam watched with regret as her tempting flesh disappeared from view. "Well, Tate?"

She looked into eyes still darkened with passion and said with all the tenderness she felt for him, "I love you, Adam."

"That was lust, not love."

Tate winced at the vehemence with which he denied the rightness of what had just happened between them.

"Besides," he added, "I like my women a little more experienced."

Adam did nothing to temper the pain he saw in Tate's face at his brutal rejection of her. He couldn't give her what she wanted, and he refused to risk the pain and humiliation of having her reject what little he could offer.

"If what you want is sex, I'm available," he said. "But I'm not in love with you, Tate. And I won't pretend I am."

Tate fought the tears that threatened. She would be *damned* if she would let him see how devastated she was by his refusal to acknowledge the beautiful experience they had shared.

"It wasn't just sex, Adam," she said. "You're only fooling yourself if you think it was."

His lips curled sardonically. "When you've had a little more experience you'll realize that any man can do the same thing for you."

"Even Buck?" she taunted.

A muscle jumped in Adam's jaw. She knew all the right buttons to push where he was concerned. "You get the hankering for a little sex, you come see *me,*" he drawled. "*I'll* make sure you're satisfied, *little girl.*"

Tate pulled the sheet free of the mattress and wrapped it around herself as best she could. "Good night, Adam. I think I'll sleep better in my own bed."

He watched her go without saying another word. The instant she was gone he pounded a fist into the mattress.

"Damn you, Tate Whitelaw!"

She had made him wish for something he could never have. She had offered him the moon and the stars. All he had to do was bare his soul to her. And take the heart-wrenching chance that she would reject what little he could offer in return.

Seven

The tears Tate had refused to let Adam see her shed fell with a vengeance once she was alone. But she hadn't been raised to give up or give in. Before long Tate had brushed the tears aside and begun to plan how best to make Adam eat his words.

If Adam hadn't cared for her at least a little, Tate reasoned, he wouldn't have been so upset by her taunt that she would seek out Buck. She was certain that Adam's jealousy could be a powerful weapon in her battle to convince him that they belonged together. Especially since Adam had admitted that he was willing to take extreme measures—even making love to her!—to keep her away from Buck. Tate intended to seek Buck out and let the green-eyed monster eat Adam alive.

It was with some distress and consternation that Tate realized over the next several days that Adam had somehow turned the tables on her. He was the one who found excuses to send her off alone with Buck. And he did it with a smile on his face.

Where was the green-eyed monster? Was it possible Adam really *didn't* care? He was obviously pushing her in Buck's direction. Was this some sort of test? Did he expect her to fall into Buck's arms? Did he *want* her to?

If Tate was unsure of Adam's intentions, he was no less confused himself. He had woken up the morning after making love to Tate and realized that somewhere between the moment she had first flashed that gamine smile at him and the moment he had claimed her with his body, he had fallen in love with her. It was an appalling realization, coming, as it had, after he had insulted and rejected her.

Loving Tate meant being willing to do what was best for her— even if it meant giving her up. He had made the selflessly noble— if absurd—decision that if, after the way he had treated her, she would rather be with Buck, he would not stand in her way. So he had made excuses for them to be alone together. And suffered the agonies of the damned, wondering whether Buck was taking advantage of the time to make love to her.

One or the other of them might have relented and honestly admitted their feelings, but they weren't given the chance before circumstances caused the tension-fraught situation to explode.

Adam had gritted his teeth and nobly sent Tate off with Buck to the Saturday night dance at the Grange Hall in Knippa, not realizing that they were stopping to pick up Velma on the way.

Tate didn't lack for partners at the dance, but she was on her way to a wretchedly lonely evening nonetheless—because the one person she wanted to be with wasn't there. She refused a cowboy the next dance so she could catch her breath. Unfortunately, that gave her time to think.

She found herself admitting that she might as well give up on her plan to make Adam jealous, mainly because it wasn't working. If he truly didn't want her, she would have to leave the Lazy S. Because she couldn't stand to be around him knowing that the love she felt would never be returned.

An altercation on the dance floor dragged Tate from her morose reflections. She was on her feet an instant later when she realized that one of the two men slugging away at each other was Buck Magnesson.

She reached Velma's side and shouted over the ruckus, "What happened? Why are they fighting?"

"All the poor man did was wink at me!" Velma shouted back. "It didn't mean a thing! There was no reason for Buck to take a swing at him."

When Tate looked back to the fight it was all over. The cowboy who had winked at Velma was out cold, and Buck was blowing cool air on his bruised knuckles. He was sporting a black eye and a cut on his chin, but his smile was broad and satisfied.

"Guess he won't be making any more advances to you, honey," Buck said.

"You idiot! You animal! I don't know when I've ever been so humiliated in my entire life!" Velma raged.

"But, honey—"

"How could you?"

"But, honey—"

Tate and Buck were left standing as Velma turned in a huff and headed for the door. Buck threw some money on the table to pay for their drinks and raced outside after her.

Velma was draped across the hood of the pickup, her face hidden in her crossed arms as she sobbed her heart out.

When Buck tried to touch her, she whirled on him. "Stay away from me!"

"What did I do?" he demanded, getting angry now.

"You don't even know, do you?" she sobbed.

"No, I don't, so I'd appreciate it if you'd just spit it out."

"You didn't trust me!" she cried.

"What?"

"You didn't trust me to let that cowboy know I'm not interested. You took it upon yourself to make sure he'd keep his distance.

"You're never going to forget the fact that I strayed once, Buck. You're always going to be watching—waiting to see if I slip up again. And every time you do something to remind me that you don't trust me—like you did tonight—it'll hurt the way it hurts right now.

"I won't be able to stand it, Buck. It'll kill me to love you and know you're watching me every minute from the corner of your eye. Take me home. I never want to see you again!"

Velma sat on the outside edge of the front seat, with Tate in the middle during the long, silent fifteen-minute drive west to Uvalde from Knippa. When they arrived in Velma's driveway, she jumped out and went running into the house before Buck could follow her.

Buck crossed his arms on the steering wheel and dropped his forehead onto them. "God. I feel awful."

Tate didn't know what to say. So she just waited for him to talk.

"I couldn't help myself," he said. "When I saw that fellow looking at her...I don't know, I just went crazy."

"Because you were afraid he would make a move on Velma?"

"Yeah."

"Is Velma right, Buck? Didn't you trust her to say no on her own?"

Buck sighed. It was a defeated sound. "No."

There wasn't anything else to say. Buck had thought he could forgive and forget. But when it came right down to it, he would never trust Velma again. The risk was too great that his trust would prove unfounded.

"I don't want to be alone right now," Buck said. "Would you mind driving up toward the Frio with me? Maybe we can find a comfortable place to sit along the riverbank and lie back and count the stars. Just for a while," he promised. "I won't keep you out too late."

Tate knew Adam might be waiting up for her, but Buck had promised he wouldn't keep her out late. Besides, Adam's behavior over the past few days—throwing her into Buck's company—suggested that he no longer cared one way or the other.

"All right, Buck. Let's go. I could use some time away to think myself."

They found a spot beneath some immense cypress trees, and lay back on the grassy bank and listened to the wind whistling through the boughs. They tried to find the constellations and the North Star in the cloudless blue-black sky. The burble of the water over the rocky streambed was soothing to two wounded souls.

They talked about nothing, and everything. About childhood hopes and dreams. And adult realities. About wishes that never came true. They talked until their eyes drifted closed.

And they fell asleep.

Tate woke first. A mosquito was buzzing in her ear. She slapped at it, and when it came back again she sat up abruptly. And realized where she was. And who was lying beside her. And what time it was.

She shook Buck hard and said, "Wake up! It's dawn already. We must have fallen asleep. We've got to get home!"

Buck was used to rising early, but a night on the cold hard ground—not to mention the events of the previous evening—had left him grumpy. "I'm going, I'm going," he muttered as Tate shoved him toward the truck.

Tate sat on the edge of her seat the whole way home. She only hoped she could sneak into the house before Adam saw her. She could imagine what he would think if he saw her with grass stains on her denim skirt and a blouse that looked as if she had slept in it—which she had. Adam would never believe it had been a totally innocent evening.

When Buck dropped her off, she ran up the steps to the front door—a better choice than the kitchen if she hoped to avoid Adam— and stopped dead when he opened it for her. Adam stood back so she could come inside.

"We fell asleep!" she blurted. "Oh, Lord, that came out all wrong! Look, Adam, I can explain everything. Buck and I did fall asleep, but we weren't sleeping together!"

"I wouldn't have let you sleep, either," he drawled. "Not when there are so many more interesting things to do with the time."

"I mean, we didn't have sex," she said, irritated by his sarcasm.

"Oh, really?" It was obvious he didn't believe her.

"I'm telling you the truth!"

"What makes you think I care who you spent the night with, or what you did?" he said in a voice that could have cut steel.

"I'm telling you that absolutely nothing sexual happened between me and Buck Magnesson last night," she insisted.

Adam wanted to believe her. But he couldn't imagine how Buck could have kept her out all night and not have touched her. He didn't have that kind of willpower himself. His mouth was opened and the words were out before he knew he was going to say them.

"I made you an offer once, *little girl*, and I meant it. If you're looking for more experience in bed, I'll be more than happy to provide it."

Tate's eyes widened as she realized what Adam's harsh-sounding words really meant. He was *jealous!* He *did* care! If only there was some way of provoking him into admitting how he really felt! Of course, there was something that might work. It was an outrageous idea, but then, as her brother Faron had always preached, "A faint heart never filled a flush."

Tate sat down on the brass-studded leather sofa and pulled off one of her boots. When Adam said nothing, she pulled off the other one. Then she stood up and began releasing the zipper down the side of her skirt.

"What are you doing?" he asked at last.

"I'm taking you up on your offer."

"What? Are you serious?"

"Absolutely! Weren't you?" She looked up at him coyly, batted her lashes, and had the satisfaction of seeing him flush.

"You don't know what you're doing," he said.

"I know exactly what I'm doing," she replied.

Her skirt landed in a pile at her feet, and Tate was left standing in a frilly slip and a peasant blouse that was well on its way to falling off her shoulder.

Adam swallowed hard. He knew he ought to stop her, but was powerless to do so. "Maria will be—"

"You know Maria isn't here. Sunday is her day off."

Tate reached for the hem of her blouse and pulled it up over her head.

Adam gasped. He had never seen her in a bra before—if that's what you called the tiny piece of confection that hugged her breasts and offered them up in lacy cups for a hungry man's palate.

Tate watched Adam's pulse jump when she stepped out of the circle of her skirt and walked toward him. His hand was warm when she took it in her own. "Your bedroom or mine?" she asked.

"Mine," he croaked.

Adam allowed himself to be led to his bedroom as though he had no will of his own. Indeed, he felt as though he were living some sort of fantasy. Since it was one very much to his liking, he wasn't putting up much of a struggle—none, actually—to be free.

"Here we are," Tate said as she closed the door behind her, shutting them into Adam's bedroom alone.

"I've never been made love to in the morning," Tate said. "Is there any special way it should be done?"

What healthy, red-blooded male could resist that kind of invitation?

Adam swept Tate off her feet. From then on she was caught up in a whirlwind of passion that left her breathless and panting. But now he led and she followed.

Lips reached out for lips. Flesh reached out for flesh. She was aware of textures, hard and soft, silky and crisp, rigid and supple, as Adam introduced her to the delights of sex in the warm sunlight.

This time there was no pain, only joy as he joined their bodies and made them one. When it was over, they lay together in the tangled sheets, her head on his shoulder, his hand on her hip, in a way that spoke volumes about the true state of their hearts.

Tate was aware of the fact Adam hadn't said a word since she had closed the bedroom door behind them. She didn't want to break the magic spell, so she remained silent. But it was plain from the way Adam began moving restlessly, tugging on the sheet, rearranging it to cover and uncover various parts of her body, that there was something he wanted to get off his chest.

"I don't want you to go out with Buck anymore," he said in a quiet voice.

"All right."

"Just like that? All right?"

"I don't want Buck," she said. "I want you."

Adam groaned and pulled her into his arms, holding her so tightly that she protested, "I'm not going anywhere!"

"I can hardly believe that you're here. That you want to be here," Adam said with a boyish grin. "I've been going crazy for the past week."

"Me, too," Tate admitted. "But everything is going to be perfect now, isn't it, Adam? You do love me, don't you?"

She didn't wait for an answer, just kept on talking.

"We can be married and start a family. Oh, how I'd love to have a little boy with your blue eyes and—"

Adam abruptly sat up on the edge of the bed.

Tate put a hand on his back and he shrugged it off. "Adam? What's wrong?"

He looked over his shoulder with eyes as desolate as an endless desert. "I thought I'd made it clear that I wasn't offering marriage."

"But you love me. Don't you?"

Instead of replying to her question, he said, "I was married once before, for eight years. It ended in a bitter divorce. I have no desire to repeat the experience."

Tate couldn't have been more shocked if Adam had said he was a convicted mass murderer. "Why didn't you ever say anything to me about this before?"

"It wasn't any of your business."

"Well, now it is!" she retorted, stung by his bluntness. "You don't have to make the same mistakes this time around, Adam. Just because one marriage failed doesn't mean another will."

He clenched his teeth, trying to dredge up the courage to tell her the truth. But he wasn't willing to risk the possibility that she would choose having children over having him. And he refused to offer marriage while his awful secret lay like a wedge between them.

"I want you in my bed, I won't deny it," Adam said. "But you'll have to settle for what I'm offering."

"What's that?" Tate asked. "An affair?"

Adam shrugged. "If you want to call it that."

"And when you're tired of me, then what?"

I'll never get tired of you. "We'll cross that river when we get to it."

Tate was shaken by the revelation that Adam had been married. She wished she knew more about what had gone wrong to make him sound so bitter. Her pride urged her to leave while she still could. But her heart couldn't face a future that didn't include Adam. With the naïveté of youth, she still believed that love would conquer all, that somehow, everything would work out and that they would live happily ever after.

"All right," she said at last. "An affair it is."

She snuggled up to Adam's back. He took her arms and pulled them around his chest.

"It's a good thing my brothers can't see me now," she teased.

"I'd be a dead man for sure," he said with a groan.

"Just thank your lucky stars that I've been using a false last name. They'll never find me here."

"Let's hope not," Adam muttered.

The conversation ended there, because Adam turned and pulled Tate around onto his lap. He still didn't quite believe that she hadn't stalked out in high dudgeon, that she had chosen to stay. He straightened her legs around his lap and slipped inside her.

Tate learned yet another way to make love in the morning.

It was a mere three weeks later that their idyll came to a shocking and totally unforeseen end.

Eight

Tate was pregnant. At least she thought she was. She was sitting in Dr. Kowalski's office, waiting for her name to be called so she could find out if the results of her home pregnancy test were as accurate as the company claimed. She was only eight days late, but never once had such a phenomenon occurred in the past. Who would have thought you could get pregnant the first time out!

It had to have happened then, because after that first time she had gone to see Dr. Kowalski and been fitted for a diaphragm. She had managed to use it every time she had made love with Adam over the past three weeks—except the time she had seduced him after spending the night at the river with Buck. So maybe it had happened the second time out. That was beginner's luck for you!

"Mrs. Whitelaw? You're next."

Tate sat up, then realized the nurse had said *Mrs.* Whitelaw. Besides, she had given her name as Tate Whatly. So who was this mysterious *Mrs.* Whitelaw?

The tall woman who stood up was very pregnant. The condition obviously agreed with her, because her skin glowed with health. She had curly blond hair that fell to her shoulders and a face that revealed her age and character in smile lines at the edges of her cornflower-blue eyes and the parentheses bracketing her mouth.

Tate found it hard to believe that it was pure coincidence that this woman had the same unusual last name as she did. Jesse had been gone for so long without any word that Tate immediately began weaving fantasies around the pregnant woman. Maybe this was Jesse's wife. Maybe Jesse would walk in that door in a few minutes and Tate would see him at long last.

Maybe pigs would fly.

Tate watched the woman disappear into an examining room. She was left with little time to speculate because she was called next.

"Ms. Whatly?"

"Uh, yes." She had almost forgotten the phony name she had given the nurse.

"You can come on back now. We'll need a urine specimen, and then I'd like you to strip down and put on this gown. It ties in front. The doctor will be with you in a few minutes."

Tate had had only one pelvic examination in her life—when she had been fitted for the diaphragm—and all the medical hardware attached to the examining table looked as cold and intimidating as she remembered. The wait seemed more like an hour, but actually was only about fifteen minutes. Tate had worked herself into a pretty good case of nerves by the time Dr. Kowalski came into the room.

"Hello, Tate. I understand the rabbit died."

The doctor's teasing smile and her twinkling eyes immediately put Tate at ease. "I'm afraid so," she answered.

The doctor's hands were as warm as her manner. Tate found herself leaving the doctor's office a short time later with a prescription for prenatal vitamins and another appointment in six weeks.

Tate was in the parking lot, still dazed by the confirmation of the fact she was going to have Adam's baby, when she realized that the woman who had been identified as Mrs. Whitelaw was trying to hoist her ungainly body into a pickup.

Tate hurried over to her. "Need a hand?"

"I think I can manage," the woman answered with a friendly smile. "Thanks, anyway."

Tate closed the door behind the pregnant woman, then cupped her hands over the open window frame. "The nurse called you Mrs. Whitelaw. Would you by any chance know a Jesse Whitelaw?"

The woman smiled again. "He's my husband."

Tate's jaw dropped. "No fooling! Really? Jesse's your husband! You've got to be kidding! Why, that means he's going to be a father!"

The woman chuckled at Tate's exuberance. "He sure is. My name's Honey," the woman said. "What's yours?"

"I'm Tate. Wow! This is fantastic! I can't believe this! Wait until I tell Faron and Garth!"

Tate sobered suddenly. She couldn't contact Faron and Garth to tell them she had found Jesse without taking the chance of having them discover her whereabouts. But Jesse wouldn't know she had run away from home. She could see him, and share this joy with him.

With the mention of Tate's name, and then Faron's and Garth's, Honey's gaze had become speculative, and finally troubled. When Honey had first found out she was pregnant, she had urged Jesse to get back in touch with his family. It had taken a little while to convince him, but eventually she had.

When Jesse had called Hawk's Way, he had found his brothers frantic with worry. His little sister Tate had disappeared from the face of the earth, and Faron and Garth feared she had suffered some dire fate.

If Honey wasn't mistaken, she was looking at her husband's little sister—the one who had been missing for a good two and a half months. The prescription for prenatal vitamins that Tate had been waving in her hand suggested that Jesse's little sister had been involved in a few adventures since she had left home.

"I have a confession to make," Tate said, interrupting Honey's thoughts. "Jesse—your husband—is my brother! That makes us sisters, I guess. Gee, I never had a sister. This is great!"

Honey smiled again at Tate's ebullience. "Maybe you'd like to come home with me and see Jesse," she offered.

Tate's brow furrowed as she tried to imagine what Jesse's reaction would be to the fact that she was here on her own. On second thought, it might be safer to meet him on her own ground. "Why don't you and Jesse come over for dinner at my place instead?" Tate said.

"Your place?"

Tate grinned and said, "Well, it's not exactly *mine*. I'm living at the Lazy S and working as a bookkeeper for Adam Philips."

"Horsefeathers," Honey murmured.

"Is something wrong?"

"No. Nothing." Except that Adam Philips was the man she had jilted to marry Jesse Whitelaw.

"Well, do you think you could come?"

If Tate didn't realize the can of worms she was opening, Honey wasn't about to be the one to tell her. Honey was afraid that if she didn't take advantage of Tate's offer, the girl might run into Jesse sometime when Honey wasn't around. From facts Honey knew— that Tate obviously didn't—it was clear the fur was going to fly. Honey wanted to be there to make sure everyone came out with a whole skin.

"Of course we'll come," she said. "What time?"

"About seven. See you then, Honey. Oh, and it was nice meeting you."

"Nice meeting you, too," Honey murmured as Tate turned and hurried away. Honey watched the younger woman yank open the door to the '51 Chevy pickup her brothers claimed she had confiscated when she had run away from home.

"Horsefeathers," she said again. The word didn't do nearly enough to express the foreboding she felt about the evening ahead of her.

Meanwhile, Tate was floating on air. This was going to work out perfectly. She would introduce Adam to her brother and his wife, and later, when they were alone, she would tell Adam that he was going to be a father.

Boy was he going to be surprised!

Tate refused to imagine Adam's reaction as anything other than ecstatic. After all, just as two people didn't have to be married to have sex, they didn't have to be married to have children, either. After all, lots of movie stars were doing it. Why couldn't they?

Long before seven o'clock Tate heard someone pounding on the front door. She knew it couldn't be the company she had invited, and from the sound of things it was an emergency. She ran to open the door and gasped when she realized who was standing there.

"Jesse!"

"So it *is* you!"

Tate launched herself into her brother's arms. He lifted her up and swung her in a circle, just as he had the last time they had seen each other, when she was a child of eight.

Jesse looked so much the same, and yet he was different. His dark eyes were still as fierce as ever, his black hair still as shaggy. But his face was lined, and his body that of a mature man, not the twenty-year-old boy who had gone away when she was just a little girl.

"You look wonderful, Tate," Jesse said.

"So do you," she said with an irrepressible grin. She angled her head around his broad chest, trying to locate Honey. "Where's your wife?"

"I came ahead of her." Actually, he had snuck out behind Honey's back and come running to save his little sister from that sonofabitch Adam Philips. Jesse had never liked the man, and now his feelings had been vindicated. Just look how Philips had taken advantage of his baby sister!

"Faron and Garth have been worried to death about you," Jesse chastised.

"You've been in touch with them? When? How?"

"Honey talked me into calling them when she found out for sure she was pregnant. Is it true what Honey told me? Are you living here with Adam Philips?" Jesse demanded.

"I work here," Tate said, the pride she felt in her job apparent in her voice. "I'm Adam's bookkeeper."

"What else do you do for Adam?"

Tate hissed in a breath of air. "I don't think I like your tone of voice."

"Get your things," Jesse ordered. "You're getting out of here."

Tate's hands fisted and found her hips. "I left home to get away from that kind of high-handedness. I don't intend to let you get away with it, either," she said tartly. "I happen to enjoy my job, and I have no intention of giving it up."

"You don't have any idea what can happen to a young woman living alone with a man!"

"Oh, don't I?"

"Do you mean to say that you and Philips—"

"My relationship with Adam is no concern of yours."

Jesse's dark eyes narrowed speculatively. His little sister glowed from the inside out. He was mentally adding one and one—and getting three. "Honey said she met you in the parking lot of Doc Kowalski's office, but she didn't say what you were doing there. What were you doing there, Tate? Are you sick?"

Jesse was just fishing, Tate thought. He couldn't know anything for sure. But even a blind pig will find an acorn once in a while. She had to do something to distract him.

"Honey's a really beautiful woman, Jesse. How did you meet her?"

"Don't change the subject, Tate."

Jesse had just grabbed Tate by the arm when Adam stepped into the living room from the kitchen. "I thought I heard voices in here." Adam spied Jesse's hold on Tate, and his body tensed. He welcomed the long overdue confrontation with Tate's brother. "Hello, Jesse. Would you mind telling me what's going on?"

"I'm taking my sister home," Jesse said.

Adam searched Tate's face, looking deep into her hazel eyes. "Is that what you want?"

"I want to stay here."

"You heard her, Jesse," Adam said in a steely voice. "Let her go."

"You bastard! It'll be a cold day in hell before I leave my sister in your clutches."

Adam took a step forward, eyes flashing, teeth bared, fists clenched.

"Stop it! Both of you!" Tate yanked herself free from Jesse's grasp, but remained between the two men, a human barrier to the violence that threatened to erupt at any moment.

"Get out of the way, Tate," Jesse said.

"Do as he says," Adam ordered.

Tate put a firm, flat palm on each man's chest to keep them apart. "I said stop it, and I meant it!"

"I'm taking you home, Tate," Jesse said. But his words and the challenge were meant for Adam.

"If Tate wants to stay, she stays!" Adam retorted, accepting the summons to battle.

Tate might as well not have been there for as much attention either man paid to her. She was merely the prize to be won. They were intent only on the conflict to come.

There was a loud knocking at the door, but before any of them could move, it opened and Honey stepped inside. "Thank goodness I got here in time!"

Honey stepped between the two men who fell back in deference to her pregnant state. "What are you two doing to this poor girl?"

She slipped a comforting arm around Tate's shoulder. "Are you all right, Tate?"

"I'm fine," Tate said. "But these two idiots are about to start pounding on each other!"

"He's got it coming!" Jesse growled. "What kind of low-down hyena seduces an innocent child!"

"Jesse!" Tate cried, mortified as much by his use of the term *child* as by his accusation. Jesse might still remember her as a child, but she was a woman now.

Adam's face had bleached white. "You're way off base, Whitelaw," he snarled.

"Can you say you aren't sleeping with her?" Jesse demanded.

"That's none of your damn business!" Adam snapped back.

Honey stepped back a pace, taking Tate with her, beyond the range of the animosity radiating from the two powerful men.

Tate turned to plead peace with her brother. "I love Adam," she said.

"But I'll bet he hasn't said he loves you," Jesse retorted in a mocking voice.

Tate lowered her eyes and bit her lip.

"I thought not!" he said triumphantly.

Tate's chin lifted and her eyes flashed defiance. "I won't leave him!"

"He's just using you to get back at me," Jesse said. "The reason I know he can't love you, is because *I* stole the woman *he* wanted right out from under his nose."

"What?" Confused, Tate looked from her brother to her lover. Adam's eyes were dark with pain and regret.

Tate whirled her head to look at Honey. The pregnant woman's arms were folded protectively around her unborn child. Her cheeks flamed. She slowly lifted her lids and allowed Tate to see the guilt in her lovely cornflower-blue eyes.

It couldn't be true! Adam wouldn't have done something so heinous as to seduce her to get back at her brother for stealing the woman he loved. But none of the three parties involved was denying it.

Her eyes sought out Adam's face again, looking for some shred of hope that her brother was lying. "Adam?"

Adam's stony features spoke volumes even though he remained mute.

"Oh, God," Tate breathed. "This can't be happening to me!"

Jesse lashed out with his fist at the man who had caused his sister so much pain. Adam instinctively stepped back and Jesse's fist swung through empty air. Before Jesse could swing the other fist, Honey had thrown herself in front of her husband.

"Please don't fight! Please, Jesse!"

It was a tribute to how much Jesse loved his wife that he held himself in check. He circled his wife's shoulder with one hand and held out the other to Tate.

"Are you coming?" he asked.

"I...I'm staying." At least until she had a chance to talk with Adam in private and hear his side of this unbelievable story. Then she would decide whether to tell him that she was going to have his child.

Honey saw that her husband was ready to argue further and intervened. "She's a grown woman, Jesse. She has to make her own choices."

"Dammit, this is the wrong one!" Jesse snarled.

"But it is my choice," Tate said in a quiet voice.

Honey slipped her arm around her husband's waist. "Let's go home, Jesse."

"I'm leaving," Jesse said. "But I'll be back with Faron and Garth." He yanked open the door, urged his wife out of the house and quickly followed, slamming the door after him.

Tate felt her stomach fall to her feet. She had been surprised to see Adam stand up to her brother—overjoyed, in fact. But if all three of the Whitelaw brothers showed up, there was no way Adam would be able to endure against them. Her brothers would haul her back home before she had time to say yeah, boo, or "I'm pregnant."

"You might as well say goodbye to me now," she said glumly. "When Faron and Garth find out where I am they'll be coming for me."

"No one—your brothers included—is going to take you from the Lazy S if you don't want to go," Adam said in a hard voice.

"Does that mean you want me to stay?"

Adam nodded curtly.

She didn't want to ask, but she had to. "Is it true, what my brother said? Did you love Honey?"

That same curt nod in response.

Tate felt the constriction in her chest tighten. "Would you have married her if Jesse hadn't come along?"

Adam shoved a hand through his hair in agitation. "I don't know. I wanted to marry her. I'm not so sure she was as anxious to marry me. I asked her. She never said yes."

That was small comfort to Tate, who was appalled to hear how close Adam had come to marrying her brother's wife.

"Is that why you can't love me?" Tate asked. "Because you're still in love with her?"

The tortured look of pain on Adam's face left Tate feeling certain she had hit upon the truth. But she didn't despair. In fact, she felt a great deal of hope. Adam must realize that he could never have Honey Whitelaw now. Time was the best doctor for a wound of the heart. And time was on her side.

She very carefully did not bring up the subject of Jesse's accusation that Adam had made love to her to get revenge on her brother. In her heart she knew Adam would never use her like that. He might not be able to say he loved her—yet—but she was certain that one day he would.

"I need a hug," Tate said.

Adam opened his arms and Tate stepped into them. She snuggled against him, letting the love she felt flow over them both. But his body remained stiff and unyielding.

"Adam, I'm…" The word *pregnant* wouldn't come out.

"What is it, Tate?"

His voice sounded harsh in her ear, his tone still as curt as the abrupt nods with which he had acknowledged his love for another woman. Maybe Tate would just wait a little while before she told him she was carrying his child.

"I'm glad you want me to stay," she said.

He hugged her harder, until his hold was almost painful. Tate felt tears pool in the corners of her eyes. She blamed the phenomenon now on the heightened emotions caused by her pregnancy.

But the devil on her shoulder forced her to admit that unsettling seeds of doubt had been planted concerning whether everything would turn out happily ever after.

Nine

Tate spent the night in Adam's arms. He couldn't have been more comforting. But for the first time since they had begun sleeping together, they didn't make love.

When they met across the kitchen table the next morning, an awkwardness existed between them that had not been there in the past.

"You must eat more, *señorita*," Maria urged. "You will not make it through the day on so little."

"I'm not hungry," Tate said. Actually, she had already snuck in earlier and had a light breakfast to stave off the first symptoms of morning sickness. Under Maria's stern eye, she dutifully applied herself to the bowl of oatmeal in front of her.

Tate's concentration was so complete that she paid no attention to the subsequent conversation Maria conducted with Adam in Spanish.

"The *señorita* has been crying," Maria said.

Adam glanced at Tate's red-rimmed eyes. "Her brother came to visit yesterday, the one she hasn't seen since she was a child."

"This brother made her cry?"

"He wanted her to go away with him."

"Ah. But you did not let her go."

"She chose to stay," Adam corrected.

"Then why was she crying?" Maria asked.

A muscle worked in Adam's jaw. At last he answered, "Because she's afraid I don't love her."

"Stupid man! Why don't you tell her so and put the smile back on her face?"

Adam sighed disgustedly. "I don't think she'll believe me now."

Maria shook her head and clucked her tongue. "I am going to the store to buy groceries. I will not be coming back for two—no, three hours. Tell her you love her."

Adam's lips curled sardonically. "All right, Maria. I'll give it a try."

Tate had been making shapes with her oatmeal and had only eaten about three bites when Maria whisked the bowl out from in front of her.

"I need to clear the table so I can go shopping," Maria said. She refilled Tate's coffee cup. "You sit here and enjoy another cup of coffee."

She refilled Adam's cup as well and, giving him a suggestive look, said, "You keep the *señorita* company."

Maria took off her apron, picked up her purse and left by the kitchen door a few moments later.

When she was gone, the silence seemed oppressive. Finally Adam said, "What are your plans for today?"

"I guess I'll input some more information on the computer. What about you?"

"I'm moving cattle from one pasture to another."

"Your job sounds like more fun than mine. Can I come along?"

"I don't think that would be a good idea."

"Oh."

Adam saw the look on Tate's face and realized she thought he was rejecting her—again. He swore under his breath. "Look, Tate. I think we'd better have a talk."

Tate rose abruptly. This was where Adam told her that he had thought things over and he wanted her to leave the Lazy S after all. She wasn't going to hang around to let him do it. "I'd better get going. I—"

Adam caught her before she had gone two steps. He took her shoulders in his hands, turning her to face him. She kept her eyes lowered, refusing to look at him.

"Tate," he said in a voice that was tender with the love he felt for her. "Look at me."

Her eyes were more green than gold. He couldn't bear to see the sadness in them. He grasped her nape and pulled her toward him as his mouth lowered to claim hers.

It was a hungry kiss. A kiss of longing for things that ought to be. A kiss fierce with passion. And tender with love.

Adam wanted to be closer. He pulled her T-shirt up and over her head, then yanked the snaps open down the front of his shirt and pulled the tails out of his jeans. He sighed in satisfaction as he closed his arms around her and snuggled her naked breasts tight against his chest.

"Lord, sweetheart. You feel so good!" He cupped her fanny with his hands and lifted her, rubbing himself against her, letting the layers of denim add to the friction between them.

His mouth found a spot beneath her ear that he knew was sensitive, and he sucked just hard enough to make her moan with pleasure.

Adam froze when he heard the kitchen door being flung open. He whirled to meet whatever threat was there, pulling Tate close and pressing her face against his chest protectively.

Tate felt Adam's body tense, felt his shoulders square and his stance widen. She knew who it was, who it had to be. She turned her head. There in the doorway stood her three brothers, Faron, Jesse and Garth. And Garth was carrying a shotgun.

Tate felt her face flush to the roots of her hair. She was naked from the waist up, and there could be no doubt as to what she had been doing with Adam. Or, from the looks on their faces, how her brothers felt about it. She closed her eyes and clutched Adam, knowing her brothers planned to tear them apart.

"Make yourself decent!" Garth ordered.

Tate reached across to the chair where Adam had slung her T-shirt, and with her back to her brothers, pulled it over her head. When she turned to face them, Adam put an arm around her waist and pulled her snug against his hip.

The three men crowded into the kitchen. It soon became apparent they hadn't come alone. An elderly gentleman wearing a clerical collar and carrying what Tate supposed to be a Bible followed them inside.

"You have a choice," Garth said to Adam. "You can make an honest woman of my sister, or I can kill you."

Adam cocked a brow. "That's murder."

Garth smiled grimly. "It'll be an accidental shooting, of course."

"Of course," Adam said, his lips twisting cynically. "What if Tate and I aren't ready to get married?"

"Man gets a woman pregnant, it's time to marry her," Jesse snarled. "I made a point of seeing Doc Kowalski on the way home last night and told her Tate was my sister. She congratulated me on the fact I'll soon be an *uncle!*"

Adam froze. He turned to stare at Tate, but she refused to meet his gaze. His hand tightened on her waist. "Are you pregnant, Tate?"

She nodded.

Adam's lips flattened and a muscle worked in his jaw. He grabbed hold of her chin and forced it up. "Whose child is it? Buck's?"

"Yours!" Tate cried, jerking her head from his grasp.

"Not mine," he said flatly. "I'm sterile."

Tate sank into a kitchen chair at one end of the table, her eyes never wavering from Adam's granitelike expression.

Meanwhile, Tate's brothers were in a quandary.

"We can't force him to marry Tate if the child's not his," Faron argued.

"But it must be his!" Jesse said. "Look how we found them today!"

Garth handed the shotgun to Faron, then crossed and sat down beside Tate on the opposite side of the table from Adam. He took Tate's hand from her lap and held it in his for a moment, gently rubbing her knuckles. "I want you to be honest with me, Tate. Have you been with another man besides Adam?"

"No! I'm carrying Adam's child, whether he believes it or not!"

"Adam says he's sterile," Garth persisted.

"I don't care what he says," Tate said through clenched teeth. "I'm telling the truth."

Garth and Faron exchanged a significant glance. Garth stood and confronted Adam. "Can you deny you've made love to my sister?"

"No, I don't deny that."

"Then my original offer still holds," Garth said.

"Given that choice, I suppose I have no choice," Adam conceded with a stony glare.

"What about me?" Tate asked. "Don't I get a choice?"

"You'll do as you're told," Garth commanded. "Or else."

"Or else what?"

"You come home to Hawk's Way."

Tate shuddered. There seemed no escape from the ultimatum Garth had given her. At least if she went through with the wedding, she would still have her freedom. Once her brothers had her safely married they would go back where they had come from—and she could figure out what to do from there.

"All right. Let's get this over with," she said.

"Reverend Wheeler, if you please?" Garth directed the minister to the head of the table, arranged Tate and Adam on one side, and stood on the other side with Faron and Jesse.

He told Adam, "I had to cut a few corners, but I've taken care of getting the license." He gestured to the minister. "Whenever you're ready, Reverend."

If Reverend Wheeler hadn't baptized Tate and presided at her confirmation, he might have had some qualms about what he was about to do. Never had bride and bridegroom looked less happy to be wed. But he firmly believed in the sanctity of home and family. And Garth had promised a large donation to build the new Sunday school wing.

The reverend opened the Bible he had brought along and began to read, "Dearly Beloved..."

Tate listened, but she didn't hear what was being said, spoke when called upon, but was unaware of the answers she gave. She had fallen into a deep well of despair.

Tate had never really thought about having a big wedding, but a white T-shirt was a poor substitute for a wedding gown. She wouldn't have minded giving up the festive trappings, if only she were sure the man standing beside her wanted to be her husband.

Adam did not.

How had things gone so wrong? Tate had never meant to trap Adam. It was clear he thought she had slept with Buck, and that the baby wasn't his. She knew from her experience with Buck and Velma that a marriage that lacked trust—on both sides—was in deep trouble. If Adam believed she had lied about the child's father, wouldn't he expect her to lie about other things? Would he, like Buck, overreact from now on if she so much as looked at another man? Of course Buck was jealous because he loved Velma. Tate wasn't so sure about Adam's feelings. He had never once said he loved her.

Tate would have given anything if she had just told Adam about the baby last night. Then, they would have had a chance to discuss things alone. Such as why a man who was obviously able to sire children thought he was sterile.

"Tate?"

"What?"

"Hold out your hand so Adam can put the ring on your finger," Garth said.

What ring? Tate thought.

"With this ring I thee wed," Adam said. He slipped the turquoise ring he usually wore on his little finger on the third finger of Tate's left hand.

Tate was lost. What had happened to the rest of the ceremony? Had she said "I do"?

Reverend Wheeler said, "I now pronounce you man and wife. You may kiss the bride."

When neither of the newlyweds moved, Faron said in a quiet— some might have said gentle—voice, "It's time to kiss your bride now, Adam."

Adam wanted to refuse. It was all a sham, anyway. But when Tate turned her face up to him she looked so bewildered he felt the urge to take her in his arms and protect her.

Garth cleared his throat at the delay.

Adam's jaw tightened. Tate already had three very efficient guardians. She didn't need him. But he found himself unable to resist the temptation of her lips, still swollen from his earlier kisses. Her eyes slid closed as he lowered his head. He touched his lips lightly to hers, taking the barest taste of her with the tip of his tongue.

If this had been a real wedding he would have wanted to cherish this moment. From the shuffling sounds across the table, Adam was reminded that it was real enough. So he took what he wanted from Tate, ravaging her mouth, letting her feel his fury and frustration at what her brothers had robbed them of when they had insisted on this forced marriage.

As soon as he lifted his head Adam saw that Garth had crossed around the table. Instead of the punch in the nose Adam expected, Tate's oldest brother held out his hand to be shaken. To Adam's further surprise, Garth had a grin on his face.

"Welcome to the family," Garth said. He gave Tate a fierce hug. "Be happy!" he whispered in her ear.

Faron was next to shake Adam's hand. "How about a drink to celebrate?" he asked. "I've got champagne on ice outside in the pickup."

"I guess that would be all right," Adam said, still stunned by the abrupt change in attitude of Tate's brothers.

Faron headed outside as Jesse approached Adam. The two men eyed each other warily.

At last Jesse held out his hand. "Truce?"

When Adam hesitated, Jesse said, "Honey will kill me if we don't make peace." When Adam still hesitated, Jesse added, "For Tate's sake?"

Adam shook hands with Tate's middle brother. They would never be good friends. But they were neighbors, and now brothers-in-law. For their wives' sakes, they would tolerate one another.

The wedding celebration was a lively affair. Now that Adam had done the right thing by Tate, her brothers were more than willing to treat him like one of the family.

As the morning wore on and Adam had a few glasses of champagne—and more than a few glasses of whiskey—he began to think maybe things hadn't turned out so badly after all.

Now that he and Tate were married, there was no reason why they couldn't make the best of the situation. He couldn't feel sorry about the baby, even if it meant Tate had lied to him about sleeping with Buck. He had always wanted children, and this one would be especially beloved because it would belong to him and Tate.

After he made love to his wife, Adam would tell her that he loved her. They could forget what had happened in the past. Their lives could begin from there.

Tate's brothers might have stayed longer, except Honey called to make sure everything had turned out all right. When Jesse hung up the phone, he said to his brothers, "I know you don't want to be reminded, but I have work that has to get done today."

Faron guffawed and said, "Tell the truth. What you're really concerned about is getting home to your wife."

The three brothers kidded each other good-naturedly all the way out the door. Once they and the preacher were gone, Tate closed the door and leaned her forehead against the cool wood frame.

"I'm sorry, Adam."

He crossed to her and slipped his arms around her waist from behind. "It's all right, Tate. It wasn't your fault."

"They're *my* brothers."

"They only did what they thought was best for you." Despite the fact he was a victim of their manipulation, Adam could sympathize with her brothers. If Melanie had lived...if he had found her in the same circumstances...he might have done the same thing. And hoped for the best. As Adam was hoping for the best now with Tate.

He kissed her nape and felt her shiver in his arms. "Come to bed, Tate. It's our wedding day."

She kept her face pressed to the door. She was too intent on giving Adam back his freedom to hear the message of love in his words and his caress. "I can't stand it—knowing you were trapped into marrying me." She felt his body stiffen, and said, "I promise I'll give you a divorce. As soon as the baby is born I—"

Adam grabbed her by the arm and jerked her around to face him. "Is that the reason you agreed to marry me? So you can have a name for your bastard?"

"Please, Adam—"

"Don't beg, Tate, it doesn't become you."

Tate had slapped him before she was aware she had raised her hand. She gasped when she saw the stark imprint her fingers had left on his cheek.

Adam grabbed her wrist. Tate could feel him trembling with rage. She waited to see what form his retaliation would take.

"All right," Adam said in the harshest voice she had ever heard him use. "I'll give you what you want. Your baby will have my name and you can have your divorce. But there's something I want in return, Tate."

"What?" she breathed.

"You. I want you in my bed every night." His grasp on her wrist tightened. "Warm. And willing. Do I make myself understood?"

Oh, she understood, all right. She had offered him the divorce hoping he would refuse. His ultimatum made it clear what he had wanted from her all along. Well, she would just show him what he was so willing to give up!

"Believe me, you're going to get what you're asking for, Adam," she said in a silky voice. *And a whole lot more!*

He started for the bedroom, his hand firmly clamped around her wrist. Tate hurried to catch up, afraid that if she fell, he would simply drag her behind him.

When they arrived in the bedroom he closed the door behind her. Only then did he release her. "Get undressed," he ordered. He crossed his arms and stood there, legs widespread, staring at her.

Tate held herself proudly erect. Sooner or later Adam was going to realize the truth. The child she carried was his. Meanwhile, he was going to get every bit of what he had demanded—and perhaps even more than he had bargained for.

Tate had never stripped to tease a man. She did so now.

The T-shirt came off first. Slowly. She let it hang by one finger for a moment before it dropped to the floor. She looked down at her breasts and saw the aureoles were pink and full. She reached down to brush her fingertips across her nipples, then returned to tease the pink buds until they stood erect.

Adam hissed in a breath of air.

Tate didn't dare look at him, afraid she would lose her nerve. Instead she smoothed her hands over her belly and down across the delta of her thighs, spreading her legs so that her hand could cup the heat there. She glided her hands back up the length of her body, feeling the textures of her skin, aware of the prickles as her flesh responded to the knowledge that Adam was watching every move she made.

She shoved her hands into her hair at the temples and then gathered her hair and lifted it off her nape, knowing that as she raised her arms her breasts would follow. She arched her back in a sensuous curve that thrust breasts and belly toward Adam.

She actually heard him swallow. Then she made the mistake of looking at him—at his bare chest. His nipples were as turgid as hers. As she relaxed her body into a more natural pose, she met blue eyes so dark with passion they were more the hue of a stormy sky.

His nostrils were flared to drink in the scent of her. His body was wired taut as a bowstring, fists clenched at his sides. His manhood was a hard ridge that threatened the seams at the crotch of his jeans. As his tongue reached out to lick at the perspiration on his upper lip, she felt her groin tighten with answering pleasure.

Tate felt exultant. Powerful. And oh, so much a woman. Encouraged by her success, she reached down for the snap of her jeans.

Adam's whole body jerked when it popped free. The rasp of her zipper as she slid it down was matched by the harsh sound of Adam's breathing.

She slowly turned down each side of her jeans in front, creating a V through which the white of her panties showed. Then she spread her legs, stuck her thumbs into her panties and let her fingers slide down inside the jeans, pulling her underwear down and slowly exposing a V of flesh on her belly.

Adam swore under his breath. But he didn't move an inch.

Tate took a deep breath and shoved both panties and jeans down low on her hips, revealing her hipbones and belly and a hint of dark curls at the crest of her thighs. She put her hands behind her and rubbed her buttocks, easing the jeans down a little more with each circular motion.

She stuck her thumbs back in the front of the jeans, and met Adam's gaze before skimming her fingers across her pubic arch. A pulse in his temple jumped. His jaw clenched. But otherwise he didn't stir from where he was standing.

Tate smiled, a feminine smile of enjoyment and satisfaction. She gave one last little shove and both panties and jeans began the slide down to her ankles, where she stepped out of jeans, panties and moccasins all at once.

At last Tate stood naked before Adam. Her body felt languid, graceful as it never had. She realized it was because Adam adored her with his eyes. Because he desired her with his body. She made no move to hide herself from him.

It wasn't until she took a step toward him that Adam finally moved.

He glided toward her like a stalking tiger. Tate felt the sexual energy radiating from him long before their bodies met. His kiss was fierce, consuming. His hands seemed to be everywhere, touching, demanding a response. She arched against him, feeling the swollen heat and hardness beneath the denim.

Adam didn't bother taking her to bed. He backed her up against the wall, unsnapped his jeans to free himself, then lifted her legs around him and thrust himself inside.

Tate clung to Adam's neck with her arms and to his hips with her legs. His mouth sought hers, and his tongue thrust in rhythm with his body. His hand slipped between them and sought out the tiny nubbin that was the source of her pleasure. His thumb caressed her until he felt the waves of pleasure tightening her inner muscles around him. He threw his head back in ecstasy as his own powerful orgasm spilled inside her.

Then his head fell forward against her shoulder as he struggled to regain his breath. He finally released her legs so that she could stand, but found he had to hold her to keep her from falling, her knees were so wobbly. He lifted her into his arms and carried her to bed, throwing the sheets back and setting her down gently before joining her there.

He pulled the covers up over them both and found he could barely keep his eyes open. But there was something he wanted to say before he fell asleep.

"Tate? Are you awake?"

"Mmm. I guess so," she murmured against his throat.

"You can admit the truth about sleeping with Buck. It isn't going to make a difference in how I feel about you." *Or the baby,* he thought.

Tate pushed herself upright. The sheet that had covered her fell to her waist. "I'm telling the truth, Adam, when I say I never slept with Buck. Why won't you believe me?"

Adam levered himself up on his elbow and met her gaze with a flinty one of his own. "Because I have the medical tests to prove you wrong."

"Then your tests are mistaken!" Tate retorted. She leaned back against the headboard and yanked the covers up to her neck.

Tate had never looked more beautiful. Adam had to lie back and put his hands behind his head to keep from reaching for her again. The three hours Maria had promised to stay gone were nearly up, and he had no doubt the housekeeper would come looking for him to find out whether he had told Tate that he loved her.

He was glad now that he hadn't. At least he had been spared the humbling experience of confessing his love to a woman who had married him only to have a name for her child. Adam lay there trying to figure out why Tate persisted in lying about the baby.

"Does Buck know about the baby?" he asked.

"He guessed," Tate admitted. Buck had known from the glow on her face that something was different and had confronted her about it. She had told him the truth.

"I suppose he refused to marry you because he's still in love with Velma," Adam said.

Tate lurched out of bed and stomped over to where her clothes lay in a pile on the floor. She kept her back to Adam as she began dressing.

"Where are you going?" he asked.

"Anywhere I can be away from you," she retorted.

"Just so long as you stay away from Buck, I don't care—"

Tate whirled and said, "Buck is my friend. I'll see him when and where and as often as I please."

Adam shoved the covers out of the way and yanked on his jeans. "You took vows to me that I don't intend to see you break," he said

"You're a fool, Adam. You can't see what's right in front of your face."

"I know a whore when I see one."

Adam was sorry the instant the words were out of his mouth. He would have given anything to take them back. He was jealous, and hurt by her apparent devotion to Buck. He had said the first thing that came into his head that he knew would hurt her.

And he was sorry for it. "Tate, I—"

"Don't say anything, Adam. Just get away from me. Maybe someday I'll be able to forgive you for that."

Adam grabbed his shirt, underwear, socks and boots and left the room, closing the door quietly behind him.

Tate sank onto the bed, fighting sobs that made her chest ache. This was worse than anything she had ever imagined. She had ample evidence in Buck's case of how suspicion and mistrust could make a man act irrationally. She had just never expected to see Adam behave like a jealous jackass.

What was she going to do now?

Ten

Adam had ample time all through the day and overnight to regret his outburst. Tate had spent the rest of the day in the office, then retreated to her own bedroom for the night. He had decided it would be best to meet her over the breakfast table and try to mend fences when Maria was there to act as a buffer.

But morning sickness had once again brought Tate to the kitchen early. Instead of waiting to have coffee with Adam, she left the house to go for a walk, hoping it might settle her stomach. Buck waved to her from the loft of the barn, where he was forking down hay. After looking back once at the house, Tate headed toward the barn to talk to him. She had better give him fair warning that Adam was on the war path and looking for scalps.

Adam's mood wasn't improved when he realized, after sitting at the table for half an hour alone, that Tate wasn't coming to breakfast. He had snapped at Maria like a wounded bear when she started asking questions, and now she wasn't talking to him, either. He shoved his hat down on his head and headed out to the barn to work off some steam by cleaning out stalls.

Adam's eyes had barely adjusted to the shadows in the barn when he spied Tate standing next to the ladder that led to the loft. His heart gave a giant leap—then began to pump with adrenaline when he realized that Buck was standing right beside her. And that the lanky cowboy had his arm around Tate's shoulder.

Adam marched over to Buck and ordered, "Get your hands off my wife."

Buck grinned. "Jealous, huh? You've got no reason—"

Adam thought he had damned good reason to be jealous. After all, his wife was carrying Buck's child. His fist swung hard and fast, straight for Buck's nose.

Buck fell like a stone, his nose squirting blood. Tate quickly knelt beside him, grabbing the bandanna out of her back pocket to staunch the bleeding.

"You idiot!" she snapped at Adam. "Go stick your head in a bucket of water and cool off!"

Adam wanted to yank Tate away from the other man's side, but it was plain he would have a fight on his hands if he tried. His pride wouldn't allow him to ask her nicely to come with him. Not that he could have forced the words past the lump in his throat. "Do as you please," he snarled. "You always have."

With that, he turned and marched right back out of the barn. They heard gravel fly in the drive as he gunned his pickup and drove away.

"Who put a burr under his saddle?" Buck asked, dabbing gently at his nose with the bloody bandanna.

"How did you like the way he treated you?" Tate asked.

"Damn near hated it," Buck replied.

"Think about it the next time you see Velma with another man and decide to take a punch at him. Because that's what an unreasonable, mistrustful, paranoid sonofabitch looks like in action."

Buck's lips quirked at the corners. "Are you saying that's the way I act around Velma?"

"Bingo."

Buck tested the bridge of his nose to see if it were broken. "Maybe this bloody nose wasn't such a bad thing after all."

"Oh?"

"Adam might have knocked some sense into me. I know damn well he has no reason to be jealous, even though he thinks he does. He should have trusted you." Buck struggled to his feet. "Maybe I'll just go see Velma again."

"Is there any chance she'll speak to you?"

"If she's been as miserable as I have the past few weeks, she will," Buck said, a determined light in his brown eyes.

"I wish you luck," Tate said.

"I don't think I'm going to need luck," Buck said. "I've got something even better."

"What's that?"

"I think I just might have had some trust pounded into me."

Tate gave Buck a hug, which he was quick to escape with the excuse of dusting the hay off his britches.

"I may have become a trusting soul," he said, "but Adam's still crazy as a loon. No telling when he'll turn right around and come looking for you. I'd feel a mite safer if you go on back to the house."

Tate did as he asked. She hoped Buck's experience with Adam had shown Buck once and for all the folly of being needlessly jealous. Because if Buck could learn to trust Velma, there was some hope that Adam would one day come to trust her.

Meanwhile, Adam had driven north toward Fredericksburg and was almost into the hill country before he calmed down enough to look around and see where he was. He made a U-turn in the middle of the highway and headed back the way he had come.

Jealousy. Adam had never before had to cope with the feeling, and he had been doing a pretty rotten job of it so far. He could spend the little time he and Tate had together before she sought out a divorce condemning her for what was past. Or he could simply enjoy the company of the irrepressible, lively hoyden he had come to know and love. Between those two choices, the latter made a whole lot more sense.

When Adam arrived back at the ranch house he sought Tate out first in the barn. He found Buck working there.

The lanky cowboy leaned on the pitchfork and said, "You finally come to your senses?"

Adam grinned ruefully. "Yeah. About that punch—"

"Forget it." Buck had been working out how he could use his swollen nose to get Velma's sympathy, and then explain to her the lesson it had taught him. "Believe me, I can understand how you must have felt when you saw me with Tate."

"Because of Velma?" Adam remembered how devastated Buck had been when he had found out his wife was cheating on him.

"Yeah."

"Uh, have you seen Tate?" Adam asked.

"She went back to the house. Look, Adam, you don't—"

"You don't have to explain, Buck. It doesn't matter." Adam

turned and headed back to the house. He found Tate working in his office at the computer.

"Busy?"

Tate jumped at the sound of Adam's voice. She looked over her shoulder and found him leaning negligently against the door frame, one hip cocked, his hat in his hands. The anxious way his fingers were working the brim betrayed his nerves.

"Not too busy to talk," she said. She turned the swivel chair in his direction, leaned back, put her ankles on the desk and crossed her arms behind her head. It was a pose intended to be equally carefree. In Tate's case, her bare toes—which wiggled constantly—gave her away.

In his younger days, Adam had ridden bucking broncs in the rodeo. His stomach felt now as it did when he was on the bronc and the chute was about to open. Like the championship rider he was, he gave himself eight good seconds to make his point and get out.

"I'm sorry. I was out of line—with what I said last night and today with Buck. I'm not asking you to forgive me. I'd just like a chance to start over fresh from here."

Tate sat there stunned. *Adam apologizing?* She had never thought she would see the day. But like Velma, once burned, twice chary. "Does this mean you're rescinding the bargain we made?"

Adam swallowed hard. "No."

So, he still wanted her, even though he was convinced the baby was Buck's. And he was willing to keep his mouth shut about her supposed indiscretion—and give his name to Buck's child—in return for favors in bed.

A woman had to be out of her mind to accept a bargain like that.

"All right," Tate said. "I accept your apology. And I agree to abide by the bargain we made yesterday."

Adam noticed she hadn't forgiven him. But then he hadn't asked for forgiveness. More to the point, she had agreed that their marriage continue to be consummated.

Tate thought she must be an eternal optimist, because she took Adam's appearance at her door as a good sign. She hadn't given up hope that she could somehow convince him of the truth about the baby, and that they would live happily ever after. It might never happen, but at least now they would be living in amity while they tried to work things out.

"It's beautiful out today," Adam said. "How would you like to take a break and come help me? I still have to move those cattle from one pasture to another." Work that hadn't been done yesterday because they had gotten married instead.

A broad smile appeared on Tate's face. "I'd like that. Just let me save this material on the computer."

She dropped her feet and swiveled back around to face the computer. She was interrupted when Adam loudly cleared his throat.

"Uh. I didn't think to ask. Did Dr. Kowalski say everything's okay with the baby? There's no medical reason why you can't do strenuous exercise, is there?"

Tate turned and gave him a beatific smile. "I'm fine. The baby will enjoy the ride."

Nevertheless, Adam kept a close eye on Tate. When he saw her eyelids begin to droop late in the afternoon he suggested they take a siesta. He led her to a giant live oak that stood near the banks of a creek on his property. There he spread a blanket he had tied behind the saddle and provided a picnic he had packed in his saddlebags.

Tate pulled off her boots and wiggled her toes. Then she lay back on the blanket with her hands behind her head and stared up at the freckles of sun visible through the gnarled, moss-laden limbs of the live oak. "This is wonderful! A picnic! I had no idea you had this in mind when you asked me to come with you today."

Actually, Maria was responsible for the impromptu picnic. Adam had thought of the blanket himself. The delight on Tate's face was its own reward. Adam sat down cross-legged across from her and passed out ham and cheese sandwiches, deviled eggs and pickles. There was a thermos of iced tea to drink.

"I don't usually care for pickles," Tate said, crunching into the sweet gherkin in her hand. "But you know, this tastes pretty good."

Adam smiled to himself. In his experience, pregnant women had odd cravings. He had once had a patient who'd eaten liver with peanut butter.

Soon after she had finished her lunch, Tate yawned. "I can't believe how tired I feel lately."

"Your body is going through a lot of changes."

"Is that a medical opinion, Doctor?" Tate asked, eyeing him through half-closed lids. But she didn't hear his answer. The moment she laid her head on her hand and closed her eyes, she fell sound asleep.

Adam cleared away the picnic and lay down beside her to watch her sleep. He had never realized how very long her lashes were, or how very dark. She had a tiny mole beside her ear that he hadn't detected before. And dark circles under her eyes, which he also hadn't noticed.

As a doctor he knew the strain pregnancy put on a woman's body and her emotions. He made a vow to himself to take care of Tate, to make sure that the dark circles disappeared and that the smile stayed on her face.

He knew how she would resent it if she thought he had taken on the role of caretaker. After all, she had fled her brothers because they had been overprotective. He knew he would have to be subtle if he were going to get her to rest. Like the picnic today. He was sure she had no idea she was being manipulated for her own good.

When Tate awoke, she stretched languorously, unaware that she had an appreciative audience. When she blinked open her eyes she realized it was nearly dusk. She sat up abruptly and made herself dizzy.

Adam was beside her instantly, his arm around her shoulder to support her. "Are you all right?"

"Just a little woozy. I guess I sat up too quickly. Why did you let me sleep so long?"

"You were tired."

Tate leaned her head on his shoulder. "I guess I was. Hadn't we better head back now?"

He nuzzled her neck, searching out the mole near her ear. "I don't have anything planned for this evening. Do you?"

Tate chuckled. "No, I can't say that I have."

Adam slowly laid her back down and found her mouth with his. He brushed his cheek against her long lashes and slid his hands into her hair, smoothing it back where the breeze had ruffled it into her face.

As the sun slipped from the sky, Adam made sweet love to his wife. They rode home by moonlight, and after they had taken care of the horses, Adam made sure Tate went right to bed. In his room. With his arms around her.

"I'll have Maria move your things to my room," he murmured

in her ear. "It'll be more convenient since you'll be sleeping in here."

Tate opened her mouth to object and shut it again. After all, she wanted this marriage to work. It made sense that the more time she spent with Adam, the better chance she had of making that happen. She intended to become absolutely irreplaceable in his life.

But as the days turned into weeks, and the weeks into months, the invisible wall of mistrust between them did not come down. Though she made love with Adam each evening, the words "I love you" stuck in Tate's throat whenever she tried to say them. It was too painful to expose her need to him. Especially since she didn't want to put him in the position of feeling he had to say the words back. Which she was afraid he wouldn't.

Adam was equally aware of how much he had gained when he had moved Tate into his bedroom, and how little things had really changed between them. He found himself enchanted by her constant delight in the baby. He tried to be happy with each stage of her pregnancy. Mostly he was successful.

But he watched her and wondered if she ever thought of Buck. The cowboy hadn't been spending much of his free time around the ranch lately. But Adam was watching. Which meant that he still didn't trust her not to seek Buck out if she got the chance.

Meanwhile, he had waited for Tate to tell him again that she loved him. She hadn't said the words lately. Not once, in fact, since they had gotten married. And he found he wanted—needed—to hear those words.

Tate was in bed with Adam when she felt the baby move for the first time. She grabbed his hand and placed it on her belly. "Can you feel that? Kind of a fluttery feeling."

"No." He tried to remove his hand.

"Wait. Maybe it'll happen again."

"Feel here," Adam said, putting her hand on his arousal. "I think I've got a little fluttery feeling of my own."

Tate couldn't help giggling as Adam's body pulsed beneath her hand. "You've got a one track mind, Dr. Philips."

"Oh, but what a lovely track it is," he murmured, kissing his way down her body. His head lay against her belly when he felt a slight movement against his cheek. He came up off her like a scalded cat.

"I felt it! I felt the baby move!"

Tate smiled triumphantly. "I told you so!"

Adam found himself suddenly uncomfortable. As a doctor he had described the stages of pregnancy to his patients hundreds of times. Yet he found himself overwhelmed by the reality of it. That feather-light touch against his cheek had been an actual human being. Growing inside Tate. A baby that would have his name. A baby that Tate planned to take away with her when she divorced him.

Adam was reminded why he shouldn't let himself care too much about either Tate or the baby. It was going to be bad enough when Tate left him. He wouldn't be able to bear it if he got attached to the child, as well.

Adam didn't say anything about what he was thinking, but from that night onward Tate noticed a distinct difference in his behavior whenever she mentioned the baby. Adam seemed indifferent. Nothing she said got him excited or brought a smile to his face. It was as if the baby had become a burden too heavy for him to bear.

Tate had conveniently forgotten that she had promised Adam a divorce as soon as the baby was born. So she was certain the only possible explanation why Adam wasn't allowing himself to get involved with anything having to do with the baby was because he believed it wasn't his child. She decided to try, once more, to convince him that he was the baby's father.

She chose her moment well. She and Adam had just made love and were lying with their bodies still tangled together. Their breathing had eased and Adam's nose was nuzzled against her throat. The baby was active now, and she pressed her belly against his, knowing Adam couldn't help but feel the movement.

"Adam?"

"Hmm."

"The baby's kicking a lot tonight."

"Hmm."

She threaded her fingers through Adam's hair. "You know, I think he's going to be a lot like his father."

She felt Adam stiffen.

"Like you, Adam. He's going to be a lot like you."

Adam's voice was weary as he said, "You don't have to do this Tate. It's not necessary to try and make me believe the baby's mine. I—" *I'll love it anyway.* Adam bit his lip on that admission. No sense revealing the pain she would be causing him when she took the child away.

"But the baby *is* yours, Adam."

"Tate, we've been through this before. I took tests—"

"What about your wife? Did she take tests, too? Maybe it was her fault and not yours."

"Anne was tested. There was nothing wrong with her."

"Maybe they got your test results mixed up with someone else's," Tate persisted. "I mean, you're a doctor. You know those things happen. Did you see the results yourself?"

"Anne called me from the doctor's office," Adam said.

"You mean you weren't there?"

"I had a medical emergency. I—"

"Then she could have lied!" Tate said.

"Why? She wanted children as much as I did. What earthly reason would she have had to lie?"

"I don't know," Tate said. "All I do know is that a child is growing in my body, and the only man who's put his seed inside me is you!"

For an instant Adam felt a wild surge of hope. Maybe there had been some mistake. Maybe Anne had not lied, but been mistaken. He couldn't believe she would have lied about a thing like that. He had seen her tests himself. The problem did not lie with Anne. So something must have been wrong with him for them to remain childless for eight years.

He felt the hope die as painfully as it had been born. "You're making wishes that can't come true, Tate," he said. "This child isn't mine. I'm sterile."

Tate could have screamed, she was so frustrated. "Is that why you refuse to get involved with anything having to do with the baby?" she demanded. "Because you think it isn't yours?"

"Have you forgotten that you promised me a divorce as soon as it's born?" Adam reminded her.

"What if I said I didn't want a divorce? Would you feel differently about the baby then?" Tate persisted.

"What do you want me to say, Tate? That I'll be a father to your child? I will. What more do you want from me?" The words seemed torn from someplace deep inside him.

Tate felt frozen inside. It was clear Adam wouldn't ever be able to accept the baby she carried as his own. And she wouldn't subject her child to a lifetime of rejection by its father, the one person who should love and protect it above all others. That knowledge, on top of her doubts about whether Adam loved her, made it plain that she would be better off away from here.

She didn't say another word, just allowed Adam to pull her into his embrace and hold her one last time. Once he was asleep, she carefully disentangled herself. She turned and looked at him once before she left the room—and his life—forever.

Eleven

Garth and Faron were shocked—to put it mildly—when Tate showed up on the doorstep at Hawk's Way.

"What happened?" Garth demanded. "What did that bastard do to you?"

"You look awful, Tate," Faron said, putting an arm around her shoulder and leading her inside.

"If that man hurt you I'll—"

"Don't, Garth!" Tate pleaded. "Just leave it alone. Adam and I are both better off this way."

"Do you want to talk about it?" Faron asked.

"I just want to go to bed and sleep for a week," Tate said.

Faron and Garth exchanged a sober look. There were deep shadows under Tate's eyes. Her face looked gaunt and unhappy.

"He'll pay for the way he's treated you," Garth said.

"No! Listen to me!" Tate said, her voice sharp with fatigue and anxiety. "You have to trust me to know what's best." There it was again. That word *trust*. "This marriage was a horrible mistake. I'm going to file for a divorce."

"Don't be hasty," Faron urged.

"You're dead on your feet. You have no idea what you're saying," Garth countered.

"Stop it! Both of you! *I'm a grown woman.*" She laughed hysterically. "Don't you see? I'm going to be a mother myself! Surely it's time for you to admit that I can manage my own life. You have to love me enough to let go.''

Tate didn't wait to hear whether they were willing to concede to her wishes. She was too distressed to deal with them anymore. She ran up the stairs to her bedroom, her rigid bearing defying either one of her brothers to come after her.

"She's changed," Faron said.

"And not for the better," Garth noted.

Faron frowned. "I'm not so sure about that. She's grown up, Garth. She's not a little girl anymore. Six months ago she wouldn't have stood up to you like that. I think she had to be in a lot of pain to leave here in the first place, and a helluva lot more pain to come back. I think maybe we're at least partly responsible."

"I blame the bastard who got her pregnant," Garth said.

"None of this would have happened if she hadn't run away from home. And she wouldn't have run away from home if we hadn't kept such a tight rein on her."

"It was for her own good."

"It doesn't seem that way now, does it?" Faron asked. "I think maybe our little sister grew up in spite of us. And I, for one, am not going to interfere anymore in her life."

Adam had been scowling ever since he had woken up to find Tate gone from his bed—and his life. The first thing he had done was to go hunting Buck. His fury had been boundless when the lanky cowboy was nowhere to be found. Finally, one of the other hands told him Buck had been spending nights with his ex-wife.

That news had confounded Adam. He had doggedly made the trip to Velma's house and knocked on the door in the early hours of the morning. Buck had answered the door wearing low-slung jeans and scratching a head of auburn hair that stood out in all directions.

"Adam! What are you doing here this hour of the morning?"

"Where's Tate?"

"How the hell should I know?" Buck retorted.

By now Velma had joined him, wearing a flashy silk robe, and with her red tresses equally tangled. "What's going on, Adam?"

It was obvious to Adam that Tate wasn't here. But he didn't know where else to look. "Do you mind if I come in?"

"Come on in and I'll make us some coffee," Velma said. "You

can tell us what's got you running around at this hour like a chicken with its head cut off.''

While Velma was in the kitchen making coffee, Adam put his elbows on the table and wearily rubbed his forehead. Buck waited patiently for Adam to speak his piece.

"Tate's gone. Run away," Adam said at last.

Buck whistled his surprise. ''Thought that little filly loved you too much ever to leave you.''

Adam's head came up out of his hands. "What?''

"Sure. You and that baby of yours was all she ever talked about.''

"*My* baby?''

"Sure as hell wasn't mine!'' Buck said.

Adam's eyes narrowed. "She spent nearly the whole night with you. Twice.''

Buck laughed in Adam's face. "We were here at Velma's house the first night. And we fell asleep on the banks of the Frio after Velma and I had an argument on the second. There's only been one woman for me. And that's my wife.''

"You mean your ex-wife.''

Buck grinned and held up his left hand, which bore a gold wedding band. "I mean my wife. Velma and I got married again last Sunday.''

"Congratulations. I guess.'' Adam was confused. "But if you're not the father of Tate's baby, then who is?''

Buck pursed his lips and shook his head. "I would think that has to be pretty obvious even to a blind man.''

"But I—'' Adam swallowed and admitted, "I can't father children.''

"Whoever told you that,'' Buck said, "is a whopping liar.''

"But—'' Adam shut his mouth over the protest he had been about to make. Was it really possible? Could Anne have lied to him? It was the only answer that would explain everything.

Adam jumped up from his chair just as Velma brought in the coffeepot.

"You're not staying?'' she asked.

"I've got to get in touch with someone in San Antonio.'' He was going to see the doctor who had done those fertility tests and find out the truth for himself.

"When you're ready to go after Tate, I have a suggestion where you might look," Buck said.

"Where?"

"I figure she went home to her brothers. You'll probably find her at Hawk's Way."

"Damn."

Buck laughed. "I'd like to be a fly on the wall when you try to take her out of there."

Adam wasn't able to think that far ahead. Right now he had a doctor to visit in San Antonio.

Early the next afternoon Adam came out of a glass-walled office building feeling like a man who had been poleaxed.

"Your sperm count was low," the doctor had said. "But certainly still within the range that would allow you to father children."

"But why didn't Anne and I ever conceive children?" he had demanded.

The doctor had shrugged. "It was just one of those things that happens with some couples."

Anne had lied to him. Whatever her reasons—maybe she just hadn't wanted to keep on trying—she had lied to him.

I'm going to be a father! Tate is pregnant with my child!

The realization was only just hitting him. Adam was floating on air. He had always intended to love the child because it was Tate's, but the knowledge that the baby Tate was carrying was a part of him filled his cup to overflowing.

There was only one problem. Tate was at Hawk's Way. And he was going to have to fight her brothers to get her back.

An hour later, he was in his pickup traveling north.

Adam shouldn't have been surprised when he discovered the vastness of Hawk's Way, but he was. The cliffs and canyons in northwest Texas were a startling contrast to the rolling prairies found on the Lazy S.

The ranch house was an imposing two-story white frame structure that looked a lot like an antebellum mansion with its four, twenty-foot-high fluted columns across the front and its railed first- and second-story porches. The road leading to the house was lined with magnolias, but the house itself was shaded by the branches of a moss-laden live oak.

Adam was glad to see that the barn and outbuildings were a good distance from the house. He was hoping to catch Tate alone and talk with her before he had to confront her brothers. He went around to the kitchen door, knocked softly and let himself inside.

Tate was standing at the sink peeling potatoes. She was wearing an apron, and sweat from the heat of the kitchen made her hair curl damply at her nape.

"Hello, Tate."

Tate dropped both potato and peeler in the sink and turned to face Adam. Once she had wiped her hands dry, she kept them hidden in the folds of the apron so Adam wouldn't see how much they were trembling.

"Hello, Adam," she said at last. "I was just peeling potatoes for tonight's pot roast."

"You look tired," he said.

"I haven't been sleeping much the last couple of days." She swallowed over the ache in her throat and asked, "What are you doing here, Adam?"

"I've come to get you. Go upstairs and pack your things. I'm taking you home with me."

"I am home."

"Like hell you are! This is where you grew up, Tate. It isn't your home. Your home is with me and our child."

Tate felt her heart racing with excitement and with hope. Adam's words now were a far cry from what she had heard a mere forty-eight hours ago. It appeared he intended to be a father to the baby after all.

Before Adam could say more, the kitchen door opened and Tate remembered she had told her brothers to come to the house early for lunch because she wanted to take a long afternoon nap. She quailed at the confrontation she knew was coming.

"What the hell are you doing here?" Garth demanded.

"I've come for my wife."

"Tate's not going anywhere," Garth said.

Adam wasn't about to be said nay. He grabbed Tate by the wrist. "Forget your things," he said. "We can get them later." He dragged her two steps, but could go no farther.

Faron and Garth were blocking the way out.

"Get out of my way," Adam said.

"Look, Adam," Faron began in a reasonable voice. "If you'll just—"

But Adam was in no mood to be reasonable. He twisted around to shove Tate out of the way, then reversed the arc with his fist. Faron was felled by the powerful blow, which caught him completely unprepared to defend himself.

Adam stood spread-legged, facing Tate's eldest brother. "I'm telling you to get out of my way."

"You're welcome to leave," Garth said. "But Tate stays here."

"I'm taking her with me."

"That remains to be seen."

Tate knew her brother's strength. He had at least three inches of height and thirty more pounds of muscle than Adam. "Garth, please don't—"

"Shut up, Tate," Adam ordered. "I can handle this on my own." He was fighting for his life—the right to cherish his wife and raise his child—and he had no intention of losing.

The fight that followed was vicious, but mercifully short. When it was finished, Adam was still standing, but it was a near thing. He grabbed Tate's wrist and helped her step over Garth's body on the way out, letting the screen door slam behind her.

Once Tate and Adam were gone, the two brothers, still sprawled on the floor where Adam had left them, had trouble meeting each other's eyes. Two against one and they were the ones dusting themselves off.

Garth cradled his ribs as he sat up and leaned back against the kitchen cupboards. He pulled his shirttail out and pressed the cloth against a cut over his cheekbone.

Faron stretched his legs out in front of him as he leaned back against the refrigerator. He rubbed his sore chin, then opened his mouth and moved his jaw around to make sure no bones were broken.

"Guess our little sister is married to a man who loves her after all," Faron said.

"One with a damned fine right hook," Garth agreed, dabbing gently with his shirttail at the bruised skin around his eye.

The two brothers looked at each other and grinned. Garth yelped when his split lip protested.

"Guess that's one suitor you couldn't scare off," Faron said.

"I always said Tate would know the right man when he came along."

"Seems you were the one needed convincing," Faron said, eyeing Garth's battered face.

Garth guffawed, then moaned when his head protested. "By the way, who do you think's going to be godfather to that baby of hers?"

"Me," Faron said, hauling himself off the floor. "You get to be godfather to Jesse's firstborn."

"Jesse's next oldest. It ought to be him."

"Jesse and Adam don't get along. I'm a better choice," Faron said.

The two brothers headed out to the barn, arguing all the way. Neither of them mentioned the fact that they had been relegated to a new role in Tate's life. Their little sister had found a new protector.

Meanwhile, Tate was aware of every move Adam made, every word he spoke. She had him stop at the first gas station they came to with the excuse she had to use the bathroom. She used the opportunity to clean the blood off his face and bought some bandages in the convenience store to put across the cuts on his cheek and chin.

Once they were back in the car, she said, "You were wonderful, you know. I don't think anybody's ever beaten my brother Garth in a fight."

"I had more at stake than he did," Adam mumbled through his split lips.

Tate's spirits soared at this further evidence that Adam's attitude toward both her and the baby had somehow changed.

It was a long ride back home to the Lazy S, broken frequently by stops to allow Tate to use rest room facilities.

"It's the baby," she explained.

"I know about these things," Adam replied with an understanding smile. "I'm a doctor, remember?"

It was dark by the time they arrived back at the Lazy S. Maria greeted them both at the door with a big hug.

"It is so good to see you back where you belong, *señora!*"

In Spanish she said to Adam, "I see you have put the smile back on her face. You will tell her now you love her, yes?"

"When the time is right," Adam said.

Maria frowned. "The time, she is *right now.*"

Adam refused to be pressed. He excused himself and ushered Tate to his bedroom. He lifted her into his arms and carried her across the threshold.

"Our marriage begins now," he said, looking into her eyes. "The past is past."

Tate could hardly believe this was happening. "I love you, Adam."

She waited for the words she knew he would say back to her. But they didn't come.

There was nothing very difficult about saying those three little words, but Adam felt too vulnerable at the moment to admit the depth of his feelings for Tate. He hadn't really given her a choice about coming back with him. It seemed more appropriate to *show* her that he loved her, rather than to tell her so in words.

He made love to her as though she were the most precious being in the world. He kissed her gently, indifferent to his split lip, tasting her as though he had never done so before, teasing her with his teeth and tongue. Her soft whimper of pleasure rolled through him, tightening his body with need.

His hand slid down to her rounded belly. "My child," he whispered in her ear. "Our child."

"Yes. Yes, our child," Tate agreed, glad that he was ready to accept the baby as his own.

"I mean, I know it's mine," Adam said.

Tate was jerked abruptly from her euphoria. "What?" She turned to face him, her eyes still wide and dilated with pleasure. "What did you say?"

Adam's thumb caressed her belly as his eyes met hers. "I went back to that doctor in San Antonio. The one who did the fertility tests on Anne and me. I'm not sterile, Tate. Anne lied to me."

Tate's eyes widened in horror as she realized what this meant. No wonder Adam hadn't said he loved her. He hadn't come to Hawk's Way for her at all. He hadn't fought Garth for the purpose of getting her back. He had fought to get back his child!

Twelve

Tate pleaded fatigue from her pregnancy as an excuse not to make love to Adam, and the damned man fell all over himself being understanding. Naturally he wanted to make sure she took good care of herself so *his child* would be born healthy!

But the next morning, when Adam stood blocking her way into the office—because she shouldn't have to work in her delicate condition—Tate let him have it with both barrels.

"I'm just as capable of working with *your* child growing inside me as I was when it was just *my* child!" she snapped.

"But—"

"No buts! I'll eat right, get enough rest and come through this pregnancy with flying colors. Even if it is partly *your* child growing inside me and not just *mine*."

Adam wasn't sure what he had done wrong, but Tate obviously had a bee in her bonnet about something. "What's all this *your* child and *my* child business? What happened to *our* child?"

"That was before you found out you can father as many children as you want. Well, you can go father some other fool woman's kids. This baby's *mine!*"

With that, she shoved him out of the office and slammed the door in his face.

Adam could hear her crying on the other side of the door. He tried the handle and found it was locked. He pounded on the door. "Tate, let me in!"

"I don't want to talk to you. Go away!"

He pounded on the door again. "If you don't open this door, I'm going to break it down," he threatened.

He had just turned his shoulder toward the door when it opened, and he nearly fell inside. "That's better," he said, walking in and shutting the door behind him. "I think maybe we better talk about this...difference of opinion. What's important—"

"I'm not a baby that needs coddling. I'm fully capable of taking care of myself. You have to trust me to—oh, what's the use?" she said, throwing up her hands in disgust. "Trust was never a part of our relationship in the past. I don't suppose that just because you've found out I didn't lie to you about the baby, it's going to change anything between us."

"What does trust have to do with this?"

"*Everything!*" Tate was quivering she was so upset. "Buck and Velma—"

"Whoa there! What do Buck and Velma have to do with this?" Adam was getting more confused by the minute.

"It doesn't matter," Tate said.

Adam grabbed her by the shoulders. "It obviously *does* matter. Now I want an explanation and I want it now!"

"You sure about that? Food for thought gives some folks indigestion!"

Adam shoved Tate down in the swivel chair and settled his hip on the desk in front of her. "Settle down now. This kind of agitation isn't good for the baby. I—"

Tate leaped out of the chair and poked a finger at Adam's chest. "*The baby! The baby!*" she mimicked back at him. "That's all you really care about, isn't it? I'm nothing more than a vessel for your seed. I could be a test tube for all the difference it would make to you! Well, I've got news for you, *buster!* I want more than a father for my child, I want a husband to love me and hold me and—" Tate choked back a sob.

"Tate, I do love—"

"Don't say it! If you really loved me, you've had plenty of opportunities to say so. If you say it now I'll know you're just doing it to calm me down for the sake of the baby."

"I'm telling the truth!"

"So was I! When I told you months ago that this baby was yours and mine—*ours!* But you didn't trust me then. And I don't believe you now! Just like Buck and Velma—"

"Are we back to them again?"

"Yes-s-s!" she hissed. "Because Buck and Velma are a perfect example of what happens when there's no trust in a relationship. You hurt each other, and you're miserable and unhappy together.

"If you love somebody you have to be willing to trust them enough to be honest with them. To lay yourself open to the pain of rejection by admitting how you really feel about them. And you have to trust in their love enough to know that they would never do anything purposely to hurt you. Like lying to you. Or sleeping with another man.

"Without trust, love will just wither and die." Tate swallowed another sob and said, "Like it did with Buck and Velma."

"Are you finished?" Adam asked.

Tate sniffled and wiped her nose with the hem of her T-shirt. "I'm finished."

"First of all, I think you should know that Buck and Velma got remarried on Sunday."

Tate's eyes went wide. "They did?"

"Second of all, whether you believe me or not, I do love you. I've loved you for a long time. I never said anything because…"

"Because you didn't trust me," Tate finished in a small voice.

He couldn't deny it, because it was true. "I guess it's my turn to point to Buck and Velma," Adam said ruefully.

"Why?"

"Aren't they proof that people can change? That mistakes aren't irrevocable?"

Tate's brow furrowed. "I suppose."

"Then will you give me a chance to prove how I feel? To prove that I do love you enough to trust you with my heart?"

Tate felt her throat swelling closed with emotion. "I suppose."

"Come here." Adam opened his arms and Tate walked into them. He tipped her chin up and looked deep into her eyes. "We start from here. Our baby, our marriage—"

"Our trust in each other," Tate finished.

They shared a tender kiss to seal the bargain. But it turned into something much more. Or would have, if Maria hadn't interrupted them.

"Señor Adam, there is a man here with the new rodeo bull he says you must sign for."

"I'm coming, Maria."

Adam gave Tate another quick, hard kiss. "Until tonight."

"Until tonight." Tate managed a smile as he turned and left her. He had given her an awful lot to think about. But it was better to confront these issues now, before the baby came, than later. Garth had always said, "If you have a hill to climb, waiting won't make it smaller."

As Adam began to realize over the next several weeks, it was one thing to believe yourself trustworthy; it was quite another thing to earn someone's trust.

He made love to Tate each night, revering her with words and gestures. But he never told her that he loved her. It was plain from the cautious way she watched him when she thought he wasn't looking, that she wasn't yet ready to hear the words—and believe them.

Maria got thoroughly disgusted watching Señor Adam and Señora Tate tiptoe around each other. She nagged at him in Spanish to tell Señora Tate he loved her and be done with it. "If you say it often enough, she will believe it," Maria advised.

"Do you think so?" Adam asked. "Even if she thinks I'm lying through my teeth?"

"But you would not be lying!" Maria protested. "She will see what is in your eyes. And she will believe."

Adam truly wished it were that simple. He was beginning to despair of ever convincing Tate that he loved her enough to want her both as his wife and the mother of his child.

The situation might have gone on unresolved, with both Adam and Tate less than happy, if Maria hadn't decided to take matters into her own hands.

As far as Maria was concerned, it was as plain as white socks on a sorrel horse that Señor Adam loved the little señora, and that she loved him. The problem was getting the two of them to recognize what was right in front of their noses.

So right after lunch one day she sent Señor Adam off to the store to buy some spices she needed for dinner. She waited a half hour, then raced into the office where the señora was working.

"Señora Tate, come quick! There's been an accident! Señor Adam—''

By the time Adam's name was out of Maria's mouth, Tate had already left her chair. She grabbed hold of Maria's sleeve and demanded, "How badly is he hurt? What happened? Where is he?''

"It was the new Brahma bull, the one he has penned in the far pasture," Maria said. "He was not watching closely enough and—''

"The bull stomped him? My God! How did you find this out? I never even heard the phone ring! Has somebody called an ambulance? We have to get Adam to a doctor!''

"Señor Buck has already called the doctor. He is with Señor Adam now.'' Maria smiled inwardly. She hadn't even had to invent an injury for Señor Adam. The *señora* had done that herself. She said, "Señor Buck—''

"Thank God, Buck's with him!'' Tate headed for the kitchen to get the keys to her pickup from the peg where she usually left them. But they weren't there.

"Where are my keys? Maria, have you seen my keys?''

Maria closed her hands around the set of keys in her pocket. "No, *señora*. But your horse, she is saddled already for the ride you wished to take this afternoon.''

"That'll probably be faster anyway. I can go cross-country. Thanks, Maria. You're a lifesaver!''

Tate had barely been gone ten minutes when Maria heard Señor Adam's pickup pull up in back of the house. She sniffed the onion she had ready and waiting and went running out to the truck, tears streaming, waving her hands frantically to attract his attention.

"Señor Adam! The *señora!* Hurry!'' Maria hid her face in her apron and pretended to cry.

"What's wrong, Maria? What happened to Tate? Is she all right?'' He didn't wait for an answer, but bounded up the back steps toward the house.

"She is not there!'' Maria cried.

Adam's face bleached white. "She's gone? She left me?''

Maria saw she had made a serious mistake and said, "Oh, no! But she went riding toward the pasture where you are keeping that big-humped bull. Her horse must have been frightened. Señor Buck found her there on the ground.''

"She's hurt? Has she been taken to the doctor?''

"She is still there. Señor Buck is with her—"

Adam didn't wait to hear more. He jumped back into his pickup and gunned the motor, heading down the gravel road, hell-bent-for-leather toward the opposite end of the Lazy S.

Maria dabbed with her apron at the corners of her eyes where the onion had done its work. Well, she would soon see the results of her meddling. If she was right, there would be more smiles and laughter around this house in the future. When *el bebé* arrived, Tía Maria would tell the story of the day Papa rescued Mama from the big bad bull and brought her home to live here happily ever after.

Tate managed to get through the gate that led to the new bull's pasture without dismounting, but she still begrudged the time it took the mare to respond to her commands as she opened the metal gate and closed it behind her.

Once she was inside the pasture she kept a sharp lookout for the huge Brahma. She wasn't sure what Buck had done to secure it after it had stomped Adam. The chance that it might still be roaming free in the pasture made her shudder in fear.

Tate hadn't gone far when she heard the sound of a truck spinning gravel somewhere beyond the pasture gate. There was no siren, but she thought it might be the ambulance. Maybe they would know exactly where to find Adam. Tate turned the mare back toward the gate and headed there at a gallop.

She was almost to the gate when she realized the huge Brahma bull, with its thick horns and humped back, was standing there, apparently drawn by the sound of the truck, which usually brought hay and feed.

When the bull heard the horse behind him, he whirled to confront the interloper on his territory. Tate found herself trapped, with no way out. She yanked the mare to a halt, holding her perfectly still, knowing that any movement would make the Brahma charge.

Adam swore loudly and fluently when he realized Tate's predicament. He slammed on the brakes, grabbed a rope from the bed of the truck, and hit the ground running.

"Don't move!" he yelled. "I'm coming."

"Wait!" Tate yelled back. "Don't come in here! It's too dangerous!"

Adam didn't bother with opening the gate, just went over the top and down inside. The rattle of the fence had the bull turning back, certain dinner was about to be served. He stopped, confused when he saw the man on foot inside the fence. He nodded his lowered head from Tate to Adam and back again, uncertain which way he wanted to go.

Adam shook out the lasso and started looking for something he could use as a snubbing post. Not too far away stood a medium-size live oak.

Adam didn't hesitate. He walked slowly toward the Brahma, which began to snort and paw at the ground in agitation. The bull's attention was definitely on Adam now, not Tate.

"Please don't come any closer, Adam," Tate said quietly.

"Don't worry. I've got this all worked out." If he missed his throw, he was going to run like hell and hope he got to the fence before the Brahma got to him.

But Adam's loop sang through the air and landed neatly around the Brahma's horns. He let out the rope as he ran for the live oak. He circled the tree several times, enough to make sure the rope was going to hold when the bull hit the end of it.

By then, Tate had realized what he was doing. She raced her mare to the live oak, took her foot out of the stirrup so Adam could quickly mount behind her, then kicked the mare into a gallop that took them out of harm's way.

The Brahma charged after them, but was brought up short by the rope that held it hog-tied to the tree.

Tate rode the mare back to the gate, where Adam slipped over the horse's rump, and quickly opened the gate for her. Once she was through, he fastened the gate, and reached up to pull her off the mare.

They clutched each other tightly, well aware of the calamity they had barely escaped. As soon as their initial relief was past, they began talking at the same time, amazed by the fact that they had found each other alive and well and unhurt.

"Maria told me the bull had stomped you!"

"She told me you had been thrown from your horse!"

"I wasn't thrown!"

"I wasn't stomped!"

The realization dawned for both at the same time that they had been manipulated into coming here under false pretenses.

"I'll kill her!" Adam said.

"I think you should give her a raise," Tate said with a laugh.

"Why? She nearly got us both killed!"

"Because she made me realize I've been a fool not to believe what I know in my heart is true."

"I do love you, Tate," Adam said. He pulled her into his arms and kissed her hard. "I do love you."

"I know. And I love you. When I thought you might be dying—or dead—I realized just how much."

"When I thought something might have happened to you, I felt the same," Adam said. "I should have been saying 'I love you' every day. I love you, Tate. I love you. I love you."

Adam punctuated each statement with a kiss that was more fervent than the one before.

Tate was having trouble catching her breath. She managed to say, "Adam, we have to do something about that bull."

"Let him find his own heifer," Adam murmured against her throat.

Tate laughed. "We can't just leave him tied up like that."

"I'll send Buck and the boys back to take care of him and to pick up your mare. We have more important things to do this afternoon."

"Like what?"

"Like plotting how we're going to get even with Maria."

As they drove back toward the ranch house, Adam and Tate plotted imaginative punishments they could wreak on the housekeeper for lying to them. It wasn't an easy job, considering how they had to balance her dubious methods against her very satisfying results.

"I think the best thing we could do is have about five children," Adam said.

Tate gulped. "Five?"

"Sure. That'll fix Maria, all right. She'll have the little devils sitting on her lap and tugging at her skirts for a good long while!"

"Serves her right!" Tate agreed with a grin.

Adam stopped the pickup in front of the ranch house, grabbed Tate's hand and went running inside to find the housekeeper.

"Maria!" he shouted. "Where are you?" He headed for the kitchen, dragging Tate along behind him.

"Here's a note on the refrigerator," Tate said.
"What's it say?"
Tate held the note out to Adam.

Dear Señor Adam,
Tell her you love her. I'll be gone for two—no, three—hours.

Love, Maria

Adam laughed and pulled Tate into his embrace—where the first of Maria's little devils promptly kicked his father in the stomach.

*   *   *   *   *

THE COWBOY AND THE PRINCESS

One

He was a man who loved women. Blond or brunette, freckled or dimpled, witty or shy, Faron Whitelaw made it his business to discover the facet of each woman that made her uniquely beautiful. Needless to say, women found Faron irresistible. Even if he hadn't been handsome, which he was, they would have loved him for the innate thoughtfulness that always made him give as much as he took. Any woman who passed through Faron Whitelaw's life—whether in bed or out—received a gift that would remain with her a lifetime: the knowledge that she was a very special, desirable human being.

In fact, Faron had never known a woman he didn't like. Until now. At the age of thirty he had finally encountered the exception to the rule. He not only didn't like Belinda Prescott, he was prepared to hate her with a passion. Because, despite the fact he had never laid eyes on her, the woman was personally responsible for turning his life upside down.

"Want some company?"

Faron looked up at his eldest brother from the chair where he sat slouched with a whiskey in his hand. "Not particularly."

Garth snorted. "Too damn bad." He poured himself two fingers of whiskey and took the chair opposite Faron's in front of the stone fireplace. He put his feet up on a sturdy rawhide-covered stool that had held generations of Whitelaw boots. "I can't believe you're making so much out of this."

Faron's gray-green eyes narrowed. His lips twisted into a bitter smile. "You're not the one who just found out he's a bastard."

Garth laughed. "Hell. I've been called a bastard all my life."

"That's how you act. It's what I *am*."

Faron's voice was stark as he asked, "How could Mom have done such a thing? Having an affair with some rich sonofabitch.... Did Dad know?"

Garth's lips flattened. "He knew." He paused and added, "So did I."

Faron stared into his brother's dark eyes, stunned by the realization that Garth had lived for years with this awful knowledge. "How long have you known that I was only half your kin?"

Garth looked away into the fire before he answered. "Since you were born."

"And you treated me like a real brother?"

"You *are* my brother!" Garth snapped. "Nothing's going to change that. Dad's name is on your birth certificate. He raised you. Nothing else matters."

Faron sneered. "You haven't read any of those letters from the widow—my stepmother—asking when I'm coming to claim my inheritance from my *father*."

"Forget it," Garth advised. "There's plenty of Hawk's Way for both of us. You can stay right here in Texas, and we'll keep on raising and training quarter horses, just like we always have."

Faron shook his head. "I've got a mind to meet Belinda Prescott. The lawyer said she was the one who talked my fa—Wayne Prescott into putting me in his will. Said she *insisted* I get half of everything. Otherwise, I might never have known what Mom..." Faron's voice trailed off as his throat tightened up on him.

He had been feeling too much since he had found out that his beautiful mother had indulged in a tawdry affair with a millionaire rancher visiting Texas from Wyoming and had borne a bastard son. It was a stunning revelation to Faron that he was only related *on his mother's side* to his older brothers Garth and Jesse and to his younger sister Tate. He felt bereft, wrenched from the bosom of his family. An outsider. And it was all that Prescott bitch's fault.

"I never figured the money would mean so much to you," Garth said in a quiet voice.

Faron's gray-green eyes turned cold. "It's a good thing I grew up knowing how distrustful you are of everybody's motives. Otherwise I'd have to stand you up and knock you down for saying that. I'd have given anything not to know the truth. I don't want half that old man's fortune. I just want things to be the way they were."

The way they never would be again.

Garth swallowed half his glass of whiskey. But he didn't apologize. Faron hadn't expected him to. He began to understand a little better what had made Garth so cynical about women, why his older brother refused to trust the species, let alone love one of them. Faron might have felt the same way himself, if he had grown up knowing his mother had betrayed his father.

Both his parents were dead now. His mother had died giving birth to his sister, Tate, when Faron was seven. His father had broken his neck coming off an ornery bronc when Faron was fifteen. He felt ill equipped to deal with this secret that had been kept from him for so many years.

Faron tried to remember if his father—or mother—had treated him any differently than Garth or Jesse or Tate. But it was too painful to even think about that right now. He was still too shocked. And angry. And frustrated. He felt battered and needed to escape.

Faron played with the frayed seam at the knee of his jeans. "I just want to see the place where my fa— Where *he* came from," Faron said. "I can't explain it except to say that I feel like there's a hole inside me now that needs filling. Maybe I'll find something in Wyoming that'll give me the answers I need."

"Give my regards to Belinda Prescott," Garth said with a caustic smile.

"Your greetings will have to wait," Faron said grimly. "I've got a few things to say to Mrs. Prescott myself."

Belinda Prescott felt guilty as sin. She should be in mourning. Her husband of eight years had been buried a mere four months ago. She should be home wearing black and recounting the memories of her too-brief marriage. Instead she was riding the fastest horse in the stables across Wayne's Wyoming ranch, King's Castle, enjoying the early spring sunshine and feeling finally, at long last, *free*. Because for six of the past eight years, The Castle had been a prison and Wayne her jailer.

It hadn't started out that way, of course. She had met Wayne when she was a waitress in a short-order diner in Casper that he frequented. She had worked the graveyard shift trying to make ends meet, and he had often come in for a midnight breakfast. They had started talking, and one thing had led to another.

Wayne had found out that she was supporting three sisters. He was more than willing to accept a beautiful and youthful bride in exchange for a substantial trust fund for each of her siblings. She and Wayne had each known exactly what they were getting into. Twenty-year-old Belinda had willingly said her wedding vows with a man old enough to be her father. It was a small enough sacrifice to make so her sisters could have better lives.

She had been too young and desperate at the time to realize the ramifications of selling herself—body and soul—for money. In the years since, she had regretted her devil's bargain, but never so much as now, when she was finally free of Wayne and ready to go on with her life. Belinda had given up something besides her youth to marry Wayne—she had lost her innocence. She was no longer credulous, gullible or naive. She would never trust another man. The lessons Wayne had taught were hard, and he had been brutally thorough.

She spurred the mare beneath her into a lope and lifted her face to the sun. She didn't want to remember. But she couldn't forget.

Wayne had been such a gentle husband. At first. Then his heart had started causing him trouble. He had needed to take medication to keep him alive, and the medication had made him impotent. He had felt less a man and had sought other ways to relieve his frustration. He had begun to gamble. Then he drank to forget his huge gambling losses.

Slowly but surely he had become less gentle and more unreasonable in his demands. His fortune had dwindled until all that was left was The Castle, the land and a few prime head of breeding stock. And a twenty-eight-year-old wife who had learned that sometimes the price of security comes too high.

Belinda pulled the mare to an abrupt stop and wiped tears from eyes that were too blurred to see the grassy prairie around her. Her chest felt leaden—not because of sorrow, but because she felt none. God help her, she had felt only relief when the heart attack killed Wayne. It was difficult for her to look Wayne's mother, Madelyn, in the eye. Because Madelyn truly grieved, and Belinda could not.

At least she had been able to do one good thing. She had convinced Wayne to leave half of everything to his son. If it hadn't been for Wayne's mother, Belinda would have urged Wayne to leave his entire ranching empire to Faron Whitelaw. But Belinda had no money of her own. She hadn't had any trust fund put in her own name when she had married Wayne. He had gambled nearly everything else away. She had to have some way to take care of Madelyn, who had become as precious to her as her own mother.

Over the years, as Wayne had become more cruel, Madelyn had often stepped in to act as a buffer between her son and his wife. Madelyn had been appalled when she caught Wayne slapping Belinda. She had threatened to call the police if her son ever threatened Belinda with violence again. The two women had never spoken about Wayne, but they had shared other confidences, other hopes and dreams. Which was why Belinda had been determined to light a fire under her stepson that would goad him into moving north as soon as possible.

Belinda wondered what Faron Whitelaw would do when he learned the other conditions of Wayne's will. Her brow furrowed in concern. She had to hope that he would want his half of King's Castle enough to do what had to be done. She was counting on it. She was willing to do her part. She only hoped he would be willing to hang around long enough after he showed up to do his.

Otherwise they were both going to lose everything.

Two

Faron spoke softly as he unloaded the quarter horse gelding from the trailer. He had pulled his pickup well off the highway near a pasture gate. "I know it's been a long trip, Sonny. We're both tired of traveling. Just take it easy, boy. According to that old man at the gas station in Casper we're standing on Wayne Prescott's land. Just be patient a few more minutes until I get you saddled up, and we'll take ourselves a look-see."

The horse nickered as though he understood Faron and stood patiently while Faron brushed him down and saddled him up. It had been a long drive from northwest Texas to northeastern Wyoming. As Faron stepped into the saddle he thought of what the white-haired gent at the gas station had told him about his father's land.

"Mr. Prescott had him a kingdom, all right. Called his spread King's Castle. Miles and miles of the prettiest grassland you ever did see," the old man had said. "That big old house is set off in the middle of nowhere. Near three stories high, made of gray stone, with them little pointy things on the roof like some storybook castle. Even called it The Castle, Mr. Prescott did."

Now, as Faron surveyed his father's domain, he was humbled by its vastness, awed by its richness. On this warm, surprisingly summerlike day in May, blue grama grass and wheatgrass flowed in waves over the rolling hills as far as the eye could see. This was cattle country, but there was a wealth of riches under the ground, as well. Oil. Natural gas. And coal.

Faron gave the horse his head and let him run. He felt the power of the animal beneath him, taking him farther into an untamed wilderness. He urged the animal on, as though by running faster he could escape the oppressive feelings that had haunted him since he had learned the truth about his birth.

It had taken him a week to put his things together after he had told Garth he was leaving. He had received yet another letter from Belinda Prescott asking him whether he was coming. She had sounded desperate. It made him wonder why she was so anxious for him to visit King's Castle. He had unbent enough to tell her he was coming, but he hadn't given her a definite date. His wire had simply said, "I'll be there when I get there."

Faron rode some distance from the highway, until there was nothing to remind him of the civilized world he had left behind. He couldn't believe his eyes when he spied a blond woman riding a palomino in the distance. Horse and rider presented a stunning picture. Her waist-length hair, flying like a gonfalon behind her, was the same magnificent gold as the horse's mane and tail.

He shouted to attract her attention. When she turned her head to stare at him, Faron drew breath with an audible gasp. She was incredibly beautiful. Ethereal. Like some fairy princess. He wondered for a moment if he had conjured her in his imagination.

But the shock on her face was real. And the sound of the palomino's thundering hooves as she galloped her horse away was real.

Intrigued, Faron pursued his elusive golden princess. He dug his heels in and urged his mount to a run. The quarter horse was bred for speed over short distances, and Faron quickly overtook the woman. He grabbed the palomino's bridle and hauled her horse to a stop.

The woman stared at him wide-eyed, wary.

Faron smiled. It was a smile that said, "You can trust me. I won't hurt you. I find you absolutely lovely."

But his elusive princess—who else but a princess would he find on King's Castle land?—wasn't the least bit impressed.

"Let me go," she said in a breathless voice. "Please."

He let go of the bridle but said, "Don't go. Stay and talk with me."

She took her lower lip between her teeth. He could see her distress, the struggle to decide. "We're strangers," she said at last. "We have nothing to talk about."

"If we talk, we won't be strangers for long," he promised. "Please."

"I have to go home."

"What's your name?" he asked.

"None of your business."

"All right, then. No names. I'll call you Princess. You can call me…Cowboy."

He thought he saw the hint of a smile curl her lip, but she flattened it out damn quick. Faron stepped down from his horse and walked around its head to stand at her side. He tipped his Stetson back and smiled up at her. "I'll help you down."

He didn't give her a chance to object. Before she could say anything Faron had got hold of her tiny waist. He could feel the tension in her as he lifted her off the horse. She met his gaze for an instant with frightened eyes before she lowered her lashes, and he realized that she expected him to take advantage of the situation. Maybe he should have dragged her down the length of him. He sure as hell had wanted to bad enough.

She clearly had a body made for loving. She was nearly as tall as he was. Her head came all the way to his chin, which was surprising because he was well over six feet. She was wearing a long-sleeved man's shirt tucked into fitted Levi's, but both shirt and jeans showed off a figure that was fully feminine. Her boots were well used but expensive, ostrich if he wasn't mistaken.

He had to bite the inside of his cheek to keep from gasping when she glanced up at him again. She had eyes a rare violet color. Her complexion would have earned the envy of a pale pink rose. As he stared at her, stricken by emotions he couldn't name, he saw her cheeks darken to a redder rose.

"I should go home," she said. But she sounded less sure about leaving. She was worrying that full lower lip again with pearly white teeth.

Faron slipped her hand through his crooked arm, took the reins of both horses and started walking toward a meadow of spring wild-flowers. "It's a beautiful day, isn't it, Princess?"

He could feel the tension in her, and he kept talking in an attempt to show her he wasn't a threat to her. At least not yet.

"Tell me about yourself," he urged.

She eyed him from beneath lowered lashes. "What do you want to know?"

"Any brothers or sisters?"

For the first time, her lips curved in a genuine smile. Sweet and kind of sad. "Three sisters."

"Older or younger?"

"All younger. You?"

Faron opened his mouth to say two brothers and a sister, then realized he would have to qualify that—half-brothers and a half-sister. He frowned. Damned if he would. "I've got two older brothers and a younger sister."

He felt her relax almost immediately. Amazing how having a family made him seem less dangerous. Little did she know. His family was about the most unruly bunch he knew. "What are you doing way out here?" he asked.

She looked off into the distance. "Running from my problems."

He was tempted to make a flippant retort, but her honesty spurred him to equal sincerity. "Me, too."

She looked up at him again from beneath those dark lashes, to see if he was telling the truth. He realized she hadn't once looked at him directly and figured she must be used to hiding her feelings. But from whom? And why?

His lips twisted wryly. "Seems like we do have something in common, Princess. How 'bout if we run off together and leave our problems behind?"

"I can't—"

"Just for the afternoon," he urged. "What do you say? Let's throw our cares to the four winds and enjoy this afternoon together."

He felt her hand tremble where it lay on his forearm. She withdrew it and clasped her hands together in front of her. He could see she was tempted. He wished he knew what to say to push her over the brink. Nothing came to mind, so he just smiled.

Belinda knew she was making a mistake even as she nodded her head yes. She had to be crazy. She was truly certifiable. Imagine agreeing to spend the afternoon with a perfect stranger. She recognized the quality of both his horse and saddle, so she knew he was more than just some drifter. He was wearing frayed jeans, but his Western shirt appeared to have been tailored to fit both his broad shoulders and his lean waist.

But who was he? And where had he come from? She had lived so reclusively at The Castle, he might even be a neighbor from one of the outlying spreads for all she knew. "Are you from around here?" she asked.

"Just passing through."

That was some comfort. "What brings you here?"

He looked off across the prairie. "Just taking a look around. How about you? You live around here?"

She nodded. "Around." She wasn't about to be any more specific than he had been. It was safer that way.

Apparently the Cowboy gave her evasive answer a different meaning because he grinned and said, "So you're trespassing, too?"

"What?"

"Trespassing. On Wayne Prescott's land."

"Oh." Belinda knew she ought to correct his mistaken impression, but that would mean admitting she was Wayne Prescott's widow. Which would mean an abrupt end to her afternoon with the Cowboy. She wanted—needed—to forget who she was for a little while. So she said nothing.

Faron took her revealing blush as an admission of equal guilt. He smiled and said, "Don't worry. I won't let you get into trouble." After all, he owned half the place. If that bitch stepmother of his tried to make trouble, well, he would handle her. He pulled off his worn leather gloves and tucked them in his belt. Then he held out his hand to her. "I feel like walking some more. Will you join me?"

His smile made the invitation irresistible. Belinda's heart was doing a *rat-a-tat-tat* that made her want to press her hands to her chest to slow it down. She forcibly relaxed the knotted fingers she had clasped in front of her and reached out to take his hand. It was warm and callused like a working man's ought to be. It gave her a feeling of strength and security as it closed around her fingers.

At the same time, she looked up into the Cowboy's unusual gray-green eyes. They were the color of a mountain spruce, wide-set, heavily lashed and crowned with arched brows. There were webbed lines at the corners, etched there by the sun. His nose was straight and angled slightly at the tip, and he had a beauty mark—was it called that when a man had one?—high on his right cheekbone.

She had been terrified when he chased her on horseback, but he had done a good job of allaying her fears. He hadn't touched her in any except the most gentlemanly way. She had noticed his restraint when he lifted her off her horse. On the other hand, he hadn't exactly given her a choice of whether she was going to join him on the ground. She felt certain he wasn't the sort of man to be denied something he wanted.

Nevertheless, she was inclined to accept him at face value. He was an open, friendly and—she would not deny it—handsome man... who knew his way around women. She had been charmed by that ridiculous name he had called her, Princess. And it was telling that he had tagged himself Cowboy, after that chivalrous knight of the Old West.

So what did he *really* want from her? She angled her head and took a long hard look at him.

"Something wrong?" he asked.

"You look familiar somehow."

He grinned. "Maybe I'm the man you've been waiting for all your life."

Her expression sobered. She was waiting for someone, all right, but it wasn't the man of her dreams. Any day now she expected her stepson from Texas to arrive. For a horrified instant she wondered if this stranger with whom she had been flirting could be Faron Whitelaw.

But this man couldn't be Wayne's son. He didn't look a bit like Wayne. Wayne's well-trimmed hair had been almost white blond. This man had coal black hair hanging down over his collar. Nor did his gray-green eyes have anything in common with the cold sapphire of Wayne's. And the Cowboy's forearms, visible where his shirt-sleeves were folded up, revealed a warm bronze tint totally different from Wayne's light, easily freckled skin.

Did it really matter who he was? Would it be so awful if she stole an afternoon for herself with a perfect stranger? She had seen the admiration in his eyes, and it felt good. She had found him equally attractive.

He was extraordinarily tall, which was a good thing, since she had been as long-legged as a giraffe all her life. He had the rangy build of a cowboy, long, lean and strong. He had lifted her from the saddle as though she weighed nothing. And she had felt the play of muscle and sinew where her hand rested on his forearm.

Why not join in the Cowboy's fantasy? Just for an afternoon. What could possibly go wrong?

"So what are you running from?" Belinda asked as she strolled with the Cowboy toward the nearby meadow.

Faron left the two horses with their reins dragging. A cow horse wouldn't wander far ground-tied like that, and there was plenty of grass to keep the animals close.

"I think this is only going to work if we leave our problems behind us," Faron said. "We can only talk about good things this afternoon." He stopped and turned to face her. "Agreed?"

"It's a deal," Belinda said.

He lifted the hand he held, turned it over and kissed the center of her palm.

Belinda felt a streak of electricity shoot up her arm. She yanked her hand back reflexively, then laughed to cover the awkwardness it had created between them. "That tickled," she murmured in excuse and explanation.

"Yeah," he muttered back. Faron wondered if she had felt the same charge on her skin as he had felt on his lips. It had been an amazingly strong jolt to his system.

"Let's sit down, shall we?" Belinda dropped to her knees near a patch of large, daisylike flowers. Nearby was a bunch of bright blue lupine. The top of the hillside was rimmed with Indian paintbrush. "We couldn't have picked a more perfect spot for an afternoon idyll if we'd tried," she said.

Faron's eyes narrowed as he surveyed the countryside. "It is beautiful. It's a shame…"

"What?"

"Nothing." Faron wasn't about to spoil his afternoon by thinking about his father and stepmother. He sat down and realized the ground still held the chill of winter. He pulled off his denim jacket and said, "Why don't you sit on this? It'll keep you from getting cold."

"I don't think—"

Again, he didn't give her a choice. He spread his jacket on the ground, then slipped a hand around her waist and resettled her on the denim. "Thanks," she murmured.

Faron's gallantry won him a rare smile that made his heart skip a beat. "You're welcome."

Belinda immediately began making a chain from the daisylike flowers. Faron stretched out beside her, his head on his hand.

"God, you're beautiful," he said.

Belinda laughed. "Are you always so forthright?"

He felt his body tighten at the sound of her laughter. "I tend to say what I'm thinking."

She looked up at him from under lowered lashes. "Then since we're being honest, you're quite good-looking yourself."

He grinned. "Thanks."

She laughed again. He was so different from Wayne. So carefree. She ought not to be here. She ought to be home, wearing black. Mourning.

"What are you thinking, Princess?"

The Cowboy's voice ripped her from the melancholy that threatened her peace. "What?"

He smoothed the furrows on her brow with his thumb. She had to purposely hold herself still for the caress. It was the first one she had received in so long her skin seemed to come alive beneath his touch. When his fingers trailed into the hair at her temple she leaned away, and his hand dropped back to the grass.

"You looked worried," he said. "I wondered what you were thinking."

"That I shouldn't be here."

"No time for regrets now. We made a deal. Only happy thoughts." Faron sat up and leaned his wrist on one bent knee. "Let's see. What should we talk about?"

"When was the happiest time in your life?" she asked.

"It's all been pretty good," he admitted. Until lately. "I guess I'd choose the day I made love to a woman for the first time."

Faron was both surprised and delighted by the blush that stained her cheeks at his revelation.

"I can't believe you said that," Belinda protested with a laugh.

"I warned you I was honest," Faron said. "It's your turn now."

"The happiest time?" she asked. There was a long silence while she thought about it.

"It wasn't that tough a question, was it?" Faron asked.

She grimaced. "I suppose the happiest time would have been before my parents died, although life was such a struggle on the ranch..." She shrugged.

Belinda could see the Cowboy was about to ask questions she would rather not answer, so she asked, "What did you want to be when you grew up?"

"That's easy," Faron replied. "The best."

"At what?"

"Something. Anything."

"That certainly gave you a lot of room to succeed," she said teasingly. Apparently he hadn't liked the idea of being tied down to any one thing. "Are you the best at something?"

Faron grinned. "I'm a damned good cowboy, ma'am." He leaned back so she could see the rodeo belt buckle he was wearing.

Belinda laughed and realized suddenly it had been a long time since she had done so. "I should have known." She leaned over and traced the writing on the buckle with her fingertips. *Rodeo Cowboy All-Around Champion.*

No wonder he had called himself Cowboy!

Faron held his breath as Belinda traced the face of the silver buckle with her fingertips. It was as though he could actually feel her touching his skin. He wanted her hand lower. His body was doing a helluva good job of imagining all by itself.

He cleared his throat, distracting her attention. "How about you? What did you want to be?"

"I never let myself dream. I couldn't."

"Why not?"

She draped a chain of flowers around the brim of his Stetson. "My sisters and I were orphaned when my parents were killed in a car accident. I was eighteen and had just graduated high school. Dori and Tillie and Fiona were still in school. The ranch went to the bank for debts. I found a job in Casper that paid enough to feed us and keep a roof over our heads. That didn't leave much time for dreaming."

"Let's pretend you're a real princess, and you can have anything you want. What would you wish for?" Faron asked. He laid a handful of flowers he had broken off just below the bud in her lap.

She scooped up the white, yellow and blue flowers and lifted them to her nose to see how they smelled. "I'd wish for a man to love me. And for children. I've always wanted to have children."

"How many children?" he asked in a quiet voice.

"More than one," she said definitely. "I liked having sisters. I grew up knowing I never had to be alone."

"Do your sisters live close?"

"Unfortunately they're scattered across the country. Every Fourth of July we get together. That's the only time everyone can get free."

Which meant she spent the rest of the year alone, Faron deduced.

Her lashes fluttered down to conceal her eyes. "You're not wearing a ring. Are you married?"

"No."

"Do you have a girlfriend?"

"No."

"But you've had lots of them, I suspect."

Faron eyed her askance. "What makes you say that?"

"You're awfully charming, for one thing."

He shrugged. "If you say so."

She smiled. "I do. For another thing, you don't seem in any hurry to... Her cheeks felt warm. "I don't know exactly how to say this."

"Jump your bones?"

Her flush deepened. "Well, I wouldn't have said it quite that way, but—"

"The afternoon isn't over yet."

She swallowed hard. "Then I'm not safe with you?"

"As safe as you want to be," he said in a husky voice.

His eyes were more green than gray as they sought hers. Belinda was aware of a frisson of desire that began in her belly and spiraled upward. She could feel herself being drawn to him. She had already begun to lean toward him when she realized what she was doing. She jumped abruptly to her feet, scattering flowers around her. "It's getting late. I have to go."

She had already started toward her horse when he caught up to her and grasped her arm, stopping her. "Are you sure you can't stay a little longer?"

Belinda looked at the sun lowering in the western sky. Why, several hours must have passed! Where had the time gone? The Cowboy had cast some sort of spell on her to make her forget who—and what—she was. She would be lucky to get back to The Castle before suppertime. Madelyn would worry if she wasn't home by then. "I have to leave. Really, this has been lovely, but I have to go."

"Where do you live? When can I see you again?"

"You can't!" She hadn't meant to be curt, but she couldn't bear to see the look in his eyes if he ever found out she was a widow, a woman who should be in mourning. "You can't," she said more calmly, but just as firmly.

"Why not?"

"Because...please don't ask me to explain."

"All right."

Belinda breathed a sigh of relief. It turned out to be premature.

"I'll settle for a good-bye kiss."

"What?"

He didn't give her a chance to argue about it, simply pulled her into his arms and captured her mouth with his.

The Cowboy's kiss was like nothing Belinda had ever experienced before in her life. He tunneled all ten fingers into her hair. His lips softened on hers, and his tongue slipped inside her mouth to tease and to taste. For a moment she was quiescent. Then she kissed him back.

Faron hadn't known what to expect when he kissed his Princess. He had supposed from her shyness that he would be tasting innocence. For a few moments he had. But she had pulled him down to a deeper, darker well of desire than he had ever explored with a woman. A well where feelings and emotions were intimately bound with the physical act of love.

He lifted his head far enough to look into her eyes. "Princess?"

Belinda gazed up into gray-green orbs that were fierce with need. She reached up to touch the beauty mark on the Cowboy's cheek, then trailed her fingertips back down to his mouth, which was still wet from their kiss. She traced his lips with her forefinger, then looked up into eyes that had darkened with desire. She raised her mouth and touched it lightly to his. Then her tongue slipped inside his mouth to taste him.

She could feel the restraint he exercised to remain still for her kiss. It made her dare more. Her hands slipped around his neck and her fingertips teased the hair at his nape. She kissed the edges of his mouth and lingered to nip at his lower lip with her teeth. A harsh sound grated deep in the Cowboy's throat, and Belinda found herself answering with a kittenish purr of satisfaction.

He kissed his way along the edge of her jaw to her ear and caressed the delicate shell with his tongue. His breath was hot and moist and sent a shiver down her spine. Then his tongue slipped into her ear, and her belly curled with erotic sensation.

Belinda's eyes closed in surrender as her body swayed toward his. The Cowboy's arms closed around her, pulling her tight against him. She could feel the blunt ridge of his manhood against her femininity. As he rocked their bodies together, Belinda felt her knees give way.

The two of them slipped to the ground together. Belinda was aware of the cool grass beneath her, but it was the warmth above that she found so intriguing. The Cowboy held most of his weight on his arms, but their bodies were pressed together from the waist down, their legs entwined. His mouth found hers again, and this time he was more impatient.

One yank ripped the first three buttons on her shirt free. His mouth was reverent as he kissed the creamy mounds that spilled out of her lacy bra. He freed the bra itself, and his mouth latched on to a rosy crest. When he began to suck, Belinda's whole body arched up into his.

She was desperate to touch his skin, and she pulled at his shirt to free it from his jeans. She tried to unbutton the buttons, but her hands were trembling too much. The Cowboy ripped the shirt off himself, sending buttons flying. Then he pressed their bodies together, flesh to flesh. Belinda made a soft little sound in her throat as the crisp hair on his chest brushed her tender nipples.

"Princess, you feel so good. You feel so right." His hand slid down to unsnap her jeans. The rasp of her zipper coming down sounded loud in her ears. Before she could come to her senses his mouth had captured her breast again. The Cowboy sucked and nipped and sucked again so the sensual tension never let up.

His hand slid down inside her panties, through her feminine curls until he found the tender bud he sought. Belinda nearly came up off the ground as his fingers began to work their magic.

"Come apart for me, Princess," Faron crooned. "Be beautiful for me, only me."

He shoved her jeans down out of the way and unfastened his own. Belinda caught his face with both hands and brought his mouth up to hers.

"Kiss me, Cowboy. Please, kiss me."

She felt his body invade hers at the same time his tongue thrust into her mouth. He was big and hard, and her body arched up to take all of him as he thrust deeply inside her. Belinda heard an animal sound rip from her throat as their bodies surged together. He withdrew and thrust again in ageless rhythm as her hips rose in counterpoint to his.

Her fingernails dug crescents in his shoulders as her body arched up in passion. At the last instant, Belinda tried to fight the pleasure. This shouldn't be happening! She had no right!

But the Cowboy wouldn't allow her to withdraw. "Come with me, Princess. Come with me!"

Then it was too late. Her body began to convulse in wave after wave of unbearable pleasure. She gritted her teeth against the ecstasy that besieged her, holding her prisoner for timeless moments. While she was caught in the throes of passion, the Cowboy claimed her for his own. His cries were guttural as his body arched and spilled its seed within her.

Afterward, they both lay exhausted, unable to move. Belinda was aware of a fine sheen of sweat on his body and the musky smell of sex.

"I want to see you again," the Cowboy murmured as he slipped to her side and drew her into his arms. He was already asleep before Belinda could answer him.

Which was just as well.

Belinda was appalled at what she had done. But she couldn't regret it. What had passed between the Cowboy and his Princess was one brief shining moment when two souls blended into one. They might be strangers still, but they had found something more than physical satisfaction in each other's arms. She would hold this magical afternoon close to her heart forever.

But there was no way she could see him again. He would be horrified if he knew the truth about her. And she would be ashamed for him to find out. She had to escape now, while he was asleep.

She dressed quickly and quietly and led her palomino a short distance away before she mounted him, so that she wouldn't wake the Cowboy. When she was far enough away that the sound wouldn't waken him, she kicked the mare into a gallop and raced back to The Castle.

The instant she stepped inside the kitchen door, she was greeted by her mother-in-law. Belinda plowed a hand through her hair, shoving it off her face, and tried a smile. It failed dismally.

"You're late," Madelyn said. She took one look at Belinda's disheveled appearance and asked, "What happened to you?" There was more curiosity than accusation in her tone.

"I...my horse threw me," Belinda said, brushing at the grass stains on her jeans.

"Your blouse is ripped. Are you sure you're all right?"

Belinda flushed and clutched at the torn fabric. Getting thrown shouldn't have torn three buttons off her blouse. "I'll just run upstairs and change for supper." She hurried from the kitchen and practically ran up the majestic circular staircase that led to her bedroom.

"There's no hurry," Madelyn murmured to Belinda's disappearing back. There would be plenty of time before supper to ask about the love-bruise on her daughter-in-law's neck.

Three

The cool night air woke Faron. At first he didn't know where he was. It all came back to him in a hurry. As he dressed himself, one thing quickly became apparent. His Princess was gone.

Faron was furious when he realized he didn't know her name or how to find her. Nor could he track her in the dark. Besides, he had phoned The Castle from Casper, and Madelyn Prescott was expecting him for dinner.

He dressed quickly, muttering profanities when he realized half the buttons were gone from his shirt. He would have to change it when he got back to his truck. He took a look at the knees of his jeans and realized it probably wouldn't hurt to change them, either. Not that he gave a damn what the Prescotts thought of him, but he had been taught manners around ladies that were hard to shed.

Faron whistled for his horse, and Sonny nickered a response. The quarter horse hadn't drifted far. Faron mounted up and rode in the fading light of dusk back in the direction of his truck and trailer. There wasn't any chance he would lose his way. He had learned young to look back every so often when he was riding the range to mark his trail. He easily found the landmarks that took him back to the highway.

Faron had gotten directions from Madelyn Prescott, and it didn't take him long to find the formal entrance to King's Castle. If the land had awed him, the house itself—The Castle—left him speechless.

As he stepped from his pickup he couldn't help staring. Light poured from tall, narrow, leaded windows, and there were sconces on the outside stone walls that created an eerie silhouette on the plains. The house did indeed have crenels along the roofline and what appeared to be turrets at the corners.

When he cut the engine a cowhand came from the direction of the barn.

"I'm Toby, Mr. Whitelaw. Mrs. Prescott said I was to take care of your horse," the cowhand said.

Faron backed Sonny from the trailer and watched long enough to make sure the cowhand knew what he was doing before he left his horse in Toby's care.

Moments later Faron found himself on the front steps of The Castle. The three-story gray stone structure had a massive double wooden door headed by a stone arch that might once have been the gateway to a medieval castle. When Faron knocked, the imposing entrance was opened by a tiny, silver-haired lady dressed in black. He found himself looking into a pair of gray-green eyes the same unusual color as his own.

"Hello, Faron," the woman said with a smile of greeting, "I'm your grandmother, Madelyn Prescott. We've been expecting you."

Faron's hat came off at once. He leaned over and kissed the old woman on the cheek. She smelled of lavender powder. Her skin had the softness of the very young and the very old. The wrinkles on her face gave her character as well as age. Faron felt his throat tighten as he realized this woman was indeed his grandmother. It was true, then. He was a bastard.

Madelyn cupped her grandson's cheek with her hand and searched his features looking for signs of Wayne. There was nothing of her son in Faron, but there was something of her. "You've got the Halliwell eyes, I see."

"If you say so, ma'am," Faron said. "Hope I'm not too late for supper."

"Not at all. Belinda is still upstairs getting dressed. Perhaps you'd like to share a brandy with me in the parlor while we wait."

"I'd be pleased to, ma'am."

"Please, call me Madelyn."

But Faron couldn't bring himself to call his grandmother by her first name. It seemed disrespectful somehow. By what fond nickname would he have called her, he wondered, if he had known as a child that she existed? He had called his father's mother Nanaw, and his mother's mother Gram. "Would you mind if I called you Maddy?" he asked.

Her gray-green eyes quickly misted, and she pressed a fragile hand against her heart. "Why, that would be lovely, Faron."

He frowned when she seemed to have trouble catching her breath. "Are you all right?"

"My health isn't what it used to be. My heart, you know."

"I didn't know. Have you seen a doctor?"

"Oh, yes. I'm afraid in my case it's just a matter of age catching up with me. Come along now. Belinda will be down soon, I'm sure."

As Faron followed Madelyn, he stepped into a world of days gone by—an open drawing room with walnut woodwork, nineteenth century furniture of polished cherry and oak, lace curtains and brilliant chandeliers of sparkling crystal. Two broad stairways formed a sweeping arc leading to the upper floors.

Faron frowned at what he saw only because it represented his father's wealth, which was the source of the current calamity in his life. It was not the setting in which he had expected to find his ogre of a stepmother. It felt too much like a home. He couldn't help but admire the sense of history that was represented in the antique Western furnishings.

Faron and his grandmother had gotten only as far as the stairs when they heard the echo of footsteps.

"That will be Belinda," Madelyn said.

Faron followed her gaze up the stairs. The composed, graceful young woman who came walking down the sweeping staircase was a far cry from the ugly stepmother found in fairy tales. In fact, she was his very own Princess.

Her glorious golden hair, which he had grasped in his fists while he came inside her mere hours ago, was bound up now in a stylish twist. Her sleek black silk dress showed off a lush figure with which he was intimately familiar. A long black chiffon scarf circled her neck and floated on the air behind her. But there was nothing of the wanton woman he had loved reflected in the cool violet eyes that met his gaze.

It would be difficult to say which of the two lovers was more shocked to see the other. It was equally apparent that neither of them was willing to do or say anything in front of Madelyn that would upset the old woman.

"Good evening, Mr. Whitelaw," Belinda said, extending her hand. Her heart was pounding, and she felt as though she were going to faint. When the Cowboy took her hand, he held it longer than he should. His mouth had formed into a smile, but his gray-green eyes looked wintry.

"It's a pleasure to meet you at last, Mrs. Prescott. Please call me Faron. If you don't mind, I'll call you...Belinda."

Faron's anger had returned with a vengeance. Here stood a woman he had hated sight unseen—but with whom he had just experienced an incredibly passionate assignation. He wanted to ask her why she had made love to him when her husband—his father—was barely cold in the ground. But his lips clamped tight on the question. What they had done was awful enough. He had no intention of embarrassing his grandmother with revelations that would have to be distasteful to her.

Beyond being angry, Faron was hurt. His stepmother had made a fool of him. He had called The Castle from Casper hours ago, so she must have known he was coming. Which meant she also must have known who he was when she had made love with him. No wonder she hadn't wanted to give him her name! How could she have done such a thing?

But despite being angry and hurt, he was also aroused. The memory of what had happened between them was still fresh, like a green wound that ached when prodded. Even icily distant, she was still his Princess. And he wanted her as much now as he ever had.

Tension lay thick in the air. A powerful current sparked between them, threatening a shock to the first who broke it.

"Come along, children," Madelyn said at last. She led the way to the dining room, which was as richly furnished as the rest of the house. The pine trestle table was at least fifteen feet long. Three places had been set at one end with fine china and silver.

Faron held Madelyn's chair as she sat at the head of the table. Then he went around to help Belinda. Her stomach clenched when Faron leaned over to whisper in her ear and trailed his hand across her bare shoulder. When he spoke, it was his anger she heard.

"It didn't take you long to find some young stud to service you," he hissed. "Did I measure up to my father?"

Belinda's face bleached white.

"Are you feeling all right, my dear?" Madelyn asked.

"I'm a little tired," Belinda said. "I had a long ride this afternoon." She raised her eyes to meet Faron's and realized the second meaning that could be given to her words. His lips lifted in a slight smirk that made her feel physically ill.

Belinda wanted to tell him she was sorry. But she wasn't sorry. What had happened between them had been beautiful. What she really wanted was the chance to explain why she had needed what he had offered. She had been so very vulnerable. It had been so wonderful to allow herself the fantasy of loving and being loved.

Now Belinda was sure Faron Whitelaw had entirely the wrong idea about what kind of woman she was. She could feel his attraction to her, but it was laced with harsher, harder feelings. The fierce look on his face gave ample evidence that he didn't want to hear what she had to say. And that he was unlikely to forgive or forget what she had done.

When Belinda realized the road her thoughts had taken she was alarmed. Hadn't she learned her lesson with Wayne? Here she was ready to make the same mistakes again! Why should she care what her stepson thought of her? She would never give another man the sort of emotional, physical and economic hold over her that Wayne had possessed.

She ought to show Faron the door. If it had only been herself involved in the catastrophe that threatened, she would have. But there was Madelyn to think of. So she clamped her back teeth together and held her tongue.

Once Faron was seated, an older woman wearing a voluminous white apron began serving dinner. She passed out plates already laden with pork chops, mashed potatoes and green beans. The servant had hair dyed a shocking red and fingernails painted an equally vivid color. When she left the room Madelyn said, "Rue has been with the family forever. Belinda and I couldn't manage without her."

To Faron it was further proof that Belinda Prescott was the pampered Princess he had labeled her. His stepmother sat across from him looking cool and elegant and totally in control. Meanwhile, his body was hard and throbbing from the small caress of her shoulders he had allowed himself. But he would be damned if he'd touch her again anytime soon.

As he ate his dinner, Faron tried to revive the feelings of dislike he had felt toward Belinda Prescott for forcing him to confront his true paternity. But it was one thing to hate a woman you envisioned as an interfering Rich Bitch, and quite another to hate a woman with whom you've just shared the most poignant physical encounter of your life.

To compound his confusion, the woman he found so attractive was his stepmother. He had been determined not to take anything handed down to him from Wayne Prescott. Now he found there was one thing he wanted very much: his father's widow.

"Did Belinda write you about the terms of the will?"

Madelyn's question jerked Faron from his thoughts. "What?"

"The will. Did Belinda tell you the terms of Wayne's will?"

Faron's gaze swung back around the table to spear Belinda. "No, Maddy, she didn't. She did seem in an all-fired hurry for me to get here."

"Why don't you tell Faron the problem, Belinda," Madelyn said.

"If you came here expecting to inherit wealth beyond your dreams, you're going to be disappointed," Belinda began.

Faron's brows arched. "I heard my father was a millionaire."

"*Was* is the correct word," Belinda said. "King's Castle, including the land and The Castle on it, is mortgaged to the hilt. The mineral leases only provide enough income to cover the taxes, and the worsening economy has left the ranch only marginally profitable."

"So sell the ranch and move into town," Faron said.

"It isn't that simple."

"Why not?" Faron asked.

"If we could sell the property piecemeal, there might be some hope of making a profit and avoiding foreclosure. But Wayne's will stipulates that King's Castle has to be sold all in one piece. Otherwise it gets donated to charity.

"We simply haven't been able to find a buyer willing to take the whole thing—thousands of acres of land, dozens of buildings, farm equipment, the stock, the house—in short, someone willing to buy the losing aspects of the ranch along with the profitable ones," Belinda explained. "I was hoping you might have some ideas about improvements that would make the ranch attractive to a single corporate buyer.''

Faron had wondered why his stepmother had gone to so much trouble to have him included in his father's will. Now he had his answer. She needed someone with the right motivation—a promise of half the proceeds—to spend the time and energy putting King's Castle back on its feet so she could make a big killing when it was sold!

His sense of self-preservation warned him to get right back in his truck and go home to Texas. He decided to ask a few more questions first.

"How much money do you have to work with?"

"You mean cash?" Belinda asked. When Faron nodded she said, "There's just enough in the bank for food for us and the stock over the summer."

"Surely there are some jewels or furs you can liquidate," Faron said.

"Oh, dear, no," Madelyn said. "Wayne sold all those things years ago."

"Have you tried cutting the staff for the house and the number of cowboys on the payroll."

Madelyn's eyes twinkled as she laughed. "You've seen the house staff," she said.

"Rue?" Faron asked incredulously.

"We simply couldn't let her go," Madelyn said. "She's almost family."

"And the cowhands?"

"You've met Toby, I presume."

Faron nodded. When Madelyn said nothing more he realized the middle-aged cowboy was all there was. "Who takes care of things around here?" he demanded.

"Why, Belinda does, of course," Madelyn said.

Faron stared hard at his stepmother. That wasn't at all what he had expected to hear.

"I can see you two need to discuss business," Madelyn said. "So I'll just excuse myself and go upstairs and get some rest."

Faron stood and escorted his grandmother to the door of the dining room, sliding the wooden door closed behind her. Then he turned back to the woman who had become his nemesis—and his desire.

Faron stared at Belinda with narrowed eyes. "How bad is it?" he demanded.

She laced her hands together calmly. "It's as bad as you think it is. We're as poor as church mice. If something isn't done to make King's Castle salable, Madelyn and I will be penniless and homeless within the year."

Faron fisted his hands so hard his knuckles turned white. He might have been able to leave Belinda to her fate, but there was no way he could stand by and watch his own grandmother be put out in the street.

"All right," he said. "I'll hang around long enough to help put the place in shape to sell. But as soon as we find a buyer, I'm out of here!"

"No one could want to leave this place more than I do!" Belinda said vehemently. "There are no happy memories here for me!"

"No one forced you to marry my father," Faron snarled. "You made your own bed. Now you have to lie in it. Just don't expect me to join you there."

Belinda's face blanched white. She could feel his fury, his hate and his desire. She had learned from Wayne how to avoid confrontation. It didn't always work, but often enough it had saved her a bruise or a blackened eye. She put those lessons to good use now.

She lowered her eyelids to hide the anger blazing there. She rose and smoothed the front of her skirt with hands that appeared much more calm than they were. In a soft, deferential voice she said, "I believe I'll retire now."

When Faron took a step toward Belinda, her eyes flashed defiance. She would not become a victim, ever again. "Keep your distance, Cowboy!"

He took another step toward her.

"I'm warning you—"

Then it was too late. He had her in his arms before she could turn and run.

"Let me go," she cried breathlessly. "This is wrong!"

"It's a little late for that argument, don't you think, Princess?"

"I didn't know who you were! I never would have..."

"Never would have rolled in the grass with your stepson?" Faron finished for her.

Tears blurred Belinda's vision. She held herself stiff in Faron's arms. "I don't have to explain anything to you."

"No, you don't," he murmured.

The hardest thing Faron had ever done was to let her go. His body was hard and throbbing with need. It didn't matter one bit that she was his father's widow. But he had to work side by side with her over the next several weeks—or months. It was going to be awkward enough being together every day without knowing for sure that she still desired him as much as he desired her.

"Where do I sleep?" he asked.

Belinda was quivering with relief—or unsatisfied desire. She wasn't willing to examine her feelings closely enough to find out. "Follow me," she said. "I'll show you where your room is."

Once again Faron found himself staring into violet eyes that had turned to ice. He followed her up one half of the curving staircase to a room that might have welcomed some cowboy a hundred years ago. It was furnished sparingly with a maple four-poster, a dry sink, a chest and a rocker. A rag rug covered a small area of the oak hardwood floor. The lamp was electric, but it was Victorian in style.

The connected bathroom had a tub on legs and a pedestal sink. "The linens on the rack are for your use," she said.

Belinda was aware of the confines of the bathroom. She edged her way past the Cowboy and back into the more spacious bedroom. "If you need anything..."

"I'll be fine," Faron said, realizing that she didn't want to spend any more time with him than she had to. "Good night, Princess," he said. His eyes said what he didn't put in words. He wanted her. She was welcome to stay.

Belinda didn't bother to answer. She did what any self-respecting Princess would have done when the dragon started breathing fire. She fled to her room.

Four

Faron was astounded at how much Belinda knew about the business affairs of King's Castle. Unfortunately, the more he learned from her, the more grim-lipped he became. Because things were every bit as bad as she had suggested they were.

"I don't know how you've kept the bank from foreclosing before now," he muttered when he was done examining his father's records.

"Can anything be done to save King's Castle?"

Faron felt his gut tighten as he met Belinda's expectant gaze across the width of the oak rolltop desk in Wayne's study. Even now he wanted her. This morning her golden hair was confined in a single tail that fell over her shoulder, and she was wearing a Western shirt, jeans and boots. She reminded him much too much of his prairie Princess.

He leashed his memories of the previous day and concentrated on the matter at hand. "We can't do it alone," he said. "We'll have to hire some help."

Belinda wiped her palms down the length of her jeans, unaware of the way Faron's gray-green eyes followed her gesture. "I don't have money for that."

"I do."

Belinda frowned. "I can't let you spend your money."

"You can't stop me," Faron retorted. "According to my father's will I own half of King's Castle. If something isn't done, the bank is going to take my inheritance. It's no skin off your nose if I invest my money to save my half of this place."

Belinda's lip curled in a wry smile. "You'll also be saving my half," she pointed out.

"I don't want to see my grandmother put out in the street."

Belinda's smile twisted into something more cynical. "And you have to save me to save her, is that it?"

"Something like that."

"Where do we start?" Belinda asked.

Faron arched a disdainful brow. "We?"

"I presume you have some plan in mind. Things that have to be done. I want to help."

"What is it you think you can do?" Faron asked. He preferred to keep her—and temptation—as far from him as possible.

Belinda's chin came up pugnaciously. "What do you need done?"

Faron tried to think of something that would impress upon his stepmother—he had to keep reminding himself how Belinda had deceived him about her identity—how very much *work* was involved in restoring King's Castle to its former greatness.

Not one, but several ideas caught his fancy. He reached out and grabbed Belinda's hand and pulled her after him. "Come with me. I want to start with a tour of the ranch, so I can get some idea of what needs to be done." He only got as far as the back porch before he stopped and asked, "Are there enough roads to get us where we need to go, or should we do this survey on horseback?"

Belinda wasn't sure which was worse. Spending half the day on horseback together would remind them both of the events of the previous day. But if she said they ought to drive, she would have to endure an hour or more confined with him in the cab of a pickup truck. The pickup seemed the lesser of two evils.

"It would be faster and more efficient to drive," she said. "But the only pickup I have isn't in very good mechanical shape."

Faron grimaced at this reminder of the state of poverty in which his father had left his stepmother and grandmother. "We'll take my truck. Just give me a minute to disconnect the horse trailer," he replied.

It was strange seeing King's Castle through Faron's eyes. The splendor of the land, which Belinda had taken for granted, he found not only pleasing to the eye, but a definite economic asset.

"The land itself is a selling point," he explained to her. "It hasn't been overdeveloped. The grass is tall and there's lots of it."

She headed him in the direction of the small herd of Herefords that still roamed King's Castle.

"I see you're using a windmill for water," he said as he pulled the truck to a stop beside the windmill tank.

Faron got out of the truck and headed for the windmill, and Belinda followed after him. He leaned his head back and watched and listened as the wind pushed the windmill around.

"It's not running right," he said at last. "You've got a bolt or two loose up top that ought to be tightened."

She put her hands on her hips. "Who would you suggest I send up there to tighten them. Myself? Or Toby?"

Faron recalled the stature of the stocky cowhand, then gave Belinda a looking over that had a blush skating up her throat. "I guess you," he said at last in a taunting voice.

Belinda's eyes went wide. Was he serious? But if he thought she would back off from such a chore, he had another think coming. "All right," she said, pushing her sleeves up out of the way. "What is it you want me to do?"

Faron pursed his lips in chagrin. He had been certain she would defer the job to him. Now he found himself in the awkward position of having to admit that he had been manipulating the situation. He certainly didn't expect a woman to do the kind of dangerous repair job that was necessary.

He opened his mouth to tell her so and shut it again. The challenging look in her violet eyes dared him to admit he was wrong. Before he conceded the issue, Faron decided to see just how far she was willing to go.

He left Belinda and crossed to the back of his pickup where he kept a tool chest. He rattled around in it for a few moments and came back with a wrench.

"I think this is the tool you'll need."

Belinda took the wrench from him, but she hadn't the slightest idea what to do with it. What she was thinking must have shown in her face, because he stepped up beside her and showed her how to adjust it.

"This way tightens it, this way loosens it. You're not afraid of heights are you?"

Belinda stared at the thin metal ladder that was attached to the windmill. Her eyes followed it what seemed an immense distance into the air. She swallowed and said, "No. I'm not afraid of heights."

"What you're looking for is the bolt that attaches the wheel. Right now the wheel isn't at the correct angle to the yaw axis in the vane."

"What?" Belinda hadn't the vaguest notion what he was talking about.

"You do understand how a windmill works, don't you?"

Belinda wrinkled her nose. "Sort of. I understand the principle of the thing, but not exactly how the pieces fit together."

"Maybe you'd better let me do this." Faron waited for her to concede that he was the one better equipped to handle this job. He had underestimated her stubbornness.

"I can do it," she insisted. "If you'll just explain what it is I have to do."

"That's a little difficult without having the windmill down here where I can point things out," Faron said.

Belinda looked at the ladder. No way could both of them go up it together. "Let me try," she said at last. "If I can't fix it, then you can do the job."

Faron was amazed, but not amused, by Belinda's insistence on climbing to the top of the windmill. "Dammit, woman. It's dangerous to go up there."

"I'm not afraid."

"I am," he muttered. Faron wasn't about to let her endanger her life. "You've proved your point," he said. "You're willing to do what has to be done. Now give me that wrench, and let me go up and tighten that bolt."

"I'm not helpless!"

"I never said you were," Faron retorted. "Now give me the damn wrench!"

Instead, she turned and started up the ladder.

Faron put both arms around her and dragged her back down. Belinda didn't come without a fight. The wrench fell to the ground in the struggle. She kicked and hit at Faron, but he had her from behind and her efforts to free herself were useless.

At last she slumped in his arms.

"Are you done fighting me?" he asked.

"Let me go."

"Are you done fighting me?" he repeated.

"Yessss," she hissed.

Now that he could let her go, Faron realized he didn't want to. His body was way ahead of his mind. It had long since reacted strongly and certainly to the woman in his arms. Faron felt the weight of her soft breasts resting on his forearm. She smelled of soap and shampoo and woman. His hands slid down until his fingertips lay at the base of her belly.

"Faron."

Belinda bit her lip to keep from saying more than Faron's name. Oh, God, she wanted him! She wanted to lie with him, to merge their bodies, to join their souls. But she was not so far gone with desire that she couldn't see the folly of repeating what had happened the previous day.

Belinda covered the male hand on her belly with her own. "We can't do this, Faron. Please. Your father—"

His whole body stiffened. A moment later she was free.

Belinda was afraid to turn around and face him. When she did, she wished she hadn't. There was an awful look of disgust and disdain on his face. The gray-green eyes she had found so fascinating yesterday were slicing shards of cut green glass today.

She stooped to pick up the wrench, thus avoiding his piercing gaze. When she rose, she kept her lashes lowered. She held out the wrench, and he took it from her, careful not to touch her hand. Soon after, he was halfway up the ladder.

"Be careful," she whispered. She shaded her eyes from the sun and watched as Faron made his way to the top of the windmill. It didn't take him long to do what he had to do, but Belinda hardly breathed the whole time he was working. He hadn't been kidding about the danger of the job. A fall from that height would break a man in pieces.

When Faron came down the ladder she stayed out of his way. "All finished?"

"That's all I can do right now," he said. "There's a part missing. I'll have to get a replacement."

"Will it cost much?"

"Always thinking about money, Princess?"

"Don't call me that! Not like that!"

"Why not? That's what you are. A pampered, golden Princess. Living off an older man's money—"

"Stop! Stop!" Belinda put her hands to her ears. "How can you be so cruel?"

"Cruel? Princess, I don't hold a candle to you!"

Faron stalked back to the truck. He was furious with himself for losing his temper, for taking out his sexual frustration in such a— yes, cruel—way. He hadn't realized he was capable of that sort of behavior with a woman. Before Belinda... Hell, that was a lifetime ago. Before Belinda he had been Faron Whitelaw, happily oblivious to the fact he was Wayne Prescott's son. Before Belinda he had known who he was. Now, everything was so damn confused!

"Get in the truck," he said.

"I'd rather walk back to The Castle than get in that truck with you," Belinda snapped back.

"Listen, Princess. Either you get in that truck under your own steam, or I'm going to pick you up and put you there."

Given that choice, Belinda stomped over to the pickup and got in. He stepped in behind the wheel and gunned the engine. The wheels sent dust flying as they headed down the road.

There was a long silence while both of them fumed. At last Belinda said, "I don't think this is going to work. I think maybe I'll just let the bank take back the ranch. I'll go to work somewhere in town to support myself and Madelyn."

"Doing what?" Faron demanded.

Belinda shrugged. "I used to be a short order cook. I could—"

Faron snorted. "Princesses don't flip hamburgers. Besides, you may be willing to give up your half of this place, but I'm not about to give up my half."

"Now who's thinking about money?" Belinda goaded.

"It's not the money," Faron gritted out. He kept his hands on the wheel and forced himself not to put his foot down on the accelerator. "Oh, hell. I don't have to explain anything to you. Just get the idea of giving this place away out of your head. I'm here and I'm staying until King's Castle is sold. Now, if you're through pouting, maybe you'd like to tell me what else I ought to take a look at."

That was just the beginning of a very long day.

Belinda had put in a lot of hours over the past few years holding King's Castle together, but she had never worked so long or so hard without a rest. She marveled at Faron's energy at his strength, at his tirelessness. But no matter how many jobs he threw at her, she was determined not to be the one who cried mercy first.

It was nearly dusk when he decided they should clean out the tack room in the barn. The small, windowless room that held saddles, bridles and other leather tack was dark and cool. Belinda pulled a string that lit a single bare bulb hanging overhead. She was assaulted by the pungent smells of leather and horses and, once Faron stepped into the room behind her, hardworking man.

"Some of this leather could use a soaping," Faron said as he walked around the room checking stirrups and reins.

"There hasn't been much time—"

"We'll start now."

"No."

It was the first time since the incident at the windmill that Belinda had objected to anything Faron had suggested. He had been expecting her to quit long before now and head back to the house. She had amazed him with her fortitude. And slowly but surely driven him crazy with her presence.

His body had tightened as he watched her lick off a fine sheen of perspiration on her upper lip that he knew would be salty to the taste. As he watched her stoop and bend and lean in jeans that hugged her rear end like a man's hand. As he watched her cant her head and lift that golden hair up off her neck so the ever-present breeze could cool her, whipping tiny curls across petal-soft skin.

He should be glad she had finally given up, glad she would be out of his hair at long last. Perversely, he said the one thing he believed would provoke her into staying.

"Conceding the battle, Princess?"

Her violet eyes flashed with anger. "I won't dignify that comment with an argument. I'm going to get cleaned up for supper. We can start here tomorrow morning."

When Belinda tried to leave the room, Faron spread his arms and rested his palms on either side of the doorway, blocking the way out.

"Please get out of the way," she said in a controlled voice. "I want to leave."

"You surprised me today."

She arched a brow but said nothing.

"I didn't think you'd be able to keep up all day."

She still said nothing.

"I was wrong."

As an apology it lacked a lot. But it was as much of a concession as Faron was willing to make. "There's something I don't understand," he said.

"What?"

"Why would someone who's willing to work as hard as you have today marry a man twice her age for his money? It doesn't fit."

Belinda's face paled. "It doesn't have to. I don't owe you any explanation. Now let me pass." She wouldn't discuss her marriage to Wayne with Wayne's son. She wouldn't.

When Faron saw she had no intention of answering, he took his weight off his palms and leaned back against the door frame, his legs widespread. She could get out, but not without touching him.

Belinda kept her eyes lowered as she tried to skim past him. She had to turn sideways, and the tips of her breasts brushed his chest. She gasped at her body's reaction to even that brief contact.

Faron's response was powerful and instantaneous. Before Belinda could get past him, he clamped his hands on her shoulders and turned her toward him. His arms folded around her, and he drew her close.

"Faron, don't!"

"Do you think I want to feel like this?" he rasped in her ear. "It's driving me crazy, knowing how your skin tastes, knowing what it feels like to be inside you—and knowing that you were my father's wife!"

Belinda pushed at his chest with the heels of her hands. "Let me go, Faron! This is wrong!"

"You didn't think so yesterday."

"I told you, I didn't know who you were yesterday! This situation is awkward enough. Let's not make it worse."

He nuzzled her temple, let his lips trail down to her ear and felt her shiver in his arms. "And this will make it worse?"

Belinda exhaled a shuddery sigh. "What happened between us was—"

"A miracle."

"A mistake. Faron, we can't let this happen again."

Faron heard the desperation in her voice. He felt the same desperation himself. However, he could afford to be patient. He wasn't going anywhere anytime soon. Neither was she.

He dropped his hands to his sides and stood up straight so there was more space between them. "Call me when supper's ready."

She didn't answer him, just made her escape as quickly as she could. Belinda didn't run back to the house, although it took all her willpower to keep her pace to a walk.

How had things gotten out of hand so quickly? She should have known better than to let herself get cornered like that. But she hadn't been expecting Faron to confront her. She hadn't been expecting him to admit that he still desired her.

But she had been right to push him away. There could be no repetition of what had happened yesterday. Under the circumstances it was unthinkable.

Belinda stepped up on the back porch and shoved her way through the screen door that led to the kitchen. In some ways, the Castle was like any other ranch house. Friends and neighbors always entered through the back door which was usually left open, rather than the front. She stopped dead when she saw Madelyn standing in front of the stove, stirring a pot of chili.

"What are you doing in here?" she asked.

Madelyn lifted a spoonful of chili and sipped a taste of it. "Making supper."

"Where's Rue?"

"She's having one of her spells."

That was Madelyn's way of saying Rue was drunk. Once a year, on the anniversary of her son's death in Vietnam, Rue got drunk. How long the "episode" lasted depended on how good a job Belinda did of finding Rue's stash of bottles and disposing of it. "I thought we'd gotten rid of all the bottles."

"She must have had another tucked away somewhere."

Belinda came up behind Madelyn and put a hand around her shoulder. "You should be resting."

"There'll be time enough for that when I'm laid in my grave."

"I wish you wouldn't talk like that!" Before Wayne's death, Belinda hadn't been quite so aware of Madelyn's mortality. Now she worried about the older woman's health. Madelyn's heart wasn't in much better shape than Wayne's had been.

Madelyn turned and patted Belinda on the arm. "I'm sorry, dear.

Why don't you sit down and tell me how the day went with my grandson?''

That brought a wry smile to Belinda's face. "I'll make a deal. *You* sit down, and I'll tell you how the day went.''

Madelyn handed over the wooden spoon and took a seat on a bar stool next to the woodblock island in the center of the kitchen. "I'm sitting. Talk.''

Belinda turned away to stir the chili, which gave her a chance to organize her thoughts. There was no hope for her feelings, which were still in a state of chaos. "He's a hard worker,'' Belinda conceded.

"Then you two should have gotten along well,'' Madelyn said.

Belinda shot Madelyn a look over her shoulder. She was a shrewd old woman. Belinda wondered how much Madelyn knew—or suspected—about the tension between her daughter-in-law and her grandson. "We didn't argue much, if that's what you're getting at.'' Only at the very beginning and the very end of the day. "Faron has his own way of doing things. I just went along with him.''

"Go along and get along. That didn't work very well with Wayne, my dear.''

"Faron is nothing like Wayne!'' Belinda astonished herself with her outburst. She flushed and tried to backtrack by saying, "I mean, they look nothing alike.''

"And they don't act alike, either. Is that what you wanted to say?''

"I don't intend to criticize my late husband to his mother,'' Belinda said.

Madelyn sighed. "Unfortunately, I'm well aware of my son's faults. I hope you won't let what happened between you and Wayne keep you from finding another young man to love.''

Belinda dropped the spoon in the chili and turned to face Madelyn. "I hope you're not thinking about matchmaking, Madelyn. Not matching me with Faron, anyway. For heaven's sake, he's Wayne's son!''

"And quite a good-looking young man, if I do say so myself.''

"Please, Madelyn. Don't interfere. Things are difficult enough as it is.''

"Difficult? How so?''

Belinda grimaced. She should have known Madelyn wouldn't be

satisfied without specifics. But she wasn't going to get them. "We just don't get along."

"It didn't look that way to me last night."

The old woman saw too much. Belinda took a deep breath and let it out. "Suffice it to say that I don't want to get involved with *anyone* right now."

Madclyn was wise enough to know when to let well enough alone. She had said her piece. Not that she wouldn't consider a little manipulating behind the scenes. She would have a talk with her grandson and see which way the wind was blowing.

When the table was set and the corn muffins were just about ready to come out of the oven, Belinda stepped out onto the back porch and circled the triangle hanging from the eave several times with an iron rod. The metallic clang was a sound that cowboys recognized all over the West as a call to supper.

Sure enough, Faron's head and shoulders appeared at the barn door, followed quickly by the rest of him. Belinda knew she should turn around and go back inside, but she couldn't take her eyes off him.

His stride was long and his body moved with an easy grace. His face was hidden by the hat he had pulled down low on his brow. His shirtsleeves were rolled up onto his forearms and she could see the muscles move as he swung his arms in rhythm with his legs. He was almost to the porch by the time she realized he was aware that she had been staring at him.

He stopped with his boot on the first step and tipped his hat back so she could see his face. He was grinning.

"See anything you like?"

"Oh!" She whirled and headed for the door, but she didn't get two steps before he caught her arm and pulled her back around to face him.

"I wasn't complaining. In fact, I'm flattered. I can't keep my eyes off you, either."

"Faron—"

He laid two fingers across her mouth to silence her. His voice was gruff when he spoke again. "You'd better be careful how you look at me with those violet eyes of yours, Princess. I've got myself on a short tether. Don't you go untying any knots."

His fingers slid across her mouth to her cheek, and then tunneled up into her hair. Belinda found herself caught by Faron's green-eyed gaze. It was a powerful force, the desire in a man's eyes. It made a woman want to give herself up to him. Belinda felt her knees growing weak—nature's method of getting a woman down so a man could couple with her more easily. She was having trouble catching her breath, and her mouth dropped open slightly for more air.

Faron saw it differently. He perceived her open mouth as an irresistible invitation. Faron had always liked parties, and he never turned one down. He didn't now.

His head lowered slowly, and his lips parted slightly to match hers. He paused just before their mouths made contact and took a breath. Belinda felt as though he were stealing the breath right out of her. A soft moan sounded deep in her throat.

His lips were pliant against hers. And urgent. She felt his need as his tongue came searching hungrily for sustenance only she could provide. Her hands seemed to have a will of their own. They latched on to his shirt at the waist, then slid up behind his back and threaded into the curls at his nape.

She could feel the dampness where his hair was soaked with sweat. He smelled of hardworking man, a pungent odor, but one that made her think of his muscles bunching beneath cloth as he hefted a bale of hay. His body was hard where he had it pressed against her hips, and his mouth was hot and demanding on hers.

Belinda didn't want to feel so much. Didn't want to need so much. She felt the trap closing on her and at the last minute realized that she must escape. She yanked hard on Faron's hair, and when he howled in pain she let go and backed away as quickly as she could.

"No," she said. "We're not going to do this."

His eyes were feral, his body taut with need. He could still take her if he wanted to. Her aroused, aching body cried out for fulfillment. She saw him hesitate, torn between taking what he wanted or letting her go.

He whirled abruptly and headed for the sink on the back porch. He turned on the cold water full blast, yanked off his hat and threw it down, then stuck his head under the spigot. She stared as he cooled the back of his neck with the icy water. Then he stood and slung his wet hair back. His hands forked through the tangled black curls, setting them in some kind of order. Then he picked up his hat and settled it back on his head.

Water still dripped from his nose and chin and clumped on his eyelashes. But no signs of passion remained when he looked at her again. "You've got some supper ready for me, I believe."

"Yes. I— Yes." She turned and hurried inside, letting the screen door slam behind her. A moment later she heard it creak as he opened it and followed her inside.

Belinda could hardly believe the gentleman who exchanged witticisms with Madelyn at dinner was the same cowboy who had kissed her senseless on the back porch. Faron was absolutely charming. She could see he was good for Madelyn. He made the old woman laugh and even blush once. Asking him to leave was out of the question, even though it was what Belinda desperately wanted to do.

She urged Faron and Madelyn to stay in the dining room and talk while she cleared the table and washed the dishes. But she could hear everything they said through the open door to the kitchen. She cringed when she heard Madelyn ask whether Faron had ever been married.

"No," he answered.

"Why not?" Madelyn asked.

"Never found the right woman, I guess."

"What is it, exactly, you're looking for?"

There was a long pause before he answered, "I'll know her when I find her."

Belinda smiled. Maybe Madelyn had met her match. Faron Whitelaw wasn't the kind of man who could be manipulated. But she should have known her mother-in-law wouldn't easily abandon her matchmaking efforts. Madelyn's next question left Belinda gasping.

"How do you like Belinda?"

"She's a hard worker."

Madelyn chuckled. "She said the same thing about you. I suppose that's one thing you both have in common. I wonder if there are any others."

Again, that long pause.

"I admit I thought Belinda was, well, a little more pampered than she's turned out to be."

"Wayne wasn't the most considerate of husbands."

Belinda gritted her teeth. She wasn't about to let Madelyn start talking about her marriage. She grabbed the apple pie on the counter and marched back through the open doorway. "Dessert, anyone?"

Belinda kept her expression bland, but she had a feeling she wasn't fooling either of them.

"I love apple pie," Faron said. "I'll take a piece. How about you, Maddy?"

Belinda saw the flush rise on Madelyn's cheeks as Faron turned his smile on her.

"Why, I guess I will join you."

Faron turned that stunning smile on Belinda, and she felt—flustered. She dropped the pie on the table and said, "I'll go get some plates and the pie knife.

She turned just in time to keep the two of them from seeing the color race up her throat. This situation was unbearable! She had spent so many years learning to control her emotions, learning to keep what she was feeling hidden, because Wayne inevitably used it against her. All that Cowboy had to do was smile at her and she felt young and foolish again.

And desirable.

Lord, Lord, Lord, he made her feel like he wanted to lick her up like an ice cream cone on a hot Sunday afternoon.

Belinda leaned her forehead against the cool tile wall in the kitchen and took a deep breath. Then she scurried to find plates and a pie server before Faron came looking for her.

She could hear voices again from the other room.

"I'd love to play a little gin rummy," Faron was saying. "Penny a point is fine with me."

"You sure you wouldn't mind?" Madelyn asked.

Belinda could hear the worry in the old woman's voice. Madelyn didn't like being a burden on anyone. She would know if Faron was lying about spending time with her. Belinda heaved a quiet sigh of relief when she heard Faron reply, "Maddy, there's nothing I'd like better than skinning you at gin rummy."

Madelyn giggled. It was a youthful sound and one Belinda couldn't remember ever hearing from the old woman. Had their lives with Wayne been so very grim? It was hard for Belinda to be objective. But hearing Madelyn tonight with her grandson made Belinda wish that things could have been different with Wayne.

She put a smile on her face as she reentered the dining room. "Did I hear you say you're going to challenge Madelyn to a game of rummy?" she asked Faron.

"Yes, ma'am. Soon as I finish my pie."

Belinda served him a piece and set another in front of Madelyn. When she started to leave Faron asked, "Aren't you going to have some, too?"

"I'm not very hungry right now." She kept her lids lowered so Faron wouldn't find out the truth. She wanted to get away now, while she could still think rationally. She didn't want to see him being nice to his grandmother. She didn't want to see him being charming. She wanted to remember who he was and who she was and why any relationship between them other than the legal one resulting from her marriage to Faron's father was a mistake.

"I'm a little tired. I thought I'd go to bed early tonight," she said.

She was unprepared when Faron left the table and crossed to her. He stood facing her and said in a voice too low to carry back to Madelyn, "Are you all right?"

She felt breathless again. "Yes. I'm fine. Just a little tired."

He put a hand on her shoulder, and she felt the pressure of it deep in the pit of her belly.

"I made some calls while you were having lunch and hired some men to do the heavy labor. There's no reason for you to leave the house tomorrow."

Her eyes flashed up to meet his concerned gaze. "I'll do my part," she said.

"You don't—"

"I don't want any favors from you. I'll see you tomorrow morning."

Belinda jerked herself away and marched toward the spiral staircase. She felt Faron's eyes on her the entire way up to the second floor. When she reached her room, she closed the door behind her and leaned against it.

She felt like crying. Why hadn't she met Faron Whitelaw eight years ago? It was too late now for what might have been. And what made her think things would be any different with Faron? She had learned her lessons from Wayne. Things had been fine with him, too, at first. It was only later...

But Wayne Prescott had never made her feel the things Faron Whitelaw made her feel. Belinda was frightened. And excited. She felt a sort of anticipation for the days to come that she knew was dangerous for her peace of mind. Worst of all was the knowledge that she desired Faron Whitelaw every bit as much as he seemed to desire her.

She had to resist temptation. She had to make herself a regal, unapproachable Princess. Maybe that would keep the Cowboy at bay.

Belinda lifted her chin and focused her eyes on the distant canopy bed with its delicate eyelet covers. It was a bed eminently fit for a princess who had resigned herself to life in an inaccessible, remote ivory tower.

She crossed the room and sat down on the bed with her back stiff and her teeth clenched to still a quivering chin. She had survived a lot over the past eight years. By God, she would survive this as well.

Five

Over the next several weeks, Belinda kept her distance from Faron. She conversed with him at breakfast, where Madelyn provided a buffer, and he gave her jobs so she could contribute to the work being accomplished at King's Castle. But nothing she did brought her into contact with Faron.

She marveled at the improvements in the ranch. Fences lost their dilapidated look, buildings got a new coat of paint, windmills began to whir again, machinery had a well-oiled sound. She began to believe that they really might find a buyer for the ranch. And to realize that if—when—King's Castle was finally sold, she was going to miss it.

One of her jobs today was to oil all the hinges on the stalls. Belinda thought she was alone in the barn, so she practically jumped out of her skin when a voice behind her said, "What are you doing?"

She whirled, then expelled a relieved breath. "You scared me half to death!"

Faron grinned. "I usually have a somewhat different effect on women. So what are you doing?" he asked again.

She held out the oil can so he could see it. "I'm doing just what you ordered me to do this morning."

"Ordered?"

"All right, what you *suggested* I do."

He took the can out of her hand and set it on the corner of one of the stalls. "Madelyn sent me to get you. She said she needs you in the house."

If Belinda thought that keeping distance between them had diffused the sexual tension one whit, she was finding out now that she had been wrong. She was aware of Faron from the top of her head to the tips of her toes. "Did she say why she wants me?"

"No. But I noticed there's a lot of cleaning going on in the house. I asked Rue what was going on, and she said we're expecting company."

"My sisters and their families always come to King's Castle to visit during the Fourth of July holiday."

"Now I remember. You said something about that the first day—" He cut himself off. He didn't want to think back to the day he had met Belinda, when they had shared a special moment in time together. He had been trying desperately over the past couple of weeks to treat her like the stepmother she was.

It wasn't working. All he had to do was take a breath around her, and his body surged to life. He had given her things to do that would keep them apart, but once her family arrived they would be forced into social situations together. It would be hell pretending in front of her family that he didn't want her.

"When does your family start arriving?"

"Tomorrow."

Faron took off his hat, forked his fingers through his hair and tugged the hat back on again. "You could have given me a little more warning."

"Why? There's nothing you need to do. Madelyn and Rue and I will take care of everything."

If he'd had more warning maybe he could have figured out a reason to be gone from the ranch during their visit. If he left now it would look like he was running. Faron wasn't the kind of man to run from trouble. Not that he necessarily sought it out, either. But he could see trouble coming.

Still, some good might come of this visit. He would have a chance to ask Belinda's family some of the questions she had refused to answer. "I'm looking forward to meeting your sisters."

Belinda smiled. "It'll be hard not to trip over them, since they'll all be staying at the house."

By sundown the next day Faron realized that Belinda hadn't been exaggerating. Her three sisters, Dori, Tillie and Fiona, had all arrived. Dori had come with her husband, Bill, and three daughters under seven years of age. Tillie was also married. She and her husband, Sam, had two boys, five and nine. Fiona was still single, but she had brought her Abyssinian cat, Tutankhamen, Tut for short.

There were trucks on the floor, dolls on the chairs and screaming children chasing each other and the cat up and down the stairs. When they all sat down to dinner it was chaos.

It reminded Faron of home. Of the days when his mother had still been alive, and he and his brothers had argued at the table while their parents refereed. He felt his stomach twist when he realized that the picture he remembered hadn't been exactly as it had seemed.

Had his father's eyes been sad as they met his mother's across the table? Had there been any hesitancy in the way his father had lifted him up into his arms and held him in his lap? He couldn't remember.

Whatever his father had felt about raising another man's child hadn't been evident in the way Faron had been treated. He had felt loved, had known he was loved. By a woman who had been faithless to his father in conceiving him. By a man who had overlooked the foreign blood that ran in his veins.

He sat back and listened to the children around him and searched for the warm memories he knew he would find.

"Mom, Travis threw a pea at me!"

"Travis, stop throwing food at Peter."

"Dad, make Jennifer stop kicking the table."

"Jennifer, that's enough. Eat."

"Daddy, Trisha spilled her milk."

"I did not!"

"It's all over your dress."

"Is not!"

"Is, too!"

"Is not!"

"Penny! Trisha! That's enough from both of you. Can't we have a little peace and quiet here?"

No, Faron thought. There would be no peace and quiet until the kids had been put to bed. But he didn't mind. And he could see that Belinda didn't mind, either. In fact, the look in her eyes was decidedly soft—and yearning.

He remembered what Belinda had said about wanting children. He wondered why she and his father hadn't given him stepbrothers and stepsisters. Suddenly he was fiercely, selfishly glad that Belinda hadn't borne his father's children. Even if it meant she had no child to hold to her breast during this family reunion. Because he wanted to be the one to give her those children.

Until that moment Faron hadn't realized how deep his feelings for Belinda ran. He had known, of course, that he desired her physically. When he looked at her now it was with the knowledge that she was the one woman he was meant to spend his life with. With a sense of awful frustration he conceded that the unique relationship that had brought them together was equally likely to be what kept them apart.

Faron turned his gaze on Belinda. She had settled Jennifer, the youngest of Dori's daughters, in her lap and was playing patty-cake with the child. The smile on Belinda's face was easily as broad as the little girl's. When Jennifer threw her hands wide, Belinda tossed her head back to keep from getting hit. And met Faron's eyes.

He made no effort to hide what he was feeling. At first her expression softened. She shared with him the joy of holding the baby in her arms. As he continued staring, she lowered her lids and hid those expressive violet eyes from him. But it was too late. He had already seen the need, the desire, the yearning for a child of her own.

"Time for baths," Tillie announced.

"Aw, Mom!"

"Jeez, Mom!"

"I want to play some more."

Faron listened to all the complaints knowing that they were being made in vain. The children's parents slowly but surely herded their offspring up the stairs. He wasn't surprised when Belinda took advantage of the opportunity to escape with them. Madelyn excused herself to check on Rue, who had apparently found another bottle this afternoon.

That left Faron sitting at the table with Belinda's youngest sister, Fiona. Fiona had a pixie face, and from what Faron had seen, a puckish sense of humor. She was blond and blue-eyed, but considerably shorter than her eldest sister. She had a figure that curved in all the right places. If Faron had met her before Belinda, he might even have been interested in getting to know her better.

Fiona picked up her wineglass and walked down the length of the table to take a chair across from Faron. "I guess you and I are the only ones without someone to bathe.'' She paused and added with a come-hither smile, ''Unless you'd like me to scrub your back?''

''No thanks,'' Faron said, returning the smile.

''Thank goodness.''

''Pardon?''

Fiona's smile turned into a grin. ''I was just checking. I mean, I saw the way you stared at Belinda all night. You wouldn't be the right kind of guy for her if you were willing to hustle me the minute her back was turned.''

''Thanks for the vote of confidence.''

''Oh, I'm still not sure you're what she needs.''

''And what is that?''

Fiona's blue eyes bored into him. Her hands fisted on the table. ''Someone who wouldn't take advantage of her. Someone who would make her happy.''

''She wasn't happy with my father?''

Fiona gave an unladylike snort. ''Not hardly.''

Faron waited for her to say more. He didn't have to wait long.

''Wayne Prescott abused my sister. Oh, not so much physically. Although I know he hit her once or twice. But he crushed her spirit. Or at least he tried. Toward the end Belinda learned to hide what she was feeling, and he left her alone.''

Faron felt a rage such as he had never known directed at a man who was beyond his reach. ''Why didn't she leave him?''

''I asked her the same question. She said they had made a deal, and she owed him her loyalty.''

''What kind of deal?''

Fiona's eyes were bleak. ''Belinda sold herself to get the money to take care of us. Me and Dori and Tillie. When she married Wayne he established a substantial trust fund in each of our names. Dori went to UCLA and fell in love with Bill. Tillie married the doctor who put the cast on the broken leg she got skiing in Colorado. I bought a bed and breakfast in Vermont. Belinda got nothing. Except marriage to Wayne.

''Of course, all of us were too young to realize what she was doing when she did it. She told us she was in love with Wayne, and during the first couple of years they got along pretty well.''

''What happened then?''

''Wayne started to gamble. He lost big. He took it out on Belinda.

He kept her like a prisoner here, wouldn't let her go anywhere. I guess he was afraid she wouldn't come back. If it hadn't been for Madelyn, she probably would have left him.''

"What does Madelyn have to do with anything?''

"You've seen them together. Madelyn treats Belinda like the daughter she never had, and Belinda returns her affection. They both tried to curb Wayne's excesses. Sometimes I think if Belinda hadn't been there, Wayne might have taken out his frustrations on his mother.''

"Not the best father figure a man could have.''

"I'm sorry. I forgot he was your father. But he wasn't really, was he? I mean, someone else raised you. You're certainly nothing like Wayne from what I've seen today.''

"The question is whether Belinda sees my father when she looks at me,'' Faron said.

"I don't see how she could,'' Fiona said. "You don't look a thing like him. You don't act like him, either. Wayne mostly thought about himself. From things Belinda has told me about you—''

"Belinda talked to you about me?''

Fiona shrugged. "She just told me you were Wayne's son.'' Belinda had revealed a whole lot more about her feelings for Faron Whitelaw through what she had not said. But Fiona wasn't about to give away Belinda's secrets to the cowboy. She would keep her eyes open over the next couple of days and make her own judgment about whether Faron deserved a chance with Belinda.

"Guess I'd better go see if I can help get things settled upstairs. I'll be down later to help with the dishes,'' Fiona said.

Faron looked around him and realized everything was still sitting on the table. With Rue sleeping off her latest binge there was no one to handle such details. "I'll take care of it,'' Faron said.

Thus, when Belinda came downstairs she found the table cleared, the leftovers put away and Faron wiping down the counters with a sponge.

"You didn't have to do the dishes,'' she protested. "I would have done them.''

"You were busy. I didn't mind. Charlie One-Horse taught me how to stack a dishwasher.''

"Who's Charlie One-Horse?''

"A cross between hired hand, mother and father at Hawk's Way. He kind of takes care of things."

Belinda sat on one of the bar stools at the center island and leaned her chin on the heel of her hand. "When you see Charlie again, tell him I said thanks. I have to admit I'm a little tired."

"You work too hard."

"It was mostly play today. I love having my family around, but they keep things hectic."

"I spent some time after dinner talking to Fiona."

Belinda's lids lowered to hide her eyes. "And?"

"She told me why you married my father."

"Fiona never could keep a secret."

"She's grateful for what you did."

Belinda's voice was bitter as she explained. "If I had it to do over again, I wouldn't. And I won't make the same mistake twice. I'll never let another man do to me what Wayne did. I won't—"

Belinda suddenly realized who she was talking to. Wayne's son. A man it would be all too easy to allow into her life. Would she be making a mistake if she did? Or would things be different with Faron? She wished...she wished...

"Excuse me." Abruptly Belinda stood and headed for the screen door. She shoved her way outside and started walking. She didn't have any destination in mind, she just wanted to get away. Belinda didn't want to think of might-have-beens. She was tired of feeling regret. It wouldn't change what had happened. She had to forget about the past and go on with her life. Alone. That was the safest way, the best way to survive.

Faron stood in the kitchen after Belinda was gone, thinking back over what he had learned about her marriage to his father.

Belinda might have married Wayne Prescott for money, but she had done it from self*less* rather than self*ish* motives. It had become increasingly clear to him that she had bought security for her sisters at a very high price.

Now that he knew Belinda bitterly regretted what she had done, he allowed himself to acknowledge that he had been jealous of her relationship with his father. He wanted Belinda's love unbound by memories of her past. He was grateful to learn that he didn't have to compete with loving recollections of Wayne Prescott. But it had dawned on him this evening that he might have even more difficulty overcoming the damage done by his father's abusive treatment of his wife.

I won't make the same mistake twice. I'll never let another man do to me what Wayne did.

Faron was going to have to prove to Belinda that he wasn't like his father. That he was capable of loving her, of cherishing her, of treating her with the respect she deserved. He had to find a way to convince her that marriage to him wouldn't even remotely resemble her relationship with his father.

There was no time like the present to start.

Faron shoved open the screen door and marched out into the darkness after Belinda. She had already disappeared beyond the light pouring from the windows. He increased his pace and finally caught up to her at the edge of the river that ran across King's Castle.

The North Platte was narrow here, and the shallow water rushed over stones that made up the riverbed. Cottonwoods lined the water, and their leaves rustled in the wind. A zephyr cooled the night air. The cicadas chirped, and Faron heard an owl hoot in the distance. They might have been two people lost on the prairie with no one around for a thousand miles.

Or so it felt.

The moonlight created a glow around Belinda, outlining her so she was easy to find. "Why did you run away?"

Belinda whirled, surprised to find she had been followed. "I thought it was pretty obvious why I left. I was telling my late husband's son that his father was a terrible husband. Not the most proper after-dinner conversation I can imagine."

"But fascinating all the same."

"Why don't you go away and leave me alone? I've made up my mind not to get involved with another man—ever."

Her statement seemed to confirm his fears and left him feeling angry over what he couldn't control. "Are you only precluding marriage? Or do you plan to live the rest of your life as celibate as a nun?"

Belinda crossed her arms defensively. "I don't think that's any of your business."

"There you're wrong. Because," he said in a low, dangerous voice, "you're lying to yourself if you think you can live without love for the rest of your life."

"I don't need a man—for any reason."

"I think you're lying. To me. And to yourself." Faron stalked her now as he had wanted to for the past month. He was fighting for their life together. This time he wouldn't allow her to escape.

Belinda backed away slowly, but for every step she took, Faron took two. She found herself backed up against a cottonwood at the edge of the river with nowhere else to retreat.

Faron laid his palms on the bark on either side of her head and leaned down so they were eye to eye. "I'm not my father. I would never hurt you."

"That's what you say now," Belinda said in a tremulous voice. "But later—"

"Later I'll be the same man I am now. A man who desires you, Princess. A man who wants to cherish you."

It was too much what she had always wanted to hear from a man she cared for, and never had. Belinda's eyes sank closed. A moment later she felt Faron's mouth on hers. Gentle. Tender. Coaxing.

He insinuated his body between her thighs and rubbed himself against her. "Princess, open your mouth for me. Please."

He caught her upper lip with his teeth and teased it, then slid his tongue along the crease of her lips, making her gasp with the pleasure of it. He took advantage of the opportunity to slip his tongue inside, to taste, to tempt her to join him in his sensual exploration.

She put her palms on his chest, intending to push him away, but her fingers curled against the cloth instead, and she pulled him closer. Faron's arms curved around her and aligned them from breast to hip.

"I need you, Princess."

Belinda caught fire in Faron's arms. There was no denying that she wanted him. And needed him. As the prairie grass needed sunshine. As the flowers needed spring rain. Her knees would no longer support her, and she and Faron sank to the ground together.

Faron made short work of Belinda's blouse, but when he reached under her skirt he found a delightful surprise. "You're wearing nylons."

"I always wear nylons with a skirt."

Faron grinned. "I mean real nylons." His hand slid around the top rim of her nylons and followed the garter belt up to her waist. "It's been a long time since I've met a woman who wore a garter belt."

"So I'm old-fashioned. Sue me."

"I'd rather make love to you."

Faron took his time removing her nylons. By the time he had her garter belt off, they were both having trouble breathing. He unsnapped his shirt and then pulled it off over his head. He unbuckled his belt, but when he reached for the zipper, she was there before him.

She took her time, touching him as she had always dreamed of touching a man. Aware of his guttural groans of pleasure, aware of the restraint he exercised to remain quiescent under her touch. But soon, touching wasn't enough for either of them. Faron finished what Belinda had started, and in moments they were both naked in the moonlight.

"You're so beautiful," Faron said. "So exquisite."

Belinda had never felt so loved, so cared for, so much the object of a man's desire. She ran her hands across his broad shoulders, feeling the play of muscle and sinew. Then her hands slipped up his back and tunneled into his hair. She urged his head down until their mouths met.

It was a kiss of longing. Of belonging. Her to him. Him to her. It was more than sex. It always had been. It always would be. Something magical, something mystical happened between them when their bodies merged. Their souls meshed, as well.

When at last they lay sated in each other's arms, Belinda didn't feel grateful to Faron for proving her wrong about needing him. She hated him for being right. Because she was afraid to take another chance. The consequences of her relationship with Faron's father were too devastating ever to forget.

She sat up with her back to Faron and began putting her clothes on. "This doesn't change anything."

Faron sat up, but made no move to touch her. "What do you mean?"

"I'm not going to let myself get involved with you."

"You already are involved!" Faron retorted. "You can't pretend nothing just happened between us."

"It was just sex."

"Like hell it was!" Faron was angry. Even though he knew why Belinda was shoving him away, it didn't make the rejection any less painful. He stood and slipped on his shorts, then yanked on his jeans.

"I know you had a tough time with my father, but I thought we'd settled all that."

"I can't take the chance you'll turn out to be like him," Belinda said in a quiet voice.

"I'm not—"

"You're an especially bad risk, Faron. After all, like father, like son."

Belinda could see Faron was furious. She waited for a blow that never came. Instead, he sat back down, pulled on his socks and boots, then stood and retrieved his shirt without saying another word.

He wasn't like his father. She knew it. And he knew it. Yet he didn't argue with her. When he was finished dressing he turned to her and said, "I'll walk you back to the house."

"I don't need—"

"Don't argue with me, Princess."

She didn't. She stuffed her nylons and garter belt into the pocket of her denim skirt, stuck her bare feet into her shoes and headed back toward the house.

The house was dark when they returned. Apparently both adults and children had welcomed the day's end. Belinda began to think she might escape to her bedroom without any further confrontation with Faron. She almost did.

At the top of the stairs Faron caught her hand and drew her toward him.

"It was beautiful, Princess. What happened between us was beautiful. I don't know what my father did to you. I don't even want to try to imagine what it must have been like living with him. But I don't intend to let what happened between the two of you interfere with our relationship."

"But—"

He put his fingertips to her lips. "All men aren't like my father. Not even his son. Especially not his son."

He let her go, and she disappeared into her bedroom. A moment later Faron found himself facing Belinda's sister, Fiona. Faron held his breath, waiting for whatever she had to say.

"I didn't mean to eavesdrop. I was looking for Tut." The Abyssinian curled himself around her bare ankles and purred. "I think maybe you'll do for Belinda. I think maybe you'll do just fine."

Faron smiled grimly. "All I have to do now is convince your sister of that."

"You'll manage. Be patient. All it'll take is a little time." She leaned down and picked up the cat, then closed the door, shutting Faron out.

Faron stared down the hall at Belinda's closed door. He didn't have as much time as Fiona seemed to think. With the progress he was making turning the ranch into a showplace, they were bound to find a buyer soon. Once they sold the ranch, he would head back to Texas.

If he didn't get matters resolved with Belinda, he was likely to end up making the trip alone.

Faron clenched his fists in determination.

He would be damned if he'd leave her behind.

Six

Belinda managed to avoid Faron until her sisters left. She knew he was giving her space. Fiona had told her so—and a lot more besides—while they were sitting at the Casper airport. Dori's and Tillie's flights had already come and gone. She was waiting for Fiona's plane to depart.

"You can't judge every man by your husband," Fiona had said.

"What other gauge would you suggest I use?" Belinda demanded.

"Your heart."

"I don't have one."

Fiona laughed. "Don't you wish! You've got one all right. Maybe a little bruised and battered, but it's in there beating away. And if what I suspect is true, beating a whole lot faster whenever a certain cowboy is around."

Belinda was helpless to control the flush that rose on her cheeks. "All right, so I'm attracted to Faron Whitelaw. He's a handsome man."

"And charming."

"And charming. But he's also my stepson."

"A fact that makes absolutely no difference."

"How can you say that?"

"It might be different if Faron had grown up at King's Castle, if you had stood in the role of stepmother and he had been your stepson. But that wasn't the case.

"You know what I think, Belinda? I think the fact Faron is technically your stepson is just an excuse."

Belinda laughed nervously. "An excuse for what?"

"An excuse not to fall in love with him. Which you already half are, if I'm not mistaken."

That nervous laugh escaped again. Belinda lowered her eyelids to hide her expressive eyes, but Fiona exercised the prerogative of younger sisters the world over to ignore her elder sister's tender sensibilities.

"Look," Fiona said. "I say you ought to go for it."

Belinda gasped. "*Go for it?* What kind of thing is that to urge your sister to do?"

"Look, you like the guy, right?"

Fiona didn't wait for Belinda to respond.

"And he likes you."

Again Fiona didn't wait for Belinda to respond.

"So go for it. Give the relationship a chance. Get to know Faron. Let yourself fall in love—I mean, if that's what happens."

"And if nothing happens?"

"Then you're no worse off than you were before," Fiona said philosophically.

Fiona's flight was called. She rose and hugged Belinda, then picked up the cat carrier that held Tut. "Be happy, Belinda. You deserve it. Call me, okay?"

"Okay."

Belinda waved as Fiona turned and smiled over her shoulder. Before Fiona even got to the door, she had met a man traveling on the same flight. Belinda shook her head in disbelief at her sister's easy way with men as she turned and headed for the parking lot. But she used the drive back from Casper to think about Fiona's advice.

Be happy, Belinda. You deserve it.

It was wonderful advice, actually. If only Belinda knew what would make her happy, she would do it. The problem was, Belinda had no idea what she wanted. She had been honest with Faron the day she had met him. She hadn't ever allowed herself to dream. Right after her parents were buried, she had needed to work to support her sisters. After she had married Wayne, whatever hopes she'd harbored had died a sure, if not precisely sudden, death.

So what would make her happy?

A husband who loved her. A houseful of children, with Madelyn nearby, a doting grandmother.

It was all so very simple. The Princess would just fall in love with the Cowboy and live happily ever after.

But as Belinda drove up to The Castle, the old fears rose up before her. How could she be sure things would turn out happily ever after? Was she willing to take the risk of loving Faron? They had been forced by circumstance into each other's company. What if the ranch sold in the next few weeks? Would he leave her behind and return to Texas without another thought of her?

Belinda found Faron sitting in one of the rockers on the stone terrace along the side of the house with Madelyn sitting in the rocker beside him. The sun was just setting, and in the fading light Belinda saw that Madelyn's head was thrown back and she was laughing. Belinda wanted to be a part of that picture.

When she stopped the pickup, Faron bounded down from the terrace, pulled open the door and practically dragged her out.

"Come on and join us," he said. "We're having a glass of tea and exchanging war stories."

"War stories?" Belinda felt the strength in Faron's hand as he gripped her fingers and tugged her along behind him.

And yet she knew how gentle he could be. Surely he wasn't like his father. Surely...

Faron seated her in the rocker where he had been sitting and settled himself on the flagstone terrace cross-legged facing her. "I just finished my war story," he said. "It's Maddy's turn."

"What kind of war story?" Belinda persisted.

"Be still and listen, girl, and you'll find out soon enough," Madelyn chided with a twinkle in her eye. "Now, let's see. It must have been '42, or maybe it was '43. Everyone contributed what he or she could to the War Effort. I did my part. I danced for the USO."

"I didn't know there was a USO in Casper," Belinda said.

"Hush, girl," Madelyn said. "This is my story." She leaned back in the rocker and set it in motion with the toe of her shoe.

"His name was Tommy Neville. He had the bluest eyes and the blackest hair I'd ever seen. We met at the USO. He was a Navy flier headed to California, scheduled to ship out to the Pacific. It was his last night at home. He said he wanted to hold an American girl in his arms one last time, and feel the touch of her lips on his—because he might not be coming home.''

"What a line!'' Faron interjected. "So did you kiss him?''

"What kind of war stories *are* these?'' Belinda asked suspiciously.

"Hush, dear, and let me finish,'' Maddy reproved. "Of course I kissed him,'' she said with a girlish grin. "What kind of patriot would I have been if I'd let a soldier go off to war without a good-bye kiss?''

Faron clapped his hands. "Good for you, Maddy. Your turn, Belinda.''

"My turn for what?''

"We're telling romantic war stories,'' Maddy explained. "Your turn.''

"I... I wasn't dating anyone during a war.''

Faron and Maddy exchanged disbelieving looks and then burst out laughing.

"She can't be that naive, can she?'' Faron asked Maddy.

"I wouldn't have said so, but maybe she is. Perhaps you'd better explain it to her.''

"We're telling 'war' stories about our previous love affairs,'' Faron said.

"You're exchanging romantic escapades with your *grandmother?*'' Belinda asked incredulously. "Whose idea was this?''

"Mine,'' Madelyn said.

That took the wind out of Belinda's sails.

"So, are you going to play or not?'' Madelyn asked.

"I'm not!''

"Chicken!'' Faron taunted.

"Coward!'' Madelyn accused.

"All right!'' Belinda retorted. "You asked for it. You're going to get it!''

"I can't wait to hear this,'' Faron said, settling back against the short stone wall that edged the terrace.

"Me, either,'' Madelyn said with a chuckle.

"He had the biggest, brownest eyes you ever saw.''

"You like brown eyes?'' Faron asked with a frown.

"Shut up and listen,'' Belinda said. "And he had curly red hair.''

"So tell us about the date,'' Faron urged.

"We spent the whole night together,'' Belinda said.

Faron's eyes narrowed. "The whole night? Who the hell was this guy?"

"His name was Whitey."

"What kind of name is that for a redheaded man?" Faron asked disgustedly.

"It's a terrible name for a man," Belinda agreed. "But a great name for a Hereford steer."

"A steer?"

Belinda saw the moment when recognition—and relief—dawned on Faron's face.

Madelyn joined Faron's laughter. "I guess she showed us."

Belinda was glad they believed she had told her story as a joke. Because the truth was, there weren't any other men in her life. Not that she was embarrassed to admit to her lack of experience. No wonder she was afraid to take a chance on romantic love. Having never felt the emotion, she wasn't sure she would recognize it if it bit her on the nose.

"I'm going in to see if Rue needs any help," Madelyn said.

Faron jumped up to help his grandmother out of the rocker.

"You'd think I was an old lady," she muttered.

"No, just a lady," Faron said with a gentle smile.

Madelyn shot a look at Belinda as though to say, "You're a fool if you don't grab him!"

When Madelyn was gone, Faron took her seat and set the rocker in motion. Belinda joined him rocking, and the only sound for a while was the creak of the wooden rockers and the occasional lowing of cattle.

"Did you have a nice drive back from Casper?"

"Yes."

"I like your sisters."

"They are nice, aren't they?"

"Was the sacrifice worth it?"

Belinda sighed. "It was a foolish thing to do. Everything turned out better than I had a right to expect."

"Meaning your sisters ended up happy, even if you didn't."

Belinda didn't bother to respond because Faron hadn't been asking a question, he had been making a statement. The two of them rocked quietly, each caught up in his own thoughts.

Faron's sister Tate had called while Belinda was at the airport. It had been one of the most difficult conversations of Faron's life.

"I called Hawk's Way looking for you," Tate began, "because Adam and I want you to be our son's godfather. Garth said you'd gone to Wyoming, but he wouldn't tell me why. He just gave me this number and said you'd answer my questions. So what are you doing in Wyoming, Faron?"

Faron felt a lump in his throat. This is what it meant to be a part of the Whitelaw family. Caring. Concern. Curiosity. But he didn't have the right to play the role she wanted to cast him in without confessing the truth first. "Tate, I—"

She was too impatient to allow him to get a word in edgewise. "Spill the beans, big brother. What's going on up there? I'm guessing there's a woman involved. Am I right?"

Tate had been talking virtually without taking a breath, so when she finally stopped, the silence was awesome.

"Faron? Is something wrong? Talk to me."

Faron realized Garth had left it up to him to decide whether to tell the rest of the family the truth about his birth. For a moment he thought about making up some kind of story to hide what their mother had done. But Tate was a mother herself now. She was no longer a child who had to be protected from the facts of life.

"I'm here in Wyoming to meet my stepmother."

There was an absurdly long silence on the other end of the line.

"Is this some kind of joke, Faron? I don't understand."

Faron heard Tate's confusion, her anger and her fear. He shoved his free hand through his hair. "It's no joke, Tate. Mother had an affair before you were born. I was the result. My real father left me half his ranch in Wyoming. I came up here to…to see this place."

"Am I…?"

"You're legitimate, as far as I know," Faron reassured her. "I guess Mom and Dad got back together after her affair."

"I'm so sorry, Faron."

Faron swallowed over the lump in his throat. "I'll understand if you don't want me to be godfather to—"

"Oh, no! Please, Faron. You *have* to be the baby's godfather. It's what Adam and I both want. This other…thing…doesn't change how I feel about you. You're still my brother, and I love you dearly."

Faron's eyes burned with tears. He wanted to tell Tate how much her love meant to him but he couldn't get the words past his constricted throat.

"Faron? Are you there?"

At last he managed, "I'm here, Tate."

"Well, will you do it? Will you be Brett's godfather?"

"I'd be proud and pleased to be godfather to your son."

He heard a sigh of relief on the other end of the line.

"Everybody's coming to Hawk's Way over Labor Day. That's not a problem for you, is it? Because if it is, we can change the day. We need you there."

"I can make it. I might bring a couple of people along."

"So there *is* a girl involved!"

Faron grinned. "Maybe."

"I can't wait to meet her. What's she like?"

"Good-bye, Tate."

"Good-bye, Faron. And thanks again. I love you. See you at Hawk's Way. Oh. Wait. Does Jesse know?"

"I haven't said anything to him."

"Do you want me to tell him?"

Faron thought how easy it would be to say yes. "No. I'll call him. Good-bye, Tate."

"Good-bye."

Faron hadn't waited to make the call to Jesse. It seemed better to get it over with right away. Jesse was considerably more philosophical than Faron had expected him to be.

"I'm not surprised," Jesse had said.

"You're not?"

"I'm older than you. I guess I saw more than you did as a child. Mom and Dad...there were some arguments, some hard words. It went on for about a year. Then it suddenly stopped. That must have been when she was having the affair. Their marriage seemed stronger after that."

Faron marveled at how differently his two older brothers had viewed their mother's infidelity. Garth remembered only the hurt. Jesse had remembered the healing. Surprisingly, Faron felt better knowing that his illegitimate birth hadn't split his parents apart, but might even have helped draw them closer together.

Faron had hung up the phone feeling like a huge weight had been lifted from his shoulders, one he hadn't even been aware he was carrying around.

Remembering the two phone calls reminded Faron that he had already set in motion plans to get Belinda to visit Hawk's Way. Now all he had to do was convince her she should go.

"I think you'd like my brothers and sister if you ever met them," Faron said, breaking the peaceful silence between them.

Belinda was still half dreaming and murmured, "Maybe I will someday."

"How about Labor Day?"

Belinda put out a foot to stop her rocker. "What?"

"I got a call while you were gone to the airport. The family is getting together for the christening of my sister Tate's son. I've agreed to be his godfather. I thought you might like to come with me."

Belinda wasn't sure what to think, what to do. "That's two months from now. Maybe the ranch will sell, and you'll be long gone by then."

"Maybe. Maybe not."

"I couldn't leave Madelyn alone," Belinda said.

"I've already invited Maddy to come, and she's agreed."

"Maddy's your grandmother. She has a reason to come."

"I want you to come, Belinda."

Belinda searched Faron's face. "Why?"

"Because this will be an important moment in my life, Princess. And I want to share it with you."

"I..."

"You don't have to answer me now. Just think about it."

A moment later Belinda was alone. Faron had disappeared in the direction of the barn.

Over the next month Faron kept his distance from her. At first Belinda was grateful. She figured he stayed away so she wouldn't feel pressured to accept his invitation. It also allowed her to avoid having to examine her feelings for the Cowboy. However, Belinda soon realized that unless she spent time with Faron, she wouldn't have a chance to find out whether she wanted their relationship to develop further.

So when she got a call from a corporate buyer who wanted to

take a look at King's Castle, she saddled her horse and went in search of Faron. She found him working on another windmill on the northern border of the ranch.

"I thought you had hired men to do the manual labor," she said as she stepped down from the saddle.

"This just needed a little fine-tuning. Thought I'd take care of it myself."

Belinda took a moment to admire the man. He had removed his shirt, and his bronzed upper torso glistened with sweat. The muscles in his back bunched as he manhandled the wrench he was holding. He twisted it once more, then stood and threw the wrench into the tool box in the back of his pickup. He pulled a bandanna out of his back jeans pocket and used it to wipe the sweat from his brow.

He seemed to realize suddenly that she was staring at him. Only this time when he met her gaze, she didn't look away. She did nothing to hide her desire. Nothing could have been a more powerful aphrodisiac.

"Why did you come out here?" he asked.

"There was a phone call..." Belinda lost her train of thought as Faron reached out and cupped her cheek with the palm of his hand. He tilted her face up and it seemed the most natural thing in the world to lift her lips to meet his.

Warm. Welcome. Like coming home. She hadn't known she needed his kiss so much.

Soft. Receptive. She belonged to him. He must have been insane to have stayed away so long.

Faron pulled her into his arms, nearly crushing her with the strength of his embrace. He spread his legs and settled her in the cradle of his thighs.

Belinda wondered if this was what it felt like to be in love. She couldn't deny the passion that flared between the two of them whenever they were together. Touching Faron gave her as much pleasure as having him touch her.

It had been too long for both of them. He was impatient, but so was she. Once Faron had her breasts bare under the sunlight, he took his time. He bent his head to kiss her soft curves and then suckled her. Belinda arched into his caresses, and her traitorous knees once more gave way.

Faron picked her up in his arms, but the only shady spot available was already occupied by cattle.

"How about going for a ride?"

He set her back in the saddle, then mounted behind her. When Belinda started to rebutton her blouse, Faron stopped her.

"Don't. I want to hold you while we're riding." Belinda leaned back into his embrace, and Faron's hands crossed around her, cupping her breasts. Faron kicked the palomino into a lope, heading toward the river and the cottonwoods he knew they would find there.

It was the most decadent ride Belinda had ever taken. By the time they got to the river, each of them had aroused the other beyond bearing. Faron slid off the palomino's back and pulled Belinda down onto the ground. He had them both stripped in record time.

The day was hot, but the grass was cool on Belinda's naked backside. Their coupling was urgent, so quick that each offered a quite unnecessary apology to the other.

"I should have waited—"

"I couldn't wait—"

They both laughed, and then hugged each other and rolled to their sides, their bodies still joined. They lay like that a long time, until at last they separated to lie on their backs and stare at the sky through the rustling leaves of the cottonwood.

"So why did you come out to see me?" Faron asked as he nibbled on the lobe of her ear.

"We got a call from a corporate buyer. He wants to take a look at King's Castle." Belinda was close enough to be aware of the way Faron stiffened. It was still a month until Labor Day.

"When does he want to come?"

"Tomorrow."

So soon. Faron wasn't ready to leave King's Castle yet. Over the past month he had begun to see the potential of the place. With a little better management it could become a successful enterprise again. Of course, a woman alone would have a tough time managing, but a couple—a couple could do just fine.

He didn't dare mention to Belinda what he was thinking. She couldn't even make up her mind to take a trip to Texas with him. How could he expect her to consider marriage and a life spent together at King's Castle?

Faron surprised himself with how easily that thought had formed

In his mind. Was he really ready to get married? What would his family say when they heard he wanted to marry his stepmother? He could hear Garth now. His eldest brother would think Faron had lost his mind.

But Faron knew if his family met Belinda, they would understand how he had fallen in love with her. Which was why he had to convince her to come to the christening at Hawk's Way on Labor Day.

Now that they knew he had a different father, he wanted them to see that he wasn't going to allow his bastardy to separate him from his family. In fact, he wanted them to see that he had merely extended his family to include his grandmother. He hadn't figured out yet what he would say about Belinda.

"Did you tell the buyer we'd be glad to show him around?" he asked her.

"I told him we'd call him back."

Faron arched a brow. "Was there some reason you wanted to wait?"

"I just thought...what if he makes us an offer?"

"If it's a reasonable offer, we'll accept."

"Do you really want to sell the ranch?"

"Don't you?" Faron asked.

"I guess I do," Belinda said. "But it's been home for a long time. It'll seem strange to live in town."

"Is that what you'd do? Move to town?"

"Where else would I go?"

Home with me to Hawk's Way. But Faron didn't say what he was thinking. It was too soon to tell Belinda the plans he had for the two of them. He didn't want to scare her away.

It wasn't until she had told the story about spending the night with a brown-eyed, redheaded steer that he had realized just how limited her experience with men was. He knew she'd had a bad time with Wayne Prescott. He could understand her reluctance to trust another man.

But if he'd thought his time was short before, it was down to nothing now. Tomorrow. It might all end tomorrow if the buyer made an offer they couldn't refuse. So maybe he should say something to her now, let her know that he didn't intend ever to let her go.

Faron opened his mouth to declare his love and shut it again.

Belinda was asleep.

He lay down beside her and pulled her into his arms. Tomorrow would be soon enough to speak his mind. Maybe the buyer wouldn't want the property. Maybe there would be no decisions to be made right away. He would just wait and see.

Seven

"How dare you refuse an offer for this ranch without consulting me!" Belinda raged.

"He offered a quarter of what the place was worth!" Faron retorted.

"I don't care how much he offered. What I care about is the fact that you made the decision without saying anything to me. I should have been consulted."

"Both of us have to agree for this place to get sold. Since I would have refused the offer anyway, it didn't make sense to get you involved."

"Didn't make sense? I can't believe what I'm hearing! That's just the sort of thing Wayne would have said. 'No sense troubling your pretty little head with business.' I own half of King's Castle, and by God, I'll be a part of any decisions that are made regarding this ranch."

Faron realized he had made a big mistake, and he quickly sought to make amends. "I'm sorry. Next time—"

"If there is a next time!" Belinda put her fisted hands on her hips. "There aren't so many corporate buyers out there that we can afford to refuse an honest offer."

"So maybe we just won't sell!"

"Right! And when the bank comes to collect the mortgage payment what do you suggest we use for money?"

"I've got—"

"I don't want to rely on you to keep this place afloat."

"Why not?" Faron asked.

"I learned how much that sort of debt can cost when I was married to your father!"

There it was again. The comparison of Faron with his father, and it hadn't been a compliment. "I am not my father," he said quietly.

"Could have fooled me," Belinda muttered. "Tyrannical, autocratic—"

"That's enough," Faron said. "I get your point."

Belinda was still quivering with rage. And fighting tears. She had talked herself into believing that Faron was different from his father. His actions today, discounting her opinion and involvement in a way similar to what Wayne might have done, was a deep disappointment. Her romantic bubble had burst, and she was sharply, brutally disillusioned.

"I hope you're not going to use this incident as an excuse not to come to Texas," Faron said.

"I've learned never to make decisions when I'm angry," Belinda admitted. "Maybe when I've calmed down we can talk about where we go from here."

She turned on her heel and left Faron standing alone in Wayne's study. He leaned back in the swivel chair and put his boot heels up on the rolltop desk.

Was what he had done so wrong? Faron was used to making decisions on his own. Except on major issues that concerned Hawk's Way. Then he and Garth would discuss the matter... As he should have discussed the matter with Belinda, Faron realized.

If the situation had been reversed, he would have been furious if Belinda had made a major decision regarding King's Castle without him. She deserved no less consideration than he would have demanded for himself. Unconsciously he had put himself in the role of caretaker, but it was clear now, if it hadn't been before, that Belinda intended to be nothing less than an equal partner.

Which he was willing to be. Only what he wanted from her was not just a business partnership, but a deeply committed personal relationship.

Faron cursed the father who had so wounded the woman he loved. His recent error hadn't helped matters. Belinda was sure to be less trusting of him in the future. It was going to be a challenge convincing her that she didn't have to worry about repeating the mistakes with him that she had made with his father.

Meanwhile Belinda had retreated to the vegetable garden behind the house where she was on her hands and knees pulling up weeds between a row of snap beans and a row of tomatoes. She wasn't precisely aware when Madelyn joined her. The older woman wore a floppy hat to keep the sun off and gloves to protect her hands. The two women worked in silence for a while, as they had on many another day. It was Madelyn who finally spoke.

"You're going to get sunstroke working without a hat."

"Don't you start treating me like a child. I get enough of that from Faron."

"Oh?"

"He turned down an offer for the ranch without even consulting me. Just like Wayne, he—"

Madelyn's interruption cut off Belinda's tirade before it even got started. "Oh, no, my dear. He's not like Wayne at all."

"It didn't even cross his mind to speak to me before—"

"But he apologized when you pointed out his mistake, didn't he?"

"Yes, but—"

"Wayne would never have apologized. I think you should give Faron the benefit of the doubt."

Belinda dusted the dirt off her hands. "Does that mean you also think I should go to Texas with him?"

"Tell me one good reason why you shouldn't go."

"I've never been beyond the borders of Wyoming in my entire life."

"Land sakes, girl. All the more reason to go."

"I've never been on an airplane."

"Flying is a piece of cake."

Belinda resorted to the real reasons she had reservations about going to Texas. "I'm the widow of the man with whom Faron's mother had an affair. I'm Faron's stepmother."

"When the Whitelaws meet you they'll be just as fond of you as Faron is."

"Faron isn't—"

Madelyn pursed her lips and looked at Belinda across the row of snap beans. "Don't try to deny it. I've got eyes, Belinda, and I'm not too old to see what's right in front of my nose."

Belinda pulled a snap bean and broke it into pieces looking for the tiny beans inside.

Madelyn reached out and put a hand on Belinda's knee. "You're like my very own daughter, Belinda. I only want you to be happy. I think Faron could make you happy."

"If I go to the christening with Faron, it doesn't mean I'm committing myself to anything where he's concerned. I want to be sure you understand that and don't get your hopes up."

"Of course not, dear. I understand perfectly. It would just be a much-needed break from all the work here. A chance for you to get away and see another part of the country."

"That's all I'd be doing," Belinda affirmed.

A few weeks later, when she found herself facing the Whitelaws' antebellum mansion at Hawk's Way, Belinda was having second thoughts. The ranch house was an imposing two-story white frame structure with four twenty-foot-high fluted columns and railed first- and second-story porches. The road leading to the house was lined with majestic magnolias. The branches of a moss-laden live oak draped the roof of the house. It had a majesty every bit as profound as The Castle.

Faron had one arm around her shoulder and the other arm around Madelyn as he escorted them up the front steps and inside the foyer. "This is my home," he told Belinda.

She could hear the pride in his voice. The reason for it was evident in the well-kept, homey furnishings she found inside. There was tradition in this house, oak and pine furniture that had survived the rough and tumble of generations of Whitelaw sons and daughters. An ancient map framed over the mantel delineated what had once been the vast reaches of Hawk's Way in the Texas panhandle.

"It's beautiful," she said. "You must have missed being here these past few months."

Faron was surprised to realize that he hadn't missed Hawk's Way as much as he might have expected to when he left. The reason was obvious. In Wyoming he had found something to fill the hole inside him. He no longer felt the same sense of belonging here since he had staked his claim on his father's land—and his father's wife.

Faron's brothers and sister were arrayed in the parlor with their families. The two babies, Jesse and Honey's daughter and Adam and Tate's son, were sleeping in small antique cribs. From descriptions Faron had given her, Belinda easily recognized the two couples. Honey was sitting in Jesse's lap on a chair in front of the fireplace. Adam and Tate were sitting close beside each other on the couch.

Garth was standing with an arm resting on the thick pine mantel above the stone fireplace. There was another young woman in the room, but Belinda couldn't imagine who she could be.

Faron proudly introduced Belinda and Madelyn to the assembled group. "This is my grandmother, Madelyn Prescott," he said. "I call her Maddy."

There was an awkward moment when Belinda wondered whether Faron's family would accept the old woman. Tate made the first move. She jumped up from the couch and crossed with her hands extended to the older woman. "It's so nice to meet you, Maddy." She gave Maddy a quick, hard hug. Then she stood back and looked to see whether her brother resembled his grandmother. "Oh, my goodness. Faron has your eyes! Come see, Jesse, Garth."

The two large men came forward to greet the old woman and to agree with Tate that yes, Faron and Maddy had eyes the same unique gray-green color. Honey and Adam soon joined them and everyone began talking a mile a minute.

In the confusion Belinda was tempted to sneak back out the way she had come. Just when she thought Faron had forgotten all about her, he raised his hand for quiet. It took a few moments for the commotion to die down.

You could have heard a pin drop when he said, "And this is Belinda Prescott, my stepmother."

"That's the ugly stepmother?" Jesse whispered. His wife elbowed him in the ribs to shut him up.

It was Garth who took control of what could have become a very awkward situation. "I'm pleased to meet you, Belinda."

But Belinda didn't think he was at all pleased. She didn't know when she had ever met such a granite-faced man. His greeting was formal and his manner stiff. Belinda felt like crying. She didn't belong here. She wasn't part of this family in any way, shape or form. When she would have turned and run, a beautiful young woman with long blond hair and widely spaced gray eyes reached out and grasped her hand.

"Hi. I'm Candice—Candy Baylor. I guess you and I are the only two people here who aren't family."

Candy smiled, and Belinda immediately felt better.

"I've been working at Hawk's Way this summer, and I can imagine how you must feel, meeting this rowdy bunch for the first time."

"They are a little overwhelming," Belinda conceded.

"I don't know if you remember me," Faron said, extending a hand to Candy. "I'm Faron." Faron shot a look at Garth as though to say "What's she doing here?" But Garth's face remained stony.

"Of course I remember you," Candy said. "Last time I was here with my father you yanked my braids at the breakfast table."

Faron grinned. "Guilty. Was that only three years ago? You've grown up a little since then."

Garth interrupted, saying, "I think it's time you showed Maddy and Belinda where they'll be staying."

Faron was intrigued by Garth's possessive attitude toward Candy. That was a situation he intended to find out more about later. "Come on upstairs, ladies, and I'll show you to your rooms."

After taking Maddy to her room, Faron led Belinda to hers.

Belinda was relieved to see that she and Maddy were staying on a wing of the house that was separated from the rest of the family. She felt less pleased when she saw that Faron had settled Maddy in a room that was at the opposite end of the hall from hers. She looked at the room next to hers and said, "Who sleeps there?"

"I do," Faron answered.

Belinda turned startled violet eyes on him. "I thought the family was on a separate wing."

"The rest of them are."

Belinda stared at him for a moment. "Faron—"

He leaned over and gave her a quick, hard kiss. "Don't ask me to move you somewhere else, Princess. I want you close to me."

He didn't plead, he didn't cajole. Just that simple request. Belinda remembered Fiona's advice. And what Madelyn had said. It was time to act on her feelings for the Cowboy. Time to take a chance. "All right," she said at last. "I'll stay here."

She heard his exhaled sigh of relief and smiled inwardly. So, he wasn't as confident as he had led her to believe. Somehow that made her feel better. "Do you suppose there's something I can do to help with supper?"

"As soon as you finish unpacking, come on downstairs to the kitchen, and I'm sure Charlie will put you to work."

"I can't wait to meet the man who taught you how to stack a dishwasher," Belinda said with a grin.

Faron kissed her again, then turned and left her. If he didn't go now, he was afraid he wouldn't go at all.

The chaos in the kitchen seemed familiar to Belinda, who had so recently been visited by her siblings and their families. Everyone was there pitching in to get things on the table except Garth and Candy, who had headed for the barn to check on a mare that was expected to foal in the next day or so.

Belinda was amazed and amused at the contrast between Faron's family and her own. Maybe it was because she had sisters, but there seemed to be a lot more roughhousing among Faron's clan. Even Tate, Faron's youngest sister, could hold her own with her brothers. When Faron threw a handful of potato peelings at her, she responded by throwing an entire peeled potato back at him.

Faron simply caught the potato and tossed it to Jesse, who tossed it to Honey, who tossed it to Adam, who tossed it back to Tate. She handed it primly to Charlie One Horse, who cut it into four pieces and dumped it into the pot of boiling water on the stove. Belinda didn't know when she'd had so much fun making a meal.

It was harder for Belinda to cope with her feelings when she watched Honey and Tate nursing their babies after supper. They sat in the parlor, a blanket thrown over their shoulders in deference to her presence, and suckled their children in full view of the Whitelaw men and Tate's husband, Adam. As though it was the most normal thing in the world for two nursing mothers to be sitting in a roomful of cowboys.

And it was.

Belinda's chest ached with the feelings that assailed her. She met Faron's eyes across the room. For the first time in eight years, Belinda allowed herself to imagine what her life might have been like if she had waited to fall in love and marry. It was a wonderful picture, full of love and laughter...and children.

Suddenly she couldn't stay any longer. She rose as quietly as she could and left the parlor, heading upstairs. She felt, as much as heard,

Faron coming up the stairs behind her. She pretended she didn't know he was there, just kept putting one foot in front of the other until she reached her bedroom. Just as Faron caught up to her she stepped inside her bedroom and closed the door behind her.

She leaned back against the door, closed her eyes and listened. She could hear him breathing on the other side of the door.

"Princess," he whispered. "Are you all right?"

"I'm fine," she whispered back. "Good night, Cowboy."

She could almost feel the tension on the other side of the wooden panel. She had known what memories it would conjure if she called him Cowboy. She felt her body rouse as she remembered their love-making.

"Princess." His voice was hoarse. "Open the door."

She turned and pressed her forehead against the cool painted surface. Her hand was on the knob. She would have turned it, except she heard Maddy call to him.

"Is Belinda all right?"

"She's fine, Maddy. Just a little tired, I think."

"I'm a little tired myself. Good night, Faron."

"Good night, Maddy."

Belinda waited and listened. A moment later she opened the door. But Faron was gone.

I should have opened the door right away, as soon as he called. I should have invited him inside. I want him here with me. I don't want to be alone tonight.

All she had to do was go downstairs and find him. All she had to do...

Belinda stripped and found her nightgown. But she didn't put it on. Instead, she slipped naked between the sheets. And dreamed of a certain cowboy making love to a woman he called Princess.

She must have been more tired than she had thought, because the next thing she knew, Faron was knocking on the connecting door between their rooms.

The connecting door!

Belinda scrambled into a sitting position on the four-poster bed and clutched the sheets to her naked body as the door opened and Faron stuck his head inside.

"When I didn't hear anything moving in here I thought I'd better make sure you were awake. The convoy to the church leaves in about an hour.''

''I can't believe you put us in *connecting* rooms!'' Belinda said.

The sheet slipped on one side as she clutched it tighter, and Faron was treated to a glimpse of a pink aureole. I've made no secret how I feel about you, Princess.''

''What will your family think?''

''My family will mind their own business.''

A call from downstairs drifted across the tense silence between them.

''Faaaarrrooon! You're eggs are done,'' Tate yelled.

''See you at breakfast, Princess.'' He grinned and pulled the connecting door closed just before the pillow Belinda had thrown landed against it.

If Belinda had thought the Whitelaws would act any more civilized at breakfast than they had at supper, she was sadly mistaken.

There was raw egg dripping down the front of the refrigerator, and the shell lay cracked and broken on a red tile floor dusted with a fine layer of flour. To her chagrin she realized she was sorry she hadn't been a part of the juvenile food fight.

''Coffee?'' Tate asked as Belinda stepped into the kitchen.

''Yes, thanks.''

''You look absolutely gorgeous!'' Tate said.

Belinda froze as every male eye in the room turned to stare at her. She had put her hair up in an elegant twist and was wearing a sheath that outlined her figure, even though it concealed her from neck to knee.

Faron was surprised at the surge of protectiveness that arose when Belinda became the object of all eyes. He slipped an arm around her waist and said, ''And she's as nice as she is beautiful.''

The warning was there. Unspoken but irrefutable. *She's mine and I protect what's mine.*

It was Charlie One Horse who diffused the tension in the room. He walked over to Maddy and said, ''I 'spect I gotta vote that this here is the purtiest woman in the room.''

Maddy blushed prettily and for a moment the glow in her eyes made her look exceedingly lovely.

Not to be outdone, Jesse announced that Honey was the sweetest in the room, and Adam countered that Tate was without a doubt the cutest one there. Until the only woman in the room who hadn't been complimented was Candy Baylor.

She stood by the stove, spatula in hand, staring at Garth and waiting.

But he offered not a word of praise to the young woman. At last he turned to Tate and said, "We'd better get moving if we're going to be on time. I'll go get the car."

He turned on his heel and stalked out the screen door, letting it slam behind him.

Candy's face paled as she stared after him.

There was a moment of awful silence before Belinda said, "It's hard to tell which needs a dipping worse, him or the floor of this kitchen."

Faron was at first stunned that Belinda would take on his eldest brother and then amused by the way she had chosen to do it. His grin soon found company, and the tension eased as everyone finished their breakfasts and divided into groups for the trip to church.

Belinda noticed that Candy avoided going in Garth's car, and she couldn't blame the woman. It wasn't until Garth had refused to play the game this morning that she had realized there was more going on between the couple than met the eye.

The christening was held before the church service began. Belinda sat in the first pew with Candy, Madelyn and the rest of the Whitelaw family. Faron stood beside his sister, Tate, and held her son, Brett, in his arms.

Belinda overheard Faron speaking to Tate as she handed the baby into his care.

"Thanks, Tate, for wanting me to be Brett's godfather even though—"

Tate had hugged him fiercely, the baby caught between them. "You're my brother, and I love you. Nothing—*nothing*—is going to change that."

Faron's eyes were moist when Tate let go of him.

Belinda was sitting at an angle where she could see Faron when he stood before the church altar. The love there, the exquisite tenderness on his face as he looked down on the child in his arms, moved her to tears. She listened as Faron promised to stand in the stead of the baby's parents in the event it was necessary, to be godfather to Brett Patrick Philips.

After the church service, the Whitelaw family was surprisingly subdued, perhaps awed by the dignity of the christening ceremony, as Belinda had been herself. But the celebration that afternoon, a picnic in the backyard under a spreading live oak, was as rowdy as any drunken brawl she had seen in the diner where she had worked in Casper. Only none of them was drinking anything stronger than ice tea.

"Having fun?" Faron asked, when he caught up to her halfway through the afternoon. She was dressed in cutoffs, a T-shirt and tennis shoes. Her hair was in a ponytail. She looked about fifteen, and he felt like a teenager with the biggest crush of his life.

She grinned and threw a Frisbee at him. "I'm having a ball!"

Faron caught it and pitched it back to her. They played for a while until Faron threw the Frisbee as far as he could beyond the crowd. When Belinda ran after it, he ran after her. When he caught her, he picked her up and threw her over his shoulder.

"Where are we going?" Belinda asked with a breathless laugh.

Faron didn't answer, just kept on walking.

"Faron? Put me down, Faron." Belinda started wriggling on Faron's shoulder, but he grabbed her legs and pinned her against him.

As soon as Faron entered the barn, Belinda knew where she was. It was dark and cool inside. It smelled of horses and hay and the pungent odor of manure. A horse nickered from one of the stalls. Faron carried her to an empty stall and shifted her off his shoulder until she was standing in front of him.

"Here we are," he said.

Belinda just stared at him. Her heart was pounding with excitement. All she did was take one step toward him and Faron gathered her close in his arms. He lifted her legs and wrapped them around him. She clutched at his shoulders and buried her face at his throat.

"You feel so good, Princess."

Faron backed her up against the stall and found her breasts through the T-shirt with his mouth.

"Faron? Are you in here?"

"Damn, damn, damn," Faron muttered. "What do you want, Garth?"

"Candy will be here in a minute to check on that foaling mare."

He had forgotten about the mare. "All right. Thanks."

Belinda was too caught up in the passion of the moment to realize they had been interrupted. Faron unwound her legs from around him and tried to stand her up, but her knees wouldn't support her. He picked her up in his arms and headed out of the barn. Garth had conveniently, considerately disappeared.

Belinda hid her face against Faron's shoulder. "Looks like our timing was a little off," she mumbled.

"Don't I know it," Faron muttered.

"Hey, you two!" Tate called. "We're going to play a game of softball. You want in?"

Faron looked down and met Belinda's rueful look. "Sure. We'll join you."

They spent the rest of the afternoon in a game of softball, then tossed the Frisbee again until it started to get dark. Madelyn kept an eye on the babies and generally supervised activities.

As they were clearing away the picnic table, Belinda watched the various couples begin to pair off. Again, her eyes sought out Faron. He was walking toward her. She felt her belly tighten as he stalked her. She stood and waited for him to come to her. He didn't stop when he passed by her, merely paused long enough to whisper in her ear.

Belinda shivered when he said, "Tonight."

Eight

Faron was in the kitchen, waiting for the house to get quiet, waiting for the right moment to go to Belinda. He hadn't *asked* if he could come to her, he had *told* her he was coming. He wished he could know for sure that when he knocked on her door this time, his Princess would let him in.

"What are you doing down here so late?"

Faron turned and found himself confronted by Charlie One Horse. The half-Indian codger was more than a hired hand. He had been part father, part mother and longtime friend to the Whitelaws. He had been a source of wisdom and knowledge all of Faron's life.

"Female problems," Charlie muttered.

Faron's lips curled in the semblance of a smile. "How did you know?"

"Only reason a man wanders the house at night instead of going to bed where he belongs." Charlie concentrated on retying the beaded rawhide thong on one of his black braids so Faron wouldn't see the concern in his eyes.

"As long as you're here, I could use some advice," Faron said.

"I'm listenin'." Charlie crossed to the refrigerator, opened the door and stood there looking inside.

"I'm in love with Belinda Prescott."

"So? What's the problem?"

"Her first marriage—her marriage to my father—was a disaster. I don't know if she's ever going to let another man get close to her."

Charlie took out a container of strawberries and set it on the counter. He got a fork from the drawer, then stood at the counter eating the ripe red berries. "Time is the best salve to heal wounds of the heart."

"I don't have a lot of time," Faron said in a tormented voice.

Charlie One Horse forked a huge strawberry and held it up so he could examine it. It was a "double," a strawberry that should have been two and had ended up one. "You'll just have to be patient. Show her that you love her. Once she realizes what love is supposed to be, she'll come to you like a filly to a hand outstretched with sugar." He stuffed the strawberry into his mouth and began munching.

Faron couldn't deny Charlie had given him good advice. But it seemed too little, too late. He could feel time running out. Tomorrow they would be headed back to King's Castle. Next time a corporate buyer showed up, he might not be so lucky. Next time the man might make an offer he couldn't—and Belinda wouldn't—refuse.

Faron crossed the room and laid a hand on Charlie's shoulder. "Thanks, Charlie. Good night."

Charlie just grunted because his mouth was too full of strawberries for him to speak.

Faron headed for the stairs, then detoured to the parlor. He wasn't quite ready yet to face Belinda's possible rejection. He slumped down into his regular chair in front of the fireplace, thinking he was alone, only to discover that Garth was there before him.

"What are you doing sitting in the dark?" Faron asked.

"I could ask you the same thing," Garth responded.

Neither man gave a reason why he was there. Neither needed to. As Charlie had noted, only a woman kept a man from his bed when he ought to be sleeping. They sat there staring into a fire that was no more than glowing embers. Occasionally Garth drank from a glass of whiskey he held in one hand.

"Did you find the peace of mind you were looking for when you set out for Wyoming?" Garth asked at last.

"It was worth the trip to find Maddy," Faron said. "She's a feisty old broad." Faron thrust his hands through his hair and tried to smooth it back down again. "And I love the land, King's Castle. I don't know how to explain it. It's so different from the canyons and gullies on Hawk's Way. There's something about those endless rolling green prairies that feeds my soul. I'm going to miss it when it's sold.''

''So don't sell.''

''What?''

''Don't sell the place. Keep it.''

''Belinda Prescott might have a few words to say about that. She wants to move into town.''

''So let her go. Buy her half of the place from her.''

''I—'' Faron didn't know how to explain to his brother that a great deal of what he found so captivating about King's Castle was the fact that Belinda Prescott lived there.

Garth shrugged when Faron made no effort to explain himself further. ''It was just an idea. So what did you find out about Wayne Prescott?''

''He wasn't a very noble character, my father.''

''You knew that before you left,'' Garth pointed out.

''He abused Belinda.''

''I'm sorry to hear that.''

It was the first time Faron had ever heard Garth utter those words. It brought a lump to his throat to realize that his brother understood Faron's anger and frustration without him having to say more.

''I don't have to ask if you love her,'' Garth said. ''It's written all over your face when you look at her. Are you sure you're doing the right thing to get involved with her?''

Trust Garth to go right to the heart of the problem. ''It's right for me. I'm not so sure about how she feels.''

''Does it bother you at all that she was Wayne Prescott's wife?'' Garth asked curiously.

Faron took time to seriously consider Garth's question. At last he said, ''Only because he treated her badly.''

''So what are you doing down here? I never thought you were a coward.''

Faron took enough umbrage to say, ''I'm not the only Whitelaw sitting alone in the dark. What's the story between you and Candy Baylor?''

''None of your business,'' Garth said brusquely.

A slow smile grew on Faron's face. "Well, well, big brother. How the mighty have fallen."

"What's that supposed to mean?"

"You figure it out. I'm going upstairs where I hope there's a lady waiting for me. You can sit here alone in the dark all night if you want. But I suspect there might be a lady somewhere waiting for you, too."

"She'll have a long wait," Garth retorted.

Faron laughed. "Good night, Garth. Sleep well."

"Get out of here and leave me in peace."

"I'll leave, but I doubt you'll have much peace until you seek out a certain blond-haired, gray-eyed woman."

Faron had just reached the doorway when he heard the loud splintering of glass against the stone fireplace. He was almost sorry he would be leaving tomorrow. He would give his eyeteeth to be around to see his cynical, misogynistic brother finally fall in love with a woman.

As he climbed the stairs, Faron was aware of the silence in the house. When he reached Belinda's door he knocked and then turned the knob. It was open, and he let himself in.

There was a light on beside the bed. Belinda wasn't there.

"Damn." He should have known she wasn't ready yet to hear what he wanted to say to her. He shouldn't have pushed so hard. He had frightened her so badly she had run. But where the hell had she gone?

Faron felt like throwing something. He settled for slamming one fisted hand into the palm of the other. He clenched his back teeth and stared out the window into the distance. He would just have to take Charlie One Horse's advice and be patient. Belinda couldn't go far. And he would be here waiting when she returned.

Faron crossed to the connecting door between the two bedrooms and yanked it open. He stomped across the threshold and stopped short. His jaw fell agape.

There, sound asleep in his bed, lay his golden Princess. She was wearing a filmy nightgown with a delicate lace trim that cupped her breasts. Her hand pillowed her head and one knee was drawn up so that the nightgown revealed the length of her from her toes to the top of her hip.

He sat down carefully beside her on the brass bed, but even that slight movement woke her. She turned lazily onto her back and looked up at him through half-closed eyes.

"Hi," she said. "I've been waiting for you."

Faron's heart began to gallop. "I'm glad you're here."

Belinda slipped a hand around Faron's nape and drew his mouth down to hers. Just before their lips met she said, "I like your family, Faron. I wish..."

"What do you wish, Princess?"

"I wish I had waited...to find you."

"I'm here now, Princess. And I'm not going anywhere."

Belinda took the initiative in their lovemaking. Faron made it easy for her. He responded to the barest touch of her fingertips. It was as though he could sense what she needed, what she desired. She urged his mouth down to hers. The kiss was gentle at first, tentative, but Belinda's need was great, and there was an answering fire in the Cowboy.

Faron encouraged her by showing her how much pleasure he found in her kisses, in her touch. She found his leashed passion as seductive as an aphrodisiac. She slowly undressed him, one piece of clothing at a time, indulging her need to feel the textures of his body. The crisp hair on his chest. The hardness of muscle and sinew. The petal softness of his eyelids and the shell of his ears.

"Take off your nightgown, Princess."

Belinda hesitated a moment, then reached down and pulled it up over her head. Finally she was as naked as he was. His eyes adored her. Then his hands and mouth followed where his gaze led. Where Belinda touched him, he touched her. Shoulders. Ribs. Stomach. Hips. Buttocks.

Faron hadn't known he could find such pleasure with a woman. He wanted desperately to speak of his love. But he knew he must be patient. He had to wait until she was ready to hear the words. He had to show her that he loved her, so there could be no doubt in her mind how he felt. She had to know that he would cherish her. That he would never abuse her as his father had.

Faron's body tensed as Belinda's hands surrounded him and urged him close. Her hips rose and he impaled her. They rolled once and she was above him, her hair a cloak that tantalized him by half hiding her breasts.

Belinda felt free to love Faron in ways she had never loved her husband. She had an unbelievable sense of her own feminine power as she caressed him. His eyes glowed with the warmth of his need and desire. Her body tightened in response to his guttural groans of pleasure. His urgent kisses made her feel wanted and loved.

He rolled her under him once more, mantling her body with his own. "Come with me, Princess. Reach for the stars."

Belinda did. She reached for the happiness she had never allowed herself to even dream of having. She let down the barriers she had put up to keep herself safe from a man to whom she had been a possession. And allowed herself to love a man who treasured her because of who she was.

Faron caught Belinda's cries of exultation with his mouth. He revered her with his hands, with his mouth, with his body. He brought her to the pinnacle, and they rose beyond it together.

Faron wasn't expecting the tears. "Princess? What's wrong? Did I hurt you? Are you all right?"

"I'm fine," she managed through a throat that was constricted so much it prevented easy speech. "I don't know why I'm crying. You were wonderful. It was wonderful."

He gathered her in his arms and held her while she cried. Belinda had a pretty good idea what was causing the lump in her throat. It was the pain of knowledge. Of regret for the years she had foolishly wasted. It was fear of the course she was determined to embark upon. And hope for the future.

Because now she could no longer deny to herself what she felt. She was in love with Faron Whitelaw.

That should have been the end of the fairy tale, and the beginning of the rest of her life. She would simply accept the handsome cowboy's proposal and they would live happily ever after.

Only the Cowboy hadn't proposed. He hadn't even said those three little words, "I love you."

Eventually the constriction in her throat eased. She grabbed a sheet and dabbed at the corners of her eyes. "Faron?"

"Hmm."

"I'm sorry for falling apart on you like that."

"Can you tell me about it?"

"I..." Belinda should have been able to tell Faron that she loved him. That she was hoping they would spend the rest of their lives together. But memories of times when Wayne had taken her tenderest emotions and ridiculed them came to mind. And kept her silent.

It was one thing to say she was going to forget the past and go on with her life. It was quite another to be able to do it. Apparently the wounds were deeper than she had believed. It might take a little longer for them to heal completely. "It's nothing you did, Faron," she said at last.

"Was it something my father did?"

Belinda's hand played across Faron's chest, winding in the black curls that arrowed downward toward his navel. Her fingertips skimmed across a male nipple, and she watched in fascination as it peaked. "I don't want to talk about Wayne. I want to make love to you."

Her fingertips skimmed down the front of him until she cupped him in her hand. His response was immediate and totally gratifying. Belinda grinned. "My, my, Cowboy. What have we here?"

"Don't play with fire, Princess, unless you're ready for the heat."

Belinda's laugh was cut short when Faron's hand slid down the front of her in imitation of her own intimate exploration. He slipped a finger inside her, then another, and Belinda arched up as his thumb sought out the sensitive nubbin that was the source of her desire.

Faron's mouth caught the cries of passion as Belinda arched up under his provocative caresses. But she would never again be a passive partner. She sought out the places on Faron's body that she knew drove him wild. The crease at his thigh, the dimples above his buttocks, the point where taut belly slid into crisp curls.

They taunted each other, refusing to be the first to give in to the sensual teasing. They laughed when they had the breath to do so. They kissed, their tongues entwining, their teeth nipping tender flesh.

And they loved. With their hearts. With their souls. With their whole beings.

But he never said, "I love you."

Neither did she.

When the sun dawned and sent the first rays of light across the tangled sheets, they were still wrapped in each other's arms. Neither wanted the fairy tale to end.

A knock on the door sent Belinda searching for her nightgown. Faron slipped on his jeans and buttoned them halfway.

"We don't have anything to hide," Faron said.

"What if it's Madelyn?" Belinda hissed. "I don't—I'm not ready to face her like this." She yanked her nightgown on, then raced for the door between the two rooms.

She was halfway there when Faron caught her and swung her back into his arms. He kissed her hard. "We have to talk, Princess."

"Later. Let me go, Faron. Please."

He let her go and she disappeared, closing the door silently behind her. Faron answered the persistent knock and found Garth at the door.

"This better be important," Faron growled.

"I thought it was. There was a call on the office phone. Somebody wants to buy King's Castle, but he needs to take a look at it tomorrow. Here's the number where you can reach him."

Faron grimaced. "All right. I'll be right down."

Garth took a look at the disheveled state of the bed and arched a brow. "Take your time, little brother. Take all the time you need."

Before Faron could protest, Garth was gone.

A second later Belinda was back in Faron's room. "Who was it?"

"Garth."

"What did he want?"

"A corporate buyer tracked us down. He wants to take a look at King's Castle—tomorrow."

Belinda sank down onto the bed. "What are we going to do?"

"*We* are going to listen to his offer."

Faron's reference to the fact it would be a joint decision wasn't lost on Belinda. "I...I suppose we should."

"Then we'll have to make a decision whether or not to sell."

The last thing Belinda wanted to contemplate right now was the sale of the ranch. Because once it was sold, Faron would be returning to Hawk's Way. Now that she had seen it, she knew there was no way Faron could prefer King's Castle to the comforts to be found here.

Furthermore, his family lived in Texas. She had seen how close Faron was to his brothers and sister. Family was important to him. Faron couldn't possibly contemplate living the rest of his life in Wyoming, separated from his family except for visits on holidays. Belinda knew how hard that was, and she wouldn't wish it on anyone.

Belinda tried to imagine Faron offering to bring her back to

Hawk's Way as his wife. Naturally, Madelyn would have to be part of the package. However, Belinda couldn't imagine Garth Whitelaw accepting Wayne Prescott's mother into his household. And she could never abandon Madelyn. Which meant Belinda could never live here, either.

"I'll meet you downstairs after you've had a chance to get dressed," Faron said. "And we'll give this guy a call."

"All right," Belinda said.

But when Faron tried to draw her into his arms she stepped back. "I need to get dressed," she said. She turned from him and walked away.

Faron didn't know what had gone wrong, but he had a pretty good idea it had to do with selling the ranch. But he would be damned if he could figure out whether his Princess wanted the place sold—or not.

Nine

It was a toss-up who heaved the bigger sigh of relief when the corporate buyer made a ridiculously low offer. Faron tried to look disappointed. Belinda matched him furrow for furrow in her brow.

"King's Castle is worth too much simply to give it away," Faron said. "Unless you're anxious to get moved into town before winter comes."

"A few months won't make that much difference," Belinda replied. "Besides, we'd be making the man a thief if we accepted his offer."

The unspoken result of their decision not to sell King's Castle was a commitment to continue the improvements they had begun. But the changes they made now went further than simple repairs to put the ranch back into shape to sell. What Faron suggested to Belinda were modifications that would transform King's Castle into a viable, profitable ranching operation.

"Can we really afford to make these kinds of investments?" Belinda asked.

"They'll pay off in the long run," Faron said. It was as close as he could come to saying that he hoped there might be a "long run," without actually saying it. Because he feared saying it would put Belinda on the defensive. He wanted her to realize that they worked well together, that they made a good team, and that they could be happy making a life together on the ranch.

First she had to learn to trust him. He wasn't going to take the chance of pushing her too fast. So he had to keep his distance from her. Because if he took her to bed as often as he wanted to, it wouldn't take her long to figure out that he was playing for keeps. He wanted a chance to build good memories with her of life at King's Castle, to replace the bad ones that had made her want to flee the ranch.

Belinda searched out Faron's gray-green eyes and was forced to drop her gaze or be singed by the need she saw there. Ever since their return from Texas there had been a palpable sexual tension between them. She kept waiting for Faron to act on it, to tease and taunt her as he had in the past. But he exercised a restraint that she wouldn't have believed possible.

She had no doubt that he desired her. It was there in the subtle electrical charge that passed between them whenever they brushed against each other. She saw it in the fierce light that came into his eyes as he gazed at her when he thought she wasn't looking. But she was confused by the signals he was sending.

He obviously wanted to be her lover. But he seemed to be waiting for her to make the first move. It was a novel idea to Belinda, who had never been allowed that option with Wayne. At the age of twenty-eight, she decided it was high time she tried her sexual wings.

She tried subtle things at first. One evening she was working at the computer station beside the rolltop desk while Faron sat in the swivel chair and examined the printout she had just made of feed projections for the winter. She stopped for a break and said, "My shoulders really ache. Could you rub them for me?"

The look in his eyes was priceless. He was a sinking man going down for the third time. "All right. I guess I could do that."

He dropped the printout on the desk, stood and crossed the few feet to where she was sitting. Belinda had her hair in a braid. "Would you mind undoing my braid first?" She saw the flush high on his cheekbones and felt a flutter of feminine satisfaction.

He took his time unraveling the braid, and when he was done his hand tunneled up underneath her long golden hair and massaged her scalp. Belinda's head rolled forward and she exposed her nape to his caresses. She could feel the strength of his hands where they worked to relax the muscles in her shoulders. She was feeling languorous, but there was a rising tension in her breasts and belly.

The moment came when he had to decide whether to continue what he was doing or escape the sensual torment caused by her request. She felt his lips on her nape, soft and slightly damp. A shiver chased down her spine as she felt his warm breath where he hovered over her.

Abruptly he stood up and said, "I need a cup of coffee. Can I get you one, too?"

She turned slightly toward him. He was standing and she was sitting and her eyes were level with the blunt ridge that stood out starkly against the fly of his jeans. She stared for a moment before she reached out a finger and traced the length of his arousal. Down. And then up.

She heard him swallow.

"Princess…"

She dropped her hand and said, "Yes, I'd like a cup of coffee. Thanks…Cowboy."

She turned back to the computer and began typing again. She could feel him standing there a moment longer, then heard his swift tread as he escaped the room and the sexual tension between them. Belinda couldn't help smiling when Faron was gone, pleased with the success of her plan. At this rate he wouldn't be able to hold out for long.

She was surprised the next morning over the breakfast table when he said, "What would you think about having a party to meet the neighbors?"

"That sounds like a wonderful idea," Maddy responded.

Belinda grimaced. She hadn't seen much of her neighbors since the disastrous party nearly six years ago when Wayne had publicly accused her of being a cold woman in bed. It was shortly after he had begun taking the heart medicine that had made him impotent. He had been drunk and had taken out his anger and frustration on her in the most publicly humiliating way possible. She wasn't sure she was ready to face any of those people ever again.

Maddy's enthusiasm was hard to stop. "I'll take care of the invitations," she said. "It's about time we had some music and laughter around here."

"But Maddy—" Belinda protested. "We're too busy to take time for a party."

"Nonsense. Rue and I will take care of everything. All you'll have to do is show up." She turned and beamed a smile at Faron. "I'm looking forward to showing off my grandson."

What could Belinda say to that?

Faron could see Belinda was less than enthusiastic about the party, but he didn't know why. But he decided that if she didn't want to confront her neighbors he wasn't going to force her into it, no matter what Maddy wanted. "We don't have to have a party, Princess. Just say the word and the plans will stop."

Belinda met Faron's concerned gaze, and if she hadn't already been in love with him she would have fallen for him then. He could have no idea why she didn't want to confront her neighbors. Yet he had been aware enough of her distress to respond to it, and in such a way that her needs and desires came before his own.

She smiled and reached out a hand to cover his where it lay on the table. "The party's a good idea. It's high time we said hello again to our neighbors."

Faron's hand turned under hers, and he lifted her hand and brought it to his lips. "Whatever you want, Princess."

What Belinda wanted in that moment was to go upstairs to bed. She blushed furiously at the thought, causing Maddy to chuckle and Faron's lids to droop lazily as he met the stark look of need in her eyes.

Abruptly he dropped her hand and stood. "Got work to do in the barn. See you later."

A moment later Maddy and Belinda were alone at the table.

"I'll be surprised if our neighbors accept an invitation to a party at King's Castle," Belinda said to Maddy. "I hope you know what you're doing." Belinda kept her eyes lowered to hide her pain as she admitted, "I'm afraid to face people after the insulting things Wayne said in public about our personal life."

"I don't think anyone ever blamed you for the way Wayne acted the last years of his life. It was plain to see that he wasn't well."

"I hope you're right," Belinda muttered. But she looked forward to the coming party with a feeling of dread.

The days before the party passed with unbelievable speed. Too soon Belinda found herself dressing with care for a party she had no desire to attend. When Faron knocked on her bedroom door to ask if she was ready to go downstairs she opened the door and said, "I can't go down there."

Faron stepped inside Belinda's bedroom and closed the door behind him. He took one look at the distress in her eyes and folded her into his arms. "What's the matter, Princess? Don't you know I'll protect you from the dragons?"

Just having him offer his support made her feel better. But Belinda knew these were dragons—of the past—that she had to face on her own. Yet there was no reason why she couldn't do so with Faron by her side. She stepped out of Faron's embrace and said, "I'm all right. I'm ready to go downstairs now."

But it suddenly dawned on both of them that they were alone in her bedroom with the door shut behind them. Faron grinned. "How about a kiss for luck?"

"Whose luck? Yours or mine?" Belinda quipped. Her apparent nonchalance was a sham. She felt breathless with excitement that was fed by the avid look in Faron's gray-green eyes.

"Ours," Faron replied. "Have I told you how beautiful you look tonight?"

"No."

"You look absolutely breathtaking, Princess." He reached out and waited until she placed her hand in his. Then he drew her toward him until they were standing only inches apart. He cupped her jaw with his hand and raised her face to his. She no longer kept her lids lowered to hide her feelings from him. Blazing in her eyes was a need more than equal to his own. He lowered his mouth to hers and sipped of the nectar he found there.

His chest was tight with unspoken feelings. "If you need me tonight, I won't be far from your side."

He reached past her and opened the door, then took her arm and put it in the crook of his. "It's time to face your court, Princess. And if any of them dares to offer insult, it'll be off with his head!"

That brought a smile to Belinda's face that was still present when they reached the bottom of the circular staircase.

Most of their neighbors were already there, curious about Belinda and Faron and the reason for this party. Their looks were speculative as they eyed the widow and the roguish cowboy, but not unkind.

A young woman about Belinda's age, with brown hair and brown eyes and a vivid scar across one cheek, was the first to approach Belinda.

"Do you remember me?" she asked.

"Of course I do," Belinda replied. She remembered being appalled at the time that such a beautiful young woman should be so horribly scarred. She had been curious about what had happened, but had never gotten to know the woman well enough to ask. "Your name is Desiree."

The woman smiled and Belinda realized that the scar wasn't so visible after all. "That's right. I can't believe you remember it after all these years."

"I remember it because you were so kind to me that night after..." Desiree Parrish had been the one who had finally stepped between Belinda and her husband.

"I only wish there had been more I could do to help," Desiree said. "I'm so glad you had this party. I've been hoping we could be friends."

This time it was Belinda who smiled. "I could use a friend or two."

"Maybe you'd like to come over next week and visit."

"Or you could come here," Belinda offered.

Desiree shook her head. "It's hard for me to find a babysitter. Would you mind?"

"Just name the day," Belinda said. "I'll be there."

The two women parted company knowing they had planted the seeds for a growing friendship.

By the end of the evening it was plain that everyone was more than willing to leave the past in the past.

True to his word, Faron stayed close by throughout Belinda's ordeal. She wasn't even aware that she was judging him, comparing him to his father.

She watched to see if he talked too loud and drank too much.
He didn't.

He nursed the same whiskey most of the evening, and while she occasionally heard his deep laughter, he was never boisterous.

She watched to see whether he told off-color jokes.
He didn't.

Whether he flirted with the ladies.
He did.

He had a way of making each woman feel special, while still making it clear that he intended their relationship to be strictly platonic.

Whether the neighbors respected him as a rancher and a businessman.

They did. Several times she caught him in discussions with the neighboring ranchers. He was as willing to take advice as he was to share his knowledge.

Whether he made snide or cruel remarks about their personal relationship.

He didn't. While he was never very far from her, he did nothing to indicate their relationship consisted of anything more than the legal connection between them.

But Belinda was mistaken if she thought her neighbors didn't see the attraction between the widow and the bastard son. What she would have discovered, if she had been watching, was that her neighbors were more than willing to accept such an alliance.

They already knew her to be a dedicated and caring rancher. Although Faron might be something of a rogue, he knew the ranching business. With a spread as large as King's Castle, it was important to have someone in authority who knew how to conserve the land.

Toward the end of the evening, Faron approached Belinda with another woman beside him. "Belinda, I think you know Pearl Teasdale. She was just telling me about a problem I thought you might be able to solve."

Pearl was a robust woman of forty-five, with gray hair she was proud of and calluses she had worked to earn. Her brown eyes were straightforward and her voice was slightly nasal from a deviated septum. "I was just telling Faron that Mrs. Webster had to resign as chairman of the Christmas pageant committee at the church when she found out she's expecting her third, only it's her third and fourth—twins, you see. So the doctor wants her to take it easy.

"Anyway, I was wondering if you might be willing to take the job as chairman and plan the pageant."

Belinda had been in the pageant as a child, and knew how much it meant to the children who participated. As a young woman, she hadn't been involved in the pageant, even though she had continued attending church.

"I—" She hesitated.

"Please say yes," Pearl urged. "We could really use the help. And Faron told me how much you love children."

"He did?" Belinda arched a brow. How could she argue with the truth? She would love spending time with the children. It was something Wayne had not allowed. "All right," she said. "I'll do it."

The smile on Pearl's face was blinding. "Wonderful!" She quickly called over several ladies, including Desiree, and they all began chattering about schedules and costumes.

Faron felt warm inside when he saw the way Belinda's face glowed with pleasure. There was light and laughter in her eyes. He frowned when he realized that he wasn't the only one admiring her. There was a bachelor or two among the assembled males, and Belinda was a beautiful, very eligible woman. He wanted to lay claim to her before some other man got ideas. However, he couldn't lay his claim in public when he hadn't made his intentions clear in private.

Faron was startled when he heard Maddy's quiet voice beside him. "So, are you going to give that girl a child of her own?"

Faron's eyes hooded. His mouth flattened. "Don't interfere, Maddy. Everything in its own good time."

"Don't wait too long," Maddy warned.

Faron scowled. Maddy's warning reminded him too vividly of his fear that Belinda might finally decide she couldn't take a chance on marriage again. Maybe it was time to let Belinda Prescott know his true intentions. He stalked right over to her and easily maneuvered her away from the crowd of women.

"Excuse us, ladies. There's something I need to discuss with Belinda."

"What is it, Faron?"

He dragged her all the way into the kitchen before he stopped. He spied the pantry and hauled her inside the small room and closed the door behind them. The pantry was lit by a bare bulb, and they were surrounded by canned goods and preserves. He pressed her up against the closed door and kissed her with all the pent-up desire he had been saving for just such a moment.

"Faron, stop. What are you doing?"

"Kissing you. Loving you. It's what you want, isn't it?"

Belinda had been teasing him for weeks. It would be foolish to pretend she didn't want him now. She did. She kissed him back with zest and passion. She felt the zipper coming down on her dress and a moment later she was naked to the waist.

"You're not wearing a bra," he said as his hands reverently

cupped her breasts. Belinda stepped out of the dress and laid it across several jars of stewed tomatoes.

"You're wearing a black garter belt," he said with a blissful sigh. He sounded a little shocked but pleased when he informed her, "Princess, you're not wearing any panties."

Belinda couldn't help the small giggle that escaped. "You sound like a teenage boy who just hit a home run with his girl," she teased.

"I feel like a kid in a candy store," he said. "I don't know what to taste first."

His mouth latched on to a nipple and he suckled strongly. Belinda arched toward him, but bit her lip to hold back the cry of ecstasy that sought voice. There was a very real danger of discovery here, which only heightened her excitement.

Faron dropped to his knees and his mouth began a foray across her belly and down into the nest of blond curls below. His fingers and tongue indulged in a sensual feast that left her quivering. She would have fallen down if she hadn't been clutching his shoulders.

When he stood and kissed her again she could taste herself. The room smelled of sex and heat and desire. He didn't bother to remove his trousers, just unzipped them and shoved them down enough to free his aroused shaft. He lifted her and with one thrust sank deep inside her.

She wrapped her legs around his hips, her arms around his shoulders and buried her mouth against his throat. Her teeth closed on flesh, but she was unaware of the marks she was leaving as she felt herself driving toward the peak of ecstasy. His fingers bit into her, holding her tight as he thrust within her.

Their mouths merged, tongues thrusting, but they couldn't breathe and kiss at the same time. Belinda hid her face in Faron's shoulder as their bodies climaxed. He pressed his mouth to her cheek to cut off his guttural cry of pleasure.

They stood there for scant moments panting, until Belinda's legs dropped down to support her.

She heard Faron's chuckle and smiled. "You're a crazy man, Cowboy," she said huskily.

"Then may I never be sane," he answered in an equally throaty voice.

To their chagrin and amusement there was a quiet knock at the pantry door. "You might want to rejoin your guests to bid them good night," Maddy said.

"We'll be there in a minute, Maddy," Faron answered her.

Belinda felt the door opening behind her. "Wait—"

A hand slipped inside bearing a damp towel. "I thought you might need this."

The door closed, and they heard Maddy walking away.

They took one look at each other and burst out laughing. Belinda put a hand on Faron's mouth. "Shh. We'll be caught."

He took the towel and put it to good use on her and himself. Belinda stepped into her dress and turned so he could zip her up. "Do you suppose they'll know what we've been doing?"

Belinda's hair had been left down tonight, but it looked considerably more windblown than when they had entered the pantry. Faron did his best to smooth it. Then he turned her around to face him, took one look at the sparkle in her eye and said, "They'd have to be blind not to know."

Belinda caught a glimpse of the satisfied smile on Faron's face and pursed her lips. "It might help if you wipe that grin off your face."

He shook his head. "Uh uh. No can do. Feels too good."

Belinda gave up and joined him. "I suppose it does."

They returned to the party at intervals as though they had long ago gone their separate ways to do errands that had only just been completed. If their neighbors suspected what Belinda and Faron had been doing while they were gone, they were too polite to say anything about it.

Over the weeks and months that followed, Faron and Belinda were seen often in each other's company. At church. At the feed store in Casper. Riding the borders of King's Castle. At the Grange dances. Though no words had been spoken between them to declare it so, they were a couple.

Belinda radiated a new self-confidence. She worked with several ladies who had taken part in the Christmas pageant in the past to make sure that she didn't forget anything. And she loved working with the children. They were delightful. Open and loving and honest. She felt an undeniable yearning—which she fought—for a child of her own.

She made love to Faron as often as she could and in as many ways and places as they could devise. She couldn't help feeling that she was living on borrowed time. That the magical fairy tale they had created simply couldn't last. She was too happy, and she couldn't help feeling that there had to be a villain somewhere—every fairy tale had one—who would strip away her happiness.

As Christmas approached, she asked Faron to save some time to help her set up the tree. They decided to do it the third Saturday afternoon in December.

The boxes of Christmas decorations were kept in a room on the third floor of The Castle. Faron hadn't been up there before, and he was amazed at the history he saw in the items stored there.

"A lot of families must have lived in this house over the years," he said. He picked up a *McGuffey's Reader* and paged through it. There was a handmade wooden wagon and a rocking horse that would have been about the right size for a child of four or five.

Belinda picked up a reticule, a purse once carried by a pioneer woman, and donned a silk bonnet. "What do you think? Am I ready for a trip into town?"

"You look ready for a kiss." He lowered his mouth to hers and their lips met in the tenderest of kisses. "Belinda, don't you want to be a part of this? To preserve King's Castle for future generations?"

"I—I thought that's what we were doing."

Faron's voice was harsh when he responded, "Are we? Or are we just fooling ourselves, playing games until a buyer comes along and snatches all this out from under us?"

"That's not fair, Cowboy," Belinda retorted in a heated voice. "If anybody's playing games here, it's you. What is it you want from me?"

Maddy's voice filtered up the stairs. "Faron? Belinda? Are you up there? There's someone here to see you."

"We'll talk about this tonight," Faron said. He didn't give Belinda a chance to argue, just grabbed her hand and headed down the stairs.

When they arrived downstairs they found a man slightly older than Faron waiting for them. He had chestnut brown hair and cold blue eyes. He was about Faron's height, but heavier in build, with a bigger chest and shoulders. He was wearing faded jeans and a ragged shirt and his boots hadn't seen polish in a month of Sundays.

"Hello," he said, extending his hand to Faron. "I'm Carter Prescott. Your brother. I'm here to take this place off your hands."

Ten

"**I** should have known that Wayne Prescott had more than one bastard son," Faron said bitterly.

"I'm not a bastard," Carter said in a frosty voice. "Wayne Prescott was married to my mother."

Both Faron and Belinda turned to Madelyn for confirmation. She nodded slowly. "It's true. Wayne was married once, a long time ago. The marriage ended in divorce, but as far as I know there were no children."

Carter smiled cynically. "I was conceived after the divorce papers had been filed and born shortly before the divorce was final. There was no love lost between my mother and Wayne Prescott. She didn't see any reason to let him know he had a son."

"Why have you waited until now to come forward?" Faron asked.

"I wouldn't have said anything even now, except I want this place and I thought I'd have a better chance of getting it as a Prescott."

Faron forked all ten fingers through his hair. "Damn. I'm not sure what the legalities are—whether you're entitled to a portion of King's Castle under the will or not."

"I don't give a damn about any inheritance I might be entitled to."

Faron frowned. "Then why are you here?"

"I want to buy King's Castle."

Faron looked skeptically at the man standing in front of him. Carter Prescott didn't look like someone who had the kind of money it was going to take to buy a ranch the size of King's Castle. "Do you have that kind of cash?"

Carter's lips curled into a wry smile. "In the divorce my mother took Wayne Prescott for half of everything he owned. Over the years I've made a few investments." He shrugged apologetically. "I'm rich as sin."

Faron turned stunned eyes on Belinda.

"I'm willing to pay you what the place is worth," Carter said. "Money is no object. Name your price. I'm just looking for some roots, and I think I might find them here."

Faron couldn't argue with that sentiment. He had felt it himself. But this was *his* place. Carter Prescott would have to find his roots somewhere else!

"I think Belinda and I need to have a discussion in private. Would you mind giving us some time alone?" Faron said.

"Sure." Carter turned to Madelyn and took off his hat to introduce himself. "If I'm not mistaken, you're my grandmother."

"I am," Madelyn said. There was a distinct chill in her voice that surprised Faron. "I never liked your mother," Madelyn said to Carter.

Carter smiled ruefully. "Not many people did, ma'am."

That defrosted a little of Madelyn's ice, but she couldn't embrace this new-found grandson when she believed he was determined to ruin the happiness of the other.

"I could use a cup of coffee," Carter said.

"Come with me." Madelyn turned and marched toward the kitchen without looking back.

Carter settled his Stetson on his head and followed resolutely after her.

Of all the forms the villain in Belinda's fairy tale had taken, it was never that of a handsome young man. "I can't believe this is happening," she said.

"It's happening," Faron said. "Let's go into the study where we can sit down and talk."

Belinda was too nervous to sit down. Once Faron was settled in the swivel chair in front of the desk, she jumped up and began pacing.

"With the money from the sale of King's Castle, you and Maddy will both have the security you wanted," Faron began.

Belinda looked at him with stricken eyes. That wasn't what she wanted to hear from Faron. She wanted to hear that he loved her and wanted to marry her and that together they would spend their lives making King's Castle what it once was.

But she couldn't force him to stay if he wanted to go. And with Hawk's Way calling to him, how could she ever have hoped he might want to stay?

"I suppose it makes sense to accept Carter's offer," she said tentatively.

"Is that what you really want to do?" Faron asked.

"I'm willing to go along with whatever you want to do," Belinda countered, her eyes lowered to hide the grief she felt at the loss that was to come. "So I guess we sell."

Faron's tone was grim, "If that's what you want to do, then that's what we'll do." He kept his eyes lowered to the hands fisted in his lap.

Neither one of them realized they were sacrificing what they most wanted in deference to the needs and wants of the other.

"Do you want to tell him our decision now?" Faron asked.

"Not yet!" Belinda didn't know why she felt so frantic, only that she did. "Let's wait until after the pageant tonight."

"Postponing the inevitable isn't going to change it," Faron warned.

"I know. Please, Faron. Just wait until after the pageant." She could keep her fairy tale alive for a few more hours. It wasn't over yet, and she didn't plan to give up her dream until she absolutely had to.

Faron didn't know what else to say. "We'd better finish getting that tree up. You've got to be at the church early tonight to set up for the Christmas pageant."

When Faron and Belinda entered the kitchen, Madelyn and Carter were engaged in a rousing argument.

"What's going on here?" Faron asked.

"I was just trying to talk Carter into attending the Christmas pageant tonight. Without much success, I might add."

"Oh, please come," Belinda said. "It's so moving."

"That's what I'm afraid of," Carter muttered. "I don't care much for that sort of thing."

"But it's Christmas," Belinda said. "Everyone loves Christmas."

Faron took one look at Carter's face and realized his stepbrother was the exception. "You don't have to come if you'd rather not."

Madelyn wasn't about to let Carter off that easily. "I'd appreciate the chance to show off *both* my grandsons. Surely you won't deny me that."

"All right, Maddy," Carter said. But it was plain his heart wasn't in it.

"The children have worked so hard. I know you'll enjoy it," Belinda said. "They do a wonderful job."

The more Belinda said about children, the more rigid Carter's face got, until she realized she was only making it worse by going on and on. She didn't know what Carter Prescott had against children and Christmas, but it was clear his opinions were long-standing. Nothing she said was going to change them.

In the awkward silence that ensued Carter said, "By the way, did you make a decision about selling King's Castle?"

Belinda and Faron exchanged an uneasy glance.

"We want to think about it a little while longer," Faron said.

"Goodness. This is no time to be worrying about business," Madelyn interjected. "Look at the time. If we don't get busy, we'll be late getting to the pageant."

Belinda was so excited, she and Faron left early for church. Carter promised to follow later with Madelyn. It had begun snowing, and while Belinda was glad for the hope of a white Christmas, she was worried that the threat of a bad storm might keep some families away from the pageant. She was proved wrong when she arrived at the church and saw the pews were already beginning to fill.

She rushed around setting robes in place on shoulders, making sure the shepherds had their staffs and the angels had their halos. At the last moment there was some confusion about whether it was all right to use a female doll to represent the baby Jesus. Belinda did some fast talking and got the youngster playing Joseph to agree to the deception.

Belinda watched the program from the sidelines, nestled in the curve of Faron's arm. "The children are so precious," she whispered. Unspoken was the wish for some of her own.

Belinda watched Faron watching the children and saw his eyes soften with tenderness as a six-year-old Mary nestled a baby doll Jesus in her arms. She watched them light with laughter as an eight-year-old shepherd scattered live sheep down the aisle of the church. And watched them glow with what she would have sworn was love as he turned to her and squeezed her hand while they sang "Silent Night."

When the pageant was over and all the children had been divested of their costumes and bundled into coats, Belinda and Faron looked for Carter and Madelyn. All they found was Maddy.

"Carter left," Madelyn said. "He said he would meet us back at the house."

"But why?" Belinda asked.

"I think it was too hard for him to stay any longer," Madelyn said mysteriously. Belinda never could get any more of an explanation from Madelyn all the way home. At last Belinda realized there must be a lot of people like herself and Carter who had pasts they would rather forget. She felt a little guilty for forcing Carter into a situation where he had been forced to confront demons he might rather have left resting in their dens.

When they got back to The Castle, they found Carter settled in front of the fireplace with a brandy. There was no sign either in his face or his greeting that suggested a reason for why he had left the church.

"If you're comfortable, Carter, I think we'll just leave you here for a while. Belinda and I need to talk privately with Maddy," Faron said.

"I'll be fine," Carter said. "Don't worry about me."

As Faron and Belinda ushered Madelyn into the study, she demanded to know what was going on. Faron refused to say anything until Madelyn was seated in the swivel chair in front of the rolltop desk.

"Why all this hush-hush secretive business?" Madelyn demanded.

"Belinda and I wanted you to hear that we've decided to sell King's Castle before I inform Carter about the deal."

"What!" Madelyn rose with a vigor that denied her age and her ailing heart.

It was apparent from her ruddy complexion and the outrage in her voice that even though Faron and Belinda were willing to be so foolish as to give up their dreams, Madelyn was not.

"I absolutely refuse to leave this house!" she said. It was more of a shriek, actually.

Faron and Belinda stared at the agitated woman who stood across from them, her hands twisting a lace handkerchief. Madelyn was having trouble catching her breath.

"Please sit down, Maddy." Faron was seriously concerned that she might make herself sick. He tried to get her back into the swivel chair.

Madelyn eluded him and marched around to stand beside the desk with her back to the wall. "Don't coddle me! I won't sit down until I hear from your own lips, Belinda, that you would even consider something as horrendous as selling this house out from under me!"

"But Madelyn, I thought you understood that was why Faron and I were making all these improvements," Belinda said.

"Well, I didn't understand!" Madelyn said in an imperious voice. She turned her irate gaze on Faron. "As for you, young man, I'm gravely disappointed in you."

Faron felt the heat on his cheekbones and wasn't sure whether he was feeling shame, embarrassment or anger. Actually, it was a combination of all three. "What is it you're most disappointed by, Maddy? The fact that I would court your son's wife in front of your nose? Or the fact that I'm willing to make Belinda happy at your expense?"

"You young idiot! Don't you see that selling King's Castle isn't going to make anyone happy? Least of all Belinda!"

"You're wrong. Belinda told me months ago that she wants to live in town. She just got through telling me she wants to sell this place."

"Foolish man! Belinda was willing to move into town to take care of me. She would never leave King's Castle if you decided to stay here with her. Ask her!"

Faron leapt up from his chair and turned to face Belinda. "Is that true, Belinda? Would you stay at King's Castle if I stayed here with you?"

"Since that isn't going to happen—"

Faron grabbed Belinda by the shoulders and shook her. "Answer the damned question!"

"Yes! I'd never leave this place if you were here with me. But Faron, that isn't possible, don't you see?"

"Why not?"

"Do you mean to say you'd be willing to leave Hawk's Way? That you'd be willing to spend the rest of your life in Wyoming?"

"I'd move to hell and set up housekeeping if you were there with me. I love you, Princess."

Belinda stood stunned. "Why didn't you ever tell me so?"

Faron shrugged sheepishly. "I didn't want to scare you away. What I want, Princess, what I've wanted for what seems a very long time, is to marry you and work this ranch and raise children here with you."

Belinda thought of the risk involved in committing herself to another man. What she discovered was that her love for Faron, and his love for her, took all the fear out of taking such a risk. Faron wanted only to make her happy, just as she wanted to please him.

"If that was a proposal," she said at last, "I accept."

Faron threw his arms around Belinda and hugged her so tightly she squeaked.

"Don't squeeze the girl to death," Madelyn chided.

Faron reached out and included Maddy in the hug. "You conniving old woman. I don't know what you're complaining about. You got exactly what you wanted."

Madelyn grinned and chortled. "I suppose I did at that. Now. What are we going to do about that young man in the parlor?"

"We have to invite him to stay for Christmas," Belinda said. "We can't send him off alone."

Madelyn's eyes narrowed speculatively. "No, we can't do that, can we?"

"You're not matchmaking again, are you Madelyn?" Belinda asked when she spied the look in her mother-in-law's eyes.

"Who? Me, dear? What makes you think that? However, Carter did mention while we were having coffee in the kitchen that he owns a ski resort in Vermont. It's located in a town not far from where Fiona runs her bed and breakfast. Two relatives should get to know each other, don't you think?"

"Carter's not related in the least to Fiona!" Belinda protested.

"No, they're not related, are they?" Madelyn murmured. "How fortunate. But I do foresee a slight problem."

Belinda knew she shouldn't ask, but did anyway. "What problem?"

"Carter doesn't like cats."

"How did you find that out?" Faron asked, amazed at how much information Madelyn had pried from her newest grandson in the little time they'd had together. "About Carter and cats?"

"Oh, we were discussing conservation. Carter's working to save the mountain lion, even though he doesn't like cats. I don't suppose Fiona would be willing to give up Tut…"

"Madelyn—"

Belinda's warning was lost as Madelyn headed for the parlor. "I'll just go get Carter and send him in here so you can give him the bad news."

When she was gone Belinda looked up at Faron and shook her head. "I don't think there's any help for it. I suppose I'll have to call Fiona and warn her what's coming."

Faron grinned. "What, and spoil all Maddy's fun? From what I know of your sister, Fiona can take care of herself."

"At least it looks like our fairy tale is going to end happily ever after," Belinda said as she gazed up at Faron with adoring eyes.

"What do you want for Christmas, Princess?"

"A baby."

"You've got it. But I think I'll go ahead and give you the gift I had planned." Faron opened the top right hand desk drawer and reached into the back of it. He pulled out a small velvet box and opened it. "This is for you, Princess."

Inside was a topaz surrounded by baguette diamonds. "It's the closest thing I could find to the daisies we picked that first day we spent together." He took the ring from the box and placed it on her finger. "Now you'll always be wearing flowers, Princess."

Tears blurred Belinda's vision. "It's beautiful. Thanks, Cowboy."

All things considered, Carter Prescott took the news that King's Castle had been taken off the market pretty well. "You know I could go to court and challenge the will," he pointed out. "I could tie up your assets so you'd have a hell of a time making ends meet."

"You could," Faron said, a muscle ticking in his jaw. "But I'd fight you every step of the way. And I have some considerable assets at my disposal."

Carter measured Faron's determination and apparently decided Faron meant what he said. Carter smiled wistfully. "I envy you, brother. Guess I'll have to keep looking for those roots."

"I wish you luck finding them," Faron said. "You'll always be welcome here. In fact, we'd be pleased to have you join us for Christmas."

Carter shook his head. "I don't think so. I don't want to intrude. In fact, I'll be leaving tonight."

"So soon?" Belinda asked. "I know Madelyn would like to spend more time with you."

Carter shook his head. "If I stay here much longer I might get to liking this place too much." He reached out his hand to Faron. "Good-bye, Faron. It was a pleasure meeting you."

Faron shook his stepbrother's hand. "I wish we had more time to get to know each other."

"Maybe I'll be back this way again sometime."

Faron and Belinda walked Carter to the parlor where they found Madelyn. She was distressed that her grandson had chosen to leave so soon, but didn't try to change his mind.

Carter hugged his grandmother. "I'm glad I met you, Maddy. I'll see you again sometime." But the way he said it didn't sound like he thought it would be anytime soon.

"Maybe sooner than you think," Madelyn said with a smug smile.

Belinda shook her head. Once Madelyn got an idea in her head it was hard to get it out. Somehow the old woman had gotten her mind set on matching Carter and Fiona. Belinda decided the best thing to do was to stand back and watch the fur fly. Considering how Carter felt about cats, that was a definite possibility when he met up with Tut.

The three of them stood at the door and waved as Carter drove away. It didn't take long for his pickup to disappear in the flurries of snow.

"Now that our company's gone, I think I'll go to bed," Madelyn announced. "I'm feeling a little tired tonight."

Faron and Belinda looked at each other anxiously.

"Are you all right, Maddy?" Faron asked.

Madelyn grinned. "Now don't you worry about me. I plan to be around long enough to dandle a couple of great-grandchildren on my knee. I just thought I'd leave you two alone so you could get started.'' Madelyn winked, then turned and headed up the stairs.

Faron and Belinda stood stunned for a second before they burst out laughing.

"I can take a hint,'' Faron said. He lifted Belinda into his arms and headed for the parlor. He set her down on the rug in front of the fireplace and joined her there. The only light in the room came from the fire and the colored bulbs on the Christmas tree.

They didn't speak, just sat and held each other, listening to the fire crackle and the wind howl as it blew snow against the house. The aroma of spruce pervaded the room, bringing the vast reaches of King's Castle inside for Christmas.

Faron kissed Belinda's cheek, and she snuggled back into his arms. "It's nice holding you like this,'' he said.

"It's nice being held.''

"Would you like to get married on Christmas Day?''

"That would be nice,'' Belinda said. "Maybe we could get your family and mine both to come here for the occasion.''

"I suspect we might be able to talk them into it.''

"I love you, Faron.''

He smiled. "You know, that's the first time you've said that to me.''

"Is it, really? I've thought it a thousand times.''

"I hope you'll keep on saying it.''

"I love you. Love you. Love you.'' She punctuated each pronouncement with a kiss.

Faron slowly lowered Belinda to the rug in front of the fireplace. "Your eyes are lit up like the Christmas tree,'' he said.

"I can't tell you how happy I feel. Maybe I can show you.''

She slowly began covering his face with kisses while her hands roamed his body seeking out the places she had learned would bring him the most pleasure.

"Let's make our baby here, now,'' she murmured. "Love me, Cowboy.''

Faron didn't need more invitation than that. They wasted no time undressing each other, and soon their bodies lay entwined like two golden stems in the firelight. Faron spread Belinda's legs with his knees and settled himself in the cradle of her thighs.

"How many children shall we have?" he murmured as he kissed his way up her throat toward her ear.

"At least a boy and a girl."

He grinned. "I knew a family that had six girls before they got a boy."

Belinda flushed. "I think I could be happy with just girls. Or just boys."

Faron's hand slipped down past her belly to the nest of curls below. She was already wet, and he didn't wait, just slid himself inside her. Then he lay there, waiting to see how long he could stand the pleasure before he had to move.

Meanwhile, Belinda was busy playing with the curls on his chest. She found a male nipple and laved it with her tongue. Faron jerked, and the friction of their bodies moving together wrought a soft cry of pleasure from Belinda's throat.

"Don't move," Faron begged. "I'm trying an experiment here."

Belinda lifted her hips and Faron groaned.

"What kind of experiment?" she asked.

"I wanted to see how long we could just lie here joined together like this."

Belinda grinned like a cat with a bowl of cream. "Not long, Cowboy."

She shifted again and Faron fought back a guttural sound in his throat. "Princess, I'm serious about this."

"So am I." Belinda reached down between their two bodies and touched him where they were joined. Her hand slid down and gently cupped the sac below.

Faron wasn't able to stay still under her onslaught. "All right, if that's the way you want to play, I'm game."

He reached down between them and found the heart of her desire. In moments his caresses had her undulating with pleasure.

"What do you say, Cowboy? Ready to cry uncle?"

"Not until you do, Princess," Faron replied.

Faron latched onto a nipple and suckled hard.

"That's cheating," Belinda rasped.

Faron was too busy to answer. Belinda threaded her hands in his hair and urged his mouth up to hers. "I want to be your woman, Cowboy. I want to have your baby."

Faron answered, "I love you, Princess. I want to make love with you tonight and tomorrow and the rest of our lives."

Their loving was like a prayer, a litany to happily ever after. As their bodies succumbed to the demands each made upon the other, their souls entwined once and for always.

With the woman he loved in his arms, Faron said a prayer that the weather would hold good over the winter so they would have enough feed to manage without buying more. And that his new wife would present him with a daughter in the fall, along about harvest time.

Belinda said a prayer that she would be a good and loving wife, and that she would present her new husband with a son in the fall, along about harvest time.

And just like in a fairy tale, both their prayers were answered.

*   *   *   *   *

THE WRANGLER AND THE RICH GIRL

Prologue

"**S**o how did Mom and Dad meet, Charlie?"

"That's a long story, Zach, and it's time for you three kids to get to bed." Charlie One Horse, the ancient part-Comanche housekeeper at Hawk's Way, ruffled the hair of the seven-year-old boy sitting on the rawhide stool at the foot of his chair. Zach Whitelaw was the spitting image of his father, Garth. He had black hair that hung over his forehead and dark brown eyes that could be equally serious and mischievous.

"I wanta hear, too," Falcon said. Garth's six-year-old son was stretched out on his belly in front of the fireplace, his head resting on his palms. He had his father's black hair, but his eyes were the same blue as his mother's. Falcon possessed bronzed skin, high cheekbones and a sharp blade of nose passed down from his Comanche great-great-grandmother.

"Me, too!" four-year-old Callen chorused. Garth's youngest child, the only girl, had her mother's delicate features, but her father's black hair and dark eyes. She wriggled around in Charlie's lap so she could see the old man's face. She put a hand on the Indian's weathered cheek and said, "Please, Charlie?"

Charlie glanced from the three children to their parents, who were sitting on the sofa across from him. Garth had his arm around Candy, and her blond head lay nestled against his shoulder. His big hand clasped hers. They were the image of a loving, caring couple. It hadn't always been that way.

"So you wanta hear how your mom and dad met, do you?"

"You bet!"

"Sure do!"

"Uh-huh!"

"And after I finish you'll all go to bed without arguin'?"

Three heads nodded vigorously.

"Well, now, let me see," Charlie began as he tugged on the rawhide that held one of his gray braids. He chose his words well, knowing there was no way he could tell those three innocent faces the truth. "Long about eight years ago, your father was a hoss wrangler, just like he is now. And your mother, why, she was a rich girl. One of them gen-u-ine Texas deb-u-tantes. Now, one day..."

Garth's hand tightened on Candy's as the old man began to speak. Their eyes met and held. As Charlie told a story of how they had met and fallen in love, the two of them remembered how it had really happened.

One

Garth Whitelaw had only one use for women, so he didn't have much to do with the decent sort, like the lady heading straight for him now. He avoided meeting the widely spaced, speculative gray eyes that sought him out along the show ring at the spring quarter horse sale in Amarillo. But he felt a definite tightening across his loins as he perused her long, jean-clad legs and sylphlike figure.

He couldn't help admiring the grace of her walk or the way her long blond hair shifted across her shoulders as she moved. His appreciation was balanced by the knowledge that where this particular woman was concerned, the growing bulge behind his fly had damn well better stay zipped in his jeans.

Candice Baylor was a genuine Texas debutante, the daughter of one of the richest men in the state. Garth had first met her three years ago, when she was seventeen. She and her father, Evan, had come to his northwest Texas ranch, Hawk's Way, to look over some championship cutting horses Garth had for sale.

Initially Garth had been amused when Candy tagged along behind him everywhere he went. He had a younger sister who had taught him patience, so he answered all Candy's eager questions with brotherly indulgence. Because she was clever and interested in everything he did, it was easy to be tolerant.

It soon became clear to Garth that his horses weren't the only thing that interested Candy Baylor. Unless he was very much mistaken, the girl had caught a bad case of puppy love. She began flirting with him, sending coy, come-hither looks from beneath lowered lashes.

Garth was annoyed by her antics because even though he knew what she was doing—and despite the fact that she was entirely too young for him—he had felt the first stirrings of arousal. He had scowled mightily at her, but even that hadn't discouraged her.

Garth frowned as he remembered how, the night before she was scheduled to leave the ranch, Candy had confronted him in the downstairs room that served as both office and parlor. She had been dressed for bed and wore a thigh-length belted aqua silk robe over matching long silk pajama bottoms. She might only have been seventeen, but Garth had seen a woman's shape beneath the sensually draped fabric.

Candy claimed she couldn't sleep and just needed someone to talk to. Garth had given her several crude, broad hints, but she hadn't left him alone. So he had settled back in his chair with a whiskey in hand to watch the show, certain he could handle anything this spoiled little rich girl could dish out.

Candy had wandered around the room touching his things—vicariously touching him. She sought out the collection of trophies he had won in cutting horse futurities and fingered the delicate designs. She picked up a photo of Garth with his two younger brothers, Faron and Jesse, and his sister, Tate, from the mantel and tenderly traced his image. Then she ran her hand the length of the pine mantel, which drew her slowly, inexorably toward where he sat in one of the two leather chairs that faced the stone fireplace.

Frustrated by the arousal he couldn't control, Garth fought fire with fire. As she stood before him, he let his gaze insolently run the length of her, stopping to admire the firm, high breasts and flat belly before following the length of her pajama-clad legs to her bare toes. When he looked back up at her face, she was blushing a fiery red.

But she didn't run. He felt a grudging respect for her because he knew the same look had warned off older, more savvy women. Candy had merely turned and strolled, hips sashaying, to the chair across from him. Instead of sitting down normally, she had curled herself into the leather chair with her feet underneath her. She had rested her elbows on the arm of the chair and cupped her chin in her hands.

"Why haven't you ever gotten married?" she asked.

Garth had fielded that question from a lot of women during his thirty-odd years. He gave her his usual cynical response. "Why buy the cow when the milk's free?"

She wrinkled her nose in disgust. "That's an awful thing to say! A man gets other things from marriage besides sex."

"There's nothing else I want or need from a woman."

"What about children?"

Garth's lips flattened. "If I could be sure they were mine, maybe I'd want some."

"What do you mean, if you could be sure they were yours? Whose else would they be?"

"Some other man's," Garth responded curtly.

"No wife of yours would—"

"You're right. No wife of mine would. I'd kill her first," Garth said in a harsh voice. "But don't fool yourself. Lots of wives cheat on their husbands." His own mother had cheated on his father. His younger brother—half brother—Faron had been the result.

"What about companionship?" Candy demanded. "A wife can be a friend, someone to share your hopes and dreams and troubles with."

"I've got lots of friends." He smirked and added, "Of course, none of them are women. I figure there are better things to do when you're with a woman than talk."

She blushed again, an enchanting pink flush that raised the ridge in his jeans. He was ready to concede the battle to her and leave the room, but she asked one more question.

"What about love?" she said in a quiet voice.

"What about it?"

"Haven't you ever been in love with a woman and wanted her to love you back?"

His lips curled in a sardonic smile. "I'm not the kind of man women fall in love with."

She swallowed hard and said, "I love you."

Her gray eyes were huge in her face. He had never seen such a look in a woman's eyes. This was different from the admiration of his physical body, his broad shoulders and narrow waist, his straight nose and mouth, his black hair and deep brown eyes, which he had often seen from the women who wanted him—for sex or his money or to show off on their arms. This was something more.

Garth felt a pain in his chest, like there was a great weight on it, making it hard to breathe. For one brief instant he wanted nothing more than to gather her up in his arms and hold her tight, to reach out and accept the love she offered.

But it was an instant only, and the fact he had even considered holding to his bosom what he knew was just one more female viper made him all the more harsh when he finally responded to her words of love.

"What you're feeling isn't love, little girl. It's good old-fashioned lust. Since you've been asking for it ever since you walked into this room, I figure it's about time you got it." He noticed his hand was shaking when he set down his whiskey glass, so he quickly balled it into a fist.

When he rose to his full height she looked up at him, frozen like a rabbit in a gunsight. Her face had bleached white and her hands had dropped into her lap. He reached out to grasp her wrists and slowly drew her to her feet.

Garth waited for Candy to stop him or show the least sign of fear or resistance. What he wanted her to do was run from him, back to her rich daddy, back to the safe haven of her room upstairs.

He was less surprised this time when she did not.

Candy laid her hands on his bare forearms. Then she turned her face up to his. Her innocent gray eyes were filled with love—and trust.

Garth had never felt so confused. His flesh burned where she touched him. Desire sent blood rushing through his body, engorging a shaft that was already rock hard. He wanted her like he had never wanted another woman. But he was equally determined that he wasn't going to take her. She was just a rich kid with a bad case of puppy love—which he was about to cure.

His mouth was hard, almost brutal, when it captured hers, and his tongue raped and ravaged the inside of her mouth.

Sweet. Dear God, she's so sweet!

Garth was disturbed and disgusted when he felt himself responding to the young girl in his arms. He was a bastard, but not enough of one to take advantage of a teenage virgin. He pressed his mouth harder against hers—hard enough to scare the bejesus out of her—until he tasted blood.

He felt her begin to struggle in his arms and reached out for her breast, the most crude, most possessive male gesture he could make. He cupped the warmth of her through the slippery silk, and in spite of the strong urge he felt to caress her, forced himself to tighten his hold beyond what a girl of her little experience would find comfortable. This wasn't making love. This was sex. Down and dirty. The kind he might have with a woman who wanted it a little rough.

"No, Garth!"

When Candy jerked away, he let her go. She nearly fell when he released her. She stood panting, her parted lips still moist and swollen from his kisses. Her eyes...her gray eyes were wounded, full of pain and disillusionment. She wiped her mouth with the back of her hand, leaving a streak of blood across her cheek. He felt acid in the pit of his stomach.

"Why?" she asked in a ragged voice. "I love—"

He cut her off with an obscene oath. "Don't use that word to me! Foolish little girl! You're just a rich kid playing grown-up. Come back and see me when you're woman enough to handle what I have to offer."

He kept his eyes hard, his lips curled into a sneer.

Even then she hadn't run. He had watched the tears brim in her eyes, watched her try to blink them back before one finally spilled down her cheek. It was plain she wanted to say something to him, but she couldn't talk because she had her teeth gritted to control her trembling chin.

For several tense moments he stood there feeling an urgent need to comfort her. He forced himself to remain where he was. What he had done was for her own good. But the tightness in his chest was back.

At last she swallowed and said, "You're the fool, Garth Whitelaw, to throw away an offer of love. You're going to end up a bitter, lonely old man.

"But I thank you for making me see that giving my love to a man like you, a man who can't—or won't—give love in return, would be like standing in front of a Brahma bull, waiting to get stomped. I know when it's time to make a break for the fence. Believe me when I say I'll be glad to put some distance between us!"

She turned and marched from the room, shoulders back, head held high with a dignity and courage he couldn't help but admire.

He hadn't seen Candice Baylor again before she left Hawk's Way or at any time since that night. Until now. Here she was headed straight toward him, a friendly smile on her face as though that night had never happened. At least they were on neutral territory at the fairgrounds in Amarillo. It was doubtful she planned to make a scene in a public place, although that had happened to him once or twice in the past with other women. His lips flattened in displeasure as he recalled such a moment.

"Hello, Garth."

He had forgotten how husky her voice was. The sound rasped over his flesh, lifting the hairs. He didn't know what to say, so he said nothing. An awkward silence followed. Candy was close enough that he could smell the perfume she was wearing, the light scent of lilacs. He felt his body tightening in instant response to her allure and swore under his breath.

She froze and her face paled.

Garth clamped his back teeth and stood in silence.

"I need to talk to you," she said at last.

"If you want to buy a horse, see the auctioneer."

"Not about that."

Garth refused to help her by asking what she wanted. He watched the expressions chase across her face. Frustration, then anger, then determination.

"I'd like you to join me for a drink at the hotel across the street," she said.

"I didn't think you were old enough to drink in a public place."

She flushed painfully, but her chin came up a notch. "I'm not. I'll have a glass of tea. I have a proposal I'd like to make to you. I thought we might as well get away from the noise and bustle of the sale. Will you join me?"

Garth listened to the auctioneer's patter over the microphone and the sounds of horses neighing. People were going right on with their lives, unaware that he was being confronted by a specter from his past.

He knew it would be a mistake to go with her. Despite the three years that had passed since he had seen Candy Baylor, he was still attracted to her. She was definitely not a child anymore. Her voice, her face, her body had all matured. She was a woman now.

And probably not a virgin anymore.

He tried not to think about that, but couldn't get the idea out of his head. He would never have taken her innocence, but now that she was an experienced woman, why not have her? He wondered if she would be willing. His lip curled cynically. Why else had she sought him out? Probably she was taking him up on his offer to come back when she was ready to have an adult relationship with him. He sure as hell wasn't going to turn her down.

"I don't have much time," he began. He watched her face closely and saw the disappointment she couldn't hide. "But I can spare you a few minutes."

The smile was back, and a brightness in her light gray eyes that made his gut twist. He wanted her. His mouth was so dry it was hard to swallow. His body felt taut, stretched on a rack of desire.

It was a damn good thing they were having a drink at the hotel, he thought. At least that way it wasn't far to the nearest bed.

Two

Candice Baylor wanted one thing from Garth Whitelaw—and it wasn't sex. That was a good thing, because from the look on his face as she had approached him, he wasn't the least bit happy to see her.

Her last encounter with Garth had cured her of her childish infatuation with the wrangler, but even so she couldn't help admiring the man. He stood well over six feet tall, and his lithe body was all muscle and sinew. He moved with the easy grace of someone who has spent his life depending on the strength and coordination of his body.

Over the years since that night in the parlor at Hawk's Way, Candy had tried to figure out what it was about Garth Whitelaw that had caused her to fall in love with him. She had watched him with the horses he bred and trained and seen that he was capable of gentleness, infinite patience and compassion. Her only mistake had been in thinking that Garth would be able to transfer those emotions to human beings. He had turned out to be a hard, harsh and unforgiving man where women were concerned.

As they headed toward Garth's pickup truck for the ride to the hotel, Candy stole glances at the man she had once thought she loved. His face wasn't conventionally attractive. It was full of hard planes and gaunt hollows. His dark brown eyes were feral, almost dangerous. He wore his black hair too long, down over his collar, and even his tan Western suit didn't make him look the least bit civilized.

His expression was brooding, his eyes hooded, his body taut with what Candy recognized as the first signs of desire. She felt a shiver run down her spine, aware of a sexual attraction to the rugged horseman which she thought had been put to rest forever.

Candy was grateful that the hotel was so close, since neither of them said anything to break the uncomfortable silence that had fallen between them in the truck. Once in the hotel restaurant, Garth took charge of ordering an iced tea for her and a whiskey for himself.

Candy didn't want to be interrupted when she told Garth what she wanted from him, so while they waited for their drinks to arrive, she asked about his family, whom she had met during her ill-fated visit three years before.

"Jesse and Tate are both married and have children," Garth said. "Faron…" He frowned and finished in a voice that didn't invite further probing, "Faron's gone to Wyoming on business."

"So you're all alone at the ranch now?"

"Except for Charlie One Horse."

"How is he?"

"As cantankerous as ever."

Candy knew Garth wasn't married, but she wanted to ask if he had a steady girlfriend. She resisted the impulse. It would bring back too many memories she wanted to forget. But she couldn't think of anything else to ask, either.

Fortunately, Garth picked up the slack. "I heard your father's big black stud won another cutting horse futurity."

Candy smiled. "You mean Comanche Moon? That horse can stop on a dime and give you nine cents change," she said proudly. "There's a good chance he'll be World Champion Cutting Horse this year. Not that it'll be easy to beat Hawk's Honor. I know your stallion has proved he's a champion the past two years, but this year the title belongs to Comanche Moon."

"Any chance your father would let me buy him?"

Candy shook her head. "Comanche Moon isn't for sale. Dad wouldn't part with him for all the oil in Texas."

The waiter arrived with their drinks, and Candy fiddled with her tea, squeezing in lemon and stirring in sweetener to postpone the moment when she would have to make her proposal to the wrangler.

"All right," Garth said after he had taken a drink of whiskey. "Spit it out. What do you want?"

"I want to hire you to teach me everything you know about breeding and training cutting horses." She rushed on before he could interrupt. "If I want to be the best—and I do—I figure I need to learn from the best. That's you. As a rider, you've won every cutting horse competition there is. As a breeder, your horses have what it takes to win championships."

Garth was stunned by Candy's suggestion. It was a far cry from the sexual invitation he had been expecting. He was surprised at the sharp disappointment he felt that she wasn't seeking him out for more personal reasons. On the other hand, he was flattered by her obvious admiration for what he had accomplished with cutting horses. He was tempted to say he would take her on and teach her what he knew.

Two things stopped him. First, having her around would be a constant distraction from his work. There was no denying the way his body reacted to her. He wanted her, wanted to be deep inside her. If she came to Hawk's Way he would have her.

However, having her wasn't the problem. It was getting her to leave when he was tired of her. It was bound to get awkward if she stuck around to learn about cutting horses long after he had lost interest in having her in his bed. It never occurred to him that his interest in her wouldn't wane. No woman had ever held his attention for long after he had bedded her.

His second reason for refusing her was equally compelling. In Garth's experience, rich people thought they could buy anything with money. His mother, for one, had been tempted into an affair by the gifts of jewels and money a wealthy man had offered her. Garth Whitelaw wasn't about to hire himself out to anybody—especially not to some spoiled little rich girl.

Garth had been staring into his drink while he thought. Now he looked up and saw that Candy had caught her lower lip in her teeth. His belly tightened as he remembered the sweet taste of her. His voice grated with need when he spoke.

"I'm not interested. You go on back to college in the fall and finish your education."

Her eyes flashed with irritation, but her voice remained calm. "In the first place, I've graduated college. I went straight through and finished early. In the second place, I'm prepared to pay—"

"Keep your money, sweetheart. Now, if you'd like to make me a different proposition…" He let his voice trail off suggestively.

"Like what?" she asked hesitantly.

"Seems to me we have some unfinished business together."

Candy realized suddenly what Garth wanted from her. She felt the heat skating up her throat. She had hoped and prayed he had forgotten her youthful indiscretion. Here it was, back to haunt her. "I'm only interested in a business relationship, Garth. If you're worried about me making any other overtures, you can relax. I wouldn't dream of imposing myself on you."

"Unfortunately, I can't make the same promise. I find you a damned attractive woman. Now that you're not a virgin anymore, I can't guarantee I could keep my hands off you."

Candy opened her mouth to tell him "I am too a virgin!" and snapped it shut again. It would be too embarrassing to discuss such a thing, and he was bound to say something that would make her so furious she wouldn't be able to talk.

"What if I made it clear I didn't want anything to do with you?" she asked.

"I've never forced myself on a woman," Garth said. "I've never needed to." His smile was slow in coming, but no less devastating to her senses.

Candy pressed her thighs together, but that did nothing to stop the growing warmth between her legs. She was still determined to get what she wanted, even if it meant she would have to deal with Garth's sexual overtures. She could handle him. Especially since he had promised no force would be involved.

"Look," she said, "I'm willing to work with you on a purely professional basis if you'll just work with me."

"That's the point, sweetheart. I don't want to work with you."

Candy gritted her teeth to keep from snapping something back at Garth that would forever close the door to Hawk's Way. "I'll give you some time to think about it and—"

"I don't need time to think," Garth interrupted. "The answer is no. Not now, not ever."

"You are the most stubborn, most arrogant sonofa—"

Garth's eyes narrowed. "I think you've said enough."

There was something in his tone of voice that warned Candy he was at the end of his rope. One look at his face told her that words weren't going to change his mind. She hid her disappointment, not wanting to give him something else to throw back in her face. "All right, Garth. If that's the way you feel, I suppose I'll have to look elsewhere for someone to teach me what I want to know."

Garth wondered who she would find. Sam Longstreet at the Double Bar Ranch was good. He was a bachelor, too. Garth felt a sudden unreasonable jealousy, but forced it down. He stood when Candy did and reached out a hand to help her from the booth.

Candy slid out on her own. Her eyes met Garth's one last time, searching for any sign that he might relent. When she found none, she said, "Goodbye, Garth." Then she turned and walked away.

Garth stared after her, wondering if he had done the right thing. He sat back down and finished off his whiskey. Then, because he was beginning to think maybe he had been too hasty, he ordered another drink and nursed it while he tried to get the image of Candice Baylor out of his mind.

Meanwhile, Candy headed upstairs to the hotel suite she shared with her father. She was glad he wasn't there, because by the time she arrived, she was on the verge of tears. Candy hadn't admitted to herself how much she had been counting on Garth Whitelaw to agree to her plan. She had tied up her hopes and dreams for the future in that one request. And it had been denied.

Candy slipped into her bedroom and closed the door behind her. She felt weary beyond words. She lay down on the bed and hugged a pillow to her chest, pressing it to her mouth to hold back the sobs that threatened.

It was dark when Candy's father knocked on her door.

"Candy? I've been waiting downstairs for you. I thought we were supposed to have supper together. Are you all right, honey?"

"I'm fine, Daddy." Candy quickly turned on a lamp and swiped at her eyes, which were red from all the crying she had done.

"Can I come in?" he asked.

She jumped up and crossed to the bathroom for a damp cloth. She dabbed at her eyes, trying to undo the ravages her tears had left. "Come on in, Daddy."

When she came out of the bathroom, her father took one look at her and said, "What happened? What's wrong?"

"It shows, huh?"

He opened his arms and Candy crossed into them. With her father's arms around her she confessed what she had wanted to do and Garth's rejection of her proposal. Of course, she didn't mention anything about Garth's personal interest in her. Evan Baylor was very protective of his daughter and would likely make things worse by confronting the younger man.

"It doesn't matter, Daddy," she finished. "I suppose it was pretty presumptuous to think he'd be willing to teach me. I'll find somebody else."

"But Garth Whitelaw is the best!" Evan protested.

Candy shrugged and managed a smile. "Then I guess I'll have to take second best."

Evan's mouth firmed. He hadn't started out as one of the richest men in Texas, and he had learned over the years how to get what he wanted. What he wanted now was to take that look of defeat and despair off his daughter's face. Which meant he had to find a way to get Garth Whitelaw to reverse his decision.

"Don't you worry, honey," Evan said. "Maybe when Garth thinks it over he'll change his mind."

"He sounded pretty definite about his decision," Candy said.

Evan didn't bother arguing with her. "You still hungry?"

"I'd rather have something sent up to the room, if you don't mind."

"Not at all," Evan said. That would give him a chance to hunt up Garth Whitelaw and see about changing the man's mind. "You order whatever you like. I think I'll go out and get myself a good steak. See you tomorrow morning."

"Good night, Daddy."

"Good night, honey." Evan gave his daughter a hug and received a kiss on the cheek. He adored his only child. She was the light of his life. He would do anything to see her happy. His eyes narrowed in calculation as he began to examine his options.

Evan headed back downstairs. Candy had left Garth Whitelaw in the hotel restaurant. There was just a chance the man was still there. Sure enough, as Evan entered the restaurant Garth was just on his way out. He had his arm around a luscious-looking redhead.

"Hello there, Garth," Evan said. "I see you've got yourself some entertainment for the evening."

"Yes, sir," Garth agreed with a grin.

"I wonder if I could take a few moments of your time before you retire. I have a proposition to make to you."

Garth glanced down at the redhead. She wasn't the woman he wanted, as Evan Baylor's appearance reminded him.

Evan took advantage of Garth's hesitation to hand the redhead a hundred dollar bill. "Why don't you go have yourself a drink?" he said.

The redhead looked from Garth to Evan and smiled broadly. "Why sure, mister. Whatever you say."

Garth's brow arched as what he saw reinforced both his distrust of women and his belief that the rich used their money to get what they wanted. He eyed Evan warily, but when the older man gestured, he joined him in a booth in the hotel bar.

"What are you drinking?" Evan asked.

"Whiskey."

Evan held up a twenty, and a waitress quickly appeared. "Two whiskeys," he said.

Garth remained silent. He knew Evan Baylor well enough to appreciate the man's shrewd business sense. He figured Evan wanted something from him, and it wasn't too hard to guess that it might have something to do with his recent conversation with Candy.

Evan didn't wait for the whiskeys. He got right down to business. "What would it take for you to accept my daughter's proposition?"

"I'm not for sale," Garth said flatly.

"Of course not," Evan placated. "But there must be something you want that you can't get on your own. Some new piece of land to expand Hawk's Way. Some new mare. Some stud you'd like to have."

"Did Candy put you up to this?" Garth demanded.

"She doesn't know I'm here. In fact, she's willing to settle for second best. I'm not. There must be something I have that you want," Evan insisted.

Garth started to tell Evan Baylor to go to hell. Then he thought of something Evan had that he wanted very much. "Comanche Moon," he said in a soft voice.

Evan hissed in a breath. "That stud's going to be World Champion Cutting Horse this year."

"That's my price." Garth was certain the old man would never pay it. That was the only reason he had even suggested it.

"Done."

"What?"

"You teach my daughter everything you know about cutting horses, and I'll give you Comanche Moon."

"What if she quits before I've taught her what I know?" Garth knew ways to make that happen.

Evan stared down at work-roughened hands. He might be rich, but he still worked from dawn to dusk each day. And he had taught his daughter everything he believed about hard work and persistence being the roads to success.

"Candy won't quit," Evan said certainly. He looked up at Garth. "I'm so sure she won't quit that if she does, I'll give you the stud anyway."

Garth shook his head. "If she quits, I buy the stud at a fair price." He didn't want to cheat Evan, and he was pretty certain Candy Baylor wasn't going to be hanging around Hawk's Way for very long. He didn't plan to make it easy on the girl if she came to live at his ranch. He had already told her there was only one thing he wanted from her. If he didn't end up fulfilling his part of the bargain with Evan because the girl couldn't handle everything he threw at her, Garth wanted to pay for the horse.

"Done." Evan held out his hand to be shaken by the other man. He knew his daughter well. Garth Whitelaw was in for a big surprise if he thought the girl would quit.

"There's one condition," Evan said. He knew how upset Candy got when he used his money to get his own way. His daughter was just stubborn enough to refuse to go along with the bargain if she found out the truth about the deal he had made with Garth. "You can't tell my daughter that I had anything to do with your change of mind."

"That's fine with me," Garth said. After all, he had just gotten through telling Candy he couldn't be bought. He wasn't willing to admit—even to himself—that he had spent the better part of the afternoon seeking some way to get Candy Baylor alone at Hawk's Way.

"One other thing," Evan said.

"Now what?"

"I know your reputation with women," Evan said.

Garth stiffened. "What does that have to do with anything?"

"I don't want my daughter hurt."

The warning was there, and the threat also. Garth wasn't offended. He had every intention of taking Candice Baylor to bed, and no intention at all of marrying her, so he could understand her father's concern. Nevertheless, Garth didn't believe Candy was going to suffer from their relationship.

"Rest assured, your daughter won't find herself in any situation she doesn't want to be in," he said at last.

That wasn't much comfort, but Evan realized it was the only reassurance he was going to get. He had a lot of confidence in his daughter. She had managed to handle herself in some pretty tight situations. "All right," he said. "I suppose that's the most I can ask. I'll make sure Candy is downstairs for breakfast tomorrow. Say about eight o'clock?"

"I'll be there," Garth said. "Don't worry. I'll take care of making the necessary excuses for my change of mind. Your daughter won't suspect a thing."

Three

***

Candy stared suspiciously at Garth. Against all reason, he had joined her and her father for breakfast in the hotel dining room. Then her father had suddenly remembered an appointment and left her alone with the rancher.

"What's going on?" she demanded.

Garth shrugged. "I changed my mind."

Candy sat stunned for a moment. Then she smiled. "I'm so glad." Her face lit up with happiness, but it didn't take long for a shadow to cloud her joy. Her teeth caught her lower lip and her brow furrowed.

"What changed your mind, Garth? My father didn't—"

"I figured I'd have a better chance of getting what I want from you if I had you closer to home," Garth said.

"Oh." Candy thought about that for a moment. The roguish grin on Garth's face left little doubt what it was he really wanted from her in exchange for the knowledge she wanted from him. "I think it only fair to warn you that I'm the kind of girl who doesn't have to be burned twice to learn it's dangerous to stick your hand in the fire."

"Meaning?"

"Meaning I plan to keep my distance from you at Hawk's Way."

"That's going to be a little difficult, considering the fact we'll be working side by side every day," Garth pointed out.

Candy gave an exasperated snort. "You know what I mean."

"I'm afraid I do. Lest there be any misunderstanding, I'm agreeing to this arrangement because I want you in my bed. I'm going to do my level best while you're at Hawk's Way to convince you to join me there. Now that all the cards are on the table, do you still want to come?"

"Oh, I'm coming," Candy reassured him. "That was never in doubt. Only, as long as we're both being so honest, I think you should know that I'm cured of the love or infatuation or whatever it was I felt for you three years ago. I won't set my heart on a platter and watch you refuse it again. You're welcome to do your best to seduce me. But I'd never have sex with a man I didn't love. If you're smart, you won't waste your time trying."

"It's my time." Garth was irritated, infuriated and not sure why. He didn't want her love. Why the hell would she think he cared whether she offered it to him? All he wanted was the pleasure two consenting adults could enjoy in bed together. Candy's opposition only increased his desire for her and made the chase that much more interesting. She would give in sooner or later. He had never met a woman yet who hadn't.

"I'll expect you at Hawk's Way by the end of next week," he said.

"So soon?"

Garth arched a questioning brow. "Is there something you need to do before you start?"

"Not really." Candy thought of the spring charity ball she had been planning to attend in Fort Worth. She would have to call Edward Vargas and break their date. "No, no problem at all," she said. "I'll be there next Friday."

On the following Friday, Garth was on tenterhooks from the moment he woke up. He couldn't sit still for breakfast, and Charlie One Horse kicked him out of the kitchen when he complained about the coffee.

"Get out of here and go to work," Charlie ordered. "Either that filly'll show up or she won't. Worryin' about it ain't goin' to change anythin'."

Garth saddled up a three-year-old quarter horse and began working him in the corral. A cutting horse was bred and trained to separate a cow from the herd and keep it from rejoining the other animals.

In olden days, as now, cutting cattle from the herd was a necessary function in order to brand animals or to dose them with medicine. Garth had the satisfaction of knowing that the sport for which he trained his horses also had a utilitarian purpose. Some horses were suited for the sport and thrived on the competition. Others didn't. The ability to stop and turn on a dime was of ultimate importance if the horse was going to be able to keep ahead of the cow.

Garth put the three-year-old through his paces, making sure to stop and back the horse at each turn so the animal kept his weight on his heels, giving his front end mobility. He gripped the saddle horn and hung on, giving commands with his knees while the horse leaped, dodged and wheeled with breathtaking speed to keep the cow at bay.

Garth was concentrating hard on what he was doing. It wasn't until he gave his horse a pat on the neck at the end of the workout that he realized Candy had been standing with her arms folded over the top rail of the corral watching him.

"He's wonderful!" she said.

"He needs more work," Garth countered.

Candy bit back the compliment she had been about to make about Garth's riding, certain he would only contradict her about that, as well.

Garth kneed the stallion toward Candy as she slipped through the wooden bars and approached him. When Garth stepped down from the saddle, Candy ran her hands knowingly over the quarter horse checking his conformation. She looked to see whether he had low hocks that could handle the abrupt stops, slides and pivots required of a cutting horse.

"He's a beauty," she said. "What's his name?"

"Stop and Go."

Candy grinned. "That certainly fits." She followed Garth as he led the horse into the barn to unsaddle him. "What were you teaching him today?"

"The basics," Garth said, unconsciously beginning the lessons he had promised to teach. "Traveling with the cow. Stopping, collecting, and moving his front end to stay with the cow."

Garth led the horse into one of the stalls. Candy closed the door behind him, then stood on the bottom rail and leaned over to watch while Garth unsaddled the animal.

"I noticed Stop and Go works with his head up. Does that slow him down?" she asked.

Garth shook his head. "All horses are different. Some work with their heads up, some down. What's most important is the stop that sets up the turn." Garth temporarily set the saddle on the side of the stall, slipped off the bridle and replaced it with a halter.

Candy stepped down off the stall door and opened it as Garth came back through with the sweaty horse.

"You can take him out back and hose him off now," Garth said.

Candy opened her mouth to say that bathing horses wasn't what she had come to learn but shut it again. She had made up her mind to follow directions and do what she was told. That way there was less chance of a confrontation with Garth.

A look down at what she was wearing made Candy grimace. The designer jeans, red silk shirt and matching red boots she had worn to travel in were a little fancy for hosing down horses. "Can you give me a minute to change?"

"Never mind. I'll do it myself."

Garth was being totally unreasonable, but Candy wasn't about to give him the opportunity to say later that she cared more about her clothes than the job. "Give him to me," she said. "I'll take care of him."

Candy accidentally brushed the crisp hairs across the back of Garth's hand as she took the lead rope from him. It felt as though she had been zapped with an electrical shock. She stared at the wrangler with a stricken expression.

Before she even considered asking Garth to teach her about cutting horses, Candy had convinced herself she was over her infatuation with the wrangler. Her reaction to the mere touch of his hand was a shock—both literally and figuratively.

Candy had believed herself no longer susceptible to Garth's powerful animal magnetism. Since she had firmly quashed the strong emotional feelings of three years ago, she had figured there was not much the cowboy could do to entice her into his bed. Thus, she was confounded by the surge of sexual excitement she had just experienced.

Candy stood frozen for a second, staring at the spot where she had touched Garth. For the sake of the horse, she forced herself to move slowly rather than jerking her hand away. But once she and Garth were no longer touching, she quickly headed out the back door of the stable.

"Don't get too wet," he called after her.

Candy shot him a look over her shoulder. "Don't worry, Boss. I won't melt." In fact, a dousing with cold water might be just what she needed to cool off.

As Garth watched the sway of two rear ends moving away from him, it suddenly dawned on him how quickly and easily Candy had insinuated herself into his workday.

One thing Garth hadn't considered when he told Candy he would teach her was whether she would be an apt pupil. It appeared that she was serious about learning the art of breeding and training cutting horses. Which added an entirely different dimension to their relationship.

All Garth's plans had evolved around the physical connection he planned to have with Candy. Now he was going to have to deal with her on intellectual terms, as well. He smiled wryly. That was certainly going to be a first for him. He had always kept business and pleasure separate in the past.

Garth stepped to the next stall and began saddling another horse, a two-year-old he had raised from birth. He soon found that he had certainly been right about the fact that Candy would prove a distraction. The third time he let the colt get away with turning before he made a stop, Garth ended the lesson. He didn't want the horse to end up with bad habits because his trainer's mind had strayed to some female.

Meanwhile, Candy had turned over the cooled-down quarter horse to one of the hands working in the stable and headed back to the house for a change of clothes. The silk blouse hadn't survived the encounter. The red boots would be fine to work in, but she wouldn't be dressing up in them again. She figured she better find out where Charlie One Horse had put her suitcases.

Candy stopped and stared at the place that would be her home for the next several months. She had fallen in love with Hawk's Way the first time she had seen it. The ranch house was an imposing two-story white frame structure that looked a lot like an antebellum mansion. It had four twenty-foot-high fluted columns along its face and railed first- and second-story porches that ran the length of the house. The road leading to the house was lined with magnolias, while the house itself was shaded by the branches of a moss-laden live oak.

For all its grandeur outside, the house was very much a home. The oak and pine furniture that had been passed down from generation to generation showed the hard wear of frontier life. However, though gouged and scraped, it was kept polished to a fine sheen.

Candy pulled the screen door open and entered the kitchen. "Charlie? Where are you, Charlie?" When she got no answer, she headed upstairs. She expected to find her things in the guest bedroom where she had stayed the last time she had come to Hawk's Way. A glance inside the room showed it was bare.

Candy pursed her lips and began a search from room to room upstairs. Each room showed the personality of its former occupant, and Candy got images of Garth's siblings—independent, uncontrolled, unpredictable—as she passed from one room to another. Each step took her closer to the end of the hall, where she knew Garth slept. Sure enough, she found her suitcases in the bedroom next to his. Candy frowned.

She walked in and closed the door behind her, muttering her displeasure as she began stripping off her wet clothes. There was nothing subtle about the message Garth was sending. It was only a step or two from her bedroom to his.

Despite her anger at Garth's blatant manipulation, she had to admire the room itself. The canopy over the bed was trimmed in eyelet lace, as was the spread. The dry sink and chest were antiques, and the back of the rocker beside the bed was hand-carved. Garth had put her in a room that held a wealth of Whitelaw heritage. Candy could almost feel the love and hate, the hope and despair of the generations of Whitelaws who had slept in this room.

The view from the window took Candy's breath away. The mountainous Palo Duro Canyon area was rugged terrain that had once provided a haven for raiding Comanches. It was a landscape as harsh and unforgiving as the man who owned it.

She was just buttoning up a blue chambray shirt when the door opened.

"Candy? It's Garth. Are you in there?"

"Garth, I—" Before Candy could say she didn't have her jeans on yet, Garth opened the door. She glared at him and said, "You could have knocked."

"I'm glad I didn't." Garth found himself treated to the sight of Candy's bare legs beneath the tails of a Western shirt. "I just came up to ask whether you'd like to take a ride with me. I have to check on some stock in the north pasture."

"I'd like that." She hesitated, then said, "I want to know why I'm not staying in the same room I used the last time I was here."

"The answer to that ought to be obvious. I wanted you close to me."

Candy's fists landed on her hips. "It's not going to make any difference where you put me. I'm not going to go to bed with you."

"Then it won't matter if you stay here," Garth shot back. His eyes slid to her legs where another inch or two of flesh had been exposed when her fisted hands gathered the shirt at her waist. His heart, which was already thudding from his race upstairs in search of her, picked up a beat.

For a few hectic minutes when he couldn't find Candy anywhere around the barn, Garth had feared she had packed up and gone home. He refused to admit how relieved he was to discover her here. He let his eyes feast on the sight of her.

"If you're through ogling, I'd like to finish getting dressed," Candy said.

Garth tipped his hat in acknowledgement of her demand, turned and sauntered out the door. He stopped just beyond the threshold and said, "If you're not at the barn in five minutes, I'm leaving without you."

Candy slammed the door behind him. She considered making him wait on her, then admitted he probably wouldn't. At which point she grabbed a pair of Levi's and jerked them on, tucked in her shirt and added a tooled leather belt. Then she sat down on the canopy bed, pulled on socks and stuck her feet into a pair of sturdy Western boots.

Four and a half minutes later she was standing at the door to the barn. Garth walked down the center aisle leading two saddled horses. He handed the reins of a bay gelding with four white stockings to Candy and led a coal black stallion out of the barn for himself.

Candy checked the length of the stirrups and the cinch to make sure it was tight. Then she mounted and followed Garth down a dirt road that led to the north pasture. She was pleased to note that Garth had put her on a spirited animal, but she felt self-conscious as the wrangler evaluated her seat on the horse. She forced herself to relax. She had learned to ride before she could walk and had been a champion herself in several eighteen-and-under junior cutting horse futurities.

Still, she breathed a sigh of relief when Garth said, "I'm glad to see you've got an easy hand on a horse's mouth. That's one less thing I'll have to teach you."

"I'm willing to take pointers on anything you think could stand improvement," she said.

"That's good to know. Because I have a suggestion."

"Oh?" Candy tensed.

"Relax. I'm not going to bite you. At least, not anytime soon."

Candy laughed. "Be careful. I might bite back." She made the mistake of looking at Garth and saw the sudden leap of desire in his eyes. "Forget I said that," she muttered.

Fortunately they had reached the pasture where several mares and their foals were grazing along with some stock that was still too young to be ridden. Candy dismounted and, following Garth's lead, tied her horse to the closest fence post. Garth's stallion whinnied at the mares, who looked up and then went back to grazing again. Candy wished she could be so nonchalant when Garth demanded her attention.

She assessed the quarter horse mares and realized she was seeing the best of the best. She whistled her appreciation. To her surprise, one of the yearling colts began trotting toward her. Then she realized Garth had slipped through the fence and was holding an apple in his palm, waiting for the colt to approach.

After sidestepping and tossing his head several times, the yearling walked over to Garth and took the apple from him. As the chestnut-colored colt stood there munching, Garth handled the animal, running his hands over its neck and chest, down over the withers and back to the hindquarters, then down the legs and up again.

"Come here," he said to Candy in a quiet voice.

Candy joined him, and he began another lesson. He stepped behind her, took her hand in his and made the same journey as before. Only this time, his hand moved hers across the colt's sleek coat, pointing out the yearling's good and bad points for her edification.

At last he moved to the colt's head. "He's short between the eye and muzzle, has a wide forehead, a nicely defined jowl and a straight profile. His eyes are wide-set, and his ears are set forward and close to each other. Damn near perfect."

Garth let go of Candy's hand at last, but he didn't step back. Their bodies were aligned so that each could feel the other's heat. Candy forced herself to focus on the horse, not the man standing behind her. She scratched the blaze on the colt's face and said, "You didn't comment on the way his neck meets his shoulder."

Garth had his right hand on the colt's withers and reached past her with his left to run a hand down the colt's neck, effectively trapping her between his arms. "It might be a bit low, but not enough to make a difference," he said at last.

Candy felt Garth's moist breath against her cheek when he spoke. She turned slightly and realized that their mouths were only inches apart. She raised her eyes to his and saw they were hooded, the dark eyes lambent. She was appalled at the desire that pooled between her legs. Her breasts felt full and achy. Her nipples were erect.

Candy stood frozen as Garth lowered his mouth to hers. She was prepared for violence. It was what she expected, and it would have freed her from his thrall. His lips barely touched hers before they retreated, only to return for another taste. She kept her mouth closed, but he made love to her lips, kissing first one edge and then the other of her mouth before sliding his tongue along the seam.

Candy moaned when she felt Garth's tongue slip between her lips. The warmth, the wetness, made her feel weak. She needn't have worried about falling. Garth's hand slid around her waist and turned her to face him, sealing their bodies together from the waist down. There was no mistaking his arousal, which only intensified her own disjointed feelings.

Candy pressed the heels of her hands against Garth's chest with the thought of pushing him away, but instead her fingers curled into his cotton shirt, clutching him tight.

Candy was in way over her head. She knew how sexually experienced Garth was, and that she had to guard against his persuasiveness. But it was that experience which made him so successful in his seduction. Whenever she seemed reluctant for him to go a step further, he backed off. So a love bite on her throat that drew a guttural groan from her was followed by teasing kisses that had her melting in his arms.

His fingers tunneled into her hair and held her still for a ravishing kiss, then slid down to her nape and gently massaged the tender flesh there.

Candy was far more innocent than Garth knew. Her disastrous experience with him three years ago had kept her from letting things get very far with the men she had dated in college. No man besides Garth had ever touched her.

So when Garth's hand slid up to cup her breast, it recalled the memory of how he had hurt her in the past. She cried out in anticipation of the pain and jerked herself from his grasp. Her cry frightened the colt, which turned and kicked up its heels.

Garth grabbed her and threw them both out of the way of the colt's slashing hooves. He took the brunt of the fall, protecting her in his arms. When they finished rolling, he was lying on top of her in the grass.

Candy stared up at him, eyes wide with fright.

"You damn fool! Don't you know better than to shout like that around a horse?" Garth said between gritted teeth.

"I was—"

"What were you yelling for, anyway? I know damn well I didn't hurt you!" he ranted.

"Not *this* time," Candy retorted.

She watched a muscle work in Garth's jaw, but his tirade abruptly ended. She gave his shoulders a push. "You can get off me now."

Garth took most of his weight off her, but he didn't free her. The grass was surprisingly cool beneath her, and several blades tickled the back of her neck. She closed her eyes and turned her face away, unable to bear the taunting look on his face. But he didn't allow her to hide from him for long. He grasped her chin and turned her face toward him.

"Open your eyes, Candy."

"No, Garth."

He lowered his body so that he was cradled between her thighs. He was aroused again. Or still. Candy didn't know which, but it hardly mattered.

"Open your eyes," he demanded.

She blinked against the sun's glare and stared at him in defiance. "Let me up."

"In a minute. First, we have a few things to get settled."

"I don't want to hear anything you have to say."

"That's too damn bad," Garth said. "I think what just happened between us proves you're not indifferent to me."

Candy's lips pressed flat. She couldn't deny the rush of passion she had felt in Garth's arms. Or the fact that she had enjoyed every moment of his kisses. But she still wasn't sophisticated enough to accept the fact that she could feel sexual desire for a man she wasn't even sure she liked.

When she remained stubbornly silent, Garth commanded, "Talk to me, Candy."

"What do you want me to say? That I enjoyed what happened? I did. That I want to repeat the experience? I don't! You're pushing too far, too fast, Garth."

Garth eased his body away from hers. Her outburst was something he understood. A woman liked a little courting before she succumbed to a man. He was willing to play the game, now that Candy had told him the rules. "Sure, sweetheart. Whatever you say."

Garth rose and pulled Candy to her feet. He began dusting her off, but she slapped his hands away. "Leave me alone. I can take care of myself."

She swatted the last of the grass from her fanny, then turned back around to face Garth. "What are you grinning at?"

"Can't a man smile when he's happy?"

Candy scowled. She marched past Garth toward where she had left the gelding tied and heard Garth following close behind her. She felt the heat of him, smelled the musky scent of aroused male that even three years later had the power to make her remember the taste of him. Candy turned, forcing Garth to stop in his tracks.

She jabbed a finger at his chest and said, "Don't push me, Garth. You won't like what I'll do."

Garth's grin widened. "Try me."

Pushed to the limit, Candy took him at his word. Her hand arced and her open palm hit his cheek with a loud crack. She was appalled at the clear imprint of her hand on his face and the dark flush that quickly followed. Garth's eyes narrowed, and his lips flattened, but he made no move to retaliate.

Candy trembled, shaken by the attack, which had surprised her as much as it had Garth. She swallowed over the sudden thickness in her throat. "I...I didn't mean..."

"Forget it," Garth snapped. "We'd better be getting back to the house. Charlie will have supper waiting for us."

Candy mounted her horse and rode back to the ranch house in silence. She couldn't imagine what had caused her to react so violently to Garth's provocation. She had never hit anyone before in her life.

When the ranch house came into sight, Candy realized that if she didn't want to have to apologize in front of Charlie One Horse she had better do it now. "I'm sorry."

Garth eyed her askance. "It's not the first time I've been slapped."

Candy flushed. "It's the first time *I've* slapped someone," she retorted. "Are you going to accept my apology, or not?"

"Apology accepted."

As they dismounted at the stable, Candy had the awful feeling that Garth wasn't the sort of man who easily forgave and forgot. She was bound to him and Hawk's Way for the next several months, at least until she had learned enough to feel confident about opening her own stable. Now they were engaged in a war of nerves. He was determined to have her; she was determined to resist him.

Candy had been certain she could hold her own against any efforts Garth made to seduce her. As she had just discovered, things weren't turning out quite like she had planned. She made up her mind that she, for one, wasn't going to be the next tempting morsel on Garth Whitelaw's plate. Because as she knew from bitter experience, the wrangler ate up little rich girls, and spit them out when he was done.

Four

Charlie One Horse was bent over, checking the pot roast in the oven, when Candy came through the kitchen on her way upstairs. She mumbled something about washing up and disappeared in the direction of the stairs. Charlie took one look at Garth's face as he stepped through the screen door and poured him a whiskey from the bottle he kept over the stove. "What you been doin' to that girl got her so mad she whacked you?"

Garth rubbed his cheek, wondering how Charlie knew he had been slapped. To his chagrin, he felt several scratches left by Candy's nails. "Stay out of it, Charlie." Garth sat down at the heavy oak table in the center of the kitchen. He downed the finger of whiskey and held out his glass for another.

"She ain't like them other women of yours," Charlie said as he poured the second whiskey.

"Candy knew what she was getting into when she agreed to come here," Garth said. "Let it go, Charlie. This is none of your business."

"Ain't nothin' ever my business, but I'm the one gotta put up with your bad temper when some female's givin' you fits."

"Charlie." Garth's voice held a warning tone that made the housekeeper look behind him. Candy was standing in the kitchen doorway.

"Are we eating in here?" she asked.

"You can forget the silver and crystal," Garth said. "You're not a guest at Hawk's Way anymore."

Candy stuck her hands in the pockets of her jeans to hide her agitation. "I wasn't expecting any special treatment. I was just asking where supper is being served."

"I'm afraid I have to disappoint you there, too," Garth said. "The food's on the stove. Every man helps himself."

Charlie shot Garth an incredulous look. That was the first he had heard of such a practice. When the family was home they ate supper in the dining room. Charlie usually served the meal, although Tate or Faron sometimes took a turn.

Charlie picked up a pair of pot holders, took the pot roast out of the oven and plopped it on top of the stove. He looked pointedly at Garth. "Here it is. Dig in."

Garth gave Charlie a baleful stare which the old man ignored.

Charlie took out two plates and filled them with roast beef, potatoes and carrots. He handed one plate to Candy and took the other for himself, then made sure they had silverware and glasses of tea. He settled on a chair on the opposite side of the table from Garth and pulled out a chair next to him for Candy.

"Delicious," Candy said as she dug in. "You really are a good cook, Charlie."

"Thanks, girl."

Garth was torn between his hunger and his pride. Finally he got up and served himself a plate of food. "We'll start work at dawn tomorrow," he said to Candy. "You might as well learn how and what we feed our stock."

"Don't you hire people to take care of that sort of thing?" Candy asked.

"Sure," Garth said. "But somebody has to tell them what to do. Parasite prevention, fresh water, proteins, vitamins and minerals and the right amount of forage are all as important as the right amount and kind of feed."

Candy felt a little overwhelmed. "Am I going to learn all that?"

"That's up to you. But it's as true of horses as it is of humans— you are what you eat. If you want healthy animals, you have to pay attention to nutrition."

Candy nodded her head in understanding. "I see what you mean. All right. Is there some sort of literature that explains all that?"

Charlie exchanged a look with Garth. Apparently there was more to the spoiled little rich girl than met the eye.

Garth had known Candy was clever. Now she had proved she was also inquisitive, which was not a bad trait for a pupil. "Sure," he said. "I've got lots of stuff you can read. If you come into the parlor with me after supper—"

Candy nearly choked on a bite of food. Charlie slapped her on the back, but it took a moment for her to stop coughing. She wasn't about to follow that beast back into his den anytime soon.

Garth swore under his breath when he realized that Candy's memory of their encounter three years ago was as vivid as his own. He stood, leaving his food half finished. "I'll put the books on my desk. You can get them on your way upstairs later. I'm going out."

"Where you goin'?" Charlie asked. "You gotta be up early in the mornin'."

"None of your business," Garth snapped. He grabbed his hat from the rack by the back door and slapped it on his head, letting the screen door slam behind him. Then he turned right back around and stomped back through the kitchen into the parlor. They could hear books dropping on his desk. A moment later he returned. "Don't stay up late reading," he snarled. Then he was gone.

"Wonder what got into him," Charlie muttered.

Candy wasn't about to explain. She was grateful for Garth's willingness to provide the books, which led her to believe that even if he intended to pursue her, he also intended to uphold his end of the bargain.

She stayed in the kitchen long enough to help Charlie with the dishes, even though the old man said he could manage. "Things are easier when there's another pair of helping hands," Candy said as she scraped the remains of Garth's supper into the disposal.

Charlie handed her his plate and said, "I didn't think rich folks did their own dishes."

Candy smiled wryly. "My father raised me to believe in the work ethic. If he spoiled me, it was by making me believe that I could have anything I wanted if I was willing to work hard enough for it."

"So why you want to go into the horse-raisin' business?" Charlie asked.

"There's a lot of history and tradition involved with cutting horses. I want to be a part of it."

"You got all the money a gal would ever need. Why not just buy up a ranch and let somebody else manage it for you?"

"I want the satisfaction of breeding my own horses and training them to be champions. That's why I came here." She refused to admit to any other reason than her stated one, even to herself.

"Then you better get on out of here and get to those books," Charlie said. "I'll finish up."

Candy didn't want to leave, but she found herself unable to fight both Charlie and the desire to dig into the materials Garth had left for her on his desk.

It felt strange stepping into the parlor. Looking back, she wondered where she had gotten the courage to confront Garth Whitelaw and tell him she loved him. She felt extreme embarrassment—and a great sense of loss—when she looked back on that evening.

The fireplace was as cold now as it had been that long-ago night, no more than a blackened hearth. She walked up to the mantel, above which hung a map that delineated the vast borders of Hawk's Way past and present. Someday she would have a place of her own, and in the years to come her children and grandchildren would be able to point back to the moment when she had taken that first step.

Candy crossed to the rolltop desk where Whitelaw business had been conducted over the past hundred years. There sat a stack of books and pamphlets nearly a foot high. She picked up the one on top and read: *Horse Feeding and Management.* And another: *Rules of Thumb for Equine Feeding.* And another: *Feed a Horse Like a Horse.* She thumbed through a thick book as she crossed to the leather chair by the fireplace. She turned on the standing lamp beside the chair, sat down and put her feet up on the rawhide stool at its foot and began to read.

Garth was calling himself seven kinds of a fool for leaving the comfort of his home to drive around in his pickup. He hadn't had any specific destination in mind when he had left, only the desperate need to escape. So naturally he found an excuse not to go anyplace when all he really wanted to do was return home. Near midnight Garth decided that Candy must surely be in bed, and he would have the parlor to himself for a drink, which he sorely needed.

Because Garth believed everyone to be asleep, he entered the house quietly. He headed straight for the parlor, but was brought up short when he realized there was still a light on in the room. He crossed the threshold with matching amounts of reluctance and eagerness, afraid of what he might find.

She was there.

Candy was sound asleep, stretched out in his chair. One bare foot rested on the rawhide stool. The other was draped over the arm of the chair. Her boots were strewn like fallen soldiers beside the stool. A book lay open across her stomach, and her cheek rested on her hand on the arm of the chair.

She looked young and vulnerable, and he felt a sudden anger that she should be there waiting for him. He approached her like a wolf drawn by the bait, but wary of the steel jaws of the trap waiting to snap shut on him.

He knelt beside the chair and softly called her name. "Candy."

She made a sound in her throat which he took to be a subconscious acknowledgment of his presence, but otherwise she didn't move.

He knew he should wake her up and send her to bed, but he couldn't resist the opportunity to look at her at his leisure. He had never before noticed the tiny wisps of hair at her temples or the mole just below her ear or the slight jut of her chin. Her lashes created a feathery coal crescent along cheeks that bore the tiniest of freckles. The fingernails that had scratched him were her own, cut short and covered with a clear polish.

He ran a finger over lips that looked as sweet as strawberries. She instinctively turned her face toward his caress, much as a baby might when nudged by a mother's breast. Garth's physical reaction was powerful and instantaneous. He bit back the oath that sought voice. The last thing he wanted was to wake her up so she could see him on his knees looking every bit like he was worshiping at her feet. Not that he was. He just found her fascinating to look at.

He picked up the book on her lap, closed it and set it on top of a stack of six or seven beside the chair. Apparently she had done a lot of reading while he was gone. The more he learned about Candy Baylor the less certain he became of who she really was. None of the growing list of adjectives he could apply to her left him feeling the least bit satisfied. He didn't want to admire her intelligence or her curiosity or her determination. He wanted to enjoy a romp in bed with her.

Garth knew he could probably arouse Candy enough while she slumbered that by the time she was completely awake she would gladly join him in bed. He found himself strangely reluctant to take advantage of her that way. Which made him wonder what it was about Candy Baylor that kept him from acting the way he normally would with any other woman.

She wasn't the most beautiful woman he had ever known, though she was pretty enough. Perhaps it was the way she looked at him with those light gray eyes of hers that caused that achy feeling in his chest. Not that she used them to flirt with—at least, not this time around. They were clear and honest and there was nothing of the deceit he had expected—and often found—in other women.

Perhaps it was the fact that she absorbed everything he taught her like a sponge. Or that she didn't mind getting her hands dirty. Or ruining an expensive silk shirt. Or eating supper at the kitchen table when he was idiot enough to suggest that that was how they did things at Hawk's Way.

He wondered what would have happened if he had taken her up on her offer three years ago. What if he had made love to her— really made love to her—both giving and accepting the love she offered in return?

Garth felt his stomach clench and recognized the feeling as cold, stark fear. He had seen how his mother's unfaithfulness eventually destroyed his father. The old man had gotten drunk every night to forget the pain. One day he hadn't quite sobered up before he went to work and had come off a bucking horse and broken his neck. Garth had been left with the responsibility of holding both Hawk's Way and the family together.

Garth had made a vow that he would never let himself care for any woman enough that she could destroy him the way his father had been destroyed. In the years since his mother's infidelity he hadn't allowed himself to even think of a woman in terms of love.

Until he had met Candy Baylor.

Garth hadn't realized the emptiness, the loneliness he had felt over the past three years until she came back into his life. It was getting harder every day to convince himself that all he felt for her was desire.

Which made him all the more convinced that what he ought to do was get her bedded and out of his life before his feelings for her made him as vulnerable to a broken heart as his father had been.

Garth considered leaving Candy where she was. One look at the awkward angle of her neck convinced him that if he did, she wouldn't be much use to him in the morning. He slid one arm under her shoulders and scooped up her legs with the other. As he stood, she rolled down his arms and settled against his chest. Her face burrowed against him, and she said something unintelligible in her sleep.

In vain, Garth fought the feelings of possessiveness and protectiveness that rose within him. He hugged her a little closer and dropped a kiss on her forehead. "Come on, sweetheart. It's time for bed."

"Good night," she mumbled.

He carried her up the stairs and down the hall. The hardest thing he had ever done in his life was to stop at her bedroom door rather than traveling two steps farther to his own. He reached out with two fingers and dragged the spread off the bed before he laid her on it. She immediately curled into a ball on her side and murmured a sigh of satisfaction.

He would have loved to undress her, but he didn't trust his willpower that far. He pulled the spread back up over her shoulder, set the alarm clock beside the bed for 5:00 a.m. and left the room, closing the door behind him.

The next morning, the look on Candy's face was sheepish when she arrived in the kitchen for breakfast.

"Did you put me to bed?" she asked Garth.

Garth grunted his assent.

"Thank you. I guess I fell asleep. I'm sorry to be a bother."

"Next time go to bed when you're tired," he said.

Candy winced at the irritation in his voice.

"Did you learn anything?" he asked.

Candy gave him an excited recitation on equine digestion that ended with, "I had no idea all of that went on inside a horse."

Garth couldn't help smiling at her enthusiasm. She talked the whole distance to the barn and asked surprisingly astute questions as he and one of the hands, a young man named Tom Handy, fed the horses in the stable.

"Who feeds the horses in the north pasture?" she asked.

"Tom will take care of that. We've got other business to do to-day."

"Oh?"

"How would you like to take a turn on Stop and Go?"

Candy stared at him. "You're going to let me ride him?"

"I'd rather you started with a horse who knows what he's doing while I teach you the basics. Then I'll give you a horse of your own to bring along from scratch," Garth explained.

Candy hadn't expected to be allowed to work one of Garth's horses so soon. Although when she thought about it, how else was Garth going to teach her to train cutting horses except to put her on an animal and give her instructions about what she was doing right and wrong?

Two hours later, Candy was having second thoughts about riding, cutting horses and Garth Whitelaw, in that order.

Garth touched her constantly. All under the guise of teaching her, of course. The position of her hands, the angle of her heels, the shape of her shoulders, nothing escaped his notice. When he wasn't touching her, he was barking orders.

"When the cow goes, you go. When the cow stops, you stop. Back the horse up to reinforce the stop!"

Candy had grabbed the saddle horn and hung on, using her knees to let the horse know what she wanted from him.

"Stay down in the saddle. Push your pelvis forward. Not like that! Hold up there."

Garth marched out to her and put a hand on her rear end and a hand on her belly. "Tuck in your rear end. Sit deep in the saddle and stay with the horse's movement. Understand?"

Candy was so flustered by the feel of Garth's hands on her where no other man had ever dared put them, that she couldn't find her voice to object.

"Understand?" he demanded.

Candy nodded. "You can take your hands off me now."

Garth seemed to realize suddenly where his hands were. To Candy's chagrin he drew them away slowly, making his touch a caress. She closed her eyes and bit her lip to keep from moaning.

When she opened her eyes again, Garth was on the other side of the fence. Apparently he had recognized the danger, as well.

"Concentrate on getting the horse to travel with the cow. Keep his head aimed at the cow's shoulder."

Candy nudged Stop and Go with her knees.

"Don't pressure the cow!" Garth warned.

Candy backed the horse off slightly.

"Now you're too late!" Garth remonstrated. "Travel with the cow. Travel with the cow!"

Candy was more exhausted than Stop and Go when the training session was over, but she believed both she and the horse were doing better. She waited for a word of praise from Garth. It didn't come.

"Unsaddle him and wash him down," Garth ordered. "When you get done come back, and you can watch me with the two-year-old I'm working."

"Yes, sir, your highness," Candy muttered as she rode past Garth out of the corral.

She hadn't thought she had spoken loud enough to be heard. An instant later Garth had yanked her out of the saddle, and she was standing on the ground in front of him.

"There's no royalty around here, sweetheart. Just hard-working cowboys. If you've got a problem with that, we can finish the business between ourselves, and you can skedaddle on home."

Garth emphasized his point by pulling Candy into his arms and kissing her hard. Candy kept her teeth clenched, but he used his hands on her cheeks to force her mouth open so he could thrust his tongue inside. He wasn't gentle, and she had the feeling he wanted her to fight him.

Candy was smarter than that. She kissed him back. She slipped her tongue into his mouth and tasted him the way he had tasted her. It was a toss-up which of them was more surprised by what she had done. Desire speared through her, powerful and demanding.

She forced herself to think, rather than feel. This was a war of nerves as much as a seduction. She was determined not to succumb to the desire that demanded satisfaction. If anybody cried uncle, it wasn't going to be her.

Every place Garth touched her, she touched him back.

Shoulders. Arms. Chest. Buttocks.

Both of them were gasping when he broke the kiss at last.

"Damn you, girl! You've left that horse standing there with the sweat drying on him. Take care of him!"

Candy was furious at Garth's accusation. He was as much responsible for the horse being left unattended as she was. But she wasn't about to lose her temper and give Garth a reason either to send her packing or seduce her further. "Next time stay out of my way!" she snapped as she crossed past him.

Garth stared after Candy as she picked up the reins and led the cutting horse back around behind the barn. He was shaken by how close he had come to having her right here in the open. Never had he become aroused so quickly or so completely from a woman's touch. When he was with her he felt like he was riding the edge of a steep cliff. It wasn't going to take much more to shove him off.

Similar thoughts were running through Candy's mind. She had never understood the power of her passions. It wasn't the least bit comforting to know that all Garth had to do was touch her and she responded. From the way things had gone today, every lesson was going to be a trial.

Over the next several weeks Candy realized that she had been mistaken about her feelings for Garth. To her horror, she discovered that the infatuation she had felt for him at seventeen wasn't gone at all. It had always been there, buried somewhere beneath the embarrassment and humiliation she had suffered that evening in his arms.

Every time Garth touched her—and he touched her as often as he could find an excuse—she was forced to deal not only with her body's instant reaction to his physical presence, but the growing knowledge that her heart and mind were equally involved with the man.

Candy knew the day was coming when Garth would push her too far, and she would have to make a choice. Candy couldn't decide whether it would hurt more to make love to him when she knew he didn't love her, or to leave and know that she could never come back.

During breakfast on the Fourth of July, Charlie One Horse announced that he was spending the holiday in Amarillo where he could see the parade and the fireworks.

"You two wanta come along?" Charlie asked.

"We've got work to do," Garth answered him.

Candy laughed. "It's a holiday. Surely we can—" The fierce look in Garth's dark eyes cut her off.

Garth turned to Charlie and said, "We'll be staying here."

Charlie shrugged. "Suit yourselves."

When Candy heard Charlie's rattletrap truck heading down the magnolia-lined lane, a frisson of alarm ran down her spine. It dawned on her suddenly that the old man had provided a much-needed buffer between her and Garth. Now that buffer was gone.

The difference was immediately noticeable. There was a subtle tension between them that made the horses skittish. Stop and Go performed badly, and Candy had to bite her tongue to keep from apologizing for what wasn't her fault.

"That's enough."

Garth's order, coming as it did long before sunset, told Candy she wasn't the only one who had noticed the difference. He followed her inside and watched her with hooded eyes while she unsaddled the horse and put away the tack. Then, for the first time since she had come to Hawk's Way, Garth joined her when she took Stop and Go out back to rinse him off.

Naturally, with Garth watching her, Candy was all thumbs.

"I'll do that," he volunteered.

Candy gratefully handed him the hose and was surprised when he turned it on her.

She stared at him aghast. Water dripped from her eyelashes, nose and chin. Her blouse was plastered to her body. "What did you do that for?" she spluttered.

Garth grinned. "I figured you needed to cool off, too."

It only took Candy two seconds to reach Garth and another two seconds to wrestle the hose in his direction. The two of them drenched each other, laughing over who was getting the wettest.

"We'd better go get dried off," Garth said at last.

Candy followed the direction of his gaze. She looked down and realized he could see her bra through her shirt. From the avid look in Garth's eyes, she knew he was seeing more than a hint of lace. If she could see his nipples through his soaked shirt, she suspected her bra wasn't doing a much better job of keeping her concealed. A flush rose from her throat to stain her cheeks.

Candy decided that going into the house with Garth right now wasn't such a good idea. "What about Stop and Go? We can't leave him here like this."

"Tom can take care of him."

Candy froze. It was unheard of for Garth to leave an animal untended that either of them had ridden.

"Let's go," he said.

Garth held out his hand to Candy. There was no mistaking where he was taking her, or what he had in mind when he got there. This was it, Candy thought, the moment of truth. Should she go with him, or dig in her heels and stay where she was? It was a decision she had been dreading for weeks.

She knew there might be pain waiting for her at the end of the road. Garth had rejected her love once before. But there was no denying the strength of her feelings, then or now. When all was said and done, Candy followed her heart. She placed her hand in Garth's. When a woman was in love, there really wasn't any choice at all.

Five

Garth headed straight for the house. They were both drenched, so to avoid leaving two sets of wet tracks on the tile floor in the kitchen or on the hardwood throughout the rest of the house, he lifted Candy into his arms and headed upstairs. He didn't even hesitate when he passed her bedroom door, just continued on to his own.

Garth set her down with her back to him and put his hands on her shoulders. Whether he did it to comfort her or to keep her from fleeing she wasn't sure.

Candy had never been in Garth's room, but she looked at it now, searching for anything that would tell her about the man she loved.

The first thing she noticed was how neat it was. That didn't really surprise her. Garth was a man who liked to be in control. He would want things where he could find them.

She was glad to see the pictures of his family, his sister and brothers, in frames on the various wooden surfaces around the room. There was also a picture of an older man, whom she supposed was Garth's father. She wondered why there was no picture of his mother.

Candy found hope in the fact that family was important to Garth. It was proof that he could care for people as much as he cared about horses. Whether he could love one woman and commit himself to her for a lifetime was another matter altogether.

His room was full of antiques, pieces of Whitelaw history that had been handed down from father to son. She had never doubted that Garth valued the traditions of his family. Which made her wonder whether he had ever considered how he could pass on those traditions to another generation of Whitelaws when he had so little respect for women and no use at all for a wife.

He slept in a huge four-poster bed covered with a patterned quilt. She stared at the bed, unable to take her eyes off it.

"Candy?"

His voice was low, intense, as demanding as it was challenging.

She suddenly had second thoughts about what she had come here to do. "I suppose there have been a lot of women in this bed."

"Yes, there have."

Candy's heart dropped to her feet as she thought of all the women Garth must have brought here.

"My mother, my grandmother, my great-grandmother—"

Her heart swelled with joy. So this bed was reserved for Whitelaw women. Surely the fact that he had brought her to this room, to this bed, meant he felt something special for her. And maybe, just maybe, she would be able to get him to admit those feelings.

Candy turned slowly to face Garth. In his dark eyes, whether he knew it or not, was a need so fierce it sent a shiver of anticipation running through her.

"Make love to me, Garth."

He had been in such a hurry to get them here, she expected him to be impatient. Candy wouldn't have been surprised if he had simply ripped off her clothes and taken her in a fury of desire. It was infinitely worse waiting the endless moments it took him to undo her shirt one button at a time.

The wet cotton clung to her skin as he pushed the shirt off her shoulders. Candy shrugged and tugged at the sleeves to help him rid her of the garment.

With practiced hands he unsnapped the catch of her bra and pushed it out of his way—reminding her how experienced he was and how little she knew about what was to come. She caught his wrist when he reached for the zipper of her jeans.

"Your turn," she said in a shaky voice. Candy reached up and began unbuttoning his shirt. Her fingers were trembling, so it took longer than it should have, but he didn't interfere with her efforts.

At long last the buttons were free, and she reached up to shove the shirt off his shoulders. Her hands skimmed across flesh that was smooth and warm. She felt his muscles bunch beneath her fingertips in response to her touch.

Intrigued by Garth's reaction, she slid her hands across his chest, playing with the dark curls there. They formed a triangle that headed down into jeans that hung low on his hips. His belly contracted as she skimmed past it.

He grabbed her wrists with enough strength that she shot a surprised look at him. His dark eyes were hooded, his nostrils flared for the scent of her, his facial muscles taut.

"Did I do something wrong?" Candy asked.

"I want to take my time," he said. "The way you were heading, things would have been over too damn fast."

Candy shivered again, only this time from the chill caused by the air-conditioning on her damp skin.

"Come on." Garth took her hand and led her toward a large, modern bathroom attached to his bedroom. Before Candy could object he had both her and himself completely stripped. She caught one quick and somewhat awe-inspiring—glimpse of aroused male before he propelled her into the shower and followed after her.

The warm water felt wonderful. Candy closed her eyes and luxuriated in the feel of it on her back and shoulders. Her eyes blinked open when she felt Garth's hands on her as well. Every feeling was new and exquisite, and yet it felt so right to be here with him that she welcomed each sensation.

Garth's hands slid over her breasts to her belly and then around to her buttocks. He tightened his arms around her, fitting their bodies together. There was no mistaking the hard length of him, even for someone as inexperienced as she was.

"Candy," he murmured. His mouth nuzzled against her brow as his hands slid up her back to hold her tight. "You taste sweet, girl."

Candy's flesh burned everywhere it met his. Her hands roamed over his back as she caressed him the way she had yearned to all those years ago. "Garth, I—"

Candy hesitated, uncertain whether she ought to admit she was a virgin. It didn't really matter, she reasoned. In a few more minutes she wouldn't be one anymore.

"What is it, sweetheart?"

"Shouldn't we be doing this in bed?" she asked in a husky voice.

Garth laughed, a deep, resonant sound she could feel because he was holding her so close. "I just wanted to make sure you didn't catch a chill."

This time Candy laughed. "Believe me, I'm warm now."

Garth wasted no time getting them out of the shower. He wrapped Candy in his white terry-cloth robe and dried himself with a large towel which he knotted around his waist. He picked her up again and carried her into the bedroom.

"I can walk," Candy protested.

"I know, but I like the feel of you in my arms." Garth stopped beside the bed and bent so she could reach the covers. "Get the quilt, sweetheart."

Candy reached out and pulled the patterned quilt away to reveal pristine white sheets. She froze, thinking how they would look stained with virgin's blood. She opened her mouth to tell him the truth, and he kissed her quick and hard. The ferocity of the kiss left her gasping.

A moment later she was in bed, and Garth was lying beside her. She might have wished for darkness, because she felt naked even with Garth's robe surrounding her. But she wouldn't have missed for anything the look in Garth's dark eyes as he reached out and spread the two halves of the robe and feasted his eyes on her.

"You're so beautiful."

Candy was overwhelmed with sensations as Garth's callused fingertips explored her body, beginning at her collarbone and heading downward between her breasts. He circled them, teasing her nipples before trailing his hand down across her belly.

Candy's body arched upward under his caresses. She pulled the towel away from his hips so flesh met flesh. Then she grabbed hold of Garth's shoulders and held on. His dark eyes never left hers as his hands, and then his warm, wet mouth, roamed her body. She made a small sound in her throat as Garth's hand slipped down between her legs.

Instinctively she tightened her thighs to prevent his invasion.

"Relax, sweetheart. You're acting just like a—"

Candy did the first thing she could think of to distract him, so he wouldn't realize the truth. Her hand slid down his belly and encircled him. She was surprised to discover he was hard and soft all at the same time.

"Whoa, Candy! Go slow, sweetheart."

Candy had no idea what the difference was between fast and slow. But she forced herself to relax, and his hand slid between her legs.

Candy gasped at the intimate contact as he slid a finger inside her.

"You're so tight. Just like a—"

Candy could see it was going to take constant distraction to keep him from getting suspicious. She did what came naturally. She pulled his head down and kissed him to shut him up. She moaned deep in her throat when his tongue mimicked the thrust and parry of lovers truly joined.

His voice was harsh when he broke the kiss. "Dammit, Candy! I want to be inside you."

"I want you, too, Garth," she murmured breathlessly.

He spread her legs with his knees and thrust hard.

Her body resisted for a second before the barrier tore, and he sank to the hilt inside her. Candy bit her lip until it bled, but a whimper of pain escaped.

Garth muttered an oath. "A virgin! I should have known. What a fool I am!"

Candy wrapped her legs around Garth and held tight to his shoulders. "It's done now, and there's no going back. Please, Garth. Make love to me."

"I'll hurt you."

"No, you won't."

Garth knew he was making a mistake. He ought to get out while the getting was good. He hadn't asked if she was protected, he had simply assumed she was. The kind of woman he normally took to bed wasn't about to take the chance of getting pregnant. Candy had been a virgin. It was a good bet she hadn't taken any precautions to prevent pregnancy, and he sure as hell hadn't, either.

But right now he wanted her with a need that was beyond anything he had ever felt before in his life. Stopping was out of the question. If there were consequences, he would deal with them. "All right, little rich girl," he said. "You've got what you wanted. Now let's see how you handle it."

Garth moved slightly and saw her wince. "Dammit! I *am* hurting you!"

He started to withdraw, but Candy stopped him again. "It's all right, really. It's just…I'm not used to… You're so big that I—"

She flushed a bright red.

Garth chuckled. "All right, sweetheart. Let's start over again."

She arched a questioning brow. "Is that possible?"

He nudged his hips against hers, and Candy felt a spiral of desire twist inside her belly. Her breasts tingled. It appeared it was more than possible.

"I'm not in any hurry," Garth said with a grin. "Let's go back a few steps."

Candy didn't understand at first what Garth meant. Five… fifteen…thirty minutes later she was writhing with pleasure beneath him. He was still inside her, but there wasn't a spot on her body he hadn't caressed, licked, bitten, sucked or kissed.

Of course, she hadn't been idle. She had learned how to touch him in ways that pushed him close to the edge. His body was covered with a fine sheen of sweat, and she could see the strain in his face as he delayed the culmination of his own pleasure to make sure she reached the pinnacle of desire.

He seemed in no hurry. He drove her to the edge only to back off again. At last she thought she would go mad if he didn't finish what he had started.

"Now!" she insisted. "Now, Garth!"

Those were the words he had been waiting to hear. Garth thrust slow and easy at first, but Candy wouldn't allow him to be gentle. Her fingernails left crescents in his flesh as she arched under him. He slipped a hand between them and found the tiny nubbin that was so sensitive by now that it took only a bare touch to set her off.

He felt her squeezing him, the tight muscles contracting around him until he could barely stand the pleasure. It was Candy's guttural cry of delight that freed him to find his own satisfaction. His head arched back and his body tautened as he released his seed in powerful racking spasms.

As Garth relaxed his weight on top of her, Candy wrapped her arms around him. She felt good. She felt wonderful. She felt loved.

"I love you," she whispered.

She felt him stiffen immediately. He took his weight on his palms and stared down at her.

"I don't want to hear that any more now than I did three years ago,'' he said in a harsh voice. ''That was sex, sweetheart. You asked for it, and you got it.''

Candy turned her head away to hide her distress. It was impossible to speak over the lump in her throat.

Fool! Fool! You should have known he had no heart. You should have protected yourself better!

Maybe he can change. Maybe all he needs is a woman to love him just for himself and not ask anything in return.

Right! And if you believe that, I've got a spavined horse I'd like to sell you.

''I'm not asking you for anything,'' she managed to say.

''That's good. Because I'm not offering anything,'' he said. ''You should have told me you'd never been with a man!''

''Would it have made any difference?''

''Damn straight! I don't make a habit of deflowering virgins!''

She smiled slightly. ''But you do it so well!''

''That isn't funny!'' he snarled.

Her smile widened. ''Oh, I don't know. I find the idea pretty amusing.''

''I could have hurt you!''

''But you didn't.'' She put her hands on either side of his face and forced him to look into her eyes. ''You brought me a great deal of pleasure. I'm not asking for any more than that, Garth. Truly I'm not. I know you don't love me.'' She swallowed to try and force down the thickness in her throat. ''But you enjoy making love to me. If it's what we both want, where's the harm?''

Garth knew where the harm was. The harm was that he wanted her as much now—more now—than he had before they made love. That had never happened to him. Once the chase was over, he usually tired of the woman quickly. With Candy, all she had to do was look at him, and he was hard all over again. At his age that was nothing short of miraculous.

He told himself he might as well take advantage of her while she was here. Once she learned what she needed to know to run her own stable of cutting horses she would be gone. He felt that same awful weight on his chest he had felt three years ago. He rolled onto his back and pulled her on top of him.

He tunneled his hands up into her hair and tugged her mouth down to his. He kissed her fiercely, letting her feel his anger and his frustration. Her hands soothed him as they spread across his chest and set him on fire at the same time. How was that possible?

His hands slid down her back to her buttocks. He grabbed hold, leaving fingerprints where his hands had been as he lifted her and impaled her on his shaft.

Garth sighed in satisfaction as he slid inside her. Wet. Warm. Tight. How could she be ready for him so soon? His lips twisted. Probably the same way he was ready for her. They were made for each other. Man and his mate.

His mate.

Garth denied the strength of his feelings for Candy Baylor. She was just like every other woman. She wasn't to be trusted. Give your heart to a female, and she would crush it beneath her high-heeled boots. Garth Whitelaw was never going to fall for any woman. Least of all some spoiled little rich girl.

Garth sat up and pulled Candy's legs around him. His hands tangled in her hair, and he held her captive for his kiss. His tongue searched her mouth for the sweetness that he couldn't seem to get enough of. He groaned as her tongue slipped into his mouth, tasting lips and teeth and seeking equal pleasure.

Garth took Candy to sensual heights she had never imagined as they made love through the afternoon. She reveled in his touch, and touched him in return. The loving was fierce and wild and left them both overwhelmed by tumultuous feelings that threatened an already-fragile relationship.

At last Candy lay asleep in Garth's arms, exhausted by the day's pleasures. Garth lay staring at the ceiling, appalled by how vulnerable he felt. He had never before experienced what had happened in this bedroom with Candice Baylor. He had exhausted himself and her, and still he wanted her. The truth could no longer be denied. His need for her was more than sexual. It seemed to come from deep inside.

He couldn't bear the thought of any other man ever laughing with her, holding her, loving her. His feelings were totally irrational, of course. But he knew he would kill the man who touched her. Such powerful emotions left him feeling agitated. And angry.

He shook Candy. "Wake up!"

Candy woke from a dream in which Garth had just told her he loved her, so there was a soft smile on her face as she looked up at him with sleepy eyes. "What is it, Garth?" Her hand smoothed over his chest, luxuriating in the feel of him.

Garth cursed when his body—wrung out from a day of making love to her—immediately hardened with need. He grabbed a handful of Candy's blond hair and pulled her head back at a painful angle.

"What's wrong, Garth?"

She didn't struggle, didn't swear or strike out against his strength. She lay there in his arms, looking up at him with love and concern. Garth felt that now-familiar tightening in his chest. He forced himself to ignore it. He was fighting for his life.

"I'm not the marrying kind," he said through gritted teeth. "I want one thing from you. Just one thing!" He laid her down and thrust inside her.

He cried out in an agony of pleasure as Candy arched up to receive him, welcoming him, taking all of him and asking for whatever more he had to give.

She was a witch, and he was ensorceled by her. That was the only explanation for the excruciating need he felt for this particular woman. There was no time for thinking once he was inside her, or for talking, either. He thrust and she parried, taking and giving pleasure, fast and hard and deep, until he heard her cry out and joined her in reaching a plateau of pleasure beyond any they had sought or expected to find.

As he lay panting above her, his body sweat-slick and musky from their lovemaking, he said, "So long as you're at Hawk's Way, you belong to me."

"All right, Garth."

Her demure response did little to ease Garth's anxiousness. "Anytime you want to cut and leave, it'll be fine by me."

"We have a deal," Candy said. "You promised to teach me what you know about cutting horses."

"And I will."

"Then I don't see that we have anything to argue about."

Garth stared at her suspiciously. There was something wrong with her logic, although he hadn't yet figured it out. "Just so we understand each other," Garth said. "From now on you'll sleep in here with me."

Candy snuggled closer to him. "All right, Garth."

Garth pulled her tight and closed his eyes. A few moments later, sated at long last, he slept.

Candy was wide awake.

She stared beyond Garth's shoulder to the framed picture of the older man, a man without a woman by his side. She knew some people would tell her she was tilting at windmills to even hope that she could change Garth's attitude about women—about having a wife.

But he had brought her here to the bed of his forebears, and when he had discovered her virginity he hadn't tossed her out. In fact, he had made love to her again and again. Sex was a strong lure, one women had used for aeons. Candy was not above using every source of ammunition she had to lay claim to her man.

She would love him so much he wouldn't be able to live without her. She would succeed where every other woman had failed. She would wait him out. Sooner or later Garth would have to admit that what they had done wasn't *having sex,* it was *making love.* Then he would ask her to be his wife.

She just had to make sure all that happened before she learned everything she needed to know to start her own stable. Otherwise, he might kick her out before she was ready to go. Well, Garth's deft, capable pupil might suddenly have to become all thumbs.

Six

"He's so savage! How can you hope to tame him?" Candy's eyes anxiously sought Garth's, then skipped back to the black stallion that was rearing and kicking and screaming his fury in the corral. "Is there a way to make him trust humans again?"

"It will take time. And patience. Maybe even that won't be enough. Señor Santos sent Midnight to me because none of his men could do anything with the horse."

"What made him so mean?" Candy asked.

"Probably somebody beat him once upon a time. Santos bought him at auction, but the horse had gone through three or four owners by then, so there's no telling, really."

Candy was aghast. "Beat him! How could anyone be so cruel?"

Garth's lips pursed. "You're living in a dreamworld if you think there aren't people out there who mistreat animals. It's too bad. Santos said if I couldn't tame that black beast he'd have to put him down."

"Oh, no, Garth! You can't let him be killed!" Candy grasped the wrangler's arm as though to stop him from such an action. She felt a jolt of electricity the instant she touched him. Candy stared up into Garth's dark eyes and saw that he was as aroused as she was by the simple contact. "You can tame him. I know you can!"

"I don't have the time to waste," Garth said. "Santos didn't tell me what bad shape the horse is in, or I never would have let him ship the stud here.''

"I've got the time!'' Candy said. ''I'll do it. If you'll just tell me what to do.''

Garth frowned. ''I don't know. You need to concentrate on learning what you came here to learn.''

Candy flushed with embarrassment. Garth hadn't said it aloud, but over the past week her learning curve had dipped considerably. She had manipulated the slowdown purposely, of course. But Garth didn't know that.

"I—I can learn,'' she stuttered. ''This is important to me, Garth. Please let me try.''

Garth scrutinized the magnificent quarter horse stallion. ''He's a good-looking animal. It would be a shame to put him down.''

"It's settled, then,'' Candy said. ''I'll work with him.'' She put her arms around Garth's waist and hugged him. ''Thanks, Garth.''

Garth folded Candy into his embrace. ''Don't think it's going to be a picnic, because it isn't.''

"Oh, I know that. But if Midnight can be tamed, you'll show me how to do it.''

"I'm glad you have so much confidence in me.'' Garth was appalled by how good her compliment made him feel. It was one more sign of what he had begun to recognize as his growing dependence on her. He wasn't sure how it had happened, because nothing had changed in his life. At least not where outward appearances were concerned.

He still worked from dawn to dusk, only with Candy by his side. After supper in the dining room—he hadn't been stubborn fool enough to insist they keep on eating in the kitchen—he and Candy would retire to the parlor where she would read and he would work on the business end of his business. Then they would retire to his bedroom, where he would make love to her once or twice or sometimes even three times in a night.

She was always willing, and she had learned enough over the past week to incite him to passions even he hadn't known he was capable of. He felt his loins tighten as vivid memories of their lovemaking replayed in his head. The tastes, the scents, the sounds all combined to bring him to full arousal.

"Damn!''

Candy looked up at him. "What's wrong?" Then she looked down and said, "Oh. Again?"

"Again. Always. Constantly."

She grinned. "I think it's kind of cute."

He shook his head and laughed. "You would." His body concealed hers from the cowboys who were working nearby. He slipped his hand between them and cupped her breast, running his thumb across the nipple, which peaked instantly.

Candy made a tiny, kittenish sound in her throat and repaid him by sliding her hand across the hard ridge in his jeans. "Two can play that game," she teased.

They touched each other, hands pressing, pinching, playing, always careful to keep what they were doing hidden from the men who worked around them.

Only they might as well not have wasted their time. There wasn't a cowhand at Hawk's Way who didn't know the boss had a soft spot for Candy Baylor, and any look crosswise at her was a sure way to find oneself booted off the ranch.

Candy was breathless by the time Garth called a halt to their sensual play. He simply pulled her into his arms and hugged her tight.

"We've got work to do, woman," he growled in her ear. He turned her and gave her a little shove in the direction of the stable.

As they fed the horses their evening ration of grain and alfalfa hay, Candy asked, "Will you tell me what I should do first, where I should start, to tame the stud?"

"I'd leave him outside in the corral, give him some room to move around. Don't hedge him in too close."

Candy nodded her head. She could do that.

"You should be the one to feed and water him, no one else. Talk to him when you do. Keep it soft, something soothing."

"All right."

"Then you can start tempting him to come closer with something sweet. Sugar works. Leave it where he can find it at first. On the fence rail, maybe. Then make him come to you for it."

"Won't he try to bite me?"

"He might. When the time comes, watch yourself."

"Then what?"

"When he starts coming to you for the sugar, you'll have a chance to touch him. Take your time. Move slow. Don't crowd him. Let him get to know you.''

"And when he gets to know me, I can put a rope on him,'' Candy concluded.

"Hell, no, woman! You'd undo everything you've done so far.''

Candy stepped out of a stall and stuck her hands on her hips. "How long before I can put a rope on him?'' she demanded.

Garth shrugged. "It'll take time. Maybe a few weeks. A month. Six months. Maybe never.''

"When will I know for sure?''

"You'll know when you know,'' Garth said. "There's no predicting these things. It all depends on the horse, on his history. If he can't let go of what happened in the past, of whatever it was that made him the way he is, he'll be useless to himself and everybody else.''

"I see,'' Candy said thoughtfully. "Oh, I see.''

Candy looked at Garth with new eyes. She couldn't help seeing the similarity between the battle she was fighting in her attempts to gain Garth's love and trust and the challenge of taming the wild stallion.

She was determined to win the stallion's confidence. She would do whatever was necessary to save the animal from destruction. And if she could win one battle, surely she could win the other.

"All right, Garth. I'll do what you say.''

"You just be careful,'' Garth said. "That beast is dangerous. He'll destroy you if he can.''

Candy was struck by Garth's warning. So, too, could *he* destroy *her*, if he only knew it. But she was her father's daughter, and she wasn't used to giving up or giving in. She would tame the stallion *and* the man. Just wait and see if she didn't!

Garth put his arm around Candy as they walked back toward the house. "By the way,'' he said, "we'll be having company for the Labor Day holiday.''

"Oh?''

"My sister Tate's son is being christened. The whole family will be coming here for the occasion.''

Garth felt Candy hesitate, then slow to a stop. She turned to face him and asked, "Where do I fit into that picture, Garth?''

"You'll be staying with me, of course. Just like you have been for the past week."

Candy shook her head. "I don't think so."

"Why not?" Garth wasn't happy about the irritation in his voice. It indicated just how great was his need to have her in his bed.

"I don't want your family thinking—"

"Don't worry. They won't say a word." He would give them fair warning that Candy was different. He couldn't—wouldn't—tolerate his brothers saying the things about Candy that they had said about other women he had from time to time brought to Hawk's Way.

"But they'll know," Candy protested.

"Know what?"

That I'm sleeping with you when you haven't once said you love me, Candy thought. She didn't dare say that aloud.

"How soon did you say they'll be here?" she asked.

"Labor Day."

Only three weeks in which to get Garth to admit his feelings for her.

Candy didn't waste any time following Garth's advice, either with the horse or with him. She kept one rule in mind at all times.

Give him some room to move around. Don't hedge him in too close. With that understood she moved on to the second point Garth had made.

You should be the one to feed and water him, no one else. She was the only one who fed and watered the stallion. Things were a little more difficult when it came to feeding Garth.

Charlie One Horse normally prepared meals. Candy decided to take the bull by the horns and tell Charlie what she was trying to do. She caught him in the kitchen preparing supper.

When she was done, the old Indian tugged on the beaded rawhide thong that held one of his braids and asked, "You really think this is goin' to work?"

"It has to," Candy said.

Charlie was skeptical that Garth would ever trust another woman after what his momma had done. Mona's infidelity had occurred at a very impressionable time in Garth's life. But he had seen with his own eyes that Garth treated Candy differently than he had other women. And Charlie had been the one to wash the bloodstained sheets that had told their own story.

"All right," Charlie said at last. "I ain't gone on vacation yet this year. I'll tell Garth I'm takin' three weeks off. But that's all. I ain't missin' the christenin'."

"I'd never ask you to do that," Candy said. She gave the old man a kiss on the cheek and watched his ruddy face turn even ruddier. "Thank you, Charlie."

"Aw. Didn't do nothin'."

"How soon can you leave?" Candy asked.

Charlie chuckled. "I'll be gone 'fore supper, if that's what you're askin'."

"Thanks again, Charlie."

"Good luck, girl," Charlie said. As she left Charlie to run upstairs and change her clothes he muttered, "You're gonna need it!"

While she cooked supper, Candy went over in her mind the rest of what Garth had said about taming the stallion. *Talk to him. Keep it soft, something soothing.*

Garth wasn't in the best of moods that evening. As Candy set his plate in front of him he grumbled, "That old buzzard didn't even give me a day of warning. Who's going to do the cooking around here?"

"I am."

Garth eyed her skeptically. "You can cook?"

"Of course I can."

"You've already got enough to do. How are you going to handle any more?"

"I'll manage," Candy said. "Don't worry about me, darling." Candy let the endearment drop in a husky, breathless voice.

Garth looked at her sharply, but he didn't deny her the right to call him by such a term. Candy joined him at the table and waited for the conversation to start. She soon discovered how much Charlie had contributed to the dinnertime talk. Charlie usually asked one or the other of them how the day had gone, and then they would answer him. Candy had never noticed before that she and Garth had been talking to Charlie, not to each other.

Their time in the parlor after supper each evening had always been comfortable because they were together, even though very little dialogue passed between them. Candy recognized the importance of Garth's lesson. She needed to talk to him, to establish some sort of communication with him beyond the exchange of knowledge that consumed their days and the lovemaking that consumed their nights.

"Tell me what it was like growing up at Hawk's Way," she said.

Garth seemed startled by the request. She was afraid for a moment he wouldn't respond. Then he said, "There was a lot of work to do. I did it."

"There must have been some time for play," Candy chided.

"Not much," Garth muttered.

"But there were so many of you—your father and your brothers and sister—to do the work, and with the cowhands—"

"We couldn't afford hired help when I was growing up," Garth interrupted.

"Oh. Hawk's Way is so large and successful now, I thought it must always have been like this."

"It's always been a big spread," Garth conceded, "but we've been through a lot of hard times. There's oil on the property, but the bottom fell out of the market, if you'll recall. We raised beef for a while, but that's another market that isn't too dependable. Then we took a chance on raising rodeo stock. It wasn't until we started breeding and training championship cutting horses that we could afford any outside help."

"I had no idea," Candy said. It gave her a whole different image of what Garth's childhood must have been like.

"I saw a picture of your father upstairs. You must miss him a lot."

An agonized look crossed Garth's face and was gone so quickly Candy thought she must have imagined it.

"He was a good father. Until my mother killed him."

"What? Faron told me three years ago that your father came off a bronc and broke his neck. Are you saying he lied?"

Candy waited for Garth to answer her question, to explain his provocative statement, but his features turned stony and he remained mute. At least she knew now why there was no picture of his mother upstairs. Finally, she couldn't stand the suspense any longer.

"I don't want to intrude on what must be a painful episode in your life—"

"Then don't," he said in a harsh voice.

Candy reminded herself this was supposed to be *soothing* talk and decided to change the subject.

"Tell me more about your brothers and sister."

Almost immediately his expression softened. "My brother Jesse's a renegade," Garth said. "We were too close in age, so we knocked heads after Dad died. Jesse left to find his own way."

"How long was he gone?"

"It was years before we heard from him again. He was a Texas Ranger until he married a widow named Honey Farrell. Now he has two stepsons and a daughter of his own, and he and Honey run their ranch, the Flying Diamond, in southwest Texas.

"My sister Tate is as independent as they come. Did you know she ran away from home?"

"You must have been crazy with worry," Candy said.

"I was. But at twenty-three she decided she'd had enough of her overprotective older brothers."

"Twenty-three!" Candy gasped. "You're kidding, right?"

"I'm afraid not," Garth said with a rueful laugh. "She was gone for a couple of months before my long-lost brother Jesse called out of the blue and told us Tate had moved in with some rancher in south Texas. My brothers and I showed up the next day and made things legal."

Candy was aghast. "You forced her to get married?"

"She was pregnant," Garth said flatly. "But it wouldn't have mattered whether she was or not. She was an innocent when she met Adam Philips. He shouldn't have taken advantage of her. Anyway, everything turned out all right. Tate and Adam are bringing their son, Brett, here to be christened."

Candy bit her tongue to keep from making the retort that leapt to mind. But if Garth wasn't making the connection between Adam's treatment of Garth's sister and Garth's treatment of her, she would be wasting her breath to point it out to him.

"What about the brother I met three years ago, Faron?"

"You mean my brother the lover?" Garth said with a chuckle.

Candy laughed as she recalled the way Faron had flirted with her. "That's the one. You said he was away on business. What kind?"

A hard, closed look reappeared on Garth's face. "Faron's in Wyoming meeting his stepmother."

Candy's brow furrowed in confusion. "What? How can Faron have a stepmother if he's your brother?"

"You figure it out." Garth's tone of voice made it clear he was done with that line of discussion. He was also finished with supper. He picked up his plate and carried it out to the kitchen, leaving Candy sitting alone.

She wouldn't have called her efforts a total success, but she had learned more personal information about Garth over supper this evening than in all the time she had spent at Hawk's Way. That achievement gave her the confidence to go on to the next step in Garth's training program.

You can start tempting him to come closer with something sweet. Sugar works. Leave it where he can find it at first. On the fence rail, maybe. Then make him come to you for it.

Candy picked up her plate and headed for the kitchen after Garth. He had already rinsed his plate and stacked it in the dishwasher and was making himself a cup of coffee.

"I'll have one of those," Candy said as she rinsed her own plate.

Garth took out another mug and poured her a cup. He handed it to her, and she took a sip before setting it down on the counter. She walked up to Garth, put her hands around his waist and leaned her cheek against his chest.

"Mmm. This feels good."

Garth said nothing. Candy's hands slid down over the contours of his buttocks and back up the center of his spine to his nape, where she played with the hair that hung over his collar. She turned her face slightly and nipped his flesh through his shirt.

"Sonofabitch," Garth muttered.

Candy released him and walked away as though she hadn't felt the blunt ridge in his jeans. She used her hands to lever herself into a sitting position on the heavy oak table. Then she spread her knees and leaned back on her palms.

Come and get your sugar, darling.

Garth approached her slowly until he stood between her legs. He grasped her thighs and pulled her toward him until the heart of her was pressed to the heat of him. Then he pressed her shoulders down until she was lying flat on the table.

When he comes to you for the sugar, you'll have a chance to touch him. Take your time. Move slow. Don't crowd him. Let him get to know you.

Candy didn't move a hair when Garth reached for the snap of her jeans. Nor did she take her eyes off him as the zipper rasped down.

He placed his hand flat on her belly and slid his thumb down so it just grazed her mound. She gasped. But she let him have his way.

He stepped back and pulled off her boots and socks. Then he reached his hands into the back of her jeans and began pulling them down. She lifted her hips slightly to help him. She lay before him naked from the waist down.

His dark eyes were almost black, hooded with desire. A muscle jerked in his cheek. He was breathing hard, as though he had been running. She wasn't breathing so well herself.

He pulled her to the edge of the table again and spread her legs so that she was totally exposed to him. Candy resisted the urge to cover herself. Instead she reached out and covered his hands where they lay on her naked thighs. She trailed her hands up his arms.

She knew what was coming. He left her plenty of time to refuse as he lifted her up and lowered his mouth to kiss her nether lips. Her hands tightened on his arms as a thrill of pleasure raced through her. Her eyes never left his face as he made love to her in this new and very different way. The sensations were exquisite, unbearably exciting, unbelievably arousing. He possessed her totally, absolutely, bringing her to a climax so powerful she trembled afterward.

She wanted to tell Garth what she was feeling. How wonderful the gift was that he had given her. But she couldn't catch her breath, and wouldn't have known what words to use anyway. She lay before him, her heart in her eyes, telling him in the only way she could that she loved him. That she wanted to spend her life with him.

How long before I can put a rope on him?

It'll take time. Maybe a few weeks. A month. Six months. Maybe never.

She managed to sit up. He was still standing between her legs. She reached out for the snap of his jeans but his hand was there to stop her. She waited to see what he would do. What he would say.

He only muttered, "Sonofabitch." Then he picked her up in his arms and headed upstairs. "Come on, woman. Let's go to bed."

Garth loved Candy with his whole body, in every way he knew and some he made up on the spot. He had nearly gone crazy when she had loved him the same way he had loved her in the kitchen. It had been wonderful. Beyond anything he had ever imagined it could be. He could feel her waiting for the words of love. He could almost hear them ricocheting off the walls. But he didn't speak them.

Neither did she.

Candy lay in Garth's arms, replete. But not satisfied.

When will I know for sure?

You'll know when you know. There's no predicting these things.

Candy had to figure out what it was that had made Garth so reluctant to commit himself to a woman. He had given her several clues. First, there was the fact that he had no picture of his mother anywhere in the house. Second, he had said that his mother killed his father. Finally, there was that story of Faron having a stepmother, because he had a different father.

It came to her in a flash, so obvious that she wondered why she hadn't suspected it before.

Apparently, Garth's mother had been unfaithful to his father. Faron had been the result. And Garth had never trusted another woman to be any more faithful than his mother.

At least now she knew what she was up against.

If he can't let go of the past, whatever it was that made him the way he is, he'll be useless to himself and everybody else.

Candy felt overwhelmed by her sudden knowledge. How was she going to change Garth's lifetime of distrust? What could she possibly do to convince him that she would never be unfaithful to him? It just wasn't possible.

She remembered the last of Garth's warnings when he had told her how to tame the big stud.

You be careful. That beast is dangerous. He'll destroy you if he can.

Candy turned into Garth's arms. She felt them close tight around her. At least for now he was hers, and she was his. She would hold him with the only ropes she had. Somehow, someday, she would find a way to reach him. She was sure of it. She would start tomorrow with that black beast in the corral and prove it could be done.

Seven

Candy had won several battles with the savage black stallion, but she was losing the war. No matter how hard she tried, the animal refused to trust her. Her failure left her feeling desolate because she had tied all her hopes for a life with Garth to her success with the incorrigible stallion. They were both turning out to be unbelievably stubborn males.

She had gotten only so far with Garth and no farther. She couldn't explain it exactly, but it seemed like the more they made love, the more distant he became. Not that he desired her any less. In fact, their loving sometimes seemed almost desperately passionate, as though they had only these moments, these very few moments, to love each other.

And maybe this summer would be all they ever had together.

Candy held out the sugar to the black again. "Come here, you big beastie. Come here and take what I'm offering you. Everything is going to be all right. No one's ever going to hurt you again."

The black horse stomped a hoof and shook his head.

"You don't believe me, do you?" She slumped against the corral. "Neither does he. He doesn't trust me any more now than he did the day I came here. He wants me. But he doesn't trust me."

Garth's family was due to start arriving any day and Candy hadn't yet made up her mind what she was going to do. She couldn't bear to have Garth's family think she was just another one of the women moving through his life. Yet he had given her no encouragement to think that she would ever play a continuing role in his future.

She stepped onto the bottom rail of the corral and leaned over, holding out her hand with the cube of sugar in it. The stallion neighed and stood his ground.

"Come here, you bullheaded mule," she crooned to him.

The horse took two steps forward and stopped.

"That's it, you willful devil," she purred. "Come and get it."

Suddenly she felt Garth's dark, brooding gaze on her. She turned to face him and lost her balance. He caught her as she fell.

The stallion raced back to the other side of the corral.

"Dammit, Garth! I almost had him," she exploded. She tried to wrench herself from his grasp, but he refused to let her go.

"Whoa, there, girl! I came to tell you Jesse and Honey are here with their kids. I thought you might like to come and meet them."

Candy took one look down at the ragged jeans and dirty shirt she had been working in all day and groaned. "Look at me. I'm a mess."

"I wouldn't say that." Garth tightened his arms around her. "You look fine to me," he whispered.

She shivered at the feel of his warm breath against her face. "You'd think I looked fine no matter what I was wearing—or wasn't wearing. I wish you'd reminded me they were coming today, Garth. I wanted to make a good impression on your family."

"Why bother? They'll be leaving in a few days anyway." He brushed her long blond hair out of the way and kissed her nape.

Candy hid her face against Garth's chest. How dense could a man be? If she married him she would certainly be seeing his family more than just this once! But that was the problem. Garth apparently didn't see a future that included her.

"Hello there."

Candy jerked herself from Garth's embrace at the sound of a deep male voice. Her face flushed scarlet as she turned to face a man she realized must be Garth's brother. She crossed her arms protectively around herself. "H-hello."

"I'm Jesse. You must be Candy Baylor. Garth was telling us about you."

Candy shot a glance at Garth. Exactly what had he been saying? She took the hand Jesse offered and shook it. "It's nice to meet you, Jesse."

She compared Jesse to his brother and noted Jesse's skin was a darker bronze, his features broader, blunter. He had the same thick black hair as Garth, the same dark eyes—only Jesse's seemed more remote.

Garth reached out to put a hand back around her shoulder, but she stepped out of his way.

"I have to go change," she said. "It's getting on toward time for supper."

She hurried past them and headed for the kitchen door.

Candy took one step inside the house and froze. It looked like an army had invaded. There was a collection of baby furniture stuck in corners and baby paraphernalia littered the counters and table. She should have realized the kitchen was the very place where everyone would congregate. To her dismay not only did she find Honey there, but Tate and her husband, Adam, as well.

She recognized Jesse's wife, Honey, right away because Garth had said she had long, curly blond hair and striking blue eyes. Tate was a delicate version of her brothers, with short-cropped black hair and friendly hazel eyes. Blond-haired, blue-eyed Adam was clearly no Whitelaw.

Candy opened her mouth and shut it again, unsure where to start.

Charlie stepped into the breach. "All you folks, this here is Candy Baylor. She's workin' at Hawk's Way this summer, learnin' all about cuttin' horses. Candy, these folks are Jesse and his wife, Honey, and Tate and her husband, Adam. Them babies in the cribs is Lauren and Brett. Honey and Jesse's two boys, Jack and Jonathan, are upstairs. You'll meet them later."

Candy shook hands with the men, and despite the condition of her work clothes, got a hug from each of the women. She resisted the urge to go look at the babies. "It's nice to meet you all," she said. "I hope you'll excuse me. I need to clean up a little."

"Sure," Tate said. "Hurry back down. I want to hear what my big brother has been doing all summer."

"Giving orders," Candy muttered.

"What was that?" Tate asked.

Honey rescued Candy from having to reply by putting a hand on her shoulder and heading her in the direction of the door. "Go on and change. We'll still be here when you get back."

Candy took her time in the shower. By the time she got back downstairs, dressed in a clean pair of jeans and a Western shirt—the same thing the two women in the kitchen had been wearing—everyone had resettled in the parlor. Apparently the two boys were still playing upstairs.

Honey was sitting in Jesse's lap on a chair in front of the fireplace. Adam and Tate were sitting close beside each other on the couch. Garth was standing with an arm resting on the thick pine mantel above the stone fireplace. They were discussing—arguing—the merits of two brands of horse feed.

It wasn't the adults who interested her. Like a lodestone, Candy approached the antique cradles in the corner that held the two babies. She tucked Brett's blanket around him, then tentatively reached down to caress the black curls on Lauren's head.

"Go ahead and pick her up," Honey said. "She won't bite."

"Are you sure you don't mind?" Candy asked.

Honey didn't answer, just got up and crossed to the cradle. She picked up her daughter and laid her in Candy's arms. "Be sure to support her head."

"What if I drop her?"

"You won't," Honey said as she settled herself back in Jesse's lap.

Candy had always loved babies. Maybe it was because she had never had any brothers or sisters of her own. Unfortunately, she had come into very little contact with small children during her twenty years. She was fascinated by Lauren's tiny fingers and her equally tiny fingernails. She laughed when the baby grasped her hand.

"She's so strong!"

Candy looked up and found herself staring straight into Garth's dark eyes. She didn't know when he had crossed from the hearth. She hadn't heard him coming. But then, she had been totally involved with investigating the baby.

Garth felt his stomach fall all the way to his toes at the sight of Candy with a child in her arms. She looked so…maternal. He had never planned to have a wife, and he would never bring a child into the world without the benefit of marriage. He had long ago resigned himself to the fact that he would never have children. He had settled for the idea of standing on the sidelines, of being a fond uncle.

Now he could see how he had cheated himself all these years. Of the joy of having his own child. Of the opportunity of sharing that bliss with a woman he loved. It hurt. Lord, it hurt.

His jaw tightened. He might never feel the joy of having his own child, but he would likewise never be destroyed by the pain of a woman's betrayal. He could survive the former, but not the latter.

"Do you want to hold her?" Candy asked.

The hell of it was, he did. "Sure," he said.

Candy laid the baby in his arms. To her surprise Garth seemed perfectly comfortable. "You look like you've done this before."

He shot a glance over his shoulder at Tate. "I put a diaper or two on my sister over the years."

Tate blushed. "Good grief, Garth. Do you have to remind me of that?"

"I somehow can't imagine you diapering a baby," Candy said to Garth with a grin.

"Mom died when Tate was born," he said in a harsh voice. "Dad fell apart and Charlie was busy with Jesse and Faron. That left me."

There was a long silence.

"I didn't know," Candy said. "That must have been hard on you."

Garth laid the baby back in the crib and returned to his place by the mantel. "She kept me up a few nights. But it was worth it."

Candy saw the look Garth exchanged with Tate. There was love there, and concern. Love for family wasn't the same as romantic love, but she couldn't help feeling optimistic. Surely there must be a way to convince Garth that loving a woman didn't have to end in disaster.

The sound of footsteps in the foyer alerted them to the fact that someone else had arrived.

"That'll be Faron," Garth said. "We're in the parlor, Faron," he called to his brother.

Candy took her time looking at the third Whitelaw brother. She had met Faron before but saw him differently now that she knew he had a different father than the other Whitelaw men. His eyes were an unusual gray-green color. He had black hair, like the rest of the White-laws, but his facial features were more refined. He was unbelievably handsome.

Faron wasn't alone. He had two women with him, an arm around each of them. "This is my grandmother, Madelyn Prescott," he said. "I call her Maddy."

The younger woman with Faron, an elegantly tall blonde with stunning violet eyes, was clearly uncomfortable. The woman seemed on the verge of fleeing the room. Faron introduced her as his stepmother, Belinda Prescott.

"That's the ugly stepmother?" Jesse whispered. His wife elbowed him in the ribs to shut him up. That saved Candy the trouble of kicking him.

Obviously the whole family knew of Faron's illegitimate birth. But it was clear there was something else going on between him and his beautiful young stepmother.

Garth spoke first in what had become a very awkward situation. "I'm pleased to meet you, Belinda."

Candy knew Garth well enough by now to hear the sneer in his voice. It was plain what he thought of the beautiful young woman who had married a rich man old enough to be her father. *Not much.*

Candy couldn't stand it. She reached out and grasped Belinda's hand.

"Hi. I'm Candice—Candy Baylor. I guess you and I are the only two people here who aren't family." She smiled, giving Belinda the welcome Garth hadn't.

"I'm working at Hawk's Way this summer, and I can imagine how you must feel, meeting this rowdy bunch for the first time."

"They are a little overwhelming," Belinda said.

Candy watched as Faron stepped up and put his arm around Belinda to support her. He reached out his hand to Candy and said, "I don't know if you remember me."

"Of course I remember you," Candy said. "Last time I was here with my father you yanked my braids at the breakfast table."

Faron grinned. "Guilty. Was that only three years ago? You've grown a little since then."

The longer Garth watched his brother flirting with Candy, the more irritated he got. Faron was a man who loved women. And they loved him. Garth wasn't about to let Faron work his wiles on Candy. "I think it's time you showed Maddy and Belinda where they'll be staying," he said.

The moment the three latest arrivals headed upstairs, Garth turned to Candy and said, "You come with me. There's a mare due to foal in the next day or so that needs to be checked."

Candy was furious that Garth had ordered her to come with him like some hired hand rather than asking her if she wanted to go. Besides, this was the first she had heard about a foaling mare. She wasn't sure Garth hadn't made the whole thing up to get her out of the room. Candy would have argued if Garth's brother and sister and their spouses hadn't been sitting there with ears perked up listening.

"All right," she said. Once they were out of earshot she planned to give Garth a good piece of her mind. But Garth was striding so fast it was all she could do to keep up with him.

The instant they reached the barn, Garth turned on her. "What the hell did you think you were doing in there?"

Candy was completely taken aback by his attack. "What are you talking about?"

"I'm talking about the way you were flirting with Faron."

"Flirting with—"

"He's right, though, you have grown up a lot in three years. I've noticed the difference myself. You're not a kid anymore, are you?"

He grabbed her wrists and pinned them over her head, then backed her up against the rough wooden wall, grinding his hips against hers. To Candy's surprise, he was aroused. To her utter horror, his violent actions caused a rush of desire to flood her body.

He put both of her wrists in one hand, then reached down to free the snap on her jeans. He unzipped them and yanked them down past her buttocks, then freed himself.

"Garth, I don't—"

"You belong to me. No one else. You're *mine!*"

He punctuated the word by thrusting inside her. Candy's body undulated to accommodate his intrusion. His mouth found hers and his tongue forced its way inside. There was nothing gentle about his lovemaking. It was hard and fast and desperate as it had never been before.

It was rough, but it wasn't rape. Because Candy participated wholeheartedly in everything he did. She sucked his tongue into her mouth and parried with her own. She arched her body into his, forcing him to give and give until at last he cried out in exultation. Her own body shuddered in response.

He released her hands at last and pulled her tight against him. He hid his face at her throat. They were both panting with exhaustion, and if either had tried to move they both would have fallen. At last he let her go.

Candy felt bereft when he turned his back on her. She heard his zipper and realized that only the tails of her shirt kept her decent. She turned away to tuck in her shirt and rearrange her jeans. What must he think of her? She had been totally wanton!

Garth shoved all ten fingers through his hair. He had never lost control like that with a woman. Never! He dared a glance at Candy and saw that her lips were swollen, her face flushed. He felt his body responding at the sight and swore loud and long.

Candy's face suddenly bleached white. She knew Garth was wishing she had never come here. She knew he was going to send her away right now, today. And she knew she would go rather than face his family when he felt about her the way he obviously did. "I guess you want me out of here," she said.

"There's a mare that needs looking after," he said. "Unless you're ready to quit and go home."

Candy could hardly believe her ears. There actually *was* a foaling mare! And he wasn't sending her away. "I'm not a quitter," she said. There were things that needed to be said about his irrational fear of Faron's charm, about the way he had made violent love to her. But she knew now there would be time enough later to say them. "Let's go see about that mare."

The pregnant mare had been separated from the other animals at the far end of the barn. In the later stages of the birth she would lie down, but right now she was restlessly pacing the stall.

"Is this the first time she's foaled?" Candy asked.

Garth shook his head. "Second. She had some difficulty the first time, but got through it all right. I have the vet on call in case she has trouble again, but I'm not expecting it."

Garth stepped into the stall and talked soothingly to the mare. "Easy there, Starlight. You're going to be fine. Take it easy, girl." As he ran his hands over the mare's sides he called to Candy. "Come in here a minute."

Candy walked quietly—if not calmly—up beside him.

"Put your hand here."

She did as he asked.

"What do you feel?"

Candy's brows rose in surprise. "Contractions."

Garth nodded. "Right. I don't like the fact she's so restless. I think I'll stay with her tonight. The company might calm her down."

"What about your family?" Candy asked.

"They're all ranchers themselves. They'll understand my stock comes first."

"If you're staying, I'm staying," Candy said. She would much rather spend the time with Garth than endure the speculative looks of his brothers and sister and their spouses.

"Suit yourself," Garth said. "If you ask Charlie, he'll fix us some sandwiches and a thermos of coffee to tide us over tonight. I'll get some blankets from the tack room."

Candy took her time getting back to the kitchen. At the last minute she checked to make sure no sign remained of her lovemaking with Garth in the barn. To her chagrin, her shirt was hanging half in and half out of her jeans. She stopped and tucked it in neatly, then shoved her hands through her hair in hopes of straightening a few of the tangles.

Candy stood at the screen door and watched the antics inside with amazement. Everybody seemed to be in the kitchen helping with supper. Perhaps *helping* was the wrong word. They seemed to be *playing* catch with a raw potato. Tate threw it to—or was she throwing it at?—Faron, who caught it and tossed it to Jesse, who tossed it to Honey, who tossed it to Adam, who tossed it back to Tate. Tate then handed it to Charlie One Horse, who cut it into four pieces and dropped it into a pot of water on the stove.

Candy took advantage of the laughter that followed to quickly step inside.

"Where's Garth?" Faron asked.

"He's in the barn," she answered. "He sent me in to let you know we're going to be spending the night there."

Faron cocked a brow. "Oh, really?"

Candy flushed as she realized Faron had misinterpreted her words. "There's a mare foaling," she rushed to explain. "Garth thinks it would calm her down to have company. So we're going to stay with her."

Faron looked at Tate, who looked at Jesse, who looked back at Faron. Garth had brought a lot of women to Hawk's Way, but he had always kept ranch business and his personal pleasure separate in the past. To be honest, none of the women Garth had ever invited to the ranch would have been willing to spend the night sleeping on a blanket in the hay, let alone baby-sitting a nervous mare.

So the three of them took a second look at Candy Baylor.

Candy tried to ignore the measuring eyes she felt on her as she crossed to Charlie One Horse. "Garth said you'd fix us up a thermos of coffee. I'll make us some sandwiches, since we won't be here for supper."

She was on her way back out the door when Tate stopped her.

"You don't have to spend the night in the barn if you'd rather not," Tate said. "My eldest brother can be something of a bully."

Candy appreciated Tate's concern, but she hurried to reassure the young woman that she wasn't acting under duress. "I came here to learn everything I can about managing a place like Hawk's Way. I'm looking forward to watching this birth. I've never seen a foal born before."

"Never?" Tate asked. "It can be a pretty messy proposition. Are you sure you want to be there?"

Candy nodded her head. "Garth will be there."

Candy didn't realize until the words were out what she had revealed to Tate. Her absolute confidence in Garth. Her absolute certainty that if he was by her side, there was nothing she couldn't handle.

Tate smiled. "Well, well."

There was nothing more Candy could say without making the situation worse than it already was. "I'd better get going. Garth will be waiting for me."

She flushed when she realized how that sounded.

"I mean," she corrected, "he'll be getting hungry."

That was even worse.

"For *supper,*" she stressed.

Tate burst out laughing. She nudged Candy out the kitchen door. "Don't worry about us, we'll all be fine. I just hope that mare delivers in time for you two to come to the christening tomorrow."

"Oh, Garth would never—"

Tate shook her head. "I'm afraid you don't know my brother as well as you think. The ranch comes first—always. You won't find anyone here who doesn't understand that. I think all of us love Hawk's Way, but to Garth... It's all Garth will ever have."

Candy heard the caution in Tate's voice. Garth's sister was telling her that while the rest of the Whitelaws might marry and have families, Garth would not. Candy was being warned not to offer Garth her heart, because he would most likely break it.

Candy understood. But she didn't agree. At least, she didn't want to agree. She had seen signs that Garth might let her climb over, step across or otherwise breach the wall he had built over the years to keep himself safe from hurt. She refused to be discouraged by Tate's well-intentioned warning.

"I'll be careful," Candy said.

Before Tate could say anything more, Candy clutched the thermos and the bag of sandwiches close and hurried out the screen door.

The contrast between the sunlight outside and the dimness of the barn left Candy blind for the few seconds it took her eyes to adjust. She called out to Garth, but got no answer.

"Garth?" she repeated. Still no answer. She felt a sudden anxiety. Something was wrong.

She rushed a few steps farther into the barn, even though she was still having trouble seeing. Which was when she tripped over the wheelbarrow.

Garth saw the sandwiches and thermos go flying in one direction while Candy went the other. He got to her just before she hit the ground. She clutched at him, and it was all he could do to keep from falling with her.

With effort he regained his balance and stood her on her feet. She was still trembling, so he kept his arms around her. His own heart was beating fast from his terror at seeing her about to crack her head on the cement floor. He tightened his grasp, aware of what a narrow escape she'd had.

"Lord almighty, woman! How did you miss seeing that wheelbarrow?" he said angrily.

"Where were you, Garth? I called and you didn't answer," she retorted no less angrily.

"I was trying to make someplace comfortable for you to spend the night," he snapped back.

They glared at each other for another moment before Candy lowered her eyes and hid her face against Garth's chest.

"I thought something had happened to you," she murmured. "I guess I panicked."

"I guess you did," Garth said in a husky voice. He felt a heaviness in his groin, a growing tension that arose from holding her in his arms. He wanted her again.

His need for her frightened him more than he was willing to admit.

Once again he pushed her away. To protect himself. And ultimately, to protect her.

Garth let Candy's feet drop and held on just long enough to make sure she was steady on them before he said, "I didn't hear the thermos hit, so maybe it landed in some hay. See if you can find it without falling down again."

Candy was stung by Garth's insinuation that she was clumsy. She marched over to the stall where the thermos had indeed landed safely on a pile of hay and picked it up.

"Here it is," she said. "Catch."

That was all the warning Garth got before she threw it to him. He had already picked up the bag of sandwiches and was forced to drop it again in order to catch the thermos.

Candy walked over, picked up the bag of sandwiches and held them out to Garth. "You dropped something," she said in a sweet voice.

Garth opened his mouth and shut it again.

Candy laughed at the look of chagrin on his face.

Garth turned his back on Candy and headed toward the stall next to the one where the mare was treading. "Come on. Let's eat."

Candy thought twice about following him. She didn't understand how Garth could be so gentle one moment and so harsh the next. And lately he had no sense of humor. But she was hungry, and going back to the house for more sandwiches would require an explanation she would rather not make.

She found Garth sitting on a thick pile of hay he had covered with a wool blanket. He was leaning back against the side of the stall. He had a cup of coffee in one hand and a roast beef sandwich in the other. Candy joined him, but kept to the farthest edge of the blanket. She helped herself to a cup of coffee from the thermos and grabbed one of the sandwiches.

They ate without conversing. Candy focused her attention on the mare.

"Starlight seems a little quieter," she said.

"Her labor's stopped."

"Is that normal?"

"It happens sometimes."

"Shouldn't we call the vet?" Candy asked anxiously.

"Not yet. We'll wait a while and see if it starts again."

But "a while" turned into several hours. Garth maintained a stony silence that discouraged conversation. Candy wasn't about to let him sulk all evening.

"Mrs. Prescott is very beautiful, don't you think?"

"Faron's stepmother? She's pretty enough."

"And very young."

Garth grunted an assent. "Not what Faron was expecting, that's for sure."

"Then it's true?"

"What's true?"

"Faron had a different father than the rest of you?"

The skin stretched tight across Garth's face. His fists bunched at his sides. "I try not to air the family linen in public."

"It must have been awful for you," she said.

"I survived," he said in a harsh voice. "I told you I don't want to talk about this."

"Why not?"

"You're asking me why I don't want to discuss the fact my mother was a whore!"

Candy scrambled to her feet. "How can you say such a thing about your own mother?"

Garth rose to his feet and towered over her. "Because it's true!"

"People make mistakes—"

"That ruin lives," Garth said ruthlessly. "My mother killed my father as surely as if she'd put a knife in him."

"He was bucked off a horse. He broke his neck. Your mother had nothing to do with that!"

"He was drunk! He was drunk a lot after he found out what she'd done."

"But he forgave her!" Candy protested.

"How the hell do you know that?"

She fisted her hands on her hips. "Tate is proof of it!"

"Tate is no proof at all," Garth countered.

"Why not?" Candy demanded. "Your father had to make love to your mother to get her pregnant again."

"He didn't make love to her," Garth said in an anguished voice. "He raped her."

Candy's face bleached white. "Oh, no. Oh, my God, no!"

"Are you happy now?" Garth put the heels of his hands to his eyes. "I've never told that to another living soul."

A moment later Candy's arms were around him. There was nothing she could say, so she said nothing.

Garth refused her comfort by physically removing her hands and stepping away from her. But now that the dam had been breached, he was unable to stop the flood of words that followed.

"Jesse and I were supposed to be spending the night with friends. I'd forgotten my jackknife, so I came back. Mom and Dad were arguing. She was begging him to forgive her, to let her make amends. He told her he would never forgive her. He could never forget, either, because Faron was there to remind him every day of what she'd done. But he still intended to exercise his marital rights.

"She told him to stay away from her. That she couldn't bear for him to touch her anymore if all he wanted was sex.

"But he wouldn't be denied. He was stronger than she was. I...I couldn't leave without being discovered. So I heard it all. Her screams. His shouts. And her tears.

"He was sorry afterward. He begged her to forgive him. You see, his betrayal of their love was every bit as wrong—as horrible—as hers had been.

"There were complications, and my mother died in childbirth when Tate was born. And my father...my father cried. He was sorry she was dead. He didn't want to live without her. I think he found a way to kill himself."

Garth's voice had become progressively more guttural, his tone of voice more bitter, more cynical, until finally it ended in a harsh rasp.

Candy had listened in shock and horror to the ghastly circumstances that had molded Garth into the man he was. She felt an awful sense of despair. After hearing such a story, how could she hope to convince Garth that he could trust her? More frightening, how could she trust him not to turn on her as his father had turned on his mother?

"Garth, I—"

"Get out of here."

"I only want to offer you—"

"Sex? Sure, I'll be glad of it. It'll help me forget. That's what you want, isn't it? To make me forget my mother betrayed my father, and that he loved her so much he got himself killed rather than live without her!"

Garth took one step and grasped a handful of her silky blond hair.

He yanked her head back so she was forced to look up at him. His arm snaked around her and pulled her tight against his hips.

Candy struggled with all her might. There was no way to deceive herself that this was love. It was something violent, something painful. And it would kill forever any feelings she had for him if she let him go through with it. She was certain Garth knew exactly how she felt, certain that he was driving her away to save her because he feared, as he had all these years, that if he ever loved a woman he might turn out to be just like his father.

"Garth, stop!" she said. "You aren't like him. You aren't! And I'm not like her. Don't make it impossible—"

"It *is* impossible! Don't you see that?"

"No!" she said fiercely. She fought back the tears that brimmed in her eyes.

"Don't fool yourself!" he said with a sneer.

"You're the fool, Garth Whitelaw. And I'm not going to stay here and let you do something you'll be sorry for later." She stomped hard on his instep. He yelped and let her go.

Candy raced from the barn, not looking back to see whether he was chasing her. She didn't stop until she reached the kitchen door. She paused then, to make sure there was no one inside to see the tears that fell in hot tracks on her cheeks.

She snuck in past the parlor where she saw the two mothers nursing their babies. It struck fresh pain in her heart to see her secret dreams played out in front of her and know she would never be a mother sitting there in front of the fireplace at Hawk's Way with Garth's baby at her breast.

She tiptoed up the stairs and closed her bedroom door behind her. She stared at the bed, knowing she would never be able to sleep.

Candy had to think what to do next. Maybe the time had come to leave Hawk's Way. She wouldn't be able to stand seeing Garth in pain and knowing he refused to reach out for the comfort—not necessarily sexual—she was willing to offer.

But maybe she ought to stay. And give him comfort whether he wanted it or not.

It was a long night. She was grateful for the sunrise, but she still hadn't made up her mind what to do. She would at least stay at Hawk's Way long enough to attend the christening. After that…well, she would see.

Eight

Candy was the first one down to the kitchen in the morning and started the bacon for breakfast. She put an apron over the simple jersey dress she had chosen to wear to the christening. It felt strange to be wearing nylons again. She had almost forgotten her other life as the debutante daughter of millionaire Evan Baylor.

Candy was soon joined by Charlie One Horse.

"Where's Garth?" he asked. "I figured the two of you would come in together for breakfast."

"I spent the night upstairs. I have no idea where Garth spent it. You're welcome to go find him. I'm cooking breakfast."

"Women," Charlie muttered. "Can't live with 'em, can't live without 'em."

They weren't alone for long. Jesse and Honey and Adam and Tate soon showed up with the babies. This time Honey's two gangly boys, Jack and Jonathan, were with them. Candy thought dinner the previous night had been chaos—breakfast was even less civilized.

Tate and Jesse starting tossing eggs back and forth. One of them missed, and Candy turned to find raw egg dripping down the front of the refrigerator. Shells lay cracked and broken on the tile floor, which was layered with a fine dusting of the flour Honey was using to make biscuits on the counter beside the stove. Both the babies were gurgling, and Madelyn was rocking their cradles, trying to keep the noise level down.

They took turns eating as the fried eggs were done. Charlie had already cracked two eggs into the pan for Faron when he realized Faron and Belinda hadn't come down yet.

"Tate, go call your brother," Charlie said.

Tate stepped to the kitchen doorway and yelled, "Faaarrrooon! Your eggs are done!"

"I could've done that," Charlie muttered.

Moments later Faron appeared. "I'm hungry as a bear. Where's my breakfast?"

"Still in the pan," Charlie replied.

"Where's Garth?" Faron asked Candy.

"Why ask me?" she retorted.

"I thought you two—"

"You thought wrong!" Candy said.

At that moment, Garth stepped into the kitchen from the interior hallway. Obviously he hadn't spent the night in the barn, either. He was dressed for church in a dark Western suit with a crisply ironed white shirt that set off his tanned skin and dark features. Lord, he was a good-looking man!

Candy pointedly turned her back on him and focused her attention on the stove.

She missed seeing the flash of pain in Garth's eyes, but Charlie One Horse did not. He shook his head in disgust and muttered, "Women."

Garth felt like a wounded animal, defensive, ready to lash out. He stared at his brothers and sister, daring them to say something, anything that would give him the excuse he was looking for to explode. Fortunately for all of them, Belinda chose that moment to make her entrance.

Every male eye in the room turned to stare at her. She had put her long blond hair up in an elegant twist, and she was wearing a sheath that outlined her figure, even though it concealed her from neck to knee.

"You look absolutely gorgeous," Tate said.

Faron slipped a protective arm around Belinda's waist and said, "And she's as nice as she is beautiful." He had obviously laid something other than a maternal claim to his stepmother, and was challenging his family to say anything about it.

This time it was Charlie One Horse who stepped in to diffuse the tension. He put a hand around Maddy's shoulder and said, "I 'spect I gotta vote that this here is the purtiest woman in the room."

Candy looked over her shoulder in time to see Maddy's blush. There could be no arguing that Charlie's compliment had made the grandmotherly woman glow.

Not to be outdone, Jesse announced, "Honey is the sweetest!"

Adam countered with, "Tate is the cutest."

That left Candy as the only woman in the room who hadn't been complimented. She stood by the stove, spatula in hand, staring at Garth and waiting.

Say it. Lay some claim to me. Name me yours, and I will be. Do it, Garth!

She willed him to speak, but he said nothing.

At last he turned to Tate. "We'd better get moving if we're going to be at the church on time. Finish up your breakfasts. I'll go get the car." He turned on his heel and stalked out the screen door, letting it slam behind him.

Candy's face paled. A moment later she left the kitchen with the excuse that she had to put on some more lipstick.

"But she hasn't eaten yet," Jesse protested.

Honey jabbed him in the ribs. "Hush."

When it came time to leave for church, there could be no doubt in anyone's mind that a rift had developed between Candy and Garth. She made a point of riding to church in a separate car. However, Faron maneuvered things so she was forced to sit in the pew beside Garth during the christening ceremony.

Candy had never been so aware of him. He was like a package of dynamite set to explode. All that was needed was a spark to set him off. Candy didn't intend to light that particular fire. She planned to ignore Garth for as long as it took to get back to the house and get her bags packed.

The incident this morning had finally made up her mind for her. Garth wasn't going to change. He could no more let go of the past than the black stallion that had refused to surrender his fear and his fury. She had learned everything she had come to learn. It was time to leave.

Only Garth apparently had other ideas.

Garth's family was celebrating the christening of Brett Patrick Philips with a picnic under the moss-laden live oak that shaded the back lawn. Candy stayed just long enough not to be rude, but excused herself from a game of softball that was forming and headed upstairs.

She was in her room packing when she heard someone knocking—pounding, really—on her door. Her heart began thumping with an equally powerful force.

"Who is it?"

"You know damned well who it is!" Garth shouted. "Open the door, Candy."

"I'm busy, Garth."

The door swung open so hard it crashed against the wall. She stood staring at him with wide, wary eyes.

He took one look at the suitcase on the bed and said, "What the hell do you think you're doing?"

What she was doing was perfectly obvious to both of them. "I'm packing."

"Why?"

Another stupid question. "Because I'm leaving."

"Starlight is in heavy labor. I need your help."

There were at least three men in the backyard who could have helped him, and she would have guessed that several of the Whitelaw women would have been equally capable of delivering a foal. Garth had the vet on call, as well. But she didn't point out to him the absurdity of his statement.

Candy supposed she owed Garth an explanation for why she could no longer remain at Hawk's Way. It wasn't going to be easy or pleasant making it, but it would allow her the mental peace she needed to get on with her life. A life without Garth Whitelaw.

She finished folding the jeans in her hands and laid them on top of the rest of the clothes in the suitcase. "All right, Garth. I'll come with you. We need to talk."

When he reached out to her, she avoided his hand. She could feel the tension in him as she crossed past him and out her bedroom door. "Have you called the vet?" she asked as they reached the bottom of the stairs.

"He's taking care of another emergency. He'll get here as soon as he can."

Candy felt a small chill of alarm. Maybe Garth's tension wasn't all directed at her. Maybe he was anticipating trouble. As she stepped through the screen door she said, "Maybe Faron or Jesse should be the one to help."

"There's nothing they know that I don't," Garth replied. It might have sounded like bragging if Candy hadn't known it was very likely the truth.

Candy stopped at the door to the barn. "What is it you need me for?" she demanded.

There was a long silence before he said, "You started this. I thought you should finish it."

His response was vague enough that he could have been referring to any number of things. "*You started this.*" Started *what?* The foaling of the mare? The taming of the stallion? Learning the art of breeding and training cutting horses? She suspected that where Garth was concerned, *this* referred to her relationship with him. Well, if he wanted to see a formal ending to the latter, she could and would provide it for him.

"All right, Garth," she said at last. "I'll see it to the end."

Her *it* was as vague as his *this.* Nevertheless, she was certain Garth understood her.

When Candy got a good look at the mare, her alarm increased. She turned to Garth and said, "She seems to be in a lot of pain, Garth. Is that normal?"

"Some pain is normal." He shoved a hand through his hair. "But not this much. There's something wrong." He whooshed out a breath of air. "I just hope the vet gets here in time to make a difference."

Candy realized suddenly why Garth had wanted her here. He was concerned about the mare. With his brothers or sister he would have had to maintain the stoic facade of uncaring. It was a mask he wore to hide his feelings—his very real and vulnerable feelings—from them. Last night had been a breakthrough of sorts. Today, for the first time—too late?—Garth was allowing her to see behind the mask.

A short half hour after Candy arrived at the barn, the mare went down. It was clear she was struggling to deliver the foal without much result.

"Shouldn't we call the vet again?" Candy asked, her fear apparent in her voice.

"He said he'd come when he can. Doc Stellan knows I wouldn't have called him if I didn't need him. He'll be here as soon as he can get here."

They were both sweating from the heat. Garth had his sleeves rolled up so he could check on the mare's progress occasionally. They left the mare momentarily alone in the stall so Garth could wash up at the sink in the barn.

"I should have called Doc Stellan the first time Starlight's labor stopped," Garth muttered to himself. "I shouldn't have waited."

"How could you have known?" Candy said, trying to ease his guilt.

"It's my job to know!" he snapped at her.

"You can't know everything!" she snapped right back.

"I sure as hell was mistaken about you," he retorted. "I thought you might be different. But you're just like every other woman—"

A screaming neigh cut him off.

"It's Starlight!" Candy cried.

The two of them set off running for the stall that contained the mare. For a moment they stood stunned.

Starlight lay on her side, clearly too exhausted to do what was necessary to complete the birth process. The tiny foal lay on the hay, still in its birth sac.

Candy had never seen Garth move so fast. He was on his knees beside the foal an instant later. He tore the sac away from the foal's mouth and nose with his hands and reached inside its mouth to clear the passage so the animal could breathe freely. But that wasn't enough.

"Breathe, damn you!" he demanded of the motionless form in his arms.

Meanwhile, Candy tended to the mare. Starlight was weak, but she was still alive. "Keep fighting, girl," she crooned to the mare. "You can make it. Keep fighting and everything will be all right."

Candy watched as Garth tried several ways to resuscitate the foal, even using his own breath to try and revive the tiny being. She could see now that the filly had a white star on its forehead that was an exact replica of the one Starlight bore.

At last Garth laid the foal down in the straw. His back was to Candy, so she couldn't see his face. But there was no mistaking the way his body heaved with silent grief. She stroked the mare the way she wanted to comfort him.

Until she realized the mare was also dead.

"Garth? *Garth?*"

Garth swiped at his eyes before he turned to face Candy. He saw the horror on her face and looked at the mare. Starlight had hemorrhaged, and he had been so busy with the foal that he hadn't noticed what was happening.

"She's dead, Garth. Starlight is dead."

"Hell. Dammit to hell!"

Candy wanted to hold Garth. She wanted to be held by him. But neither of them moved for what seemed a very long time.

"Candy, I—"

His dark eyes were full of so much pain. She crossed the distance between them on her knees. Then she was in his arms, and he was holding her tight, pressing kisses to her face and neck.

"Hold me," he said. "Hold me."

"I am. I will."

Candy didn't know how long they stayed like that. Her heart nearly broke when she felt his tears against her cheek. He *could* feel. He *did* care. Only he wasn't able to let his family see his vulnerability. He had needed to be strong, to hold his family together, to be a parent when his own parents were no longer there to do their jobs.

When at last he let her go, Candy searched out Garth's face, hoping the mask wouldn't be there. But the vulnerable man who had cried for the loss of a mare and a foal was gone. In his place was the Garth Whitelaw who wanted a woman for one purpose, and one purpose only.

In that moment she hated him. He had let her glimpse the man he could be, given her hope when she had been hopeless. And made it all the more difficult to say what she knew must be said.

"I'll be leaving in the morning."

"No one's stopping you."

That hurt. As he had known it would when he said it. Candy swallowed over the lump in her throat. "I want to thank you for everything you've taught me."

"There's more you have to learn," he said.

"It would take years to learn everything. I know enough to get started on my own. I thank you for that."

"Tell your father when you see him that he can send Comanche Moon here anytime it's convenient."

"Why would he send Comanche Moon here?"

"Your father and I had a little agreement."

Candy's lips flattened. "What sort of agreement?"

Garth shrugged negligently. "I agreed to teach you everything you wanted to know, and he agreed to sell me Comanche Moon at a fair price. The bargain is concluded the day you leave Hawk's Way."

"Were lessons in the bedroom part of the deal?" she asked in a scathing voice. "How could you? How could you blackmail my father that way?"

"He came to me," Garth countered. "And I'm paying a fair price for the horse."

"And that makes it all right?" she demanded. "I hate you! I don't think I could ever loathe anyone as much as I loathe you right now. I can't wait to get out of here!"

Candy surged to her feet and nearly fell again because her legs refused to hold her. Garth half rose to help her, and she shoved his hands away.

"Don't worry. You'll get what you bargained for. I'll make sure my father ships Comanche Moon here the instant I arrive home. Goodbye, Garth. And good riddance."

She left the barn at a walk, determined not to flee like the wounded animal she was. But her walk turned into a trot, and her trot into a run. She saw Garth's family as blurs of color as she sought out the safety of her room.

Garth stood unmoving for a long time. He didn't know why he had driven her away. He had come so close, so close to letting her see how much he cared for her. At the last instant he had turned away from the tenderness she had offered him. He was like that big black beast, unable to let go of the past. And it was destroying him, as it would one day destroy the beast.

Garth kept his distance from his family the rest of the day. He ordered Tom Handy to take care of removing the dead mare and foal. He was too afraid he might break down and cry if he saw them again. He called the vet and told him not to come.

Then Garth saddled up a horse and went riding across the vast acres of Hawk's Way, through canyons and gullies as he crisscrossed the rugged terrain. He rode without stopping until both he and the horse were exhausted.

It was nearly midnight when he arrived home. He breathed a sigh

of relief when he saw the house was dark. There was a light on in
the kitchen, but Charlie usually left a light burning in case someone
got hungry during the night.

Garth was headed for the parlor and two long fingers of whiskey,
but he ran head-on into Charlie One Horse when he stepped inside
the kitchen door.

"Where you been?" the old man asked.

"Riding."

"Case you hadn't noticed, today was supposed to be a family
celebration."

"I wasn't in much of a mood to celebrate," Garth said in a curt
voice. "I lost Starlight and the foal both."

"Candy told me what happened."

Garth didn't want to ask, but he couldn't help himself. "Is she
still here?"

"Where else would she be?"

Garth breathed a sigh of relief, although he knew he'd only had
a reprieve, not a pardon.

"Women," Charlie muttered. "You gonna marry that girl?"

Garth's dark eyes were bleak. "She's decided to leave Hawk's
Way."

"Mistake lettin' her get away."

"What am I supposed to do? Hog-tie her to keep her here?"

Charlie opened the refrigerator and began looking for something
to snack on. "You admittin' you wanta keep her?"

"I want her," Garth said.

"You wanta marry her?" Charlie asked again.

"I want her," Garth repeated stubbornly.

Charlie shook his head again. "Gotta do better than that. Else
you're gonna lose her sure. Can't get that filly without promisin'
marriage. No sirree, Bob. With a girl like Candy, it's gotta be marriage or nothin'."

"You finished saying your piece, old man?"

"I'm finished."

"Then I'll be saying good night."

When Garth was gone, the old man shut the refrigerator door and
stared at the ceiling. "Sure thought that filly had him lassoed good
and tight. Ah, well, she ain't gone yet."

Meanwhile, Garth found the whiskey in the parlor and poured

himself a glass without turning on a light. He crossed and sat in the leather chair before the fireplace and put his feet up on the rawhide stool that had held generations of Whitelaw boots. He stared into the glowing embers that were all that was left of what he was sure must have been a roaring fire earlier in the evening.

He sipped his whiskey trying to dull the pain. He thought about what Charlie had said. Would proposing marriage keep Candy Baylor from leaving tomorrow morning? He recalled the words she had shouted at him.

I hate you. I can't wait to get out of here!

Somehow he didn't think a marriage proposal would be very welcome right now.

Garth didn't know how long he had been sitting alone when Faron slumped into the leather chair beside him.

"What are you doing sitting here in the dark?" Faron asked.

"I could ask you the same thing," Garth responded.

"Women," Faron said in a tone reminiscent of the one Charlie One Horse had used.

Garth grunted an affirmation of the sentiment.

Neither of them said anything more, each caught up in his own thoughts. Occasionally, Garth drank from the glass of whiskey he held in his hand.

Without either of them knowing quite how it happened, Faron was spilling out his problems with Belinda Prescott. He had fallen in love with his stepmother but was unsure whether she loved him. They were both working hard to repair the ranch where Belinda lived so it could be sold, when all Faron really wanted to do was marry Belinda and settle down at King's Castle and raise children.

Garth urged Faron to keep the ranch. And to pursue Belinda, if that was what he wanted.

"What are you doing hiding down here? I never thought you were a coward," Garth challenged.

Faron took enough umbrage to say, "I'm not the only Whitelaw sitting in the dark. What's the story between you and Candy Baylor?"

"None of your business," Garth said brusquely.

A slow smile grew on Faron's face. "Well, well, big brother. How the mighty have fallen."

"What's that supposed to mean?"

"You figure it out. I'm going upstairs where I hope there's a lady waiting for me. You can sit here alone in the dark all night if you want. But I suspect there might be a lady somewhere waiting for you, too."

"She'll have a long wait," Garth retorted.

Faron laughed. "Good night, Garth. Sleep well."

"Get out of here and leave me in peace."

"I'll leave, but I doubt you'll have much peace until you seek out a certain blond-haired, gray-eyed woman."

Hell and damnation! Garth wanted desperately to follow his youngest brother's advice. He wanted to go to Candy, to seek forgiveness, to beg her to stay. But that would mean admitting to her, and to himself, just how much he needed her. And that was still far too dangerous a proposition.

So he would have to let her go. When he thought of the life stretching out in front of him, it seemed bleak indeed.

Garth threw his whiskey glass against the stone hearth with all the pent-up anger and frustration he was feeling. The shattering glass sounded like an explosion in the silent house. He waited for his family to rouse, to come down and demand an explanation for his violent act.

But they slept on. Unaware of the turbulence in his mind and soul as the one woman he had ever loved, would ever love, walked out of his life.

Tomorrow. Tomorrow before she left he would confront her one last time. He would tell her what he was feeling. He would lay his future happiness in her hands. He would give her his heart and wait to see if she broke it.

Nine

He was too late. When Garth knocked on Candy's door the next morning, she was already gone. Soon after that a long-distance call came for Faron and Belinda. A corporate buyer wanted to see King's Castle. They had to cut their visit short to return to Wyoming. Because the other two couples had driven to Hawk's Way from their southwest Texas ranches, they left right after lunch to try and miss the worst of the Labor Day traffic.

By late afternoon, Garth's family was gone from Hawk's Way, and he was alone. He avoided Charlie One Horse because he didn't want to hear the old man's "I told you so."

Since his brothers and sister had left the ranch and gone their own ways Garth had managed to keep the loneliness at bay. He had stayed busy, and having Charlie One Horse around gave things a sense of continuity. But after Labor Day that changed. Garth was aware there was something—someone—missing in his life. The days felt hollow, empty of all joy.

Within a week, Evan Baylor's prize stud arrived in a horse trailer, along with a note from Evan saying that once he received Garth's check for the agreed upon amount, their agreement would be fulfilled. Garth now had what he'd bargained for. But not what he wanted.

He wandered around Hawk's Way, trying to find a focus for his days, feeling the awful loneliness of the nights. For the next week, he couldn't seem to find the time to write that check to Evan Baylor. He had thought there was nothing that could make him change his mind about trusting a woman. He was discovering that in this, too, he had been mistaken.

Two weeks to the day after Candy had left him, Garth awoke with a purpose that drove him like a whip. "Hurry up with that breakfast, Charlie. I've got a lot of traveling to do today."

"You goin' someplace?"

"I'm taking Comanche Moon back to Evan Baylor."

Charlie gave Garth a speculative look. "You thinkin' 'bout makin' a trade?"

"I might be."

"Good idea," Charlie said. "You need that filly a lot more than you need that stud."

Garth grinned. "For once I have to agree with you."

The grin didn't stay on Garth's face for long. In fact, his look was downright grim by the time he arrived at Evan Baylor's doorstep. The drive to the B Bar Ranch outside of Dallas was long and grueling. The terrain was flat, the weather hot, and he had never seen a more welcome sight than Evan Baylor's Spanish hacienda.

The ranch house had thick, white-washed adobe walls that kept the heat out. He stepped through an arched doorway into a house that was dark and cool. The furniture consisted of heavy Mediterranean pieces accented by Navajo and Hopi Indian decorations. The living room was spacious and there were several arches inset along the walls adding to the Spanish flavor of the room.

Garth stood with his hat in his hand waiting to see Candy's father. He wasn't sure what his reception would be, but he was willing to insist that Evan Baylor talk to him.

Evan was cordial, if not friendly. "I'm surprised to see you, Garth. What's brought you over this way?"

"I've come to return Comanche Moon. I left him at the barn."

Evan arched a brow. "I always keep my bargains, Garth. You earned the horse. He's yours."

This time Garth heard the irritation in the older man's voice. "I didn't hold to my part of the bargain," Garth said.

"Oh?"

"I told your daughter about our agreement."

"Oh." Evan pinched the bridge of his nose. That explained

Candy's cold behavior toward him for the past two weeks. She hadn't told him much about what had happened at Hawk's Way, except to say that she had learned a great deal. And that she never wanted to see Garth Whitelaw again for as long as she lived.

"I want to talk to her," Garth said.

"What makes you think she's here?"

There was a pause. Then, "Is she?"

Evan realized the futility of that sort of deceit. Garth would keep looking until he found her. "Candy doesn't want to see you."

"Too damn bad. I want to see her, and I won't take no for an answer."

"Now, look here, young man—"

"Either you ask her to come here, or I'm going to go hunting for her."

"Like hell!" Evan said. "You'll have to go through me first."

"If I have to, I will," Garth threatened.

"That won't be necessary."

Both men turned to face Candy, who was standing in one of the arched doorways. Garth had been hungry for the sight of her, and he ate her now with his eyes. He noticed changes in her appearance. There were smudges under her eyes that told him she hadn't been sleeping well, and her jeans hung on her, which told him she hadn't been eating right, either.

But her gray eyes flashed fire, and her chin jutted pugnaciously. She might have been bucked off, but she was raring to get right back on and apparently willing to use spurs, if that was what it took to stay there.

"I'll talk to him, Daddy."

"Do you want me to stay?" Evan asked.

Garth didn't bat an eyelash.

"No, Daddy. I'll be all right."

Evan looked from his daughter to the man who had come seeking her. "Call if you need me." Evan made it plain with a look he shot at Garth that although he was leaving them alone, he wasn't going far.

Candy followed her father's progress from the room, then turned to Garth. "Say what you came to say and get out."

Garth wasn't a man used to making explanations. Nor apologies. For Candy he was willing to do both. If only he could get the words out. But wanting to explain how he felt about her and being able to do so were two different things.

"I didn't figure you for a quitter." What he had intended as a compliment came out sounding more like a taunt.

"I'm not!" Candy retorted, stung into speaking.

Garth stared at her, trying to say with his eyes what he wasn't able to express in words.

I want you back at Hawk's Way. I need you in my life.

What he said was, "If you want to be the second-best wrangler in Texas, you've got a lot more to learn."

Candy bit down on an oath that sought voice. She had control of her temper. Barely. She wasn't going to allow Garth to provoke her into losing it. She was incensed by the mockery in Garth's voice and frustrated by the fact that he seemed determined to ignore the intimate relationship that had developed between them at Hawk's Way.

Candy had hoped and prayed every night since she left Hawk's Way that Garth would see the error of his ways. She had dreamed that he came after her and asked her to marry him. Well, he was here. But he wasn't following the script she had written for him. And she was just furious enough to take him up on his challenge.

"We'll just see who's a quitter!" She marched to the door through which her father had left and called, "Daddy! Come here, please!"

Evan came on the run. He looked worriedly from his daughter to the stony face of the man who had come to get her.

"I'm going back to Hawk's Way," she announced.

"Are you sure that's what you want to do? You aren't being forced or—"

"No one's forcing me into anything." She met Garth's glacial stare with fiery eyes. "I know exactly what I'm doing."

Candy hoped she was right. The risk of giving Garth a second chance was great, of course. But the rewards, if she could get past that cynical shell he used to protect himself, would be even greater. Just coming here, she realized, had been a huge step for Garth.

"I'll go pack a few things," she told Garth. "We can leave as soon as I'm done."

Once Candy was gone, Evan eyed Garth speculatively. "Would you like a drink?"

"I could use one," Garth admitted. "But I've got a lot of driving to do yet today."

"A cup of coffee?"

"That sounds good."

Evan led Garth into the decorated tile kitchen and poured him a cup of coffee from the pot on the stove. "Make yourself comfortable." He urged Garth to sit at the small wooden table set close to the wall and took the chair across from him.

"You broke my daughter's heart," he said.

"It wasn't my intention to hurt her."

"Yet you did," Evan said. "You'd better be damn sure of what you're doing, young man. Because you won't get another chance with my daughter."

Garth took that to mean Evan wouldn't allow it. He didn't argue with Candy's father. He took a sip of the coffee, which was hot enough to burn his tongue, and kept his thoughts to himself.

Evan was worried. Candy had been miserable in the two weeks since she had returned from Hawk's Way. His gentle probing had revealed little about what had happened to bring her home. She had mentioned Garth but had refused to discuss the man. Garth's arrival explained a lot of things Evan had been wondering about.

Obviously his daughter and Garth Whitelaw had been having a love affair. It was difficult as a father to allow Candy to leave again with the wrangler. But she was a grown woman, and she knew what she wanted. Evan had always known he was going to lose his daughter someday. He would never know what Candy saw in a man as hard as Garth Whitelaw. But then, Evan hadn't known why his wife, Roberta, had chosen him, either. Nonetheless, they had enjoyed a loving and happy relationship for as long as Roberta had lived.

Evan interpreted Garth's sudden appearance at the B Bar as a good sign. The fact that Garth had returned the stallion was an even better sign. The young man's insistence on seeing Candy and his refusal to be deterred from his purpose was the best sign of all. Evan needed those signs to justify letting his daughter go with this man who had hurt her so terribly. He hoped Candy knew what she was doing. Because Evan was sure Garth Whitelaw had the power to break his daughter's heart.

"I'm ready," Candy said, joining them in the kitchen.

Garth rose and took the suitcase from her. "I left the truck at the barn." At Candy's questioning look he added, "I brought Comanche Moon back."

"He didn't keep his part of the bargain," Evan explained. "He told you I arranged for him to teach you in exchange for the horse."

"Was that all you arranged?" Candy asked.

Evan looked hurt that she would even ask. "Absolutely."

"We'd better leave if we're going to get back to Hawk's Way tonight," Garth said.

There wasn't much to see once it got dark, and neither of them wanted to listen to the radio. Candy sat with her arm resting on the open window, staring out at the shadowy landscape.

"I've been doing a lot of thinking since you left Hawk's Way," Garth said at last.

"Oh?" Candy's heart began to beat a little faster.

"I…I've blamed every woman I ever met for what my mother did to my father."

Candy remained silent.

Garth swallowed over the knot in his throat and kept talking. "I always figured that if I never let myself love a woman, she could never hurt me."

"So you never loved anyone," Candy said in a soft voice. *Not even me?* she wanted to ask. That was entirely too dangerous a question. The fact that Garth had come after her was significant. It didn't mean he had let go of the past. Only that he wanted to try.

Neither of them said anything more until they could see the lights of Hawk's Way in the distance. Candy turned to Garth and said, "What is it you want from me, Garth?"

I want you to love me. But he couldn't yet say that to her aloud. "I don't know," he said gruffly. "I want you. I always have." *I always will.*

Candy sighed. Trust a man to focus on the physical. "That isn't enough, Garth."

"I know," he admitted with a sigh easily as large as her own.

Candy took a deep breath and asked, "Do you really think you can change?"

Garth met her eyes with a bleak look. "I don't know."

It might not have been a very satisfying answer, but it was an honest one. Candy realized that only the test of time would tell whether Garth could put the past behind him.

When they arrived at Hawk's Way, Charlie One Horse was nowhere to be seen. Garth carried Candy's suitcase up to her room—

the one next to his. She looked at him askance, but he did no more than set down the suitcase and back away to the door.

"You know where everything is," he said. Then he closed the door between them.

Candy frowned. She knew Garth had been aroused. She had seen the glitter in his dark eyes, the tautness of his body when he passed by her, not to mention the ridge in his jeans. Yet he hadn't tried to seduce her. She was confused by his restraint. But not discouraged.

In fact, Garth's unusual behavior continued over the next several days and weeks. His eyes never left her, and when she caught his glance the heat was enough to warm her deep inside. But they continued tiptoeing around each other, afraid to wreck the fragile balance in their relationship.

Candy went back to work with the black stallion. She got up before dawn each day to make time for an extra session with the animal. She was close to earning his trust. She just knew it!

At last the day came when she held out her hand, and the stallion walked up to take the cube of sugar from her. Of course he instantly danced away again. But if he had done it once, Candy knew that sooner or later he would do it again. It was only the first step, but it was a big one.

"I didn't think that would ever happen."

Candy whirled to find Garth directly behind her. She smiled up at him. "He's a lot like you."

"How's that?"

"Afraid to trust."

Garth stiffened. Candy had just stepped over the invisible line they had drawn regarding discussion of their relationship. "I suppose next you'll be holding out a cube of sugar to me," he said in an acid voice.

"I would if I thought it would sweeten you up any," she retorted. When she tried to leave, Garth caught her wrist and snapped her back around to face him.

"Where are you going?" he demanded, terrified that she might be leaving him again.

"I have work to do."

"Nothing that can't wait." Garth had stayed away from Candy as long as he could. Simply touching her had brought back memories of how she felt in his arms. "Come with me." He paused and added, "Please."

"When you put it that way," she said, "I find myself inclined to join you."

Garth picked her up in his arms and headed for the house.

"Garth!" she said with a breathless laugh. "Everyone will see us."

"Let them look. I don't care."

He took the stairs two at a time, and by the time he reached his room, Candy was as aroused as he was. When Garth let her feet go, she laced her hands around his neck and urged his head down for her kiss.

The first touch of Garth's lips sent a shiver through Candy.

"Garth."

It was all she said, but it was enough to send the blood pumping through Garth's body. He wasn't feeling patient, but he forced himself to slow down. His mouth trailed over her temple, down her cheek to her ear. Her head fell back and he kissed her throat. He sucked hard enough to put a love bruise on her, branding her as his. It was a savage, primitive thing to do, but he wasn't feeling very civilized at the moment.

Candy wasn't aware of the pain, only the pleasure of Garth's mouth on her flesh. Sensation streaked through her, until she was quivering with desire.

They shed their clothes like winter coats in springtime, and then they were standing naked before each other.

"You are so beautiful," Garth said as he reached out reverently to cup her breasts. He lowered his head to suckle her, and Candy's whole body arched toward him.

Her hands landed low on his hips and slid around to his buttocks. Her fingernails left crescents as she held on for dear life.

Garth picked her up and laid her on the bed, mantling her body with his. Moments later he was inside her. She was wet and tight and welcoming.

"You have no idea how wonderful this feels," he said with a satisfied groan.

"Oh, I think I do," Candy said. She moaned deep in her throat.

Garth put his hands on either side of Candy's face and forced her to look at him. His voice was fierce, his dark eyes savage. "Don't ever leave me again, Candy. I need you."

It wasn't a declaration of love, but Candy suspected it was as close to one as Garth Whitelaw had ever come. She put her hands on either side of his face. "I love you, Garth."

She was afraid he would turn away from the words, as he had in the past. This time his face bore a look of exultation.

Garth didn't say anything more. Neither did she. But there was something different about this loving. Something deeper. More powerful. More moving than anything that had passed between them before.

Afterward, they lay close in each other's arms, until their panting eased and they could speak again.

"Will you spend the night here with me?" Garth asked.

Candy remembered what Garth had said when she had first asked him why he had never married. *Why buy the cow when the milk's free?* But she couldn't bring herself to leave him. If he didn't love her enough to marry her, she would know soon enough. And if that turned out to be the case…

She might not have a lifetime with Garth; she might have only the next few days or weeks. She planned to make a lifetime of memories for the day when she might be forced to leave him.

Candy snuggled closer to Garth and laid her arm across his chest. She angled her nose under his chin until she was comfortable and said, "I'll stay."

Garth pulled her snug against him. This felt right. It felt good. Surely it was safe to love her. Surely he would find a way to convince her that she belonged with him without having to say the words. Because it simply wasn't possible for him to speak them. It ought to be enough to prove to her how he felt.

Garth fell asleep trying to convince himself that Candy didn't— wouldn't—need to hear the words to know he loved her.

Ten

Candy succeeded beyond her wildest expectations with the black stallion. In a matter of weeks, he was not only coming to her for sugar, but she had put a halter on him and was leading him around.

"I think I'll call Señor Santos and tell him I've decided to collect on the fee he offered me, after all," Garth said when he caught Candy standing inside the corral stroking the stallion's neck.

"What fee?"

"He said if I could get Midnight to stand at stud I could breed him to the mare of my choice."

Candy stammered, "B-but we don't know how he'd act with a mare. He might savage her."

Garth grinned. "I don't think so. Midnight's problem was with humans. Nobody could handle him to get him close to a ready mare. I feel certain he'd know what to do if the situation arose."

"But—"

Garth's voice hardened. "I say he's ready. I'm going to have him cover Starlight's firstborn tomorrow afternoon."

Candy paled. Since the death of Starlight and her second foal, Candy had sought out Starlight's firstborn, a five-year-old mare out of Starlight by Hawk's Sanctuary. The mare's name was Hawk's Star and she was beautiful, a rich glossy black, with a star on her forehead. Candy had befriended the horse, and although she would have been more than happy for Midnight to prove himself, she didn't want it to be with Hawk's Star.

The thought of the savage stallion covering the mare left her feeling physically ill. "I'm afraid," she said.

"Of what?" Garth asked.

"That he'll hurt her."

"I admit the mating of two horses sounds wild and brutal, but it isn't usually. I'll keep an eye on Midnight to make sure he doesn't get vicious with Hawk's Star."

Candy swallowed hard and said, "If you're going to be there, then I want to be there, too."

Garth eyed her sharply. "Are you sure?"

"Midnight knows me best. He'll respond best to me if it's necessary to separate the two horses."

Garth snorted. "Once he's with her, his mind won't be on leaving."

"Nevertheless," Candy said, "I want to be there."

For someone who wanted to possess her own stable and breed her own stock, Candy had been strangely reluctant to observe the mating of stallion and mare. She had studied Garth's stud books to see which stallions he put with which mares, and looked to see the results in their offspring. She understood what assets Garth was looking for in an animal, and how he chose one horse to be bred to another.

But it seemed profane somehow to stand by and watch while a stallion covered a mare, even though she knew it was done for the protection of both animals. The mare might lash out with her hooves at the stallion, or he might savage her in return. In the wild, one animal could run away from the other. In a corral, there was no escape. The humans who had put them there together had to rescue the one that needed help.

It didn't help her peace of mind when Candy discovered the next afternoon that Hawk's Star had never been bred before.

"She'll be scared. She'll fight him!"

"No she won't," Garth reassured her. "She's ready. I've had them in side-by-side corrals all morning. She's been flirting with that stud like a two-dollar—" Garth cut off the vulgar reference he had been going to make and finished, "She's been flirting with him all morning."

"She's so small," Candy protested.

"She'll be fine."

"He looks so wild."

"He'll settle down."

"It's her first time."

"There has to be a first time for everyone."

The sexual tension in the animals had been transmitted to the humans. Candy's body felt stretched and full, and she was aware of every move Garth made. She wanted him, had unconsciously sent out sensual lures to him all day. Like the mare, she teased Garth and then moved away, making it necessary for him to follow her.

Garth's mouth was dry as a bone. His body was strung taut as barbed wire. He wasn't sure if Candy was aware of how she was teasing him, taunting him, but he damned sure wasn't going to wait much longer to do something about it.

If the truth were known, Garth was as anxious about putting the two animals together as Candy was. The difference was, he had previously observed the wildness, the naked ferocity of the act that was coming. She had not.

Garth opened the gate, and Candy led Midnight inside the small breeding corral. She left the halter on Midnight so he would be easier to catch, but disconnected the lead. She stepped out, and Garth closed the gate behind her. Tom Handy was there to help, if help was needed.

But Hawk's Star wasn't in the least shy. And Midnight knew exactly what he wanted. The stallion quickly covered the mare. Even with both horses willing, Candy was unprepared for the violence of the coupling. She couldn't bear to stay and watch. She headed for the house at a brisk walk. As soon as she was out of Garth's sight, she broke into a run.

Garth was torn between his duty to stay and his desire to go.

"I'll keep an eye on the horses," Tom offered.

Garth nodded abruptly and headed in the direction Candy had gone. Charlie's truck was missing, so he knew there was no one else in the house besides Candy. Garth ran up the stairs and stopped to catch his breath in front of Candy's bedroom door.

"Candy? I'm coming in." Garth didn't wait for an invitation because he wasn't sure he would get one. Candy was curled up on her bed, her face hidden in her pillow. He sat down beside her and touched her shoulder. "Candy?"

The instant he touched her she turned and launched herself into his arms. "Oh, Garth!"

Garth had never had much to do with crying women and now he knew why. A man felt downright helpless in the face of a woman's tears. All he could do was hold her tight and tell her everything would be all right. Garth felt her anguish, and if there had been a way to do it, he would have taken her pain on himself. He had to be content with murmuring words of comfort.

"Even though it looks wild and rough, the coupling isn't hurtful to the mare," he said.

Garth pushed the hair back from Candy's face and kissed her brow. Then he kissed away the tears at the corners of her eyes and on her cheeks, until his lips found their way to her mouth.

It was the gentlest, the softest kiss Candy had ever felt, and it touched her to her core. A steady warmth built inside her. She shivered when she heard the stallion's neighing scream and the mare's sharp whinny in reply.

Candy looked into Garth's dark eyes and saw a fierceness there every bit as savage as the stallion. And like the mare, she had no intention of denying him. Candy returned Garth's kisses with an urgency she didn't understand. She only knew it was necessary to couple with Garth now, to love him as she had never loved him before. Because time, her precious time with him, was finally running out.

"Love me, Garth. Please, love me." It was a plea from the heart, an urgent wish not just for the physical act, but for an emotional commitment.

Garth didn't answer her in words. She hadn't expected him to. He stripped her and himself and laid her out naked for his admiration.

"You are so perfect," Garth said in a husky voice. "Your breasts high and firm. Your belly flat. Your legs strong and slender."

He worshipped her with words. His hands adored her. His mouth cherished her. His loving was as tender as it had ever been.

But the passions running high between them put tremendous pressure on Garth's restraint. Until at last he gave rein to the demands of his nature. Man's possession of his mate was every bit as violent as that of any other animal.

Candy arched up to receive Garth as he covered her with his body. She gasped as his thrust impaled her. Her hands clutched at his shoulders as he began to move inside her. Candy was insensate with desire as she undulated beneath him.

Her fingers clawed at him.

His hands grasped at her.

Her legs circled him and held on.

His mouth claimed hers and clung.

At the moment of ultimate pleasure, Candy's wild cry of fulfillment urged Garth to his own release. His shout of exultation was no less feral than hers.

The tumultuous coupling expressed all the unspoken love each felt for the other. But in the aftermath, only she was able to say the words that expressed what they had shared.

"I love you, Garth."

There was a long silence, one that begged for words of response. Candy waited. But Garth remained silent.

Candy lay in his arms and felt only despair. Her dream that Garth would one day love her seemed doomed to remain unfulfilled. Oh, he could desire her. And he could demonstrate that desire. But because of his past, he was unable to trust—ultimately to love—any woman. She had to face the fact that he never would and go on with her life.

Candy slipped out of Garth's embrace and left the bed, looking for the clothes he had scattered when he had torn them from her.

Garth's eyes were closed, his body completely relaxed. He was enjoying the languor of a sexually satisfied male. He was aware Candy had left the bed, but he expected her to return at any moment. His arms felt empty without her. He knew she had wanted him to speak his love aloud. But it was still a very new emotion, and he felt too vulnerable to say the words.

But he knew now that he loved her. He felt almost giddy with the knowledge. Someday he might even be able to tell her so. Garth took a breath and let it out.

When Garth felt the weight on Candy's side of the bed, he thought she was returning. Then he heard two clicks. He shot bolt upright and stared at what he found.

Candy was completely dressed. She was packing her suitcase to leave.

He grabbed for his jeans and yanked them on, leaving them half-unbuttoned as he stalked around the bed to confront her. "What the hell do you think you're doing?"

"I think it's pretty obvious what I'm doing. I'm packing."

"Why?"

"I'm leaving."

"Why?"

Candy closed her eyes and took a deep breath. She let it out, opened her eyes and said, "I thought I could wait forever for you to love me. I can't. It hurts too much."

"I care for you," Garth managed to say.

"Oh, Garth." Candy knew it was more than he had ever said to any woman. But it wasn't enough upon which to build a lifetime together. "That's not enough," she said at last.

"What do you want from me?" he demanded. "I've done everything I can to show you how I feel," he said in a savage voice.

"I want the words. I want you to say it out loud. I wouldn't even mind if you shouted it to the heavens," she said with a sad, wry smile.

But Garth said nothing.

Candy returned to packing.

Garth wanted to rip the clothes from her hands. Wanted to throw the suitcase across the room. Wanted to fold her in his arms and never let her go.

He watched her close the suitcase and snap it shut on the bed. When she walked out that door, he would lose her forever.

Garth faced a moment of truth. He had to let go of the past—or let go of Candy. When it came right down to it, the choice was amazingly easy.

"I love you, Candy."

The words had a harsh, grating sound, but they were the sweetest Candy had ever heard. She stared at Garth, her heart in her throat. She was afraid to believe what she had heard. "Say it again."

"I love you."

"I wasn't hearing things?"

"No, you weren't. I love you, Candy."

"Oh, Garth!" She launched herself into his arms from halfway across the room. He caught her and swung her around with abandon. His mouth found hers and his tongue thrust inside, laying claim to her.

"You're mine, now," he rasped. "Now and forever."

"And you're mine," she said just as fiercely. "Now and forever."

"We'll have children, lots of them," he promised.

"Oh, I hope so," she said. "In fact, I think we already have one on the way."

Garth stared at her, stunned even though he had always known it was a possibility. "What?"

Candy laughed. "I said we already have one on the way."

Garth sobered, only now realizing just how much had been at stake. And how close he had come to losing it all. He would never take that chance again. He would say the words often, until Candy would never again doubt his love.

"I love you, Candy."

"And I love you, Garth. Everything will be all right. You'll see."

He took her to bed again. This time the loving was tender. At the moment of climax he said the words that sealed their fates together.

"I will always love you," the wrangler promised her.

"As I will love you, always and forever," the rich girl promised in return.

Epilogue

"**E**ight—uh—nine months later you was born, Zach. Three months after that, Hawk's Star foaled a fine colt with a star on his forehead."

"And Mom named him Midnight Star," Falcon piped up.

"Yessiree, that's the one." Charlie One Horse looked down at the little girl asleep in his arms. Zach lay sprawled on the floor in front of the fireplace. Falcon sat cross-legged at Charlie's feet. "And that's the story of how your mom and dad met and fell in love."

Zach rolled over to face his father and asked, "Is that how it really happened, Dad?"

Garth kissed Candy softly on the mouth and said, "Trust your uncle Charlie, boy. It happened just the way he said. I took one look at your Mom, and I knew she was the woman for me. Now it's time for all of you to get to bed."

"Do we hafta?" Falcon asked.

"You can barely keep your eyes open," Candy chided. "Come on now."

She herded the two boys ahead of her while Garth retrieved his daughter from Charlie's lap.

"She's sleepin' like an angel," Charlie said as he gave up his burden. The old man marveled at how tenderly Garth held the girl. He wanted to be a fly on the wall when the first beaus came calling on Callen Whitelaw.

Garth caught up with Candy and slipped his arm around her waist.

Charlie heard them laughing together as they followed their sons up the stairs.

"Yep," Charlie muttered to himself as he watched them disappear, "that sure is the way it happened, all right. And the wrangler and the rich girl lived happily ever after."

*　*　*　*　*